THE M
VES

To Ken,

Best wishes,

Peter Lud

To Len

THE MOURNING VESSELS

PETER LUTHER

First impression: 2008
© Peter Luther and Y Lolfa Cyf., 2008

Cover design: Peter Luther and Y Lolfa

The publisher acknowledges the support of the Welsh Books Council

ISBN: 978 184771 050 5

Printed on acid-free and partly recycled paper
and published and bound in Wales by
Y Lolfa Cyf., Talybont, Ceredigion SY24 5HE
e-mail ylolfa@ylolfa.com
website www.ylolfa.com
tel 01970 832 304
fax 832 782

This captures him

The two visitors had crossed the threshold with smiles of sympathy and with a promise that they could make the numbing, endless pain go away. Now in Marion's sitting room, with her dead husband looking on from the photographs on the polished dining table, they took their positions.

The young woman in the tweed suit had introduced herself as Sorrel Page and her scent carried the aroma of country apples, reminiscent of gymkhanas and village fetes. She took a seat next to the widow as her colleague Jasper Wells, a pale, elderly man in a grey suit that seemed too big and too heavy for his frail bones, began his patrol of the room.

"You have some interesting pieces," he remarked, picking up a porcelain soldier – a drummer boy in red – and glancing at the serial number on its base. His voice was hoarse as if his mouth and throat were unable to make saliva.

"They're Royal Worcester," Marion answered, her exhausted expression brightening as she touched upon her obsession. "Henry took me to the Royal Worcester Museum last year and…"

"His or yours?" he asked, not seeming to hear her.

This seemed an odd question: they had acquired everything together.

"Was it your idea to collect the porcelain, or his?" Sorrel qualified in a gentle voice. Her face had been veiled by the gloom of the porch but in the glow of a side lamp, the only light in the room, Marion saw that the young woman with the short red hair was probably in her early thirties. She was strikingly beautiful; the configuration of her eyes, forehead and nose could have been drawn mathematically to achieve such symmetrical perfection.

"They're mine, I suppose," Marion muttered. "Henry wasn't really bothered." A calling card was in her hand and she saw that it said: *The Divine Sentiment, established 1862*. There was a charity registration number and a royal crest. "The Divine Sentiment," she murmured. "Why are you called that?"

"We're an old society," Mr Wells replied. "The founding member was a religious scientist and deeply devout. He understood…" and he lifted the handle of an ornamental coal scuttle from near the electric fire, examined its lines and returned it to its brass bucket with a shake of his head "… he understood *suffering*."

"As *you* suffer," Sorrel whispered, taking her hand. She was so petite that she reminded Marion of the puppets on children's TV but her grip was stronger than her frame suggested. "Tell us about your dear Henry. What did he do?"

"He worked in Pembroke Dock. He was a rigger…"

"Backbreaking work," Mr Wells remarked. He was now behind the settee studying a small Welsh dresser that boasted an impressive dinner service in Sandringham porcelain, its blue borders etched with intricate gold leaf. He briefly revealed an array of long, yellow teeth in deep-rooted gums as he turned. "The dresser … yours?" he inquired.

Marion nodded. "Henry always worked the overtime shifts," she said, then smiled, fondly. "Sometimes we'd argue but we never let the sun go down on our wrath. That's something I taught my two children: never let the sun go down on your wrath."

"And where are your dear children now?" Mr Wells asked, as he walked out into the hallway.

"John's in London, he's a dentist," she called after him. "Clare lives in Scotland. Her husband's family are based in Edinburgh."

"London … and Edinburgh. It takes a lifetime of hard work to send your children so *far* into the world…" His voice trailed off as he stopped at a longcase grandfather clock that occupied the narrow hallway. The moon dial was twisted and broken, it would always show 'High Water at Cardigan Quay', but from the twitch of the brass hands he could see the time mechanism was still working.

"His or yours?" he called.

"What?" Marion snuffled, dabbing her eyes with the hem of her skirt, revealing heavy, varicose legs as she thought of the children she so rarely saw.

"The clock. His or yours?"

With a tremor in her stomach she looked towards the hallway, wishing that she could hear Henry saying *It's just me, Marry*, as he always did. She would tell him not to put his cap on the sideboard, that there was a hook; he would call her an old misery.

"The clock. His or yours?" Wells repeated, a slight edge in the croak of his voice.

"It's Henry's," she answered. "He found it in a junk shop and it never cleaned up properly. I think someone spilled some grease or varnish on it once." She sighed. "He made it his hobby to get it working: it took him years."

Wells nodded thoughtfully, noting the discoloration in the reclaimed oak. From the modern screws and fittings it was obviously a replica of some older and grander model, but handmade nevertheless and probably constructed by an enthusiast working from a photograph, for its back was simply a piece of plywood. The carvings around the tall and elaborate hood were of roses and thorns, requiring a delicate instrument and loving hands. "So it's *his*, and he *cared* for it?"

"Oh, Henry lived for his old clock."

Two long fingers of a liver-spotted hand traced the clock face as a finger of the other hand followed the carvings. Involuntarily, Wells let out a sigh that was a combination of anguish and pleasure.

In the sitting room, Sorrel sensed her colleague's excitement at having found what he was looking for. She squeezed Marion's hand and said, "Shall we speak to him?"

"Speak to...?" Marion muttered.

"Speak to Henry," Sorrel clarified, with a twitch of her freckled nose. "He's still here, in this room with you, held by your love and your sorrow."

At Sorrel's prompting the two women bowed their heads, as if in prayer. In those few seconds of silence, Marion was aware of the dead tap and thump of the clock's mechanism in the hallway, as if the attentions of the old man had awoken it.

"He says: 'Remember the ironed newspaper?'" Sorrel whispered.

Out of the silence, the dead tap and thump seemed louder; Marion had frozen.

"He's recalling your honeymoon, in Bournemouth," Sorrel continued, massaging Marion's knuckles. "There was a landlady with wrinkled stockings and blue hair, and the B&B was dirty and the food was greasy. Yet ... yet she ironed the newspaper. The first one slipped under your door had ink smudges and a hole in the back page." There was a pause. "Oh my, it's a precious memory for you, for this was the first time you laughed together ... in bed. After being so ... embarrassed." Sorrel gave a sigh of pleasure. "Your marriage started with that laugh."

A sound alerted Marion and, with a stunned expression, she turned to look at the dining table where Wells was now standing, having selected a photograph of Henry. It was a close-up head and shoulders portrait showing a large man sucking in his lips with irritation at being snapped unexpectedly; it wasn't a flattering likeness but she could remember his exact words after she had taken it.

Grow up Marry, for pity's sake!

He had come home from the club; he was happy and ready for his newspaper but didn't like to be bothered when he had been drinking.

"Does this capture him?" Wells asked.

Marion nodded, her mind still poring over the private memory of her honeymoon. Wells still held the photograph high, his expression blank. She had the feeling they were waiting for her to say something: something specific. That it would be courteous of her to say something.

8

"This captures him?" he asked once more.

"This captures him," she said, her words more a helpless admission than agreement. She shuddered as the three words left her mouth and she imagined a lock turning in her head.

Sorrel murmured something under her breath. The mumbled reflex sounded almost like a ritual incantation – as Marion would murmur *and also with you* when her vicar led the Eucharist at church. Marion saw the woman's eyes were closed. They snapped open.

"Listen to me very carefully, Marion Coates," Wells said. He had returned the photograph to the table and was polishing the fingernails of his left hand with the forefinger of his right. "We won't tell you to live for your memories or to be thankful for the time you've had. We won't deal with you with the indifference of your children, or your church."

Marion shook her head in surprise and confusion.

"Understand that we can solve your grief," he said to his fingernails.

Her eyes held a question.

Solve?

"Yes, yes we can," Sorrel purred, with a tight smile and wide eyes. "We can *solve* it…"

The large man waiting across the street, hunched behind the wheel of his Land Rover, pretended an interest in Pembroke's castle a hundred yards along the hill as the Trustees of the Divine Sentiment, Sorrel Page and Jasper Wells, emerged from the house and walked to their vehicle. This was a long hearse painted brilliant white with the side and rear windows blacked out, which he had nicknamed *the removal wagon* as it was raised and widened with off-roader suspension. He held his breath as it slid through the reflection in his side mirror, Wells at the wheel, and then glided smoothly down past the castle before it turned out of town.

Releasing his breath and hoping he hadn't been seen, his attention returned to the end of terrace in his side mirror as he took out his business cards with his name, occupation and mobile number. He considered the top card, which read:

Tristyn Honeyman
Scrap and junk

He slid the card to the bottom of the pile. He was yet to talk to the widow and was unaware of her financial situation, but at the door she had looked like a proud soul who wouldn't admit to owning anything that needed to be thrown away. The next card read:

Tristyn Honeyman
Antiques

He studied the front door in his mirror, noticed the paint peeling off it, and shook his head. The bay window had a few ill fitting leaded panes and he suspected they let in a chill in the winter. Returning to his cards, he shuffled through them until he found:

Tristyn Honeyman
Double-glazing

He grunted and placed this card in the top pocket of his overcoat as he opened the vehicle door.

A curious bequest

"You'll find something," had been the promise that accompanied Ellen as she inspected and itemised the very corners of her late father's townhouse. "You'll find something and you'll grieve."

It could be small and insignificant, a trivial throwaway thing; a forgotten Christmas present perhaps, a broken toy or some well-thumbed girls annual with pop stars and horses. Something of no value even, an empty box of sweets with a story behind it, or a punched cinema ticket. She had a wonderful image of sagging to the floor as she found this hidden treasure and the tears came at last.

Yet the assurances of her university counsellor had proved worthless as she had coolly prepared the house inventory, resoundingly unmoved. There was no magical box or enchanted garden waiting to be found, no secret altar where she could set down her grief.

"I'm not going to feel guilty about it," she said to her reflection as she tugged at her hair with her hairbrush. She glanced over at Cody for confirmation. From her high-backed wicker chair, Cody was patiently facing the bedroom window that looked out over Tenby's North Beach. Cody had wondrous eyes, so large and so blue that they seemed to be reflecting the sea.

"I mean, we hadn't really talked since Mum died and it's not as if he gave a damn about me anyway, not really," she continued, though knowing that for Cody her father could do no wrong. "Didn't come to my graduation … didn't even keep the graduation

11

photograph I sent him." A particularly severe tug of her straight, blonde hair prompted a wince of pain around her mouth.

I'm unable to mourn my own father. There must be something cold, something hard and bitter, buried deep inside me.

She paused to consider the face in the tall oval mirror, as if it held a clue to her true character. The cautious reflection looked back with heavy-lidded eyes, which she supposed were okay, and a prominent cupid bow to her lips that she *knew* was pretty good. Neither feature compensated for a nose far too long and a forehead way too high, which as a teenager she had regularly measured, convinced that she was turning into some kind of genetic mutation. She considered her appalling physical imperfections with a suspicious air as she stepped away from the mirror.

"Will I do?"

Cody's thick, honey blonde curls could just be seen over the rise of the high chair and her tiny left hand was visible on the armrest. She didn't answer.

"D'you think I should be wearing jeans?" she queried, glancing down at her long, skinny legs. Sod it, she thought, with a shrug. Mr Hobbs was the family solicitor, not royalty. She turned to the inventory waiting on the bed, the reason for the appointment with the solicitor, and frowned. Preparing it this morning had brought home to her how many of her father's things were missing. "All his books have vanished," she murmured to Cody, picking up the list. "And his Viennese music box. He kept all his old watches in that: watches Mum gave him. He *loved* that box. Why would he throw it away?"

She considered the inventory sullenly. The description of this room, the bedroom on the second floor, read:

My room. Everything in this room is mine except for a double bed, a dressing table with oval standing mirror (Edwardian I think), a high-backed wicker chair (not antique but Dutch and expensive), wardrobe (empty apart from blankets and coat hangers), 2 chests of drawers, leather trunk (some cigarette burns).

Cody's description followed underneath, for she was the

permanent resident of this bedroom. Her father had reminded her of this in severe terms when she had announced that she wanted to take her back to her Cardiff digs.

"She belongs here, Eleanor. Here!" he had rasped, almost summoning up the energy to rise from his armchair in the day room.

One porcelain bisque doll, circa 1880s, 32" tall. A French Jumeau Bébé (with face of little girl) 'Cody' (long-faced), with original pink satin chemise. Almond-shaped blue paperweight glass eyes, honey blonde (mohair) curls, blush cheeks. She has a soulful expression. Delightful.

An elaborate description, she supposed, for a list that would only be read by lawyers and taxmen. It was certainly unnecessary to flag the wistful raise of the feathered eyebrows that, together with the reluctant smile in the small mouth, gave the long-faced doll what she regarded as a *soulful expression*.

"But you're worth a big description, aren't you?" she murmured, her hand passing over the mohair wig, prompting the porcelain eyelids to close, then gently rock open. The mechanism was broken and erratic, the eyes and eyelids only moved when the wooden body was disturbed. It was a detail she had omitted from the inventory: she didn't like the idea of anyone thinking of the doll as less than perfect.

She walked out onto the small landing, where another precious object waited. Here a wall had been reserved for her mother's photograph, a vibrant colour portrait in an unframed plate of smoky glass. As she passed it on the stairs, it had become an automatic habit to put an index and middle finger to her lips and then touch the glass with those kissed fingers.

No matter what her mood, she never forgot to kiss the picture with her fingers and no matter what the condition of her hands, the fingers never left a smudge or stain.

The faint aroma of percolated coffee that nobody would drink was rising from the ground floor kitchen to the day room on the first floor. Tarn, the young housekeeper, had made the morning coffee on the instructions of the estate agents, to give the house that 'lived in' feel. Now she was strategically positioning the floral tributes against the legs of the grand piano and the armchair and sofa of the Sheraton suite. There were fewer than half a dozen bouquets but two of them were very large, and with the Sheraton dressed in a dramatic green regency stripe, the room was awash with colour and confusion.

"The flowers have come back from the church," Tarn told her as Ellen went to the sideboard to collect her keys. Ellen knew her bouquet was one of the large ones but she wasn't sure whether it was the lilies or the roses: on the telephone, she had left the arrangement to the florist's discretion, reading out her message ('love from your daughter, Ellen') with the same passion that she gave out her American Express card details.

On the sideboard, she noticed the pile of mail allowed to accumulate since the funeral. Many were handwritten. She decided to give the letters to the solicitor.

"They probably didn't know he had passed on," Tarn remarked sadly, looking at the mail. "I didn't know who to contact. Neither did your uncle."

"Well I couldn't be everywhere," Ellen said, as she flicked irritably through the envelopes. She had returned home to Tenby only the evening before the funeral and then in a rush with no time to speak to anyone.

"Oh I know, I'm just saying…"

"I had important course work to do. Had an essay."

"Yes, your uncle mentioned the essay…"

Ellen nodded. "Besides, I thought you had everything in hand. My mistake, I suppose. I mean, if I'd been here I'd have pointed out that my father wanted to be cremated."

"But didn't the will…?"

"I don't care about the will." Ellen picked up a window-envelope circular, considering it. "I'm telling you, he wanted to be cremated. He was terrified of being buried. He was trapped in a coal fissure once. Couldn't move his arms and legs and had to wait twenty-four hours before he was cut out." She looked round. "Did you know that?"

"No, I didn't know that," Tarn conceded uncomfortably. In a smoothing motion a hand now went to her black hair which was tied tightly back from her face.

She looks like her mother, Ellen reflected, thinking that, like her mother's, Tarn's hairstyle was far too severe for someone so painfully thin and with such sharp features. She had met the imposing Mrs Hughes at the wake and with her beak nose, gangly legs and sharp, sudden movements, she resembled a large bird of prey. When they were introduced, Mrs Hughes had protectively taken the shoulders of her only daughter, calling her *my Tarny.*

All is vanity, Ellen could almost hear her thinking, as Mrs Hughes surveyed her black Prada outfit, low cut cream top and diamonds with contempt. Her uncle had told her that the Hughes family were strict churchgoers.

"Anyway, your father would have loved your flowers, Eleanor," Tarn said, having earlier located Ellen's card and read the message with a surprised raise of her eyebrows. The bouquet was a magnificent feast of roses, the best that plastic could buy.

Ellen closed her eyes, shaken for a moment by the thought of her short, scribbled note. "It's Ellen," she said, returning to the post. "I don't like being called Eleanor. No one calls me Eleanor. Okay?"

"Oh, sorry, I didn't know. That's what your father called you."

To her surprise, Ellen thought she felt something like tears forming and angrily rubbed at her eyes, her back to the housekeeper. "Had long chats about me, did you?"

Tarn took a deep breath. "He didn't really have much to say at all," she answered quietly.

The doctors had been unable to diagnose Mr Sorensen's disability but Tarn knew there was a force at work in his illness, a power that had defeated medical understanding. A care worker who popped in occasionally had come closest to the mark when she described it as *grief and loneliness … so acute it's debilitating.*

She surveyed the flowers and sighed, thinking that the care worker's description only scratched the surface. Mr Sorensen's mind and body were in outrage; outrage that he was still alive, that he hadn't chosen to die.

"What's this?" Ellen asked, holding up a white business card.

"Oh, he called yesterday, when you were out," Tarn replied, glancing at the card and recalling the large bearded man in the long overcoat who had left it. "He said he'd call back."

Ellen frowned. The card read:

Tristyn Honeyman
Probate valuations

"He won't have much of a job, will he?" she muttered. "I mean, there's nothing here to value, is there?"

Tarn shrugged. "There's the piano…"

"Belonging to my father, I mean," Ellen clarified. "I mean, everything's gone. A collection of Charles Dickens, all first editions, was stacked … *right there*." She pointed to the largest table of a three-piece nest as if this were incontrovertible proof of a crime.

"The house is how I found it," Tarn returned defensively, catching the innuendo. In her mind, the housekeeper said a prayer to absolve her lie, seeking absolution on the basis that she was conflicted by a vow.

Swear on your god! Nigel Sorensen had demanded, with a fist raised in weak defiance.

And she had.

"Perhaps he got rid of them when he threw out my graduation photograph?" Ellen remarked coldly. "The one I sent him. That was in August. You were working here then, weren't you?"

Tarn didn't reply but, without any movement of her head, her eyes slowly closed then opened again. The mention of the graduation had triggered a series of thought processes.

"What?" Ellen insisted.

"There *is* something missing," Tarn said, to herself.

"Missing? What?"

"Your father's typewriter." Tarn paused. "Strangest thing…"

"What's strange?" Ellen asked.

"No, I mean I've only just realised that it's gone."

Tarn recalled that the typewriter had been kept on the kitchen table but in the weeks leading up to his death Mr Sorensen had tired of it and consigned it to one of the kitchen cupboards. She had cleaned all the kitchen units this morning and only now had it occurred to her that there was no typewriter.

"So where is it?" Ellen whispered, tears starting in her eyes this time, before she could stop them.

"I honestly don't know," Tarn answered cautiously, surprised and puzzled by the sudden onset of tears.

Ellen collected the mail with purposeful nods of her head, unable to speak, and walked quickly out of the house. Tarn heard her footsteps fade as she hurried down the stone steps to the road.

Ellen had run the length of the road above North Beach and was approaching the steps that would take her up into the town when she brought herself to an abrupt halt. She grabbed the rails, gasping for breath as she looked out over the sea.

"Fuck," she whispered, her breath sticking in her throat like jagged glass.

The typewriter…

"Fuck," she blubbered again as she angrily pawed the tears away from her eyes and cheeks, looking round to check no one was watching her.

She took a deep breath. The prediction that something would open the floodgates had come true after all, but Tarn had found it, not her: the housekeeper, not the daughter. When she had prepared her inventory this morning it hadn't even occurred to her that the typewriter was missing, even though it was her last link with her father.

It was over a hundred years old, a second-generation prototype or something, she wasn't sure, but she knew that her father had paid a small fortune for it. He had found it in the cellar of some defunct company he was investigating; it must have been a forgotten investment. It was at first a quirk and later a sense of stubborn pride which made him only correspond with this machine, albeit expertly refurbished, steadfastly ignoring the age of word-processing and e-mail.

She took out the letter folded in her purse, the last one she'd ever received, which had arrived on her graduation day. It was on narrow paper, specially made to fit the odd dimensions of a typewriter designed before the advent of A4 and B5, and the faint impress of the old refurbished keys read, simply:

I am so very proud

She nodded as she re-read the letter in her mind. This was all that he could manage, evidently. All her friends had their parents there at the ceremony, beaming and waving, dressed up to the nines and snapping their digital cameras. What did she have? She had this five-word letter and an American Express card.

"Stupid fucking machine," she said, holding the letter away from her so that it was framed against the sea. It had a crinkled rice paper design with a large S watermark, for Sorensen, and against the cold October waves it resembled a weathered sail in treacherous waters.

"I am so very proud," she read. She was thoughtful for a moment then crumpled up the paper and threw it over the rails, down on to the sand. The tide was coming in and would take it.

"That wasn't enough," she murmured, with a shake of her head. She considered the beach for a few moments, the letter having already been abducted by a brisk sea breeze, then turned and walked forlornly away from the rails.

The West Wales seaside town of Tenby had used the centuries to spread far beyond its ring of curtain walls, towers and gateways and *the Five Arches*, once the guarded entrance of the Barbican tower for the west gate, was now a central landmark. It was here that poor Mr Sorensen had collapsed, Tarn had explained as she described

18

her one attempt at taking him out of the house. They had been going to see his solicitor, Mr Hobbs, whose offices were in Upper Frog Street.

Well it wasn't so much a collapse, she conceded, rather he simply sank to the floor and curled up. It took much coaxing to get him up again and lead him through the arches into the narrow shopping centre, his eyes fixed on the cobbles of the uneven road, his heartbeat in a vein in his forehead.

"The silly old solicitor can come to you," she had declared at last. "I'm taking you home."

Sitting in the reception of Hobbs, Solicitors & Notary Public, Ellen pondered on her father's motives in changing his will. Mr Hobbs' letter had mentioned a 'bequest' that he needed to discuss with her 'face to face', but only after she had prepared her inventory. She knew that 'bequest' was legal-speak for 'gift' and it was obvious who the lucky recipient was.

Yes ... *my Tarny*, the holy and self-righteous housekeeper...

"My dear, dear girl. Now how are you?"

She turned as Timothy Hobbs, a balding, red-faced man in his early sixties, appeared from his office and walked over. She stood up, noticing the coloured waistcoat and smelling the overdose of aftershave, thinking that he hadn't changed a bit. The thought precipitated a small smile.

"I'm fine, thank you, Mr Hobbs," she replied. He took her hands in both of his and bit his lip with a sad and perplexed shake of his head. She wondered whether he had the same expression for her father last year over her mother's estate.

With this thought, she was back in the small hospital interview room, now with Father's strong hand in hers. The words *brain tumour* were never used, the unpronounceable Latin name offered in their place the hood of an assassin.

Yes, the specialist conceded on being pressed, *it could be described as a cancer...*

She had felt the cold death in her father's hand at that moment, the grief already setting in as surely as rigor mortis.

"Through! Through!" Hobbs declared, turning towards his door and gesturing her forward with a theatrical ushering of his hands. In his office his desk was clear except for the will, a ruled A4 pad and a Mont Blanc ballpoint pen of which he was clearly rather proud as the presentation case was nearby. She had visited the office as a little girl with her mother when they moved to the house overlooking North Beach and she remembered the reek of Cologne. Now, some fifteen years on she glanced around, realising that he still had the same pictures: she remembered the framed cartoon of the two barristers fighting, entitled 'settling out of court'.

"When you met him … for the last time…" she began with difficulty.

"He'd lost a lot of weight," the solicitor replied, coming to her rescue. He had a wistfully sad expression. "He was greatly changed: completely reliant on his housekeeper."

"Really," she muttered.

"Yes, that's young Tarn Hughes. Nice girl." He wrote something inconsequential on his pad, picking up the ill will. "I wouldn't read too much into that, my dear," he said gently. "We oldies tend to latch on to our carers. Your father probably didn't ask you to look after him because he didn't want to be a burden."

"It wouldn't have been a burden," she said quietly. She bit her lip, fighting an unexpected impulse to run out of the office, down to the beach and find her father's letter.

"You were in the final year of university and I'm sure he wouldn't have threatened that for the world. Not for the world." He paused diplomatically, noticing the girl's distraught look.

Ellen took a deep breath. "So how much does she get?" she asked, regaining her composure.

"I beg your pardon?"

"Tarn Hughes. How much did he leave her?"

The solicitor looked at her blankly for a few moments then chuckled deeply from his belly. "Oh I see, that's what you… No. The will leaves her nothing, although I know your father paid her three months' salary in advance, which I've honoured. Your father confined himself to a few words of thanks. Would you like me to read them?"

"No, that's okay." She was confused and shifted her position in her seat uneasily.

"As the main beneficiary of the estate I'm sure you'd like to hear what he had to say."

"No, honestly…"

"I wish to record my deepest gratitude to Tarn Hughes," he read from the will, "my constant and faithful companion." He put the will down, clearing his throat with a flash of his eyes.

Ellen read his message: the will is for the deceased as well as the beneficiaries; Mr Sorensen wanted to say something and you'll hear it whether you like it or not. She swallowed, once more the little girl hanging on to her mum's hand. "I've made the inventory, as you asked," she said, taking the list from her bag and handing it to the solicitor. He took a generous helping of breath and held it in, his habit when reviewing an important document.

"I remember seeing the skull when I visited," he murmured, having come to the entry that read, simply, *old skull*. "Your father wouldn't discuss it."

"Don't ask me either. It's new." The skull, which was a grey fossil with tiny lines etched into the bone, occupied a small oval table on a pedestal next to the front door. Tarn called it *Mr Sockets*.

"I think it's got something to do with phrenology," he mused.

"Whatever," she said, uninterested.

Turning the inventory over and finding it blank, he released his breath with dissatisfaction. "I expected to see a lot more on this list. And I distinctly remember a typewriter: a very unusual, antique typewriter." He cleared his throat. "I think we need a professional valuation."

"There's nothing *to* value," she protested. "The house has been stripped."

"I'm not suggesting your list is inaccurate, my dear, but this skull … well, phrenological artefacts can be quite valuable." He stretched round to locate his address book.

"Someone's already called, if it helps. Probate valuations guy."

He paused for a moment, puzzled, and then with a nod put the address book back. "Ah, your uncle must have already put it in hand."

She shrugged.

"Who is this valuer?" Hobbs asked.

She located Tristyn Honeyman's business card and slid it across the desk.

"Never heard of him," Hobbs remarked, glancing at the card and passing it back. "It's a mobile number," he added, thoughtfully, scratching his neck before he returned to the will. "Well, back to the gift in the will. It's a curious bequest, and it was the second alteration your father made. The first alteration, as you know, was a direction that he be buried, rather than cremated."

She returned the business card to her bag. "So who's it to?"

"The Divine Sentiment," he said, glancing up to observe her reaction.

"Divine...?"

"Sentiment. Yes, odd name, isn't it? They're a registered charity."

"Charity? What sort of charity?"

"They're bereavement counsellors."

"Bereavement...?"

He nodded and read, "To the charity The Divine Sentiment, in recognition of their services following the death of my beloved wife..."

She frowned. "I was here in Tenby when Mum died. It was the summer vacation and I was between digs. I didn't see anyone come to the house."

"Were you at home *all* the time, my dear?"

She opened her mouth to speak, but shook her head instead. After the funeral, she had spent some time living with a school friend, following the first major row with her father. It had been horrible because she had to sleep on the settee of the one bedroom flat, while her friend knocked the wall with a stream of boyfriends. The hours had turned into days, which turned into three weeks as she stubbornly waited for her father to call. When she eventually stormed back home, broke and in need of a decent shower, she announced imperiously that she had only come back for her things and that she was going to stay in a hotel.

Her father had changed in those three weeks. He seemed exhausted and just nodded, raising no protest and muttering that he would pay for whatever she needed. The onset of the nameless, agoraphobic disability that would claim him was only a few weeks away.

"So what's he left them? Money?"

"This is the curious part." Hobbs paused. "Any two moveable items from my house," he read, "whether they be of value or junk, large or small, old or new, family heirlooms or sentimental gifts. Two items of their choosing and their choosing alone, from a free selection of all the chattels and moveables in my home, without exception, at the time of my death." He took a theatrical breath to communicate his great dissatisfaction with the clause, which he then softened with a sigh that said *the client is the client*.

"What does it mean?"

"What it says, my dear. The charity is to select two items from the house, which it can take, free of tax."

"Two? Which two?"

"Any two. Your father gave me no contact details for these people, saying they'd prefer to get in touch themselves." He scratched his neck. "Presumably they'll read my announcement in the *Gazette* or the charities journal, or perhaps they check the obituaries."

She considered this. "They'll take the piano," she remarked.

"It seems likely," he agreed sadly. "It's a beautiful instrument, that Steinway. I heard your mother play on it once." He smiled at a pleasant memory.

"If the piano's *there*, when they visit, I mean," Ellen suggested mischievously.

If she was hoping for a look of understanding she was disappointed. He looked at his notepad and cleared his throat. "I have the inventory, remember," he said. A flash of his eyes told her: *Don't you dare! These are your father's wishes.*

She wondered whether that had been Mr Hobbs' true purpose in asking her to prepare her own inventory before telling her about the bequest in the will: to trap her with a list of contents. She supposed it might have something to do with legal ethics if her father had given him explicit instructions, but that didn't lessen her annoyance. After all, Mr Hobbs' fee was coming out of the estate, which was her money.

"They'll take the piano," she repeated, lacking the courage to make her displeasure known. "It's the only thing left in the house of any value, apart from…"

Her stomach twitched as she remembered her list. Her Jumeau doll was on that list, her beloved Cody, and hardly described in understated terms.

A soulful expression … delightful…

Oh no…

She mastered her sudden panic with a rapid assessment of the situation. She would explain that she had adopted the doll after her mother's death, brought it down to her own bedroom to help her grieve. They were a charity, nice people who would understand. They were bereavement counsellors, for Christ's sake. She smiled and nodded. For bereavement counsellors to take away her doll in the face of such protests would be like a surgeon taking away the morphine.

"I've got some letters and stuff," she said, taking the post from her bag. "Could I give them to you?"

The solicitor accepted them with a smile and shuffled through them, with a nod at first as he examined official letters, but then with hesitation as he came across the handwritten envelopes. Then he shook his head. "This one's yours," he said, passing a letter back across the table.

"Mine?" she murmured, taking the letter.

"It's addressed to you."

The letter had what appeared to be a stamp impressed in the top right hand corner, though it resembled a smudged thumbprint. It was a single piece of small paper folded tightly in two. She stared at the letter as Hobbs efficiently sliced open his envelopes with a silver letter-opener he had produced from a drawer. Her stare was unblinking.

"Everything alright, my dear?" he asked after a while.

She blinked now, nodded mutely and put the letter in her bag. Instinct told her to keep her shock to herself.

"Fine," she said, managing a smile.

The letter was on crinkled rice paper and bore an S watermark, with a faint type she had recognised immediately. It was addressed to:

Miss Eleanor Sorensen

II

Missing

The contents of the letter, which Ellen opened in private, had bewildered her. She slept badly and woke to the sound of the front door; the faint click of the lock turning was enough to open her eyes.

In the kitchen, she found Tarn washing up the cutlery and crockery she had brought with her; it was dusty from the church's vestibule cupboard where it had been stored after the wake. As Ellen strolled in, she idly picked up a dishcloth and a plate from the drainer and walked the few feet from sink to counter.

"Saw the solicitor yesterday," she remarked casually after a time. "He thinks there's stuff missing."

Tarn didn't reply, but there was a moment of hesitation in her hands.

Those busy hands, Ellen thought, liking the phrase she had invented to describe her housekeeper's activities.

"The house is as I found it, when I started working here in June," Tarn said wearily. "Except for the typewriter, as I said. I don't know what's happened to that."

Ellen walked to the sink. Tarn stepped away to let Ellen replace her plate before putting a pot on the drainer.

"Sorry," Ellen muttered, returning to the counter with an unfriendly smile.

Tarn quickly took a handful of cutlery from the drainer. "You don't have to help me with this, Ellen. It's what I'm being paid for." Crouching down she tried the first of three unpainted wooden drawers below her to her left, but had trouble pulling it out. She tried the middle drawer and this one came out easily, but it was wobbling because it was too small for the runners. The third drawer was jammed tight and broken at the side, as if a heavy instrument had been used to align the drawer.

"Are they new?" Ellen asked, remembering that there used to be a space under the sink for the bin.

"My brother fitted them. I think they need oiling or something." Tarn raised her eyebrows at her own understatement.

"Handyman, your brother, is he?" Ellen asked, remembering Tarn's slow-looking brother from the wake. The counter had all the fitted drawers and it occurred to Ellen that Tarn had tried the new ones under the sink simply to avoid having to come over and ask her to move. She pressed her bottom firmly against the counter surface, pleased at having established a territorial zone of fear.

"He enjoys it. He likes working with wood and … well…" and Tarn raised her eyebrows again "… hammering things. He made these drawers himself. He didn't buy a kit or anything."

"Don't doubt it." Ellen walked back over to the sink and collected some of the clean cutlery from the drainer.

"Really Ellen, I can manage here."

"No, I want to help." Ellen made a point of letting her drawer glide open smoothly. "I've been in digs for three years: I'm no stranger to washing up."

"I'd love to have gone to university," Tarn remarked, standing up.

"Why didn't you?" Ellen asked in an uncertain voice, surprised at the comment.

The housekeeper smiled, a little sadly. "It wasn't my path. What were you studying?"

"Business Studies and Politics – look, that doesn't matter. I want to know what's happened to this fucking typewriter."

Tarn dropped her dishcloth as if she had received an electric shock. "Don't do that," she said in a cold voice Ellen hadn't heard before.

"Do what?"

"*That*. Swearing … profanity."

"Oh for fu… For goodness sake…" Ellen replied, with a curious smile, yet feeling her stomach flutter as she realised the housekeeper was deadly serious.

They spent the next few moments looking at the dishes in the sink, as they regrouped. Ellen was the first to speak.

"So you *are* one of those born-again Christians," she said, recalling a comment that her uncle Martin had made at the wake. The Sorensens were churchgoers but her uncle thought there was a fundamental distinction.

Some people walk a closer path, Ellen…

Tarn was recovering her composure. "What I am doesn't concern you. Just don't swear around me, that's all I ask."

Ellen tried to dispel the uncomfortable sensation at having been so successfully chastised. Outwardly, she shrugged. "Whatever," she conceded.

"So, tell me about this typewriter," Tarn suggested. She had retrieved her dishcloth, her tone confirming the uneasy armistice.

"Mr Hobbs remembers it because he was involved with the paperwork when Father was in the negotiations about buying it," Ellen replied sulkily. "And it's not a typewriter, but a *type write*, one of the first prototype typewriters ever made, before Sholes & Glidden were taken over by Remington Arms." She paused to check that she was relaying the solicitor's description correctly. "In other words, it's very, very valuable."

"That old thing? I had no idea." One soapy free hand smoothed back her hair.

Ellen now abandoned the pretence of washing up and walked over to the stove where she lit a cigarette on the hob. "So, did he sell it? Advertise it?"

Tarn waved away the smoke. "How would he advertise it? Your father was just as afraid of telephones as he was of going out."

Leading off from the kitchen was a pantry; it had never been converted, despite the age of refrigeration, and its shelves were empty apart from a half-full tin of paint and some tools. Guarding the entrance to the pantry, on a small, circular table was a 1930s telephone cast in ebony bakelite with gold circular trim. They both looked at it.

"He never used the telephone, believe me," Tarn insisted, following Ellen's eyes. "Don't get me wrong, he loved that thing, he really did: he was always talking about his retro telephone and telling me to polish it." She sighed, wearily. "Polished it so often … so hard … he wasn't satisfied until he could see his face in it. He made me go out and buy this special wax … he even insisted that I get maintenance men in to check the wires to the speakers and everything…" and she paused thoughtfully, wondering now at all these instructions, "…but he never used it and it never rang. It never rang, Ellen. I think he had the number changed so no one *would* ring." She shook her head. "Check the telephone bills if you don't believe me."

"They're with the solicitor," Ellen replied.

"Well, did you get through when *you* tried to ring him?" Tarn's eyes narrowed a fraction. "When *did* you last try to ring him?"

Ellen stubbed out her cigarette. The answer was about six months ago. "So, if he didn't sell it, where is it?"

"Maybe he broke it and threw it out. Can't you claim on the insurance? Why do you need to find it?"

"Because I want to find out who's writing to me."

Tarn hesitated, then carefully folded her dishcloth and put it down. "Writing to you?" she asked quietly.

Ellen nodded. "That's how I know the typewriter isn't here and that it isn't broken." She reached into the back pocket of her jog pants and presented the envelope side of the letter, which read:

Miss Eleanor Sorensen

In the top right hand corner was the stamp, a rough square thumbprint in the centre of which was typed:

13p

"That's from your father's typewriter," Tarn whispered, her eyes widening.

"It's certainly his paper," Ellen agreed cautiously. "There's no such thing as a thirteen pence stamp, by the way, and it's not a real stamp anyway. I checked. This has been hand delivered."

Tarn nodded, perplexed. "I recognise the type as well. It's so faint you can barely see it." She took the letter in both hands with a cautious reverence, as if handed a baby for the first time.

"You *recognise* it?"

"He typed a letter while I was working here. One letter, that's all. It took him all day."

"What letter? Can I see it?"

"You've already seen it: it's the letter he sent you for your graduation. He asked me to post it."

"*That* thing?" Ellen remarked incredulously. "Just those five words?" She made a face. "I am so very proud," she recited robotically, with equal emphasis on every word, as if it were some meaningless phrase from a randomising computer.

"Yes. That thing."

"You're seriously telling me that took him *all day*?"

Tarn sighed. "You really have no idea how ill your father was, have you?"

"Five words?" Ellen repeated, ignoring her taunt. "So what was it? One key stroke every half hour? Every twenty minutes?"

There was a pause.

"Something like that."

Tarn's statement provoked a silence that glittered like a knife as Ellen briefly imagined her father staring bleakly at the typewriter, his hand poised. Tarn turned the letter over. It read, simply:

lie S

"So who sent me the note, Tarn?"

Tarn shook her head in confusion as she mouthed the word *Lies*.

"It was someone who knew me as *Eleanor*, not Ellen."

Tarn looked up.

"Perhaps it was Father," Ellen suggested, with an ironic chuckle. "Perhaps that's why he could only manage to hit four keys."

"Don't…"

Ellen sounded a long yawn and then extended her index finger. She brought it down slowly through the air. "Thump," she said.

"Stop it."

She repeated the motion.

"Thump. Thump. Thump."

Tarn considered her with resentful eyes and Ellen speculated on what she was thinking. She supposed the housekeeper imagined she was sharing the kitchen with an apostate of Hell; she caught the smoke in her mouth and let it trickle out in white wisps and curl around her, to complete the sulphurous image.

Ellen's eyes snapped open, as she woke with a start.

Sunlight was beaming into the bedroom, a strong sea wind playing havoc with the half-drawn curtains of an open window. It must have been mid morning; she had drunk a lot the night before, spending the evening with her mobile and two bottles of red wine.

She was sure she hadn't been dreaming; that it wasn't a nightmare that had woken her so suddenly. Indeed, she had the feeling that she had been in the deepest and heaviest of sleeps where no dreams visit, but as she felt back through the vague corridors of her sleeping memory, she found a door that opened to a cold room and a tiny voice.

The tiny voice was the frantic imploring of a little girl.

Wake up! Please Ellen, you must wake up!

She choked and reared up, pulling the sheets up to her chin in an instinctive gesture of defence. Her mouth was dry.

Cody had been staring directly at her. Her eyes were at their widest extreme, the eyelids fully retracted. The impression was that the doll had just seen something frightful.

Ellen considered the open window and supposed the wind

must have shaken the doll, activating the mechanism in the same way as when she brushed her hand across her hair or gave her little Jumeau a hug or a kiss. She had seen the eyes move from right to left before but never with the eyelids retracting in the same instant; their natural position was about a third closed and she had always assumed that the lever couldn't operate the eyes and eyelids at the same time.

"You scared me," she whispered, reaching down the bed. Cody's eyes switched deftly to the left, then back to the right, as Ellen's hand brushed lightly over her strong, wiry hair. She sat back in dismay for a time, wondering why her doll refused to be comforted and then slid back under the sheets. But seconds later she again jumped in alarm.

The gold and ebony telephone in the kitchen had a rusty trill ring, much like the bell on a bicycle. Her father had long ago connected the telephone up to speakers in every room but this was the first time it had rung since she had been home. He must have changed the speaker settings for the ring was so loud it sounded as if a giant had parked his bicycle in the house.

DRING-A-DRING!

She realised that she was hung over, remembering she only had the composure to take her jeans off before she slumped into bed, but the shrill summons that would go on sounding every fifteen seconds was too loud to ignore. Much as she would have loved to snuggle back into her pillow she groaned and pulled herself out of bed.

DRING-A-DRING!

She found her feet unsteadily with a face of dehydrated exhaustion. "Far too much wine," she moaned as she stumbled slowly out towards the landing.

DRING-A-DRING!

"Shut the ... up!" she muttered, reluctant as always to swear in front of Cody. Passing her mother's portrait, she automatically kissed her two fingers and put them to the glass, but her hangover was evil this morning, making her misjudge the pressure of her hand. The photograph was knocked from its hook.

The drop was about six feet onto the rough wood of the staircase, a bare edge with hammered nails bordering the centre carpet, and the small glass plate seemed to have a sense for just the worst angle to take. It landed unevenly on the curving edge of the step, and almost bounced away. It found another bounce two steps down, striking at another awkward angle. A third bounce had it twisting in mid air.

"Nooooo!" she screamed, helplessly following the trajectory of the fall. One spare cell in her brain, the only one not fully occupied with the drama of her mother's falling portrait, was aware of a small commotion in her bedroom. The wind must have started up again.

The picture found another unusual angle on the turn of the stairs as it nimbly changed direction. Accelerating with the force of repeated trauma it rocketed towards the floor of the hall, leaving her field of vision.

"Oh my God, please no," she whispered as she made her way frantically down the steps. Her mother's image wasn't a photograph in a glass frame, the image was *in* the dark smoky glass, there being no negative of which she was aware. It was irreplaceable.

DRING-A-DRING!

She didn't even hear the telephone now as she found the picture lying mournfully face down on the floor of the hall. She paused, registering a curious inquiry from her subconscious as to whether the portrait was *dead*, then took a deep breath and picked it up.

"Oh thank God," she sighed, for the colour image was undamaged. It was a very natural photograph: her mother pretending to be annoyed but with laughter already in her eyes. She could even hear her imagined words, the ones she always used when she caught Father in some harmless deceit.

You! You scamp!

The surprise on her mother's face now seemed highly appropriate, as if she had actually experienced the fall. With a smile of relief, Ellen examined the dark glass, especially the edges where the picture had met the wood during the violent series of impacts.

33

She raised her eyebrows and shook her head, finding no damage at all. Not a mark or chip on the glass. Not even a smudge.

She was perspiring and she put a sweaty palm over part of the dark surround. Taking it away, she saw that her hand left no mark on the glass and she now realised that she had never had to clean or wipe it.

It must be specially treated, she thought.

Perhaps it was some kind of highly resistant lacquer.

That must have been why Father prepared it in this way, she reasoned. Perhaps there was one of her, possibly her graduation photograph. Maybe that was why she couldn't find it, because he had been in the process of developing it. The speculation made her ponder on how similar she looked to her mother; they both had the high forehead and long nose, although her mother was much prettier, she believed, with those lovely brown locks which gave her a Romanesque…

DRING-A-DRING!

"Oh, coming," she muttered, balancing the picture carefully on the corner of the pedestal that held the skull; the care with which she handled the photograph was perhaps a little unnecessary, she supposed, given the rough and tumble it had so effortlessly survived. With her head a little clearer, she trotted down the stairs to where the antique telephone waited. It managed one final ring as she crossed the kitchen.

Dring-a-dring.

There were no speakers in the kitchen and the bicycle bell was a lament in a small mono. It seemed a little timid without the creaking amplification and she was reminded of that *Star Trek* episode where the little boy tries to frighten Captain Kirk and his crew by projecting himself through a fearsome alien dummy.

"Yes, hello," she gasped, unclipping the small gold-plated receiver and putting it to her mouth, then flicking back her hair and positioning the built-in earpiece. She muttered a curse, used to phones that rested in the palm of her hand operated with just her thumb.

"Yes, hello," she repeated. "Can you hear me?"

There was a swift hiss in the receiver, like the valve of a car tyre when an air pump is removed. It sounded like someone sucking air through their teeth.

"Hello?" she asked again quietly, unnerved by the noise.

"Miss Sorensen?" came the voice of a man whose throat sounded dry as a desert. "Is that Miss Sorensen?"

The connection was remarkably clear.

"Speaking."

"My name is Jasper Wells. I'm a Trustee of The Divine Sentiment."

"Oh … oh yes … you're the…"

"May I offer my condolences?" he croaked.

"Oh yes, yes thank you." She repositioned the telephone on her lap. Pulling a chair over with her foot, she sat down.

"Our society was founded on a phrenological society," he continued. "That science is long dead, but our purpose now is to bring comfort to the grieving…"

She was preoccupied with making herself comfortable, but something he said made her glance at the wall opposite, where there was a chart entitled PHRENOLOGICAL MIRROR.

"I know about the clause in the will," she said at length, "but I should tell you that there isn't much here of any value. My father seems to have given everything away."

The man didn't answer.

"Would you prefer a small donation?" she asked hopefully.

"We don't accept money."

"Why not?" She thought all charities accepted money.

"Our service is completely free and carried out by dedicated volunteers, of which I am one."

"I see," she muttered, becoming angry at the thought of her father seeking comfort from strangers: first the housekeeper, now these people. "You don't accept cash, but you're doing pretty well out of it, aren't you? I mean there's a grand piano here that's easily worth over ten thousand pounds. Did my father realise you might take that when you asked him to change his will?"

"Oh yes, the piano," Wells said, unperturbed by her tone. "I remember the piano."

"I bet you do."

He had started to hum something; it sounded like a tune in an ascending triplet, she couldn't quite make it out. "My fellow Trustee, Mrs Page, has a talent," he remarked. "She played for your father."

"She played ... for my father?"

"Yes ... now what was it that she played? Yes ... yes ... ah, the Moonlight Sonata. The music made your father cry, I'm sad to say."

Ellen nodded.

Yes, it would have.

Father must have told them that it was Mum's favourite piece.

"The piano's very fine," he added, "but we won't be taking it."

"Why not?" she asked suspiciously. "It's the most valuable thing in the house."

"It seems you have the lowest opinion of us, Miss Sorensen." A choking release of air made her imagine his teeth being bared and his eyes coming alive with oxygen. "We require merely a keepsake, something unique and cherished by your parents ... something of *them*, if you will. The monetary value's of no consideration whatsoever."

"Well, the solicitor says I have to respect my father's wishes," she conceded. "I've given him a list which he can send on to you."

"I think it'd be better if we came to the house. Dealing through the solicitor will simply add to your legal bill."

She thought about this. "Okay," she said. It was fine by her if they wanted to bypass her probate inventory, which after all contained Cody's extravagant description and the screaming advertisement of her value. Better to let them visit and hide Cody away in a wardrobe: yes, Cody would still be here and a wardrobe was a perfectly acceptable place for a doll, so she couldn't be accused of cheating anyone. It wouldn't be her fault if they missed her.

Her eyes darkened as she thought of her Jumeau. She wouldn't mention her attachment to the doll unless it proved necessary but she decided to prepare the ground, just in case.

"Look, I know you're not looking for anything valuable and I can see now that you're a respectable organisation. I mean, you would have snapped up the piano otherwise."

There was a pause as she waited for the acknowledgement of this compliment. It didn't come.

"So, obviously," she continued, "if you picked something but then found out that it was of sentimental value to one of the relatives, I mean really *important*, then you wouldn't take it. Would you?"

"Could you be more specific?"

Her teeth bit down on her lower lip as she searched for an example. "Well, photographs, for example. Things that are worth nothing to you, but a lot to *us*. The relatives, I mean."

"Yes, photographs are of great value, aren't they? The loved one captured, forever. For that reason, Miss Sorensen, we always give a memento to the family: photographs, cast in glass."

She pictured her mother's photograph. "*You* gave my father that?"

"We cast it in that fashion from one of his photographs. We use a special process that makes it very durable."

She nodded thoughtfully. "You said *photographs*: there's more than one?"

"Yes, we made a set. We always make a set."

She frowned, thinking this dispelled the notion that her father had set aside her graduation photograph for special treatment. A cold wave of disappointment swept over her. "I haven't got a glass picture of my father," she said glumly.

"Oh but you have."

"I'm telling you I haven't."

"It must have been misplaced." He didn't sound perturbed by the news that one of the charity's sentimental gifts had gone missing.

She shrugged. "So do you want to come round today?"

"A little too soon, I think. Find the second photograph first."

"Look, I'm sure…"

His laugh was rueful. "The elderly are covetous, Miss Sorensen, and cunning. You'd be amazed at the things that are found … secreted away…"

"Well, I'll have another look but I really don't think…"

"Good. Ring me when you've looked. In the meantime, something will be delivered to you."

"Delivered? What?"

"We believe in fair trade. We wouldn't take two items from your house without giving you two things in exchange."

He now gave her a telephone number; she didn't need to get a pen because it was so easy to remember. The number, assigned by the charity register with a special dispensation from BT, was 1331. He asked her to repeat it.

"No, I've got it," she said.

"Please repeat it, Miss Sorensen," he rasped, with an edge to his tone.

"Thirteen thirty-one," she said uncomfortably and a shiver ran down her spine. The number seemed to click into place in her brain as if it were a multi-levered lock; in the background, she thought she heard a woman's voice mutter something as if chanting.

"Is someone there with you?"

"Remember the number," he said, ignoring her question and terminating the connection.

On the landing, she carefully repositioned her mother's portrait, kissed it with her fingers and stepped back to check that it was level. With a satisfied nod she walked backwards into her bedroom, but when she turned, her heart missed a beat: Cody was sprawled face down on the floor.

Barely a second had passed before she had turned the doll over. There was no damage but the doll's eyes were staring directly ahead with the eyelids completely retracted; the expression was not of pain or fear, but of stunned surprise and shock.

"My poor darling," she whispered, hugging the doll to her shoulder and glancing evilly at the open window that must have let in the rogue gust of wind, recalling the noise in the bedroom as the photograph had dropped. She returned Cody to the wicker chair and closed the window, but paused as she secured the latch.

The chair hasn't fallen over.

How did Cody get on the floor if the chair didn't topple?

Inside the doll's metal and porcelain brain a tiny lever that had been meeting resistance finally clicked into place and the eyelids settled into their peaceful expression, about a third closed. Ellen turned and considered the glass portrait on the landing, thinking that her mother's startled expression had the same beat of shock that she had seen in Cody's face, in her glass eyes, as she had turned her over.

Just as the voice of the little girl had woken her in time for the telephone to ring, a waking thought now explored an impossible coincidence.

The doll had fallen at exactly the same moment that the portrait had hit the first step on the stairs.

III

My great unhappiness

The man lying in the iron tub, his head wrapped in swaddling towels and flopped onto his shoulder, was not quite dead. His remaining energy and his last instinct for life had raced to his fingers, which still gripped the pen and the petition.

The artist must have had a forensic eye for detail, for this petition was the lure with which his murderess, one Charlotte Corday, a Royalist, had sought her audience. The light fell softly on the dying man's face, the eyes peacefully closed, yet harshly on the document and on the knife near the drooping right hand, where the feather nib was poised in the martyred act of kindness, the answering of a petition at this the most inconvenient of times. The light itself recorded both the murderess' perfidy and the dying man's nobility, as if the elements themselves were outraged by the crime.

The beginning of Corday's handwriting could be made out on the petition and had been faithfully reproduced by the artist. It read, in French: *My great unhappiness gives me a right to your kindness...*

The large bearded man in the overcoat leaned forward towards the painting hanging over the fireplace, balancing himself by clasping his hands together and stretching them far behind his back.

"My great unhappiness..." he read, then paused, raising two bushy eyebrows.

At least that is what it *should* have read...

"What do you think?" asked a man who had approached with a glass of punch in each hand, the only alcoholic beverage on offer at the small wake. "Valuable?"

The overcoat glanced at the drinks then straightened up with a grimace, only apparent from the dark pinpoints of his eyes for his mouth could barely be seen under his moustache. A heavy head of brown curls and an enormous beard specked with grey made even his expression difficult to gauge. Hidden in one massive hand was a small notebook, which he now snapped shut and put inside one of the many pockets of his grey woollen overcoat. His hands followed the notebook into the coat.

"Drink?" the punch man asked, one of the drinks now being half-offered. He was a man in his early fifties sporting a deep tan, a crew cut and a wide toothsome smile. Waiting to break out under his sober black suit was a frilled white snooker shirt and a tie with piano keys.

With a slow wink of his right eye, the overcoat shook his head. A hand appeared to perform a brisk handshake.

"Honeyman," he said.

"Neville Parry," the punch man replied, "I'm Lawrence's nephew." There was a pause as he shook out his hand behind his back, which had gone numb from the man's grip. "How did you know Uncle Lawrence?"

"I didn't," Honeyman replied, taking a business card out of his pocket; he offered it to Neville as his attention returned to the painting. The card read:

Tristyn Honeyman
Antiques dealer

"Antiques dealer," Neville read, his face lighting up. "So, Mr Honeyman…"

"Just Honeyman."

"Hah ha." Neville brought out a short humourless laugh. "So, Honeyman, how much do you think it's worth?" He paused. "That's why you're here, right? Because you knew about the painting. I'm the sole beneficiary and executor of the will, so you can deal directly with me."

"Is this the only original painting in the house?"

"So it's not a reproduction?" Neville asked slyly.

"It's an original reproduction," Honeyman qualified.

"So where's the original?"

Honeyman, realising he was being tested, popped two sticks of chewing gum in his mouth with just an eye twitch of mirth.

"We've got a food buffet," Neville remarked, pondering on why the man had declined the punch.

"No, I'm not family or friends. Your uncle didn't know me and I'm not invited."

"Well *I'm* inviting you, right?"

Honeyman smiled but returned to the painting. "*The Death of Marat,*" he announced quietly, "by Jacques-Louis David. The original is in the Musees Royaux des Beaux-Arts, in Brussels." He paused. "Did the painting belong to your uncle?" His North Wales accent, which tended to a weighted pause in the middle of sentences, naturally placed a long emphasis on the word *belong*; nevertheless, the word as spoken seemed to carry a special significance.

"Well everything *belonged* to him when he died. But it was my aunt's painting, if that's what you mean."

"Your aunt?"

"Yeah, she only died a few months ago. None of us took her seriously when she said she was ill." The mention of his aunt prompted a grin. "There was always something that was going to kill her. Colds that took you away in the night if you kept the windows open, bugs that destroyed your nervous system if you ate the wrong food, right? When she woke up paralysed from the stroke we all said *fuck, she fooled us that time.*"

"Really," Honeyman murmured, caring neither for the man's language nor his joviality on the subject of his aunt.

"Yeah, anyway, she died a few days later in hospital. Uncle Lawrence went downhill pretty quickly after she popped it. Surprising, really."

"Surprising? Why?"

"We never thought that they liked each other that much, Uncle Lawrence and Aunt Jessica." His smile widened. "Hah ha. They didn't much like anyone, the miserable old coots. Stiff-necked bible bashers: I mean, even their own daughter…"

Honeyman's eyes darted to him. "A daughter? So you're not…?"

"She lives in Australia now. She's not here." He gave a fatalistic shrug. "She got pregnant when she was young and they cut her off."

Honeyman returned to the painting, a wrinkle trench in his forehead signalling his sadness. One of his hands went to the canvas as if in appeal, before he pulled it back. "They must have been very unhappy," he murmured. He considered the dying man awhile and asked, "Was your aunt Jessica fond of this painting?"

"Yeah, she loved this thing. Hah ha. She believed she was related to Charlotte Corday. She had a family tree prepared and all that crap."

"Ah…" Honeyman sighed, "did she now?" He leaned forward as he considered Marat's sleeping countenance. "Did she now?" he repeated.

"But Uncle Lawrence used to say that she only liked it because Marat was a martyr on the verge of death. You know, just like Aunt Jessica with her hypochondria, right?"

Honeyman nodded grimly and in Marat's final dying breath he imagined the eyes flicking open. He tried to will himself to look away: he was looking too hard now; he was intruding.

He gasped and his eyes widened.

"You alright?" Neville asked.

Honeyman straightened up quickly. "Yes, thank you," he said, rescuing himself with deep gulps of air. "Just a touch of angina." He took more gentle breaths as he regained his composure. "So … is the painting being sold with the house?" he asked, a few rapid blinks of his eyes finally dispelling the trouble.

"No, I'll sell this separately. Put it into auction maybe. But I can't sell it just yet."

"Why not?"

"There's a clause in Uncle's will that gives two items in the house to this charity: they describe themselves as bereavement counsellors. The money-grabbing lawyer says the clause is legal and I can't sell anything until they've made their selection." Neville found a sneer particularly reserved for members of the legal profession, whom he considered either muggers or robber barons, depending on the price of their suit. "Two people from the charity have been once already but I've fobbed them off."

"A tall old man with bad teeth and a very attractive young woman?"

Neville grinned. "Yeah, d'you know them?"

Honeyman nodded. "When did they visit?"

"Two days ago. They're coming back next week but I'm not going to let them take the painting if it's valuable. So, what do you think? Is it worth putting into auction?"

Honeyman's eyes wandered down to the petition in Marat's hand. "It's very accomplished ... almost a perfect reproduction."

"Right," Neville agreed, "that's what Aunt Jessica always said..." He paused. "What do you mean by *almost*?"

"Look at the petition."

"What, is there a blemish or something?" Neville put down both glasses of punch on the fireplace and peered at the painting. He shook his head, unable to find any imperfection.

Honeyman said, "The petition should read: 'My great unhappiness gives me a right to your kindness'."

"So?"

"But you'll see that it reads: 'Treize trent et un. Treize trent et un.'"

Neville's knowledge of French was virtually non-existent, but he knew these words didn't sound right.

"Thirteen thirty-one," Honeyman clarified. "Thirteen thirty-one."

Neville was silently repeating the translation as he stood up. "Well fuck," he decided at length. "The fucking artist must have been having a laugh."

"Possibly," Honeyman said, distastefully.

"You'd have thought that Auntie would have spotted it, though. I mean she spoke French…"

"Did your uncle also have an interest in art … or antiques?" Honeyman inquired.

Neville shook his head despondently, deeply upset over the revelation of the French script and wondering whether the painting was jumble sale fodder.

"Did he have anything else you'd like me to value?" Honeyman pressed hopefully.

"There's some sort of laboratory skull," Neville replied, still distracted. "And some books which look pretty old and scientific." Seeing a request in Honeyman's eyes, he shrugged his agreement. "Be my guest," he said, a finger flicking towards the ceiling. "I've put them in the upstairs bathroom."

The home of Lawrence and Jessica Parry was only a few hundred yards from Saundersfoot's fishing harbour, but in spite of the sea air finding its way through the open windows the bedrooms had a stale, crypt-like atmosphere. The plastic Anaglypta – the thick embossed wallpaper so popular in the 1970s and which continued through the entire house – had turned off-white and even yellow in places.

Hanging on the wall of the landing were two small colour portraits of Lawrence and Jessica Parry, cast in a dark smoky glass. Lawrence, a balding man with high cheekbones was annoyed over something and had his attention elsewhere, his eyes yet to register the camera. Jessica was very conscious of having her photograph taken, her face sinking into the puffy folds of her neck as if she were trying to escape from the shot.

Not their best likenesses, Honeyman thought, as he leaned forward to examine them. He had noticed many photographs of the Parrys downstairs: Lawrence was invariably smiling to show off the large white teeth that he was clearly proud of and which he shared with his nephew; Jessica tended to raise her neck in an attempt to look slim and elegant. They would have been a very handsome couple when they were younger.

A question occurred, prompting him to take the notebook out of his coat. He wrote:

Why are the photographs never posed?

Realising this might be important he closed his eyes and took careful, measured breaths. There was no clear pattern to his attacks – they were not always warnings but sometimes simply rebukes for his bad manners, as when he had looked too hard at the painting a moment ago – but a consistent feature was that they always took him by surprise. If he was prepared, as now, it wouldn't happen.

The danger having passed, he opened his eyes and furtively looked behind him; the landing was in full view of the open plan house. He returned the notebook to his pocket and, from another pocket, with his large frame hiding the portraits, brought out a sharp screwdriver. Holding Lawrence's glass portrait in place, he chiselled a tiny hole in the bottom right corner of the glass. He repeated the exercise with Jessica's portrait, making a second chisel hole then, with another glance behind him, returned the screwdriver to a pocket and retrieved his notebook.

He gloomily considered the chisel holes as he turned to a page entitled:

PARRY

Already written underneath was

The Death of Marat (hers)

My great unhappiness...

Trieze trent et un

and with a long sigh he wrote:

Photographs switched two days ago.

He stood dejectedly in front of the photographs awhile, thinking that he never seemed to get to the family in time, then went into the wooden-clad bathroom. On a shelf that should have contained soaps and shampoo he found two books, the first entitled *System of Phrenology* by George Combe and the second *The Phrenological Mirror* by H. Lundie. He flicked the pages of the books briefly, noting that they were reproductions of the nineteenth-century originals and crisp off the press. The pages had that sweet, paper-factory smell; he suspected the books had not even been opened, let alone read.

"Mr Combe and Mr Lundie," he said to himself, with an approving nod. "A pleasure to meet you again, gentlemen." Returning the books to their shelf he glanced around, looking for the phrenological heads. Leaning forward towards a commode, his arms behind him for balance, he found a plaster bust representation of a head. The cranium was exaggerated in length with the features smoothed away so as not to interfere with its purpose, which was clearly as a scientific tool. Schematic squares, words and numbers appeared in messy ink on the enlarged cranium, and on the square base of the bust, written in proud large letters, was 'PHRENOLOGY by L. N. Fowler'.

Another artefact, nestling in newspaper, was a grey fossil skull with similar markings. The nephew had presumably kept the heads out of sight because he didn't like them, or perhaps he thought that keeping them in his aunt's commode would be a good joke.

Honeyman scribbled the titles of the books into his notebook, and made a record of the skull and the Fowler bust. He always accurately recorded the phrenological materials even though he didn't believe it was necessary to do so. They were simply the Trustees' brand merchandise; they gave out phrenological relics as Debenhams gives out perfume samples.

Returning to the landing, he stood once more in front of the glass photographs. With the doors open, sections of both bedrooms were in view; he could see a sideboard with a plastic clock in the second bedroom and a portable television and a framed print of *The Laughing Cavalier* in the main bedroom.

He shook his head. What he was looking for didn't have to be old or original, nor did it have to be valuable, in working order or even intact. There were just four criteria that would make the object – what the Trustees referred to as *the vessel* – eligible. These key features, as compiled in the back pages of his notebook, were as follows:

It would be unique.

It would have a means of communication, however limited or obscure.

It would have been coveted by the owner.

And finally, the criteria that usually allowed him to find the vessel with such ease:

It would be in clear view of the photograph.

He discreetly rotated a full circle on the top step, able to see most of the open-plan living area and the entrance to the conservatory from this vantage point. "Lawrence Parry, where are you?" he murmured. "I know you're here somewhere." A thought occurred. The object he was looking for had to be in the line of sight of Lawrence Parry's photograph, he reasoned, but it could be concealed.

Yes, concealed with a cloth perhaps. Maybe the nephew had wanted to cover it to avoid it being damaged during the wake. As there was nothing conspicuously covered, it followed that it might be some kind of table; it would be something that would accept a tablecloth and blend into the background.

With new eyes, he examined the dining area. Eventually he settled on something just inside the door of the conservatory extension: it was a square table, about the size of a generous coffee table, and covered with a tablecloth. There were bumps in the cloth as if there were objects underneath a few inches tall, pushing up like tiny ghosts.

A couple with their daughter, a little girl about eight years old, were standing near this table. The mother noticed Honeyman as he walked over and discreetly lifted the cloth in one fluid motion, so delicately that he didn't topple any of the six figurines he found underneath. There was a zest in his eyes as he considered what he had found.

"Wow, look at that," the father declared.

The figures were head and shoulder carvings in silver, each with a different colour base: red, yellow, white, green, blue and purple. They were Cluedo pieces; the silver busts were modelled on the faces of the original 1946 cards. A pack of those cards was face up on the board sitting between blue and green transparent dice and two tall leather beakers. The top card showed the original Miss Scarlett with the blonde ruffle of hair and red blush cheeks; three cards were hidden in a black leather envelope, the murder envelope, in the centre of the board.

"How about that!" the man remarked, his daughter instinctively reaching out to pick up one of the pieces.

"Don't touch, sweetheart … valuable," her mother said, her last word a half-question as she looked at Honeyman. He nodded then winked at the little girl; she smiled back, the slow squeeze of his eye seeming both playful and sincere, but took her father's leg.

"Valuable," he agreed, stepping back and considering the most beautiful handcrafted Cluedo board he had ever seen. It was laid out in soft Dauphin leather, the small move squares alternating between black and ivory, while the rooms each had their own colour leather, except for the Billiard Room, which was inlaid in green felt. It mirrored the simple elegance of the original design and in the centre square of the board was written: *Geoffrey Parker, essentially English since 1958.*

"Handmade," he murmured, picking up one of the silver figurines. It was heavy, too heavy it seemed for something so small. He returned it to its place on the board with a feeling of relief.

"Ah, you've found it," Neville said, coming up behind him. Honeyman looked round and nodded, wondering if the word *valuable* had a whistle frequency to Neville's ears.

"I put a cloth on it because of drinks, you know," Neville said, looking suspiciously at the little girl.

"Oh, absolutely," the mother said, touching her daughter's shoulder.

"Your uncle seems to have had a passion beyond the bible after all," Honeyman remarked.

Neville gave a shrug of reluctant concession. "He did love his Cluedo."

Honeyman nodded thoughtfully, quite taken with the bespoke game board, which conjured up happy childhood memories of Christmas. "When you played this as a child," he murmured, "did you ever wonder what sort of scientist Professor Plum was?"

Or what sort of churchman Reverend Green was, for that matter.

He grimaced as a painful memory of walking down the aisle of his church, in disgrace, resurfaced.

"Honeyman, can I have another word?" Neville asked, ignoring the question and putting a hand to Honeyman's arm to lead him out of the conservatory. "Is there anything you can tell me about these charity people? Anything I need to know?"

Honeyman reluctantly glanced back at the conservatory to see that the mother and father had gone into the garden to light cigarettes. The mother was watching her daughter with a cautious smile: the little girl had knelt down and having examined with delight the crafted faces of the suspects was now carefully considering each of the cards to the Cluedo set.

"Have they picked out what they want?" he asked, turning back to Neville.

"No ... well, they couldn't really. I put dust sheets over everything."

"The Cluedo board and the Marat picture too?"

"Those especially. I told them the living room was being redecorated, right? Let them have a wander upstairs though ... nothing valuable up there."

Honeyman glanced once more at the little girl: she was whispering to herself, closing her eyes as she stored away each card's information. Her mother, puffing at her illicit cigarette, was still watching her from the garden.

"That seems like an elaborate hoax," he remarked, turning back to Neville before asking the question that he knew would give the man sleepless nights. "Why not just move the things out of the house before they arrived? Wouldn't that have been easier?"

Neville lost his smile: the idea of moving the Marat picture and the Cluedo board before the Trustees had arrived hadn't even occurred to him. A mental exclamation mark told him to find a reason.

The Cluedo board looked far too heavy ... yes far too heavy ... and the picture ... well, the picture just belonged on the wall. It belonged there...

"Maybe I will, next time," he muttered uncomfortably. "Depends on what they want, right? Look, what can you tell me about these people?"

"I can tell you they'd have known you were hiding things from them," Honeyman replied, snatching another glance at the conservatory. The little girl's mother, tired of watching her daughter play with the Cluedo cards and satisfied she wasn't going to damage the board, was discussing the garden with her husband, both attempting to keep their cigarettes concealed. The little girl now reached for the murder envelope where three cards were hidden: a suspect, a weapon, a room. She was muttering the murder solution to herself.

"No, you're wrong, they took it hook, line and sinker," Neville insisted. "They weren't angry at all." He remembered how the stunning female Trustee had wrinkled her nose in farewell while the other one, the gaunt old man, had muttered something about returning when the walls had dried.

"They had other business last time."

Neville's eyes narrowed. "Really? What other business?"

Honeyman hesitated then shook his head to indicate his remark wasn't important. It would be a bad idea to tell Neville about the photographs: he was suspicious now, would go straight to the glass portraits and find his chisel marks.

"Now listen to me, Mr Parry," Honeyman said, buttoning his overcoat. "The Trustees will come back and this time they will collect their inheritance. When they tell you they want the painting and the game board I suspect you'll try to handle matters yourself, but take my advice and give them up willingly."

"Bollocks. I'm going to see a fucking barrister about that clause, right? Solicitors don't know shit."

Honeyman was shaking his head as he walked towards the hallway. "Save your money. Having the entire High Court of Justice in your pocket wouldn't help you now. No, the Trustees will take the painting and the game board." He paused. "At the end you'll be begging for them to be taken." Ignoring Neville's scowl he took a last look at the conservatory. The Cluedo board was unattended, the three cards in the murder envelope sticking half way out.

"Are you in league with them?" Neville rasped, his tone now thin with anger. "Is that a fucking threat?"

Honeyman didn't answer.

"Get out before I call the police," Neville decided. "Go on – fuck off." His insistent hand on Honeyman's shoulder met resistance: the shoulder was like a stone wall.

Honeyman's attention was elsewhere, barely aware of Neville's hand attempting to steer him into the hall. He was looking at the little girl in the garden, wailing pitifully, her parents trying in vain to console her.

IV

Lies

On the morning her uncle was due to return home, Ellen received a delivery. Inside an anonymous cardboard box, packed in straw, was a plaster cast bust of a head. She glared at the bust for a while without touching it, suspiciously considering the smooth rudimentary features and the numbers etched in the cranium, then pushed the box into the small cupboard under the stairs, re-arranging some magazines to make way for it. She realised it was the promised delivery from the charity.

The exertion over, her eyes fell on the skull near the front door, the fossil that Tarn called *Mr Sockets* with tiny numbers etched within lined sections of the bone. The Trustee had also mentioned an exchange: two things in fair trade. Perhaps they gave two heads for the two gifts in the will.

On her doormat, she found something else. It was another business card from Tristyn Honeyman, Probate Valuations, with a scribbled message saying he would call on Friday afternoon if that was convenient. She nodded and made a mental note to be in; she wanted to get Mr Hobbs' list sorted out so that she could get back to Cardiff.

When her uncle arrived, he considered the bust with perplexed amusement. "Perhaps your father belonged to a scientific society, was on some kind of mailing list," he suggested. He gratefully accepted the offer of coffee and followed his niece down to the kitchen.

"Heart attack…" he mused as he leaned back against the cooker, holding his mug of coffee in two hands. He was thinking there was no heart disease in his family: he was Nigel Sorensen's identical twin and didn't even have a high cholesterol count.

"Heart attack," Ellen agreed, finding conversation difficult. She had been close to her uncle but years of separation had taken their toll.

She was nine when the brothers had their argument. She had only caught snapshots but it had something to do with her father working abroad while her grandfather was dying, and Martin nursing the old man even though he only had her father's name on his lips. The argument had been brewing for years and the allegations had landed like blows, each participant blanching with shock and pain before taking up a larger weapon with which to respond.

After only a few days her uncle opened up peace talks, but her father received him coldly.

"He's your twin, Nigel," she remembered her mother saying, "but he was born first so he thinks he's your older brother. D'you think he'd humiliate himself like this otherwise?"

Her father's face had darkened over. He wasn't going to feel guilty about travelling in his twenties and had only spoken the truth when he said his father was ashamed of Martin's homosexuality. That wasn't his fault and he wasn't going to take it back.

Eventually it became too late to relent, and only embarrassment and shame grew in the weeds of confusion and rage. The brothers had met years later at her mother's funeral but there were still no apologies, no words of regret. Her father snapped at Martin's partner, Mikey, when he attempted a diplomatic intervention. Nigel Sorensen was bitter by this time, finding things to hate.

"So are you sure you've got everything in hand?" Martin asked. "Can you manage with the solicitors, the estate agents...?"

"Oh that's all okay."

He nodded. "D'you need any financial advice? Investments? Tax planning?"

"At some point, I suppose," she conceded. "Haven't really thought about the money..."

"No, of course…"

She nodded and considered her coffee. Her uncle used to visit when she was much younger and she was always the spoilt and pampered observer, never feeling the need to speak. Now it was just the two of them and she felt embarrassed and shy, it making no difference that Martin was her father's identical twin. There were admittedly some physical differences. Her father had undoubtedly been the more handsome of the two brothers, his face longer, better suiting the square chin and close-set Sorensen eyes; Martin was also the brother with the bad eyesight, wearing spectacles and, having always mistrusted exercise in any form, proudly carrying a paunch. Yet these variations were immaterial: only people who know twins could understand how important personality, character and temperament are to shaping a face. Her gentle, sensitive and mildly spoken uncle was as different from her father as anyone could be.

"Thanks for … well arranging everything," she managed eventually.

"Oh, it was nothing."

She took a sip of her coffee, knowing that it was far from nothing. Meeting with the solicitor and the estate agents post-funeral was just about moving around the money. Her uncle had made all the arrangements that were intimately concerned with the death: visiting the hospital morgue and obtaining the death certificate; organising the notices; choosing the wood, the design and the price of the coffin; deciding which clothes her father should be buried in.

She had wanted no part of that and had stayed holed up in her Cardiff digs while her uncle had travelled from East Anglia to do the rounds of the registry and the local undertakers. She was too busy, she had tearfully explained to him over the telephone; she had a make or break essay, one that had been deferred until after her graduation on account of her mother's death, but which had to be finished on a deadline or her degree could be taken back. Mum would turn in her grave if her education were to go to waste, if she were to fall at this last hurdle.

The lie was so polished, so padded out with background scenery, from the edit notes of the essay itself to the doom-laden warnings of her tutor, that she had almost come to believe in the existence of the essay herself. The myth of the post-graduation essay was now firmly in place in her legend and she knew it would follow her through life; she wanted to believe in it as an agnostic wants to believe in God.

You are a bad daughter ... selfish and deceitful...

That was the disturbing message that the agnostic God muttered to her in the darkness.

"I'll be getting back then." Martin raised his mug in praise of the coffee then swilled it in the sink.

"Actually, there is one thing, Uncle Martin. I was going to ring you, in fact."

He nodded, urging her to continue.

She thought about how to begin. "What's your opinion of Father's housekeeper, Tarn Hughes?" she asked cautiously.

"I found her very helpful. Why do you ask?"

"Well, Father had loads of stuff and it's all gone. Just about all of it."

Martin glanced sadly around the kitchen; he had thought many times how bare the house looked since he had returned to Tenby. "It's been a long time since I saw your father, Ellen. We ... had a falling out, years ago, as you know."

"I appreciate that, but believe me this house was full of his things. Antiques, books ... you know."

He nodded. "I remember Nigel started his Dickens collection before he went abroad." He touched the bridge of his spectacles. "I was surprised not to see those."

"Exactly."

"What's this got to do with young Tarn Hughes?" His jaw straightened with realisation. "Oh come now, Ellen. You're not suggesting she's light-fingered, are you?"

"Why not?" she asked, annoyed that her uncle had immediately sprung to the little housekeeper's defence, just as Mr Hobbs had done. "I think she's got busy hands," she muttered.

He smiled at the phrase she had coined. "Ellen, she seems like a nice girl and these are serious allegations, for which you've got no proof. Besides, I think she was devoted to your father."

"What do you mean?"

"I've met a lot of carers in my time, good, bad and disinterested. Tarn was passionate, I think, about your father's health."

"She's not a professional carer … she's just a housekeeper."

"She was a *carer*," he said, giving the word a visceral meaning beyond the acquisition of qualifications.

Ellen's face was sullen; her uncle was a chiropractor and she supposed he was qualified to make the assessment. "What about her brother then?"

He shrugged. "He's … well…"

"Slow?"

"Now I wouldn't go that far. He's not the sharpest knife in the rack, I'll grant you, but that doesn't make him a thief." He paused. "Your dad seemed to trust him, anyway. Didn't he do odd jobs round the house?"

"Well he did *that*," she remarked, motioning with her coffee mug to the three wooden drawers in the ill-fitting runners to the bottom left of the sink.

"Yes indeed," he agreed, suppressing a smile. "Being a bad workman doesn't make him a thief either. As for your father's things, perhaps he … well…"

"What?"

"Just got rid of everything."

"Why would he do that? Why?"

"Because your father wasn't himself towards the end, Ellen. Mr Hobbs, as well as Tarn and her brother, have told me what he was like in the final months. And … and I *saw* him … you know, when I made the arrangements. I barely recognised him." He shook his head sadly.

"Doctors thought he was faking, to tell you the truth," she said.

"Faking?"

"Well he didn't qualify for an attendance allowance or anything. He had to pay for the carers with his own money. He had a string of them too, grumpy as he was. Until Tarn came along," she admitted, reluctantly. "He seems to have been okay with her, although perhaps by then he was just too weak to argue any more."

There was a pause as they both considered the care Tarn had given Nigel Sorensen. For Martin it was with gratitude, pleased that his brother hadn't been alone in his final months; for Ellen it was with resentment, which wasn't fully explained by the notion that the housekeeper might also be a thief. Perhaps Wendy would help when she got back to Cardiff; she pictured her counsellor, smiling patiently without speaking, but there were no answers in that little room with the Yucca plant and the pastel drawings of flowers.

"There's something else," Ellen said, anxious to change the subject. "Something I'm a bit worried about." She explained about the clause in the will and recapped her telephone conversation with Jasper Wells. She had written down the telephone number of the charity on a scrap of paper, which she handed it to him.

"That's not a telephone number," he said, looking at it.

"It is. It's a special number they've got because it's easy to remember."

"It's not a telephone number," he repeated, with a smile. "It's only four digits." Seeing that she was unconvinced he said, "Try it, if you don't believe me."

"I don't want to speak to them right now," she protested.

"Just see if it rings."

With a shrug she collected her mobile, snapped it open and tapped in the four numbers. She put the handset to her ear, waited a while and then folded it up. "Okay, so it's not a number," she agreed, taking a breath. "Now I'm spooked. Why would they give me a number that doesn't exist?"

"You must have written it down wrong."

"No way. They even made me repeat it."

Made me *say* it.

She remembered clearly the chill down her spine when she repeated the number – *thirteen thirty-one* – and it had clicked into place in her head, like a complex lock.

"It's probably an extension number, then," he suggested. "Maybe they assumed you already had their landline number."

She nodded with a measure of relief, thinking this was a good explanation. "I only mentioned the telephone number because I'm wondering whether it's connected to this letter I've received."

"Letter?"

She collected the letter written on her father's typewriter. He took it curiously, sitting down at the table as he did so. He'd recognised the typeset and the paper immediately, having received many letters from his brother before their estrangement.

"Look, there's a link between the stamp and their telephone number," she said. "Well, the first half of the number."

"Thirteen thirty-one?" he asked, with a puzzled face.

"Right," she confirmed uneasily, realising that she didn't even care to hear the number spoken. "Maybe that's just a coincidence, but I *am* sure that Tarn's involved in this somehow. Maybe she stole the typewriter and gave it the charity, and they're trying to warn me not to trust her. That's what *Lies* means…"

"This isn't a real stamp," he remarked.

"I know."

He was thoughtful for a moment then shook his head. "Forget about the charity and forget about Tarn. This is some crank who has somehow got his hands on Nigel's typewriter. Can I take this away with me? I'll ask Mikey to have a look at it."

She nodded eagerly, she'd been hoping he would suggest this. Mikey had what she had always regarded as a highly glamorous job in a forensics lab.

"Perhaps we'll get some fingerprints," Martin murmured. "I think it would be a good idea if you went back to Cardiff for the time being. Have you got a boyfriend or someone who can keep an eye out for you?"

"There's Hugh, I suppose," she said. "We've been … sort of

59

together … for about six months." She guiltily considered Hugh's texts, saying how much he was missing her, which she hadn't got round to answering: he was an accountant some ten years her senior, but she thought of him as a little boy.

Martin's eyes registered surprise at the words *six months*. "Didn't he want to come to the funeral?"

"Well I didn't invite him," she answered, as if this was the most reasonable of explanations. A quick shake of her head removed her mainly platonic relationship with Hugh from the conversation. "Anyway, I'm not sure about going back just yet. The estate agents said I'd get a better price for the house if it was lived in."

Martin returned to the letter with a troubled expression. "There are more important things than money, Ellen. The house'll sell whether you're here or not."

"The estate agents do have a key," she conceded, starting to warm to the idea. "Tarn could still pop in every morning, to air the place and everything." She smiled sardonically. "And there's not much left for her to steal."

"I'd feel happier with you out of the house," he admitted, ignoring the aside. "I'm sure this note is harmless but this place can't be doing you any good."

"I've got to speak to these charity people before I go."

"They can go through the solicitor. Just give Mr Hobbs a ring and he can arrange everything. That's what he's getting paid for."

"Suppose so," she murmured, unhappy with the idea of Mr Hobbs showing the Trustees around the house. Mr Hobbs wouldn't care what the charity took away with them. He wouldn't protect Cody…

Yes, the doll is in the second bedroom, she heard him say, studying the contents inventory as he stepped through the front door with a deep inhalation of air and a theatrical gesture towards the upstairs floor. She saw the list flutter between his chubby thumb and forefinger, the shadow of Jasper Wells gleefully reading Cody's description over the solicitor's shoulder.

… *she has a soulful expression … delightful…*

Wells' hand briefly caressing the fossil skull, while her doll screamed hysterically in the bedroom with the voice of a little girl.

"Soulful ... delightful," she heard Wells croak above the screams.

Ellen shuddered, then a new thought struck her. If she left Tenby, she could tell Mr Hobbs that she had taken Cody with her but that the Trustees would be welcome to visit her in Cardiff. She might get time to see them, though she had a hectic social life and was very busy. They could make an appointment.

"Yes, I'll go back to Cardiff," she agreed, her voice low and purposeful. "In fact I'm going to pack and go back tonight."

Nigel Sorensen had been buried near his wife, Nia, in the small church in Penally where they had been married and Martin decided to make this a short stop before he got onto the motorway. He hadn't appreciated how demanding the role of funeral organiser had been. As he stood now at his brother's grave, alone and without any duty to occupy him, he realised that he hadn't really had the opportunity to grieve.

"So here you are, you stubborn old bugger," he muttered, surprised to find his grief contained both anger and resentment. It was a fallacy, then, that death was the great leveller where all things would be forgiven and forgotten. They had lost twelve years, just because of an argument.

One stupid, senseless argument...

Nia's funeral would have been the opportunity for a re-conciliation, but they had only exchanged a few words, the muted dialogue about the grey flannel morning suit Nigel was wearing, the one Nia had loved. Nigel muttered his instructions: the next time he wore it would be at his own funeral, so he would be wearing it when he met her again. A year on, the suit was dutifully delivered to the undertaker, though it was now three sizes too large.

It was several minutes before Martin's expression softened.

"I know you didn't mean the things you said," he said to the plot of earth. He knelt down and tidied the flowers by the headstone, which marked out Nigel Sorensen as a loving father and husband, and noticed that the stone had angled back ever so slightly. Kids playing in the graveyard had moved it a fraction, he supposed. With a groan of effort he straightened the stone then tidied the flowers once more; the roses and lilies were tired and had only a day or two more left in them at most.

A chill breeze glittered in the leaves of the sycamores that cast this sheltered part of the graveyard into a mosaic of small brown shadows. As he stood up his eyes went to the earth of the plot, dark with raked peat. Something was there, in the earth: a small white triangle, perhaps a corner of a piece of paper, sticking up from the ground as if it were a tiny white shoot. He pulled it out and dusted it off. It was a folded letter with a thumbprint stamp, identical to the letter Ellen had given him this afternoon, except for one difference.

It was addressed to him.

Mr Martin Sorensen

The earth didn't cling to the paper as he dusted it off; there wasn't even the faintest of brown marks. He unfolded the letter. It read, simply:

g

Perplexed, his finger traced the outline of the odd oblong paper with its prominent S watermark, wondering who would plant such notes in a grave. His eyes returned to the plot and he made out another white triangle, buried a little deeper. He pulled a second letter out of the ground, detaching it with ease from the umbilical peat. This one read:

giv   e

"Give?" he murmured. "Give what?" With a finger to the bridge of his spectacles, he closely examined the stamps on the letters. As with Ellen's letter, the first bore the price 13p but the second had a stamp with the price 31p. He recalled Ellen's odd telephone number, wondering if there was a link. Whoever had planted them must have known he would visit the grave. Perhaps the crank had been following him.

With a shiver of suspicion, he looked around the graveyard and noticed a secluded clearing about a hundred yards away that had a view of the entire church. It was easy to miss in its angled wedge and he had to look carefully past the sycamores to find a solitary bench, cast in leafy shadows. The clearing was empty.

He turned back to the grave and walked round the edge of the plot. Behind the headstone he found the third letter, barely the tip of its corner showing as if it was seconds away from being pulled into the earth. It resisted him, but when it came out it was clean and the stamp was numbered:

13p

It read:

Forgive me

Martin's face was without expression as he stared the message. He swung round as the shadow of a large man behind him flickered in the soft brown leaves of the trees.

That evening Ellen discovered she couldn't leave her father's house. She was lying in bed in the darkness with her eyes half open, Cody a dim outline in the wicker chair, as her rational mind attempted a healing process. When she woke in the morning logic would have found a way to pack the experience away in a box, never to be opened.

The experience of trying to leave the house, with the doll in her arms.

She telephoned her uncle first thing to announce casually that she had decided to stay in Tenby for the time being, that she wasn't worried about any crank notes. Her uncle didn't attempt to talk her out of it but said he would ring her every day to check on her. The muted conversation was hesitant on both sides, and as it stumbled to a close he asked her whether she had been to the grave since the funeral. She said that she had, to lay some flowers, but this was untrue, for all the new flowers were from Tarn and her brother. Along with the myth of the essay this was yet another lie that she needed to slot into her belief system and so it came easily and naturally.

As she uttered the lie she wondered whether that letter from her father's typewriter ... *lies* ... was referring not to Tarn Hughes at all, but to herself. Once more resentment against her father boiled up inside; resentment that he should make her act this way and hate herself.

Martin suggested that she should avoid visiting the grave for a time because if she was being stalked that might be a vulnerable place. There was a clearing, he explained, where someone could easily hide. She shrugged, not concerned in the slightest but happy to take that suggestion as a royal command. There couldn't be any guilt if she had been ordered to stay away.

In truth, she had never cared for that plot in the churchyard and on the day of her father's funeral had secretly resolved never to return. On more than one occasion she had attempted to visit her mother's grave and all the memories were painful. It never felt right, being there; it was as if in visiting the grave she were shopping in an empty warehouse or planting seeds in a marsh.

She didn't understand the empty, useless feeling she experienced when she stood by the grave, unsure what to say and feeling a little stupid when she did say something.

Sometimes she had the surest feeling that her mother simply wasn't there.

V

This persecuted science

The Trustees, their eyes closed in concentration, were watching the visitor from afar. They were following his feet, each footstep through the house, ready to pounce with the suffocating image of the end that waited for him if he trespassed too far.

"Just Honeyman," the visitor murmured at 2 pm precisely on Friday afternoon, after he had introduced himself to Ellen.

Ellen considered his business card as she led him into the day room. "I'm assuming you read about my father in the paper?"

"My sincerest condolences," he said by way of reply. His hand was poised over a notepad, surveying the few ornaments in the room. She watched him work for a few minutes; sometimes he would pause and the page would be flipped over with the precision of an electric typewriter.

"Can I get you a cup of tea?" she ventured.

He acknowledged the offer of tea with a quick shake of his head, and a glance of thanks.

"My Mum's," she said, referring to the Edwardian figurines, the only ornaments left to the room.

He nodded and walked further into the day room.

"That's a Steinway," she said as he peered inside the mechanism of the piano. With his outstretched arms he made a ruler as he measured the instrument's length.

"It's a baby grand," she clarified.

He glanced at her and said, "Baby grands are just under six foot.

65

This is just over. It's a *parlour* grand." Her mouth formed an 'oh' as he wrote in his notebook. "Steinway parlour grand in mahogany satin. Circa nineteen fifties and expertly reconstituted. Turned legs and fretted desk, sostenuto third pedal for chord sustain." He paused. "Twenty thousand pounds," he decided, tapping his full stop into place.

"That much?" she whispered.

"It's in beautiful condition. I recognise the dealer; unless I'm very mistaken this was purchased in Vienna."

"Are you a musician?" she asked, shaking her head in amazement. Her parents had found the piano on their honeymoon, which was indeed in Vienna, her mother having often reminisced about hearing the most wonderful concerts of Mozart and Strauss in the Golden Hall. The book guides were still in one of the drawers upstairs.

He scribbled for a few moments with his pencil as he surveyed this end of the room then snapped his notebook shut. "An enthusiast, not a musician," he answered. "Yes, if I owned a passport my job title would have to say ... *enthusiast*. Many things fascinate me, Miss Sorensen, and some would say that I have far too much miscellanea rolling around up here." He tapped his head with his finger. "I've never understood how people can fail to be fascinated by things that are unique, in this disposable society with its fifteen-second attention span." He stepped away from the piano with a sigh of appreciation. "Was it your father who played?"

"No, that's Mum's again," she said, liking her visitor.

"Is there anything in this room that was exclusively your father's?" he asked, in a casual tone.

"Does that make a difference? For tax, I mean?" she asked with a frown.

He quickly popped something in his mouth and said, "No difference. I'm just curious, that's all."

"There used to be loads of stuff, now that you mention it. He had a collection of Dickens to start with, first editions..."

"Ah, the incomparable Mr Dickens."

"First editions," she repeated. "Sailing watches, a music box, a dressing case, lead soldiers…" she took a breath of effort "… lithographs, paintings, antique globes, a really fancy orrery, that's a clockwork model of the solar system, you know…"

"I know," he confirmed, with a shift of his moustache.

"Historical parchments – he had a genuine print copy of the signatures to the execution of Charles the First – old coins, some Roman coins in fact … a period reproduction of an Archimedes water clock … he was really proud of that and it used to be right here in this room. Then there was a Russian balalaika and lots of smaller musical instruments from around the world…"

She hesitated; it was like trying to remember the contents of a conveyor belt on a game show. She was tempted to say *cuddly toy*…

"All gone?" he queried, seeing that she was finished.

"My uncle thinks my father just threw everything out."

"Does he? Does he now?" he muttered and was thoughtful for a few moments. "Before we go any further is there anything…?" He faltered.

"What?"

"Is there anything in particular that you want me to see?"

"Such as?" She had a curious expression.

"Anything unusual," he replied quietly, without making eye contact and with his hand drifting over the lid of the keyboard. "Anything you've had trouble throwing out? Or perhaps taking out of the house?" He glanced at her and saw that the colour had drained from her face. "Everyone has problems throwing certain things out," he explained quickly. "When there's a bereavement, I should say. There are so many things of sentimental value, you understand."

"Oh I see." She shrugged.

"Nothing bothering you then?"

"What could be bothering me?" she asked, with a smile.

His eyes were still on the piano and he seemed to reach a decision, indicated by a gentle wave of his hand. He wiped the keyboard lid, then lifted it. "Well that's fine then," he said. He put his ear, completely hidden within his shaggy mane of hair, next to the side of the piano and closed one eye in concentration. Straightening up with a grimace he pressed a key with his long index finger; it answered him with a sonorous note. He waited for it to fade, then shook his head.

"Does it need tuning?" she asked.

"Oh no, it simply needs to be played." He saw that the keys were dusty. "When did your mother die?"

"A year ago," she replied.

"A year? A whole year?"

"Just over. September last year."

There was surprise in the brown pinpoints of his eyes.

"What?" she asked.

"That's a long time," he said. "A long, long time," he murmured to himself. His moustache indicated an understanding smile. "That's a long time for your father to have been alone, I mean."

"I suppose," she said, but not understanding what he meant. People could be widows or widowers for decades; a year didn't sound that long.

"He was a … your father was a…"

"What?"

He was searching for the right words. "Was he a strong character?"

"Why d'you ask? Who've you been talking to?"

"Only briefly to your housekeeper when I called before. She mentioned he had some disabling condition."

"Oh, you've spoken to *her*, have you?" She took this as a cue to light a cigarette. "We don't know what my father had, to tell you the truth. We thought it was MS or something at first but blood tests gave him the all clear." Her eyes narrowed as the smoke rose. "He didn't even come to my graduation," she muttered, something in the visitor's manner encouraging her to open up. "I mean, what sort of father doesn't come to his own daughter's graduation? He could have come in a wheelchair or something. Would that have been so hard? And he threw out my graduation photograph. Just

... threw it out. He didn't give a damn about me," she concluded sulkily.

Honeyman breathed in through his nose then briefly closed his eyes and she had the strangest notion that he had ingested her words in order to absolve them, like neutralising a poison. "Don't be so quick to judge him," he remarked. "It sounds as if he was very ill."

"Ill…" she sneered. "He was as tough as old boots."

He nodded thoughtfully. "You weren't close to your father?"

She took a long drag of her cigarette to indicate that he was correct in his assessment, though she was thinking about her visitor's accent. She repeated his sentence in her head…

You weren't *close* … to your *futhur*…

…and placed him in North Wales.

"When you were younger, perhaps?" he ventured.

"Up until Mum died, I suppose, but we used to fight a lot. So many things he did really pissed me off and I'm sure he did them just to get up my nose … like when he used to call me *Ellie Sweet*."

"Ellie Sweet?"

"Yeah. I *hated* that name." In truth she had loved it until she reached the age of nine.

Honeyman raised his eyebrows. "Perhaps you were too much alike," he suggested.

She laughed briefly. "No way. I'm like Mum. Everyone says we looked alike."

He seemed to find this answer amusing. "But your parents were close?"

She nodded. "At least they're together now, I suppose."

"You believe that?" he queried, something hopeful in his tone.

She looked at her cigarette. "I don't know. Suppose so. My parents believed in all that and maybe some of it has rubbed off on me but what I meant to say is that they're in the same plot, you know, side by side." She flicked her ash. There were no ashtrays in the house and out of longstanding habit she was using a small cake foil, which she tended to carry round with her when she came back to Tenby. The ash had turned the weary silver foil black, and it was the thought of ashes that prompted her next remark. "I'm surprised though because he always wanted to be cremated. Father wasn't afraid of anything or anyone, but he had a sort of phobia about being buried. He was trapped once when he was investigating a coalmine in Poland for his work. It surprised me when I heard he'd changed his will."

Honeyman was testing the rail mechanism on the curtains. "Changed his will?" he asked in a distracted voice.

"Yeah, to get rid of the cremation clause. He said he wanted to be buried instead."

Honeyman froze. When he turned round his notebook was back in his hand but he looked confused, appearing at a loss to know what to write. "When your father changed his will he specified that he should be *buried*, rather than *cremated*?"

She nodded.

"Even though he dreaded being buried?" he pressed.

"That's right," she said, looking suspiciously at the notebook and then stepping back. Something had happened, for his eyes were widening in fear. "Are you okay?" she asked.

He was clutching his chest, forcing his breathing to return to normal. "Just a little angina," he muttered, with a shake of his head. He took a deep breath.

"You sure?"

"I'm fine, thank you." He scribbled something in his notebook, shut it and, with a pained expression, beckoned her out to the hall.

Two new minds were now alive to the visitor's presence on the first floor of the house. The intrusion had woken them with a jolt.

The mind upstairs was rocking precariously on the edge of a thin, metal lever, as a gymnast balances on a wire. It heard the visitor's breath, read the visitor's heart and stored the information away for future deliberation. All these deliberations were coded and filed to one end only.

To keep the occupant of the house safe.

Down below, in the ground, tiny hammers lifted slowly, as a frail child would lift a sledgehammer, and banged down in response.

The visitor's breathing was slowly returning to normal. "Just angina," he repeated, his attention now turning to the skull in the hall, which he had noticed on the way in.

"The housekeeper calls it *Mr Sockets*," Ellen said following his eyes.

He leaned forward. "Does she now?" he murmured. His nose came within a few inches of the skull, darting over the etched lines and intersections on the cranium. He nodded. "Does she now?" he repeated.

"What is it, exactly?"

"This isn't just any skull, but a phrenological skull." He threw her a glance to check her reaction. "Did your father have any books on phrenology?"

She shrugged and shook her head.

"Are you sure?"

"Positive."

With a raise of his eyebrows, he ventured back into his notebook. "No books," he said, as he wrote.

"My solicitor used that word … phrenology. What's phrenology, Mr Honeyman?"

"Just Honeyman," he responded, automatically. "Phrenology: it's a Victorian science of the mind, which reasoned that different emotions and aspects of the personality are stored in separate lobes of the brain. You see the etched lines and the tiny numbers?" His fingers moved over the skull but without touching it. "Those are the lobes, the different sentiments."

"I don't understand."

He straightened up with a wince in his eyes and considered the pedestal surface, noting that that there was a circle of dust surrounding the skull. "Phrenologists believed that the brain was like a warehouse, with different rooms if you like. Think of it as

71

different parts of the personality, *sentiments*, being stored in these separate rooms."

"Sentiments," she muttered, her thoughts turning to the charity, which was called The Divine Sentiment. She had assumed that *sentiment* in that context had a sympathetic connection, as you might expect from bereavement counselling, but she wasn't so sure now. "That's true, though, isn't it?" she remarked. "Different things are stored in different parts of the brain. Like, well, if someone has a stroke on the left side it means that something's gone wrong with the *right* side of the brain. And I saw a programme once which explained which of the lobes control speech and stuff."

He was nodding as she spoke. "Of course," he said. "Different parts of the brain have different functions and in many respects the nineteenth-century phrenologists were on the right track. The phrenologists believed that the size of a lobe is evidence of its power, for example, and modern science has established that as being generally correct." He shook his head. "But the lobes themselves were imaginary. Pure invention and fantasy, the phrenological tables created through trial and error, and mostly error." A short grumble in his throat signified both his amusement and his disdain. "Common sense caught up with the scientific world by the latter part of the nineteenth century but all the leading phrenologists went to their graves refusing to believe that their theories had been disproved. They called it *this persecuted science*."

"So, phrenology is all about the brain, not the skull?"

"No, no, it's very much about the skull. The brain fits inside the skull, so the skull is the map of the brain, they believe. It can be read. So reading someone's skull will tell you the size of their lobes. For example, a phrenologist could tell by reading your skull whether you have a large benevolence lobe, hence, whether you're a good person. Not only elements of your character but your various skills could be found in the different lobes."

"Sounds like fun," she said, with a crooked smile.

He raised an eyebrow. "Just finished your exams, have you?"

"That's right."

"Done okay?"

She looked bemused. "Hope so. Got good grades in the course work."

He nodded. "You see, you wouldn't think phrenology was 'fun' if you had a job interview and instead of looking at your exam results your prospective employer took a reading of your skull."

There was a pause. "Seriously?" she asked.

"Fathers used to take their sons to phrenologists for readings. To find out whether a hapless young man was destined for the law or for the navy, for example."

"Just on…?"

"Just on the reading of their skulls." He sighed. "I've often wondered how many lawyers were out in the stormy Atlantic, pulling in yard arms when they should have been poring over their books; how many sailors were sat behind dusty old desks, dreaming of the open sea."

She was smiling in spite of her herself, for his accent gave the musings a lyrical quality, with the emphasis on *sailors* and *dreaming*. After three years in Cardiff, having chosen not to adopt the city's unique but raucous twang, she had lost what had always been a faint West Wales lilt. She now spoke in a very neutral accent that approximated to somewhere fictional in southern England. "Their fault for letting their fathers choose their life," she suggested amiably. "And for seeing quacks," she added.

"All these phrenologists were amateurs," he agreed. "Quacks, as you say: gentlemen of leisure who just picked up a book or went to a meeting and then fancied themselves as scientists." He paused. "That was one of the abuses."

"One of them?"

He nodded and said, "The Devil rejoices in misguided science."

"The Devil?" she asked, incredulously.

"Just a saying, you know," he said, with a casual wave of his hand. "Just a saying."

She wasn't convinced by the wave, for there had been too much conviction in that last remark. "Are you a churchman or something?" she asked cautiously.

He hesitated, his small eyes settling on her as he mulled something over. "Used to be," he confirmed at length, then smiled with a sideways twitch of his moustache. "Before I started on this … this occupation."

"What, valuations and stuff?" she asked. His smile widened and she noticed he was chewing gum. "So is it worth anything? The skull, I mean?"

He sighed. "Possibly. Most phrenological tools are plaster cast busts but the early phrenologists used actual skulls with all the sentiments etched into the bone. I'm guessing now, but the discolouration would suggest that it's well over a hundred years old."

"D'you think it's the skull of a criminal or something?" she wondered. "I mean, there were lots of body snatchers around in those days, weren't there?"

He shook his head sadly. "I don't know *whose* skull this was." The admission seemed to trouble him as he looked around the hall in silence. "Is there anything else in the house in this line?"

"Busts … you mentioned busts…" she muttered. "I've got one of those too." From under the stairs, she produced the cardboard box with the plaster cast bust in the straw.

"That's a Fowler bust," he declared after he had pulled it half way out.

"Fowler?"

"Phrenology became very popular in America in the late nineteenth century, just when it was going out of fashion here. Mr Fowler, an American, made it big business. There are quite a lot of these. Mass produced, you understand."

"Oh, I see," she said, stuffing the bust back into the straw with an air of disappointment. "A charity gave it to me. Gave my father the skull too, I think."

He waited expectantly.

"They say it's a fair trade, or something," she continued, "because they've been left two things of their choosing in the will."

She shrugged, unsure of what to make of the charity's 'gifts'.

"Is this charity called The Divine Sentiment?" he asked quietly.

"Yeah," she murmured, surprised. "Have you heard of them?"

"Oh yes."

"Who are they?"

"They were established on the back of one of the nineteenth-century phrenological societies I was telling you about." His tone was cautious and measured.

"What, the amateur clubs you mentioned?"

"Yes, yes indeed."

She thought about this. "Don't really understand why they keep up with it, now that they're a charity and in the bereavement business." She frowned. "And especially as the whole thing's been discredited." She threw him an inquiring look that angled for some sort of answer.

He had been watching her carefully as she spoke. "Everything that is built must have a foundation," he said slowly and gently. "The foundation was phrenology and…"

"And?"

"And a crime," he muttered, his eyes scanning her reaction as a virus software hunts down cookies. "A crime against God," he dared. "A terrible crime committed in God's name."

She considered him, eyes narrowed; she decided she was becoming frightened and shook her head slowly to show she didn't want to hear any more. In her head, she heard Wells' voice rasping his command…

Repeat it!

…as she mentally repeated the supposed telephone number…

Thirteen thirty-one…

… the numbers clicking into place like the sliding mechanism of an alarm clock preparing to go off. She wanted to end this conversation. The lock clicking inside her head was warning her to end it.

"Whatever," she said, uncomfortably. "Is the skull valuable at least?"

Honeyman sighed, having often encountered this reaction when he first tried to discuss the charity: initial interest turning into fear, turning into feigned disinterest. "Possibly," he said.

"Because I've been thinking that I'd just like to throw it out." Her voice was defiant. "Together with this bust thing. Would that be okay?"

"They are yours, you can do whatever you want with them," he sighed.

Indeed, most of them *are* thrown out, he thought.

And the Trustees never seem to *mind*, came the afterthought.

Even though the Trustees are so careful … so covetous…

A twinge of anguish made him wince, as he felt the clop of dirt on his face, the scout party of an attack. The moment was fleeting and he maintained his composure, though his train of thought had been derailed.

I'll think about it later … when I have leisure and I'm prepared…

He brought his hands together and looked at her with two expectant eyebrows raised.

"Bedrooms?" she asked.

"Bedrooms it is," he agreed.

Along the floor of the hall, on each step, in every room and corner, in every drawer and in every cupboard, the Trustees were searching for the hidden voices, having heard their calls and in their excitement now indifferent to the visitor.

Panic spread through the house as the voices realised they were detected.

Upstairs, the mind willed itself back into slumber. In the ground, the tiny hammer stopped its passage in mid-flight.

The house held its breath.

VI

Thirteen and thirty-one

Honeyman's jottings of the third floor were scribbled quickly and wherever possible he kept his eyes towards the ceiling, as if he had the notion that being in her parents' bedroom was unseemly. He was wonderfully sweet and old fashioned, Ellen thought, thinking that she liked him a great deal, even though the conversation in the hall had unsettled her. As they walked back down to the second floor, to her bedroom landing, she kissed her mother's picture with her two fingers.

"Beautiful lady," he remarked, pausing on the stairs to admire the photograph.

"My mother," she said, liking the visitor even more.

"You *are* alike," he said, studying the photograph. One of his fingers discreetly touched the smoky mist of the glass.

"Except that Mum was prettier. Look at her – she's amazing."

He had a wry smile under his moustache now. "I'd say you're very much on a par."

"No way," she said, self-consciously running a hand across her forehead.

"You don't care for compliments, do you?"

She shrugged. "I've never seen a photograph done this way before," she said, to change the subject.

"This is wet collodian. It's a special process."

"Oh, maybe *that's* it then," she muttered, moving to lead him into her bedroom. The door, as always, was wide open.

"What do you mean?"

"I mean the thing looks so fragile, being made of glass and all. But I had an accident the other day and dropped it. It dropped right down the stairs to the first floor and it didn't chip or anything." She hesitated. "What did you call it? Wet…?"

"Wet collodian. It was a process invented by one Frederick Scott Archer and was very popular from the mid to the late nineteenth century." He paused to ask whether he was getting too technical, but saw that she was interested. "It was a method of producing photographic images on glass plate. Mr Archer was a generous soul who didn't feel he needed to patent his process. Well, he died a poor man, leaving his widow and children to the charity of the industry." He shrugged and shook his head.

"So how does it work?" she asked, not in the slightest bit interested in the fate of Mr Archer's family but very interested in anything that concerned her mother's glass portrait.

"A sheet of glass is coated in a thin film of collodian. That's gun cotton dissolved in ether. In the mid nineteenth century that produced a higher resolution, better detail, than any other process."

"Then I'm amazed they don't still use it," she declared, considering the photograph. "I mean the resolution's fantastic, isn't it? It's like Mum's there in the flesh. I mean really *there*. Better than any LCD or plasma TV I've seen."

Her words surprised her. She had at last put her finger on it, the reason why this particular photograph of her mother, for she had many photographs, was so important to her. Why it would have been so important to her father also, she realised, though for some reason he had chosen to place it here, outside her bedroom.

It was *so* lifelike. It was if Mum had been miniaturised and placed in the glass.

Captured…

Honeyman shook his head. "The nineteenth-century collodians weren't nearly as sharp. In fact, if you saw some you'd probably be very, very disappointed. These are … well, a modern example of the process."

"So the technology's moved on," she remarked, with a shrug. "Whoever did them should go into business, I mean big time. They'd make a fortune."

"Have you got one of your father?"

She shook her head and said, "That charity asked me the same question."

"They said that they'd come and visit you when the second portrait turned up?"

"They said it would turn up," she agreed cautiously.

"As with the skull and the bust, the Trustees always give these collodian portraits in pairs..." His voice trailed off. They had walked into the bedroom and he had gone straight to the wicker chair.

"She's called Cody," she declared with a beaming smile, looking as proud as a new parent.

"Is she now?" he murmured, crouching down in front of the doll. He sighed. "Is she now?" he whispered, sadly.

"She's a Jumeau and one of the few models with moveable eyes. That's eyes, not just eyelids."

"Yes, so she is," he agreed. He took a tiny bisque finger between his large thumb and index finger and the image was of a giant taking the hand of a little girl. "Very pleased to meet you, Cody," he said.

The tug on the finger shuffled something in Cody's head and her eyes closed then gently rocked open.

"She likes you," Ellen said.

He threw her an inquiring glance.

"Just my little joke," she explained, with a smile. "I virtually lived with this doll after my Mum died and I used to imagine that she spoke to me with her eyes. Opening and closing the eyes means she likes or approves of something. It was a game I played."

She heard him sigh again. He had his back to her but she thought that as he stood up he quickly brushed one of his eyes. "She's very precious," he whispered.

"I know. I only want her valued for tax purposes. I'd never part with her."

He deftly moved around to the back of the doll, gently folded down its lace collar and studied the back of the neck.

"What are you looking for?" she asked.

"Every Jumeau has a serial number," he murmured, then swallowed as he replaced the collar. "I'm afraid the Trustees may take a fancy to her."

"Well they're not having her," she said in a firm voice. "Cody is … look, I can't explain it, but…"

"Oh I understand," he said quietly. "Now, Miss Sorensen, listen to me carefully. The Trustees won't mention your doll on the first visit: not if they know you're attached to her. They'll be more interested in your portraits." With a finger, he indicated the collodian on the landing.

"No, they're not interested in photographs. The man told me that on the telephone."

"They couldn't possibly justify taking family photographs," he agreed. "They couldn't even get a will and a solicitor to make *that* appear legal and innocuous." He paused. "Don't let them out of your sight. They may try to palm you off with *real* collodian plate glass photographs, in place of yours. They wouldn't regard that as theft, you see, they'd regard it as fair trade, but as I said you might be very, very disappointed."

She blinked with confusion.

"You never shut your bedroom door, do you?" he asked, deciding to press his luck.

She now looked at him suspiciously. "Have you been speaking to my psychiatrist?"

"You see a psychiatrist?" he asked.

"Counsellor," she clarified. "Dr Wendy Ridge. Do you know her?"

With a shake of his head, he happily confessed he knew nothing when it came to Cardiff psychiatrists.

"Wendy says a fear of the dark isn't uncommon after a bereavement. That's why I leave my door open." She hesitated. "Is that how you guessed?"

"Do you leave your door open in Cardiff?"

"Can't. I share with three other girls and they bring guys back."

He nodded, choosing not to point out the missing logic in her answer. "Just remember what I said: when the Trustees visit, don't take your eyes off your collodians."

"I've only got the one."

"Your father has a portrait too and it will turn up, just as the Trustees predicted." He paused. "Now, you mentioned that your father threw everything out. Does he have *anything* left?"

She didn't answer, still turning his last few statements around in her head. "Just one thing, that I can see," she said at length.

"Ah."

"That's the telephone, the antique down in the kitchen, it's rigged up to speakers all around the house." She glanced at the speaker in her bedroom, which was just above the door.

He swivelled round and considered the speaker with interest. "A telephone?" he murmured and was thoughtful for a moment. "Yes, a telephone. How many speakers?"

She counted in her head, noticing that he had his notebook out. "Seven, including this one," she said.

He hesitated before he wrote the number down, as if he had been expecting a different answer. "Seven," he grumbled, with a dissatisfied tap of the pencil on the page. He looked up as a man who has returned home to find everything missing. "So, shall we see this telephone?"

His look of bemused dissatisfaction was still evident as he examined the ebony telephone. He tried the dials and listened at the earpiece, shaking his head as he did so, and then studied its base with a solemn frown of his moustache.

"Are you looking for anything in particular?" she asked, wondering why so many tests were needed to value the piece. He seemed to realise that he was going too far as he managed a smile and held the telephone aloft, admiring its form.

81

"Interesting piece," he said, "nineteen twenties, but with a modern mechanism. Your father was ingenious."

She shrugged, reluctantly. "I always wanted different telephones in every room, but oh no. No, no, no, that would've been far too obvious."

He chuckled but shortly his countenance became thoughtful again. "And this telephone belonged to your father?" he asked rhetorically.

"No, actually it was Mum's." She was taken aback when Honeyman's eyes darted to her. "It came through her family, you know," she clarified, finding his intense stare disconcerting. "It was Father's idea to fix up the speakers, though."

He shook his head, his eyes weary and without expectation. "There's nothing else here belonging to your father? Nothing that he collected?" He paused. "It might be very small or insignificant."

"Nothing that I can think of," she answered uneasily.

He looked around the kitchen once more. "Ah, a phrenology chart," he said at length, walking over to the chart with sectioned skulls and an index.

"Is that what it is?" she asked, following him over to the wall. "Does it match up to the skull upstairs?"

"There are all the lobes, listed," he explained. "You see? Lobe number one, the instinct for reproduction. Lobe number two, parental love. You identify the location of the lobe on the diagram." He pointed at the diagrammatic head of the pencil drawing of a man who was smiling as if he had no problem with his head being sectioned. "A rather vain and proud gentleman called George Combe was the acknowledged authority in phrenological circles. This chart contains a list of the sentiments that he mapped in the human brain." He briefly ran a finger down the index as he spoke then went to his notebook. "No books, but a chart," he murmured, with satisfaction. The notebook and pencil disappeared into a roomy pocket in his coat.

"Um, Honeyman…?" she began, finding it strange to address him by his surname, but remembering that she had already been corrected twice. He raised his eyebrows with a smile to show he was all attention. "In that list … what are numbers thirteen…" and she paused and took a breath "… and thirty-one?"

He turned to her with a cautious expression, noting her hesitation. "Why do you ask?"

"I'm just wondering whether those numbers mean anything, that's all."

"Why?" he pressed.

She sighed. "Oh it's stupid, but I've been getting some hate mail. Least I think that's what it is. Maybe someone's playing a joke on me. Warning me about *lies*."

"Lies?"

"Yeah. The stamp was the first half of a telephone number the Trustee gave me. The stamp, well, it isn't a stamp, just a thumbprint and it was … thirteen pence. Post office said there was no stamp for that price."

He shook his head, completely lost. "Stamp…?" he muttered.

"That's why I don't trust my housekeeper."

He shook his head again.

"See, it's written on my father's typewriter. It's an antique, a Sholes and Glidden prototype, and I recognise the typeface and the paper: special paper with a watermark, made to fit the machine. My housekeeper must know who my father sold it to." She shrugged. "If he sold it, that is. Wouldn't be surprised if she just swiped it."

"Typewriter?" he asked. "Belonging to your father?"

"Yeah…"

"And you say … you say you've received a *letter*?"

"More of a note," she clarified. "Barely that even."

He automatically took out his notebook but then returned it to his pocket without opening it.

"Is there something wrong?" she asked.

He shook his head, his eyes far away. "Don't mention the typewriter to the Trustees," he suggested.

"Why not?"

"Or the letters," he added.

"Why not?" she asked, now with a firm tone. The question was met with a reasonable smile.

"They don't need to know any more than they have to, now do they?"

She nodded slowly with reluctant agreement. "Anyway, what about … the numbers?" she asked, returning to the chart.

"Thirteen is the sentiment of *Benevolence*," he said, without needing to look at the chart, "and thirty-one is the sentiment of *Time*."

"What are they?"

"Well benevolence is what it says. A propensity to do good: charitable works and the like. Kindness and charity."

She found lobe 13 in the schematic diagram of the head. It was just at the rise of the cranium, the top of the forehead. "Is it significant in any way? I mean … I mean is the *number* significant?"

He nodded. "It's the first of the *superior* sentiments. There are twelve sentiments which are common to man and animals. Love of children, for example, attachment to place, appetites, cunning, covetousness and so on. All the attributes to be found in animals as well as people, but when we come to number thirteen in Combe's list the sentiments are only relevant to humans. Good works, as in benevolence, but also a tendency towards faith, wonder and appreciation of beauty. And so on…"

"So the number's a sort of cut-off point? Separating humans from animals?"

"Indeed." He paused, measuring his words carefully, knowing that he now had to tread carefully. "For a scientist in the nineteenth century it was purely a cataloguing number, but if you were a religious phrenologist you could have seen that number as significant."

"Why?"

"Most of the phrenologists were amateur scientists but some of them found in this revolutionary science proof of the existence of God." He glanced at her to see whether the explanation satisfied her, but she replied with a vacant shrug of non-understanding. "You

84

must remember that this was about the time that the church was having its showdown battle with Darwin," he continued, "which it handled very, very badly, I might add. Some of the Christian advocates loved the idea of phrenology because they could use it as a means of discrediting evolution."

As if to acknowledge this information she looked at the chart, though still not sure what he meant.

He also considered the chart and said, "There's something very neat about phrenology, don't you think? Today we know the brain to be an incredibly complex organ transmitting electrons, the pinnacle of evolution but ultimately random in its structure and form. Now, phrenology said that all the traits that make us human were neatly compartmentalised. Humour, *here*. Mathematical ability, *here*." He was indicating with his extended index finger again. "Conscientiousness, *here*." He nodded to himself. "Very neat indeed. How could such a thing *evolve*, purely by chance?"

"Oh, I think I see…" she whispered, still looking at the chart.

"Yes, the separate rooms, the chambers of the human brain were proof of a creator," he murmured, his eyes darkening, "because such a thing couldn't be a random product of evolution. And as with all belief systems, once a logical assumption is made it leads to *other* logical assumptions."

She looked at him inquiringly but he made no further comment. "What about … about the other number?"

"Thirty-one?" he queried, noting her sidestep.

"Yes."

"Thirty-one is 'time'. In this context it means the ability to judge time."

"*Judge* time?"

He nodded. "Have you ever woken up a few minutes, even a few seconds before your alarm has gone off?"

She thought about this then nodded with a frown. "It's like when I used to have a long haul in the library, absorbed with my books, you know. Before I even looked at my watch I could tell myself: I've been one hour and fifteen minutes."

"Yes, some people are better at it than others. The phrenologists would have said that you had a large thirty-one lobe."

"That's nice of them." She returned to the chart and found the 31 lobes in the diagram; there were two of them, situated over each eyebrow. The forefinger and middle finger of her right hand went to her own temple, finding the lobes. "But why would … that one … time … be particularly relevant to religious phrenologists?"

"It wouldn't be," he replied immediately, with a decisive shake of his head that suggested he had pondered this question before. "It's not an important sentiment at all. Certainly not as important as thirteen, the first higher sentiment and the lobe which gives humankind the quality of goodness: the divine in all of us."

She was thoughtfully looking at Honeyman, then the chart. "So, with this telephone number the Trustee gave me … if I'm right in thinking it's connected with phrenology… what do you think this *second* number means?"

"I don't think thirty-one is referring to the sentiment of 'time' *at all*. I think it simply signifies a reverse: the reverse of thirteen. It's thirteen reversed."

"Reversed? What do you mean?"

He answered the question slowly. "What is the reverse of benevolence? The reverse of charity and goodness … of the divine?"

She considered this.

The reverse of the divine…

"Can I see this letter?" he asked.

She shook her head, collecting her thoughts before she answered. "It's with my uncle at the moment. He's running some checks on it."

Honeyman appeared disappointed. "Perhaps next time," he suggested. "I'll have your valuation list ready in a few days and I'll come back, if that's alright with you?" As they walked out of the kitchen, he hesitated, noticing the incongruous set of drawers under the sink.

"Yes, they're new," she muttered. She blinked and shook her

head, pleased to have found an opportunity to change the subject and to remove the number 1331 from her mind. "Terrible, aren't they? That's the work of the housekeeper's brother. I saw him at the funeral ... I think he's a bit ... you know..." She swirled a finger next to her head.

He gave her an inquiring glance and then leaned forward, balancing himself with his arms. He seemed as interested in the drawers as he had been with anything else in the house.

"All of the drawers are empty, except one with a few bills," she said. "Don't know why my father thought he needed more drawers. Or why he thought Tarn's brother could fit them."

"No indeed," he whispered then straightened up. "No indeed," he repeated.

Honeyman didn't speak until they were at the front door. "You have my card with my number," he said. "I really would like to have a look at that letter."

"Sure, okay."

"And contact me when you know the Trustees are coming back. I can be here if you like..." he gave her a kind of half wink "...to keep an eye on them."

"Would you?"

"Anytime," he confirmed. "Ring me *anytime*. My mobile is always on."

She smiled as she watched him walk down the steps then cross the road, thinking that he was nimble for his size and age. She waited a while, noticing that he had parked a fair distance up the road, even though there was plenty of space outside the house. As she closed the door, she accidentally moved the doormat with her foot and felt something slide underneath. Under the mat, she found a folded letter with a thumb smudge for a stamp, addressed to *Miss Eleanor Sorensen*. She stared at it as this information filtered into her brain.

Under the mat?

Tarn had been there this morning doing her daily clean. Apart from her, Honeyman had been the only visitor.

She quickly opened the door again but only in time to catch sight of Honeyman's Land Rover heading out of the town.

VII

Tempted to stay

Sorrel Page solemnly handed Marion Coates her husband.

A trace of ether still lingered in the condensation on the dark, smoky glass as Marion took the photograph and weighed it uncertainly in her hands. Henry was captured in all his irritated glory, a little flushed after his walk from the club, his eyes bleary from the real ale. Crinkling his nose at the unexpected intrusion of the camera, his image and personality were so sharply realised it was as if he was with her again; as if she could hear his voice.

Grow up Marry, for pity's sake!

"The original photograph is lost during the process," Wells remarked from behind the settee. "It melts with the collodian."

Marion nodded, pretending to understand but fighting the sensation of nausea. Her stomach had turned when she had seen the white, hearse-like vehicle arrive outside her house for this, the Trustees' third visit.

I just won't answer the door, had been the plan she had wrapped and re-wrapped around her fingers, from the moment they had telephoned to say they were ready, that the photograph they had borrowed had been prepared. She had watched them through a chink in the curtains and they hadn't moved. Sorrel stared out in front of her from her passenger seat, just a tight smile having formed as the vehicle had come to a halt, as if she knew she was being observed. The old man gripped the steering wheel though the vehicle was stationary, also staring at nothing in particular.

With a deep breath she had pulled back the curtains, feeling too tired to do anything other than accept the inevitable. A cold shiver went down her spine as they both turned to look at her, their expressions unchanged.

"The negative is lost because he's in the collodian now," Sorrel clarified, with a momentary press of her hand on the glass.

Marion instinctively tightened her grip on the picture in a defensive manner. "I've felt him," she admitted, aware of something unpleasant building in her throat. "Since you were first here, I've felt him." She sighed and shook her head. "It's as if he's wandering behind me in the house, trying to get my attention … to talk to me. He startles me. I drop things all the time." A hand went to her forehead. "Sometimes I think he's angry with me…"

"Angry? Why would he be angry with you?" Sorrel asked.

Marion shook her head, having suffered from terrible headaches since their last visit, migraines so vicious they stopped her concentrating or even speaking to anyone. "I feel weighed down, somehow. Exhausted." She took a breath and looked at Sorrel. "What did you do?"

It was Wells who answered, as he circled the settee. "We opened up a channel of communication, to Henry, or rather amplified it a little. The channel is always open though few realise it. It's understandable you feel so tired. Your exhaustion is the burden of another soul being tied to your life force."

"Another soul…?"

"Henry's soul," he clarified. "You've asked him to stay, after all."

The glass plate photograph was now heavy in her hands. She made to speak but shook her head instead.

"So we must find a way to lighten your load," he continued, still circling. "Henry needs somewhere to rest, somewhere comfortable where he feels safe and content." He stopped at the door. "But it must be soon or you'll lose him."

Marion closed her eyes. "We speak at night. Not with words … no, not with words … but with memories. With flashes of our life. Only the two of us can communicate that way…"

"The memories will be lost," Sorrel lamented. "Lost … forever." As she took Marion's hand, two of her fingers found an edge of the collodian. The grip of her hand tightened and Henry looked up from the glass in his wife's lap with annoyance. "Only your love is keeping him here now. That and his desire to comfort you, to reassure you, yet his new life is calling him and he can't resist it for long. He has no place, no substance here anymore: his only links to the man you knew as Henry Coates are your memories of him … your love for him."

"But I'll never forget him…"

"That's not enough." Sorrel shook her head folornly. "Henry was happy in life and doesn't wish to haunt this world. No, you have to find a way of keeping him here if you're to leave this world together." She made a face of warning. "And put suicide out of your mind. That would take your soul on a detour, to recuperate, and you'd still never see Henry again."

Marion didn't answer, the unpleasant taste in her throat having become bile. The photograph in her lap was as heavy as a brick.

"We need to find a suitable home for Henry, until you're ready to join him," Wells suggested. "Somewhere he can be … *tempted* to stay."

The word 'tempted' sounded peculiar, as if another word was more appropriate to the explanation. Marion had a flash image of a mouse crawling into an electrified tube after a piece of cheese. "Why are you doing this?" she asked, shuddering as she heard the crackle of electricity in her mind.

"Because love should endure," Sorrel replied. "All powerful emotions should endure. That's what I believe, Marion. Don't you believe it too?"

Marion gave a mute nod of her head, though there was pain in her eyes.

"We're *true* bereavement counsellors," Sorrel continued. "Haven't we been a help to you, Marion? Hasn't it been a certain comfort to know that Henry still exists?"

"Yes," Marion replied helplessly.

91

"To have that certainty: the certainty which your church could never give you?"

"Yes," Marion admitted.

"And hasn't it been wonderful sharing your memories once again?"

"Yes..."

"Because he's dear to you, isn't he?"

"Yes, yes he is."

Wells now spoke from the hall. "And only you have the right to ask him to stay. Your love gives you that right." He paused. "Say it Marion ... only you have the right..."

A silence fell as the Trustees waited. Wells was studying the grandfather clock in the hall, Sorrel looking at some place in the far wall, neither seeming inclined to change their aspect. Marion's headache was more oppressive than ever but it occurred to her that just a few simple words could remove the pain. "Only I have the right," she said at length, cringing as she felt something turn in her mind.

Sorrel closed her eyes, quickly muttered something to herself and then opened them with a tight smile. Marion gave a gasp of relief, but freed from the burden of the headache she took on a furtive, worried expression.

"But I still sense your caution," Wells declared. "I believe you're hiding something from us."

The silence ticked away with Henry's clock. It seemed to be ticking too quickly, as if the mechanism had been wound too tightly.

"*Are* you hiding something, Marion?" Sorrel asked.

"Someone's visited me," she admitted and from her apron pocket produced a business card. Sorrel read it and threw an eye signal to her colleague in the hall. "He told me..." Marion began.

"Not to trust us," Wells said. "That you're to bear your loss with fortitude and place your trust in God Almighty. To seek out any other comfort would be heresy."

"Perhaps we should be burned at the stake," Sorrel remarked.

"Perhaps Mr Honeyman would burn us, if he could. Is it not an outrage to bring comfort to those who cannot be comforted … hope, to those without hope? I'm sure if he was living in the seventeenth century he'd be the Witchfinder General."

Marion nodded slowly, thinking that there was some truth in this statement. She was considering how the man who had revealed himself as an ex-minister had remonstrated with her on his last visit, when she admitted that she had contacted the Trustees again, unable to resist the temptation of communing with Henry once more. That they had taken away Henry's photograph. Her headache had been screaming as he vehemently repeated his warnings about The Divine Sentiment. All his explanations now seemed disjointed and unconvincing.

Some rubbish about a Victorian science and skulls and numbers. A temple, where souls were taken…

"Who did he pretend to be this time?" Wells asked.

"Oh my, he's a salesman of double-glazing now," Sorrel announced, holding up the business card. She turned to Marion and shook her head, slowly and repeatedly, until Marion's look of apprehension and suspicion faded. "I'll give you the name of a Baptist church: they know this Tristyn Honeyman. They'll explain that he's a very dangerous man, Marion. A fanatic."

"His church has a directive out to all the other parishes, warning congregations about him," Wells added. "He's a crude, vulgar man. The last time he was in a church he was thrown out for uttering foul obscenities."

"Obscenities?" Marion murmured, refusing to believe it.

Sorrel shook her head again. "The church will confirm everything. We don't lie, Marion … unlike this man."

Marion's eyes showed her confusion. "Have you got the telephone number?"

"I'll give you their name and you can ring them through directory inquiries, just to satisfy yourself that we haven't given you a fictitious number." Sorrel got up and collected the telephone from the table at the bay window, returning with it to the settee. "But we have to hurry now. I can feel Henry pulling away ... there's so little time."

In the hallway, Wells had removed his gloves and was running his finger down the discoloured roses and thorns of the grandfather clock. He took a deep breath, placing both hands on the wood as he closed his eyes. His eyes remained closed as Marion made her calls, then as Sorrel offered her reassurances; he knew that Sorrel was touching the collodian as she spoke, that Marion was nodding her agreement.

He waited, his eyes clamped shut.

Shortly he felt Henry Coates coming through the door, returning from the club, as in his photograph; he heard his unsteady footsteps, smelled the stale beer on his breath.

"This captures him," he murmured, then opened his eyes and stepped away from the clock with an air of wonder. He stifled a whimper of delight into his fist as his beautiful colleague's attention switched excitedly to the hall.

He nodded from the doorway. Her eyes smiled back.

The mechanism of the clock was still working but the hands were no longer moving. The hour hand was on the ornate Roman numeral I, the minute hand on the III.

Marion had tried to say goodbye as the Trustees returned to their vehicle but found that she could only manage a short wave; the bile that had been building in her throat was now in her mouth, deadening her lips like some bubbling anaesthetic on her tongue. She yearned to sit down somewhere, anywhere, preferably in the dark where she could commune with Henry.

The Trustees didn't speak until they were on the porch of the house of the late Lawrence Parry, their vehicle urging them on through the excited and satisfied voices that found substance in the purr of the engine and the creak of the leather.

"Jasper Wells of The Divine Sentiment," Wells announced. "You remember me, I trust?"

"Eh, yeah, absolutely," Neville replied uncertainly.

Sorrel didn't offer her name to Neville but rather a hand with the softest of grips. She didn't seem to mind that Neville's attention had veered to her legs and breasts, as he imagined her naked.

"We've returned to collect the two items left to us by your uncle," Wells explained. "I trust that the decorators have finished their work and the house can be viewed?"

"Yeah, everything's here."

"Very good. We'll be quick, I promise you."

"Fine, that's fine," Neville replied casually, opening the door a little but not enough to let them in. "But I should tell you I've taken legal advice and I'm told that *I* can choose your bequest from the estate, given that I'm the executor. Don't worry, I'm going to be generous and give you more than just two things; I've got a stack of mementos and photographs and stuff all packed away in a box."

Wells took off one of his driving gloves. He had long, graceful fingers and the movement reminded Neville of a snake shedding its skin. "You're very kind but we prefer to choose our mementos ourselves."

Neville shrugged, feigning disinterest. For a fleeting second, his eyes met Sorrel's and he felt her tongue licking his face. "Well do you know what you want?" he asked.

"We need to look, Mr Parry. When we have looked, we will decide."

Neville shook his head, keeping the enticing angle of the door in place. "No, you've got to tell me what you're looking for first. I'm not going to let you in otherwise. My solicitor said I should ask what you were looking to take before I let you in, that it would be illegal otherwise." He offered a shrug that said *lawyers!*

Wells removed his other glove. "Mr Parry, I suggest that you re-read your uncle's will: we're perfectly within our rights to enter and choose our legacy. In fact, you're in breach of your uncle's wishes already, in having hidden them away on our last visit. The clauses in the will are clear."

"I told you, the decorators…"

"It wasn't the decorators who hid them and it isn't lawyers

who are now telling you to keep this door closed to us. We are not fools."

Neville stepped back slightly, but still didn't open the door.

"A list of your uncle's possessions has already been prepared," Wells added wearily. "Did you think we wouldn't take such an elementary precaution as to check the household contents?"

"Who gave you a list?"

"Never mind. Just understand that we have it."

Neville's eyes darkened as he reluctantly opened the door and stood aside. He retreated gloomily to the staircase as he watched the Trustees enter and drift around the house; shortly they stopped and turned to look at him.

"Well, have you decided what you want?" he muttered.

"Oh I think you know what we want," Wells answered.

"There's the TV, I suppose. Some lead soldiers in that cabinet over there … even got a science skull upstairs in the bathroom, if you want to see it."

The Trustees didn't respond.

"Okay, I know what you're up to. You want the game board and the painting, right?" Neville took a long, angry breath through his nose. "The antiques dealer warned me you'd choose them."

"Who?"

"Is he working for you? Was he staking the place out?"

"Who?" Wells repeated.

"The antiques dealer … Honeyman…"

"Ah, so he's an antiques dealer now. Perhaps we should get this out of the way before going any further. We have some telephone numbers for you, Mr Parry. Ring them and you'll…"

"Not interested."

His remark concerning Honeyman was simply pique for he already knew that the antiques dealer didn't work for the charity. He had checked with the estate agent and she had come back to him with a report of a religious fanatic who travelled the country, gate-crashing wakes; she had left him the names of some people in the church he could speak to, if he wanted confirmation.

"So are you content for us to take the things we've chosen?" Wells asked.

"Forget it. I'm seeing a barrister tomorrow and I'm going to stick your clause up your arse. It was duress. My uncle didn't know what he was signing."

Wells examined the joint of one of his fingers. "Let me assure you that I have no intention of forcing your hand. We'll return when you're ready to comply with your uncle's wishes."

"I *am* complying with my uncle's wishes," he replied irritably. "There's no way he wanted you to have things that were so important to him. Fucking family heirlooms..."

"Ah, I understand now. Rather than bequeath them to the people your uncle knew would treasure them, you believe he intended that they be sold by you on that eBay..."

"Yeah, don't get cute. I'm his nephew, right? And I'm taking both these things to my own home tonight."

Wells pulled on the finger joint. "I think you'll find such action is beyond you. I have no doubt that your uncle's wishes will weigh too heavily on you."

Sorrel was yet to speak but her eyes were wide with excitement. As Neville glanced at her, he was struck with the image of a toy that would fulfil the most lewd pornographic fantasies, some Cindy doll in sweaty leather; he couldn't understand it, for she was wearing the frumpiest of tweed suits. "I won't change my mind," he said, walking to the door and waiting for them to leave. Her eyes flashed at him as she passed, with just a hint of sexual promise on her lips.

He smiled back involuntarily, his groin twitching.

Then he heard the whisper, the cat's hiss in his head that seemed to belong to the eyes and lips of the beautiful woman as if it were a disembodied hand. The whisper was a tiny fist that pulled his senses tight, then pulled them again, jerking his eyes into his skull.

"Look after our property," Wells called as they left, his diction measured and precise. "As you have elected to keep them, you are the custodian now."

"I am the custodian," Neville murmured uneasily, shaking slightly from the jolt in his brain and unsure why he had chosen to repeat the Trustee's words.

"I am the custodian," he repeated, feeling the lock turn.

VIII

Must find a home

Honeyman avoided hotels and even guesthouses; his present home was a bedroom in an anonymous B&B just outside Tenby, in a small village called New Hedges. The family with whom he lodged believed him to be a fly fisherman; he had some rods and tackle in the back of his Land Rover and the off-roader's often mud-soaked wheels gave some credence to this cover story.

The only item of furniture in the attic bedroom which could take his weight was the bed. Here he idly reviewed the materials he kept in lever arch files, for he had finally exhausted all avenues of research. His travelling had also come to an end and he was ignoring the e-mail alerts to his laptop, the IT research system he had set up at a cost of almost everything he owned. He had just enough money left to keep him in B&Bs, petrol and roadside meals for about another six months.

It would be enough time. He was fifty-nine years of age and it was his uneasy suspicion that he wouldn't see his sixtieth birthday, but that was unimportant; all that mattered was that it was coming to an end, one way or the other.

Surrounded by his research and technology his most essential working tool remained his small, thick notebook. It was the home for all inconsequential jottings, such as the contents of the Sorensen house, should he need to prepare a probate inventory as a cover story for his return, but the key pages were found at the front and back.

The first page was an index with a list of names. With Sorensen added there were thirteen names now which the present Trustees, Jasper Wells and Sorrel Page, had stewardship over, for they had begun their service only a short time before he had gone on the road. The first two names read:

~~Danes~~

~~Fields~~

If the name was crossed out it meant that both members of the marriage were now dead. The only name left unscathed was Coates. The death of the second partner was inevitable and swift. Mrs Danes had been obsessed with her impending death and with a book, a rare, illustrated edition of Robinson Crusoe; she had read aloud from chapter thirteen, the section where the hero discovers the grizzly work of the cannibals.

I could see the marks of horror… the blood, the bones, and part of the flesh of human bodies eaten and devoured by those wretches with merriment and sport.

"This is *my* book," she explained. "I will be devoured, blood, bones and all for the sin that I have committed."

She had told him about the Trustees but he hadn't known enough at that time to ask her the right questions. He suspected they had used some form of hypnosis or a drug, to debilitate her so completely. But before long he ruled out both mental suggestion and poison. A pattern emerged as he came across Paula Fields and the music box that was occupying all her time. She had been a dear friend as well as a parishioner and the second target in Flint: two families in his home town when there was all of Wales to choose from. He now believed that Flint had been specifically targeted just for his benefit.

He was reflective as he wondered whether Mrs Fields and Mrs Danes were suffering simply because of him. That was why he couldn't stop, no matter how often he was warned and how impossible the task seemed.

The last two names on the list read:

Coates
Sorensen

The Sorensens had simply been a lucky find, for when Mrs Sorensen had died his IT system that helped him find the families was not yet in place. He had planned an afternoon off to visit the monks at Caldey Island and, as he was savouring the sea air, he turned to see the Trustees waiting in their gleaming removal wagon on the road overlooking North Beach. He hurried down the steps to the sand but in his head he could already hear the vehicle starting up, could see Sorrel Page's tight smile.

He often suspected that the Trustees saw him but on this occasion he was in no doubt, for they were gone within seconds. He took the beach route for as far as it would allow then found the part of the road where they had been waiting. After knocking on four doors, a housekeeper confirmed that the owner, Nigel Sorensen, had sadly died only a few days earlier.

The system for finding the target families was usually far more precise. His e-mail alerts announced the first death within a married couple over sixty years of age anywhere in Wales: temples tended to be fiercely geographical and this was a Welsh temple, so this geographical limit was sufficient. The couple would be members of a Protestant church and, most importantly, they would have children who would be living far away, which he had fixed as at least fifty miles. The e-mail alert was sophisticated enough to narrow down the likely candidates to a mere handful every week, but the travelling was still arduous. He visited them all and set up waiting vigils in the hope that the removal wagon would appear. Sometimes it did, most of the time it didn't.

With thirteen names on the list, the number being significant, he saw no more point in exhausting himself travelling and waiting. Each of the families had their own page in the front of his notebook.

These contained his notes and all-important first impressions when he visited a house. The Sorensen page read:

SORENSEN

Mrs S died over a year ago.
!

Mr S was a collector but house virtually empty. Daughter believes sold or stolen. Deliberate?

Will changed to remove cremation clause. (ATTACK)

Her collodian untouched, 7 days after husband's wake. His collodian yet to appear.

Jumeau doll (hers)
~~Telephone (his)~~

No books with skull, but chart. (The Phrenological Mirror by Lundie.)

Typewriter?

(Letters?!)
Where?

As he sat in the centre of his bed studying this page he was considering the chance snippet of information from Ellen Sorensen which, most importantly, had been accompanied by an attack. Her father had changed his will. They all changed their wills, of course, to insert the bequest to the charity, but her father had also removed his instruction that he be cremated.

"Why?" he murmured, replaying his journey through the house. Then he sat upright as his door was knocked.

"Would you like a cup of tea, Mr Honeyman?" came the voice of Mrs Thomas. Every evening she offered him tea even though he had a kettle and a small fridge in his room and even though he always declined.

"That's very kind, Mrs Thomas, but thank you, no."

"Would you like *anything*? A piece of cake, perhaps? There's some lovely ginger cake: it's homemade."

"Thank you, no. I'll be going out for dinner shortly. I'm getting changed now, in fact."

The bedroom had a primitive en suite bath with rusty taps that allowed about a big toe of hot water before the immersion heater gave up with a splutter of indignation. Given that he always ate out, his existence was relatively self-contained; he never willingly allowed anyone into his room and always locked his door behind him, although he was sure that Mrs Thomas used her own key to rifle around. He had fallen into the habit of carrying his materials with him.

The intrusion over, he returned to his notebook. Sorensen's cremation: the daughter had believed her father's wishes to be cremated were set in stone. Perhaps more of the people on his list had changed their will to remove a previous cremation clause and he simply hadn't noticed.

His eyebrows raised as an idea occurred to him. He went to

his red lever arch file, which contained all the information on his thirteen families, including the death certificates. On the bottom of each certificate he had scribbled the details of the internment: who had taken the service, where the wake had been held, where the body was buried…

Buried…

"All buried," he muttered, as he considered his notes on the death certificates, then flicked through them again to double check. It hadn't occurred to him that there was a coincidence here: not a single cremation among the twenty-five deaths he had now documented. They were all buried: both the first and the second partner, without exception. Surely it was reasonable to suppose that some of them, when they had changed their will, had also inserted a burial clause just as Nigel Sorensen had done?

He put his red file on the foot of his bed then reached over to his coat and found his chewing gum. He unwrapped two sticks, one Spearmint, one Juicy Fruit, and popped them in his mouth. When he was thinking he craved his cigars more than ever, the cigars that the hospital had told him to finish with before they finished *him*; he took a long, unsatisfied breath as he conjured up the smell of cigar smoke in his nostrils, thinking he had to keep his health, just long enough.

He returned to his notebook, open at a page near the back. This was where he tested his theories. Many of the pages here were headed *Questions* and the latest page read:

QUESTIONS

Why are the collodians never posed?

Different questions always occurred to him when he visited a house, but this was the question that came to him when he had· looked at the photographs of Lawrence and Jessica Parry and realised that the collodian portraits wouldn't have been to their liking. His answer, written underneath, read:

The demeanour is natural: the person is captured.

The trick is more easily achieved.

Underneath, he now wrote:

Why are there no cremations?

He pondered the question awhile. At length he wrote:

There must be a grave.

The body must find a home.

"Must find a home," he murmured and with a sudden wince of surprise clutched at his chest. He groaned, settling back on to the bed, his eyes widening with fear as he again relived the nightmare of being in a deep, narrow hole, the earth being shovelled down on him from high above, his legs and arms broken, his cries stifled as the dirt caught in his mouth.

Just as searing heartburn would visit him when he was foolish enough to risk some butter, that terrible image of being buried alive in the narrowest and deepest of places was a dream warning waiting to become real. Usually it came when he was investigating, when he would pass it off as angina, but sometimes it would visit him in his dreams when his sleeping mind was working. He had been obliged to leave two safe and comfortable B&Bs as a result of his crying out in the night.

"The body must find a home," he repeated in between long, calming breaths, as always trying to use the warning as a tool to confirm a logic breakthrough. "Why must it find a home?"

He reached over to another lever arch file, this one black, and turned to the first page, which was a photocopy of a pamphlet circulated by The Divine Sentiment. It was dated 1862 and contained a photograph of the founding member, reproduced from a glass plate collodian for the printing press. The handsome, debonair man was Mr Thomas Wilkinson Esquire and there was a zeal in his eyes that even the smudged and bleary ink of the nineteenth-century rolling press could not suppress.

He knew this pamphlet off by heart, having studied it over and over again, for it was the only surviving publication by the society, although from his research he knew that Wilkinson had produced a second pamphlet that contained none of the idealistic fervour of the first. This initial publication, however, fortunately kept by a politician who had mistakenly deposited it with some imperial papers – for otherwise it surely wouldn't have survived to reach the archives – was no such bitter document. It was jumping with the happiness of a true believer who had been privileged to witness a miracle. The front page called attention to a discovery the society had made in the name of phrenology, and called for patronage. Wilkinson's opening statement read: *Begone, all the craven doubts that hail down from these architects of Satan who call themselves scientists and natural historians. The Lord's people are blessed with the revealed truth and know that they are home.*

"The body must find a home," Honeyman repeated, daring the warning image to confront him again. His body was still, his heartbeat returning to normal. As he considered Wilkinson's fiery image he shook his head, knowing that something obvious was continuing to elude him.

He returned to his notebook, this time to the page at the very back, which was entitled:

HOW DO I STOP THEM?

He had learned everything he could possibly learn about The Divine Sentiment, from its distant origins to its present modus operandi, and he knew every prize it had acquired under his watch.

My useless watch, he thought, for the last page, apart from the question, was blank.

He had no idea how to stop them.

No one's going to stop me taking what's mine … least of all some old fart with his legal claptrap…

Neville Parry was muttering to himself as he reversed his hatchback up the drive, manoeuvring the open boot as close as he could manage to the front door. This involved the rear wheels coming onto the grass of the handkerchief garden and flattening his aunt's prized petunias; he waited for the bumper to touch the raised stones of the porch before he pulled on his handbrake.

It only vaguely occurred to him that such elaborate preparations were hardly necessary: the handmade Cluedo set was heavy but could be dismantled, the pieces put in a bag and the board top pulled out of the leather base. *The Death of Marat* was simply large, made of canvas and not even framed. It was simply a question of carrying it out at an angle.

It was perhaps the idea that the charity might be watching the house, that they would see their chosen objects spirited away, which urged him to pull the car boot as close to the front door as possible. This was the reason he offered to himself as he considered his aunt's painting and took a deep breath.

Taking this out of the house just seems wrong.

"Wrong?" he queried, the word sounding alien on his tongue.

Wrong wasn't the right word; or perhaps it was, but it had a different meaning in this context. The word had nothing to do with playing fair and respecting his uncle's wishes; it didn't even have a legal connotation. It would be … it would be … *inappropriate*, yet amplified a thousand-fold to where the word was almost a comical understatement. To take this picture out of the house, to put it inside the boot of his car, would be like committing incest, or stabbing a baby; something that was within his power yet horrible in the act and in its consequences.

As if to test his misgivings, his hands took the bottom corners of the painting and he lifted it slightly from its hook. He felt the string still on the nail, yet with the picture disrupted his heart started to pound; he imagined Marat's eyes springing open in alarm, the water of his bath spilling over if the canvas were to be disturbed from its precise position of balance.

The picture was back on the hook.

It belongs on this wall, he decided.

It is impressive and will help with the sale, he reasoned.

He walked over to the Cluedo board with misgivings, already aware that he would be unable to dismantle it as he had planned. His rational mind came up with the same alibi.

It is impressive and will help with the sale.

Standing in the small conservatory, he was annoyed to see that someone had tampered with the pieces. The old Trustee had examined it with relish yesterday but everything had been carefully put back in its place. This morning some workmen had briefly come and gone and he supposed that they were the ones who for some reason had meddled with the board.

One of the tall leather beakers was on its side and the dice had been rolled. All the pieces had moved. He picked each one up and replaced them on their starting squares but when he came to the Reverend Green he paused, for he recognised two patterns in the way the pieces had been arranged.

The first was a moving signature: Scarlett had been moved one square, Mustard three squares, White one square, and now Green three squares. He saw that Peacock was one square on and Plum was three squares on.

The second pattern was that each piece was turned around, reversed one hundred and eighty degrees, eyes no longer seeking out the leather murder envelope in the centre but instead looking out into the living area or at the glass-panelled wall of the conservatory.

He frowned as he collected up Peacock and Plum. Plum seemed particularly heavy in his hand; it returned to its purple square as if it was magnetised.

"Heavy fucking silver," he muttered but with a large exclamation mark and an even larger question mark flashing in his mind.

His eyes were on the murder envelope as he collected up the dice and returned them to the beaker, but the leather envelope that contained the three murder cards didn't seem to have been tampered with. Later he would be annoyed with himself for not having studied the numbers on the dice before collecting them up, for he would find it significant that both dice had been rolled. He had played enough games of Cluedo in this house to know that it needed only one dice: the extra dice and beaker were simply provided for the convenience of the players.

He had to concentrate very hard to recreate the scene of the board as he had discovered it, to replay what his eyes had taken in before he had started putting everything back.

Yes, the green and red precision dice were touching. They couldn't have been rolled at all to have landed in such a position; they had surely been placed together, very carefully.

His eyes became slits of concentration as his memory strained to see the mental snapshot.

And he saw the dice.

The red dice showed one dot. The green dice showed three.

While Neville was pondering his Cluedo board, Honeyman was lying in bed thinking.

Ellen Sorensen represented his last opportunity of finding a custodian who would help him. The young girl had hinted that she had some faith and some lucky chance had prevented the second collodian appearing, which in turn was delaying the Trustees.

How much did she already know?

From her interest in her mother's collodian, he had perceived that she was trying to rationalise matters. She would be concerned over the apparent indestructibility of the glass, though she would never dare test how resistant it really was; she may have even guessed that there was a link between the collodian and her Jumeau doll. He wondered if he had gone too far in asking her whether she always kept her door open but it was always so difficult to gauge: the extent to which he would be allowed to probe would be dependent on the custodian's faith, but sometimes the custodian wasn't aware that he or she had a faith. He suspected this was largely the case with Ellen Sorensen.

He carefully replayed her reactions in his head. She had denied it when he had asked her if she had had difficulty in throwing anything away, or taking anything out of the house, but she had blanched.

"Yes," he murmured, thinking that she might soon be ready to talk to him.

She's tried to leave the house, he thought.

She's tried to leave taking the doll with her.

IX

Here lies Nigel Sorensen

I t wasn't a letter but a list, the watermarked paper torn and bearing a large coffee stain, hidden among the bills of one of Stefan's ill-fitting drawers. It was typed with the Sholes & Glidden and was a long list in two columns, the first column beginning:

> This
>
> ~~Vien m b~~
>
> ~~Dckns~~
>
> Piano N
>
> Tel N

Before the list asked its questions, it triggered the memories, its discovery making Ellen sink to the kitchen floor. 'Dckns' was undoubtedly the collection of Charles Dickens first editions, the books cloaked in red leather stacked on a table set aside in the day room, gradually acquiring companions over the years. The collection carried fond memories because of a standing joke between her parents, which she as an onlooker happily shared, for there was one book that always eluded her father.

This was a first edition of *Martin Chuzzlewit*. Just as there were sportsmen that baseball and football cards had made more important to collectors than they ever were to the sport, *the Martin*, as her mother called it, was her father's obsession. If he saw a second hand bookshop he would always find the time to visit, no matter where they were or what the circumstances.

Thinking about it now, she wondered whether her mother had called it that in joking reference to Martin Sorensen, as a continuing nudge in the ribs over the estrangement. In fact her mother never made any attempt to find it, happy for the collection to remain incomplete, and with the list in her hand Ellen nodded with the hindsight of young adulthood. Perhaps her father also was content that *the Martin* would never be found, for he could surely have tracked one down on the internet if he had really put his mind to it. The book, or possibly just the search for the book, had acquired an importance far beyond the completion of a set.

"Why would he get rid of his books?" she asked herself, turning to the questions that the list raised. That must surely have been the purpose behind this list, for it appeared to be an inventory of items to be sold or thrown away, the words shortened, presumably to save effort, like a text message. The strike out in his wavering feeble hand meant that the item was accounted for.

She had the feeling that the most precious or important items were at the top of this list, with the entry marked 'This' undoubtedly being the typewriter itself.

Vien m b...

Yes, that was precious to her father.

She remembered the music box that he had purchased in Vienna on a business trip because her mother was angry with him when he returned, refusing to accept this beautiful gift that played Mozart's Eine Kleine Nachtmusik. It was a stupid argument over a telephone call he had forgotten to make, her mother later confessed, and it remained yet another standing joke with them that the Viennese musical box was *his*: it was the present she had refused to accept.

It was his...

"His," she murmured, her smile fading. Is that what he meant by putting an 'N' next to *piano* and *tel,* which must mean the antique telephone by the pantry door? By marking 'N', was he noting that they belonged to Nia and not himself?

She remembered Honeyman asking her who the piano belonged to: her father or her mother. And the telephone. Why did it matter? Everything her mother owned had become her father's property when she died.

She shook her head. If that was the case then why did she tell Honeyman that the piano, Cody and the telephone belonged to her mother? No, even though legal ownership might change there were certain things that in essence could only belong to one person.

The telephone came from her mother's side and it had belonged to Granddad Coles, a prominent journalist in his day. Coles' legend recorded that it was the very first telephone to ring in Fleet Street with the news of the Wall Street Crash, which was fanciful in the extreme but that was the family story and everyone knew that Granddad Coles had a fondness for invention. Her mother once remarked that the speakers were rigged up around the house because Nigel said he needed to hear the telephone when the President called in. Her father and Granddad Coles hadn't got on, the irascible hack invariably reminding him that he wasn't good enough for his daughter.

This further example of her parents' sense of the absurd made her smile sadly, but the essential fact was that the telephone was her mother's. It was the Coles machine, just as the Sholes & Glidden typewriter was the Sorensen machine.

She continued on through the column, passing the rare musical instruments, the watches, the parchment of Charles I's death warrant, then on to next column to find the many antiques and novelties until it came to an end as follows:

~~Arch wtr clck~~

~~Led soldrs~~

Orrery

Edwdn figrns N

The Archimedes water clock, lead soldiers, the orrery and the Roman coins completed the long inventory of her father's unique possessions, all crossed off, save for 'This' and the odd item which had an 'N' next to it. The items bearing an 'N' were still in the house, so he had obviously decided that they didn't need to be sold or thrown out.

She frowned; the deduction was logical but it still made no sense. If he cherished Mum's memory then the music box would be just as important as the piano and the telephone. Besides, he had plenty of money and didn't need to sell anything.

And there was an important omission.

"Cody," she muttered.

If this was a checklist for every valuable or original article in the house then why wasn't the doll listed?

She shook her head, even more confused, until her eyes narrowed.

Perhaps Father didn't prepare this list.

"*She* did."

Was it the little housekeeper's list of all the valuable things she planned to steal and then sell behind her father's back? Perhaps 'N' stood for 'no' or 'no good': the piano was too big, it would be missed, while the telephone was connected up to everything.

But whoever you sold it to knew all about your busy hands, my Tarny. That's why the new owner is writing to me. Didn't count on that, did you?

She sat back and stretched her spine, her bottom having gone to sleep on the cold stone floor; she knew that she was trying to force a square peg into a round hole. After all, the *Edwardian figurines* had an 'N' next to them and they certainly wouldn't be difficult to lift. She sighed and, in the hope that it might cast some light on the riddle, she took out of her shirt pocket the latest typewriter letter, the one she had found under the mat after Honeyman had visited.

114

She considered it once more:

```
in  me
```

```
lie S
```

Honeyman was now the prime suspect in the typewriter case. No one else had been to the house and as the letter was under the mat it couldn't have been posted. Lighting a cigarette and uncrossing her legs, her right foot having gone numb, she blew out smoke in dissatisfaction as she considered the probate valuer. In spite of the circumstantial evidence, something about him inspired her trust and confidence.

She tapped her cigarette into her black cake foil and returned to the letter. Some of the ash found the letter but it slid off leaving no residue. A glance at the list, which was stained and ripped, provoked an odd statement of fact from her subconscious.

The list is subject to the rules of time and accident ... but the letters aren't...

She shook her head, just as uneasy as when Honeyman had questioned her in the hallway and a lock seemed to tighten in her brain. She returned to the letter, banishing such stupid thoughts.

In me...

"In me," she whispered.

What did that mean? *Lies* she could understand, but what was the author trying to tell her by saying *in me*?

Was the author saying that the lies were hidden in the typewriter?

Or that her father had typed letters that were lies?

A cold shadow passed over her. Perhaps *Lies* had nothing to do with untruths, but should be interpreted as *lay* as in *laid to rest*.

She tried to swallow, but her throat was dry.

"Here lies Nigel Sorensen..." she murmured.

If that was the literal meaning, then *in me* meant ... it meant...

"Father's grave."

Nigel Sorensen lies in his grave. Was that what it meant?

She turned the letter over to consider the thumbprint stamp

31p

and her heart jumped as she saw the number. She studied the smudge in which the number was set. The black rings that made up the thumbprint seemed artificial and she looked closer, concentrating her vision on one of the river contours flowing through the design. She had excellent eyesight and bringing the letter up close she thought she could make out a pattern. She concentrated even harder, with one eye closed, the other straining; her iris adjusted as she finally managed to capture the image of the stamp.

She put the letter down and realised there was no breath left in her body. She took a gulp of air, then another, and another.

"Fucking weirdo," she muttered, with a tremor in her voice. The contour of the thumbprint was made up entirely of tiny 1s and 3s, tumbling over each other in chaotic heaps so that they formed smeared lines, as particles of dust form the rings of Saturn.

Still sitting on the kitchen floor she glared at the empty middle drawer that had delivered the list, sitting awkwardly on its metal runners. Uncle Martin was right: she should leave.

But she couldn't...

She snatched up her mobile and punched one of the speed dials. Hugh answered and without saying hello or letting him speak she rattled off the discovery of the list, her fresh interpretations on the latest letter and the revelations following her examination of the smudged stamp.

"What's one and three?" he muttered with a distant voice. She guessed that he was busy with something for he was mumbling his replies, his attention elsewhere.

"Have you been listening to me?" she asked irritably.

"Course, honey."

"There's some nutter out there. He must have drawn in all these numbers using a magnifying glass or something. Would have taken him ages."

"Easy to do with computer software…" he murmured.

"How do you know? You haven't seen it." There was a pause. "Hugh?"

"And you reckon it's this valuation guy … this ex-vicar?"

"Could be. Don't know, really. He did know a lot about phrenology."

There was a pause and she made a face of impatience.

"Phren…?" he began.

"Phrenology, Hugh. It's a Victorian science, okay? There's a chart and that's where this number thirteen comes from, I think. It's an important phrenological … lobe or something."

"Lobe?" he chuckled.

"There's this thirteenth lobe which is all about the divine, or something like that."

There was a silence.

"Hugh? You still there?"

"Well that explains the thirteen thing then…"

"It doesn't explain *anything*," she snapped.

"Right," he agreed. He was all attention now.

She angrily tried to push the drawer back into the unit but found that it wouldn't go. She tried again, mentally cursing Tarn's brother, but now saw that it wasn't just bad alignment on the runners, the drawer was actually blocked; something must have fallen into the back recesses of the cabinet and had now become dislodged.

"Something's jammed back there," she muttered to herself.

"So what about this last letter?" Hugh asked, hoping to salvage something from the conversation, the latest in a series of bad conversations. He was trying to remember the information she had trotted out as he had been answering his e-mails. "So you think *in me* means your dad's grave?"

"Possibly." She had given up trying to force the drawer; instead, she was peering through the structure to identify the cause of the jam.

"Ellen, can't you see how barmy this is?"

"What, you don't think I should take it seriously?" she asked indignantly.

"If you want to take it seriously then lock up the house and come home. Leave everything to the estate agents and the lawyers. That's what they're paid for."

"I'm not leaving," she said. "End of subject."

It all seemed like a dream now, her experience of trying to leave the house. She had been excited and eager to go, having packed her case, thrown it into the back of her Mini and arranged all the keys with their labels for the estate agent. Finally she came to collect Cody, intending to put her in the passenger seat for the journey back to Cardiff.

Cody seemed to get heavier with every step that she took away from the bedroom and by the time they turned the corner in the stairs it felt as if she was made of lead. Approaching the front door, the doll's eyes were switching quickly between their extremes of right and left and this, combined with the ever-increasing weight, translated into hysteria. She had hurried back up to the bedroom, returning Cody to her wicker chair.

"You belong here," she said, rationalising the experience as her guilt over shirking her duties as the executrix of her father's estate. "If you stay, I stay." She stroked the mohair wig and it was quite a time before Cody's eyes closed then gently rocked open, in composed approval.

Anything you've had trouble taking out of the house…?

She remembered Honeyman's apparently casual inspection of her reaction, when he had asked her that question.

Had he known?

"Well shall I come up?" Hugh asked. "I don't mind taking some leave."

Her attention returned to the telephone call. "Look, don't take it personally, but I just need to be alone right now, okay? Memories of my parents, that sort of thing … you know."

A pause hinted at his dissatisfaction with this explanation. "Well, it's your call. You know where I am."

"Miss you," she offered.

He sighed. "Me too. Come home soon."

She folded up her mobile and then with two sharp tugs pulled the drawer as far out of the runners as it would go. She reached in to the cabinet and pulled out the oblong glass object that was jammed at the back between this drawer and the one below. As she touched it and found her grip, her expression changed from irritation to surprise, for she knew what it was; the cool, silky touch of the glass was familiar to her.

Her father was pulled out from behind the kitchen unit, in brilliant colour within the smoky mist of the collodian. He had a thoughtful and distracted pose and he barely noticed the camera. As the picture was snapped she heard him say:

Not now, Ellie Sweet. Daddy's busy.

It was a photograph that she had taken, she believed, and probably when she was very young because her father was not centred.

"Here lies Nigel Sorensen," she muttered, thinking that her interpretation of the last typewriter letter was strangely prophetic. She had indeed found her father but he wasn't in a grave; he had slipped behind the drawers of a kitchen cabinet, lying there waiting to be found.

She recalled the promise of the Trustee: that the second collodian would turn up. It was with a sense of unease that she waited, almost expecting the telephone to ring.

It didn't. The doorbell rang instead.

X

These busy hands

"Didn't you say that I should telephone?" Ellen remarked as they took their seats in the day room following the tour of the house. Jasper Wells found the armchair, Sorrel Page the grand piano; the petite woman, overdressed in an indigo gown with bat-wing sleeves, lifted the keyboard lid carefully and glared suspiciously at the keys.

"We were passing," Wells said. "My apologies for the short notice."

On opening the door to see the Trustees brandishing their calling cards, she was forced to think quickly. Explaining that she had left a tap running she raced upstairs and bundled Cody into a wardrobe, covering her with a few old blankets for good measure. Such had been the speed of the operation, with the adrenalin firing inside her, that only now, as she sat down on the sofa, did the mental image catch up with her.

The image was of Cody's eyes before the first blanket covered her face: jammed open, wider than they had ever been. She thought of her now upstairs in the darkness, the wardrobe door closed, and her heart went out to her.

Wells had paused for a moment in her bedroom and looked thoughtfully at the wardrobe, his long fingers caressing the highest edge of the empty wicker chair. She had the feeling he knew something was wrong; perhaps he was trying to recall the list prepared for Mr Hobbs, but if so he missed his chance as he didn't ask to look inside.

"Oh, it's no problem," Ellen said in response to the Trustee's apology, "but I thought you wanted me to find the second photograph first. You were right, it did turn up." Her father's glass portrait had now taken up residence on the kitchen counter, which seemed an appropriate place for it, just as the landing on the second floor was the right place for her mother's portrait, in view of her bedroom.

In view of my doll, she thought as she settled herself on the sofa. In a fleeting moment of revelation, it occurred to her that doll and portrait were part of each other, like a fingernail and a finger; she frowned as she recalled how Cody had fallen out of her chair when the portrait had bounced down the stairs.

Wells sat back, polishing his fingernails with an air of dissatisfaction. Behind him, Sorrel was still glowering at the piano keys and in her gown Ellen thought that she looked like a concert pianist; perhaps she had come expecting to play. She decided to break the silence that had fallen.

"By the way, that telephone number of yours is wrong. Is it an extension number or something?"

"What number is that?" Wells inquired.

Ellen hesitated and shook her head. "It doesn't matter. So, did you like the telephone?" She mentally crossed her fingers, for he had made a long and careful inspection of the telephone before putting it down with a grim expression. Sorrel had stared at it for several seconds, as it sat guiltily by the pantry door, before turning to follow her colleague out of the kitchen, a twitch around her eyes.

"That telephone was the first one in Britain to receive news of the Wall Street Crash," Ellen continued. "You've seen how my father wired it up around the house, though I think that was just to annoy my grandfather when he visited."

"This would be the grandfather on your *mother's* side," Wells remarked to his fingernails, the question rhetorical. "When we were last here your father gave us the impression that the telephone was *his*…"

"No, it's from Mum's side of the family."

"So it is. Your father fooled us, you see, with all his excitement over the speakers and the wires. He was a man full of secrets, I think."

Ellen frowned. "Does it matter that it was Mum's?"

"We seek personal keepsakes for your mother and father. The original ownership is therefore important to us."

"Okay, so can't you take the telephone on behalf of my Mum?"

"The telephone was owned by your mother, but I fear she didn't love it," he said, to dismiss the suggestion.

Ellen shrugged in reluctant agreement, deciding that she would wait for Wells to make his choice. The silence soon became uncomfortable; she thought of her doll waiting fearfully in the darkness and desperately wanted to finish this meeting.

"That plaster bust you sent me," she said, attempting conversation. "It's a phrenological bust, isn't it?"

Wells nodded to his fingernails.

"So did you give my father the skull as well?"

He nodded again and said, "In fair trade."

"Why skulls and busts? Do you have a store of them or something, from when your society started up? A surplus you're trying to get rid of?"

He gave her a glance that said that this was a reasonable assumption, but didn't answer.

"You say fair trade. Are they valuable, then?" There was a note of impatience in her voice.

"Their value is subjective. I think some would find them more valuable than others."

Sorrel took this as a cue to start playing. The piece was the Moonlight Sonata and to Ellen's ear she played it perfectly, for as her mother had sometimes remarked the temptation was always to play the sonata a little too slow.

"That was Mum's favourite," Ellen murmured, thinking it could have been her mother at the piano, such was the similarity of touch. She imagined her father's reaction when these people visited him and he heard this piece again; she pictured him with his eyes closed, groaning with the ecstasy of a moment where he could believe his wife was back with him.

I can hear you, my dear one … I can hear you…

Wells smiled salaciously, as if her thoughts were naked before him. The smile produced his long teeth and gums.

"It was good of you to say that you didn't want the piano," Ellen said, shuddering slightly at seeing the yellow decay of his teeth and considering it prudent to remind the man of their telephone conversation. The woman was playing beautifully and she feared they might take the piano after all, especially if nothing else tempted them. "Have you decided what you want?" she asked, in her most casual tone. Her fingers were tapping on her knee, impatiently.

Sorrel, yet to utter a single word, looked towards Ellen as she played. Her left ear lowered towards the keys.

"Are you sure you've shown us everything, Miss Sorensen?" Wells asked, now examining the joints of his fingers. "The house looks very bare."

"My father used to have loads of stuff. To be honest I think my housekeeper has pilfered a lot of it."

"Really?"

"Well it's one explanation." In the courtroom of her mind, where the trial was still raging, she wasn't so sure she believed it anymore. If her father had made the list she had found in the drawer then it was surely a checklist designed to make sure that he got rid of everything that he had owned. There was no reason why Tarn would incriminate herself by preparing a list on something she intended to steal. "She's one of those born-again Christians, so I don't really know," she conceded, as an offering of justice to the housekeeper.

"But she has busy hands," he suggested.

She blinked in surprise and confusion.

He thoughtfully pulled at the joint of a middle finger. "Perhaps your instincts are sound. What would the little housekeeper have been thinking when she was dusting the bed, seeing all the sparkling treasures around her, with her busy hands? These Christians can have strange ideas. Perhaps she thought she was helping your father by relieving him of the wealth that would send him to Hell."

Ellen pondered this answer, supposing that *busy hands* must be a common phrase; she was sure that she thought it up herself but she must have heard it somewhere. "Aren't you ... your charity, I mean ... a Christian organisation?"

"There are far too many Christian bereavement societies offering easy and meaningless solace. We're in the business of providing comfort to the bereaved in more practical ways." He paused. "Has your housekeeper appointed herself judge and jury of your grief?"

Her surprise increased.

He glanced at her. "I see that she has. Do you resent the fact that she lauds over you her position as your father's carer in the last months of his life? How, with those busy hands she makes you feel guilty that she was here, while you were not?"

She hesitated then nodded slightly.

"You've nothing to feel guilty about, Miss Sorensen. Nothing at all. Your father wanted you to go to university, to move away; you'd have been a burden to him at this stage in his life."

"Yes, a burden," she whispered.

"Others will make it seem as if you should have abandoned your career, your freedom, your very *youth* to play nursemaid to a tired and embittered old man."

"Yes, embittered."

"And he *was* embittered, at the end. You witnessed that after your mother passed on. You expected comfort from him, sympathy and reassurance. But he had none to give, did he?"

She shook her head in negative agreement, but her eyes flickered. She hadn't offered her father any of those things either but she had assumed that no one's grief could have been greater than hers and ... and...

"He was my father," she said. "He was supposed to look after *me*." A gasp left her body, the admission in her mouth a wound in

124

her heart. "After *me,*" she repeated, tapping her chest.

Wells nodded. "Old people can be very selfish. It's a common failing of my age group, I regret to say, and men in bereavement do less well than women, in my experience. Don't feel guilty for living your life. Take my advice: ignore the sly, hinting criticism of your housekeeper and the destructive self-analysis of your psychiatrist. Life is renewed and the young replace the old."

The words were soothing like a balm, the comfort so complete it didn't occur to her to even question the basis of the man's knowledge, how he knew not only about Wendy but all the assurances she so needed to hear. Yet the urge to dash upstairs and pull open the wardrobe doors was stronger than ever, for the music was making her anxious with expectation. She felt as if Wells was expecting something from her, some snippet of information, before she could be excused.

"Now you say there's nothing further belonging to your father?" he inquired, briefly glancing at her high forehead as if to read the turmoil in her head.

"A man has visited to value everything for the probate. I can get you a list..."

"Who is this man?" he asked of his fingernails, with a smile.

She took a hesitant breath, remembering Honeyman's cautionary warning about the typewriter.

"Is he called Honeyman?" With a croak of effort, he reached over and handed her a business card. It read:

Tristyn Honeyman
Double-glazing

"Double-glazing?" she gasped, as she looked at the card.

"We have an entire collection, if you're interested. He uses anything that will get him inside the house. We obtained that one from a very dear old lady who's recently lost her husband."

"Who is he? What does he want?"

"We've no idea what he wants but he seems fascinated with us and with the poor souls we try to help. I've written a telephone number on the back of the card where you can obtain some background information on him, first hand, from a reliable source."

She turned the card over.

"That's the telephone number for the church he used to belong to," he clarified.

She remembered that Honeyman said he was a churchman before he had found ... what was it? ... *this occupation*. Yes, that was it. So what was his occupation? Was he a conman?

With a shake of her head she discarded the explanation as being too easy. "It must be him," she murmured to herself, then looked up, distracted. "Sending me these letters, I mean. It must be him."

"Letters?" Wells inquired.

"Typed on my father's antique typewriter," she explained, freely casting aside all advice from the so-called probate valuer. She became aware that the music had finished and she looked to the piano; Sorrel looked back at her.

"Your father had an antique typewriter?" he asked quietly.

"It's missing. Perhaps the housekeeper's pilfered it." Ellen shook her head. "I don't know ... I really don't know."

"I suggest you look for this typewriter. Contact us when you've found it."

"I told you, it's gone…"

"But it will turn up, have no doubt." Wells nodded, appearing satisfied now, and a wave of relief swept over her. She remembered another warning Honeyman had made, that the charity would try to swap the collodian plates, but he was wrong on that count too, for they had drifted past the portraits with scant interest. Indeed, the idea was ridiculous: why would the Trustees make presents of the collodians just to take them furtively back?

"I think we should let you get on," Wells said, getting up.

Ellen also stood up. "Thank you, I do have to…"

"Race back upstairs, to free your doll from her prison." He patted down his grey suit with long fingers.

An explanation attempted to articulate itself on her tongue but it emerged simply as an idle gesture of her hand.

"We've seen her before," he remarked, licking his dry lips. "She's a precious little thing, isn't she?"

Her face dropped. "You won't take her, will you?" she murmured helplessly.

It was Sorrel who answered, as she took Ellen's hand with both of hers. "When you heard that piece, the Moonlight Sonata, that was your mother talking to you. Look for the typewriter, for your father wants to talk to you too."

"I don't understand," Ellen said, not caring for the woman's touch.

"It's important that we find the things our loved ones cherished," Sorrel explained. "Did your father have a pet name for you? A secret name perhaps?"

"No," Ellen lied. She could now almost hear Cody's screams as she hammered helplessly on the closed door of the wardrobe.

"Look for that secret name. Your father will use it."

"I told you…"

Sorrel took a tighter grip of Ellen's resisting hand. "There's no need to lie to us, or to hide away your treasures. We're here to help you, for we understand your pain."

"Look, I'm grateful for whatever you did for my father, but I don't need…"

"You don't need the comforting reassurance that your parents are still with you?" Sorrel queried.

Ellen shook her head. "I know what you're trying to do but I'm not sure that I believe…"

"Your mother wants you to know that she's sorry she couldn't wait."

"What…?" Ellen murmured, her expression freezing.

"That she couldn't wait," Sorrel repeated, her tight smile appearing.

Ellen was back at the deathbed, her mother heaving with lack of oxygen, her eyes almost in her sockets. The nurses said that hearing was the last sense to go, yet her father had simply held her hand, mortified and unable to speak, while Ellen had whispered *I love you* over and over again.

Her mother's lips had fluttered briefly in response, silently repeating the declaration; the unexpected rejoinder had made her run out of the ward in tears.

She was dead on her return, only a few minutes later. She hadn't waited.

At last Sorrel released Ellen's hand. "Go to her now. She's waiting for you."

Cody's eyes were almost closed as she was released from the wardrobe, the eyelids quivering as if the doll was attempting to shut out the tortures of her confinement. Safely returned to her chair it was several minutes before the eyes gently rocked open with a look of settled contentment.

"It's alright, they're gone," Ellen whispered. "I won't let them take you. I promise I won't let them take you."

She glanced past the blonde, mohair curls to the landing, to her mother's portrait, then returned to her doll with a smile, for all was right with the world again. The tiny jointed arms were put back in place; the left hand, with its delicate bisque fingers, was positioned on the wing of the chair, the right hand in the lap. In the sleeve of this right hand she found a letter, folded as before with a smudged stamp.

13p

It was addressed to *Miss Eleanor Sorensen*.

"Who gave you this?" she asked her doll, turning the letter over in her hand. "Did you find it in the wardrobe? Or did that Mr Honeyman slip it in your sleeve when he was here?" She nodded to herself. "Just as he slipped a letter under the mat when he was looking at Mr Sockets." She opened the letter and it read:

```
in  me
```

```
Ellie Sweet
```

XI

The vows that are better broken

There were no shops in Tenby's main street or cobbled tributaries that could be properly regarded as 'junk shops', but there were several that carried no particular loyalty to any article of sale and where rummaging hands could in one moment find a genuine cashmere shawl, in the next a gem globe, both at low prices. Ellen was wondering how much a first edition Dickens would attract.

"Ellie Sweet," she was muttering to herself in one such shop overlooking South Beach as she trawled through the objects d'art, the letter in Cody's sleeve having infuriated her. She regarded the use of that name, that secret, private name between her and her father, as a physical outrage. This was no stranger sending these letters but someone who knew her, or knew her father, which whittled down the list of likely candidates to just one person.

She was convinced now that Tarn Hughes was behind everything: she was the only person who knew about the name and had access to the house. It was true, she reflected, that she had mentioned the name in passing to Honeyman but the letters had started to arrive before that conversation and the name *Ellie Sweet* was no afterthought: it was planned from the very beginning, as proved by the configuration of the letters.

in me

'LieS' had a capital S, because it was part of the name.

A storage box, tucked in between some old LPs, brought her search to an abrupt end. Upside down in the box was a book and as she pulled it out and wiped the dust off its stained red cover she saw it was a first edition of *Little Dorrit*. At the counter, she asked who had brought this book in; the shop owner remembered because it had been part of a set, or at least an almost complete set. This was the last remaining book. And the price? Well…

Ellen slammed the book down on the kitchen table after she had calmly made her way down the stairs, finding Tarn at the coffee percolator. The thud of *Little Dorrit* on the oak was like a drumbeat, causing the housekeeper to spin round with surprise. Her expression became resigned when she saw the book.

"You didn't even ask for any money for it?" Ellen inquired coldly, gesturing to the leather-bound evidence on the table. "I had to buy it back for twenty quid, if you're interested, though that's a fraction of what it's worth…"

"Probably…" Tarn agreed.

"But the shop owner took pity on me, see, when I said it belonged to my dear old dad and that he'd spent his life…" and she took a breath that energised her with anger "… his whole *fucking life*…"

"Don't swear, Ellen, please…"

"Collecting these stupid *fucking* books…"

Tarn sighed and shook her head.

Ellen was glaring at her, the flat of her hand on the book. "What's the matter?" she whispered. "Did you and your brother make so much out of selling everything that you decided to give the last few things away?"

"Keep my brother out of it," Tarn replied quietly.

"Why? You've poked your nose enough into *my* family. God, I can't believe you gave away those books. My father loved those books."

"Yes, yes he did." Tarn switched on the percolator with trembling hands and then quickly smoothed back the black hair tied tightly back from her face. "He did love those books. That's why he had to get rid of them."

"Had to…?"

"Along with everything else … that he loved." She turned round.

"What are you talking about?" Ellen whispered, shaking her head.

"That's what he told me."

"What?"

"That's *all* he told me. He made me promise not even to tell you that." Tarn shook her head with a pained expression. "No, he made me *vow*."

"That's a new one," Ellen chuckled, her eyes alive with hatred. "Handy alibi."

"I don't need an alibi," Tarn said, her voice finding strength. "I'm no thief. Why do you think everything was *given* away?" She paused and Ellen's pose, though still aggressive, lost some of its certainty. "Your father told me to give them away: he knew you'd suspect me otherwise. Look in every shop in Tenby if you have to – I had to spread everything across quite a few – and all the shop owners will tell you the same. Your father simply wanted everything gone."

"Why?"

"I honestly don't know."

"So my father confided in you," Ellen remarked, ignoring the answer. "He probably thought you were a little angel, didn't he? Well, I don't believe a word of this. You can fool a senile old man, but not me."

"Your father wasn't old or senile … he was just sick."

Ellen was shaking her head, now walking around the table, circling the book in its centre. "He'd lost his mind … must have, just to have given everything away … everything gone, without a word to me. Perhaps he just wanted to deprive me of my inheritance

131

… he didn't give a damn about my feelings…"

"I wondered how long it would take before this all came back to *you*," Tarn muttered. She looked down.

"What did you say?"

"That's it really, isn't it? Perhaps if you'd been here a little more often he wouldn't have needed so much help from his housekeeper."

Ellen stopped pacing. Her jaw dropped.

"He loved you in spite of that," Tarn said grimly.

"Shut up," Ellen spat back.

"Ellen, if you're feeling guilty, then you've got to deal with it. You won't do it through me, or through a lost collection of books. And … and even I know that you never have to do an essay *after* you graduate."

"Shut up."

"Perhaps it's best if you just go. Go back to Cardiff."

"This is my house!"

"Your father didn't want you here."

A tear formed in a corner of Ellen's eye, but she pushed it away. "Is that what he said?" Her voice was not her own; it had the high squeak of a child.

Tarn hesitated. "Yes," she said reluctantly. "He didn't want you here. He told me … he told me to tell you that. Why do you think he didn't even keep your graduation photograph?"

There was a silence. "Well I'm not going," Ellen said eventually. She flicked the book with the back of her hand and sent it toppling to the floor. "Fuck him, and fuck you. This is my house and he can rot in Hell."

"Don't say that," Tarn murmured, deflated, her strength gone having now fulfilled her promise to Nigel Sorensen. She pictured him raising himself up from the armchair as he had made her promise.

Tell her I'd want her to leave! Tell her I wouldn't want her here!

"Who's got my father's typewriter?" Ellen asked sharply.

"I don't know."

"So why didn't my father tell you to give *that* away, too?"

"I don't know," Tarn repeated, with a shake of her head.

Another silence followed as they surveyed the wreckage of this discussion. "There's something you're not telling me," Ellen said slowly. "You're lying, I can see it."

Tarn was looking at the floor.

"I also know it's you who's sending me those letters," Ellen said.

"The letters?"

"He told you he called me that ... that name, didn't he?"

"I don't know what you're talking about."

"Of course you don't." Ellen left the kitchen but stopped half way up the stairs. "Oh and by the way, you're fired," she called.

"But I'm paid up until..."

"I don't care, you're fired. I don't want you here anymore." A few steps further up she paused again. "Keep the money. You've taken everything else."

Ellen went directly to her bedroom and in spite of the turmoil in her brain her kissed fingers still found her mother's portrait as she passed, her perspiration leaving no mark on the glass. Although she desperately wanted privacy, she didn't close her door: she never closed it, not even during her last visit in Easter, the one that had lasted only two days.

Those two horrible days, her father in his armchair, the carers from the hospital coming and going with pills and shrugs.

There was nothing wrong with him, they had said, making it easier for her not to talk to him.

When she left the house, having asked one of her university friends to ring her and engineer an emergency back in Cardiff, she felt as if she had escaped from prison.

She sat on the bed and considered her doll, Tarn's accusations cutting in to her.

"It's true," she whispered eventually. "I wasn't here for him."

Cody's eyes made no response; they remained fixed on the window.

"He was always so strong, you see. I always expected him to snap out of it, you know. Expected him to just turn up at my door one day, in Cardiff, saying he was better. That he was going to make it all better. I would have given him a hug, if he had. I would have, honest I would."

Tears came, sniffle by sniffle, and Cody's eyes gently opened and closed as Ellen's distress rocked the bed.

"He didn't love me. He would have come otherwise, wouldn't he?" She dried her eyes. "That's why I don't feel guilty, whatever that little cow says. He doesn't deserve it." She nodded to herself and took Cody's tiny hand.

A few minutes passed as she recovered her composure.

"I threw away the graduation letter," she admitted, with a little shake of the hand. This caused a microscopic rattle inside the doll's head, which manifested itself with an unhappy half closing of two paperweight eyes, which in spite of the hand being shaken again, stayed jammed in place until Ellen woke the next morning.

When Tarn was approached by the large, bearded man in Tudor Square, Tenby's picturesque town centre, she had a vague notion she had seen him before.

Within a few moments she would remember that he had briefly called at the house and left a business card for Ellen, something about antiques, but as he introduced himself she felt an uneasy twinge of recognition. She was always brisk when she shopped in town, focussed only on her destination, but if she could replay the corners of her vision she might have seen the man in the distance, watching her.

Peering out from over a book, perhaps, through the window of a shop; in the far aisle of a supermarket; feeding sea birds from the railings over the beach.

So it was against her better judgment that she agreed to share a pot of tea with the stranger, but it was the quietly muttered words that compelled her to follow him. He said that he knew what had been wrong with Mr Sorensen.

"So, Mr...?"

"Just Honeyman," he said, attempting to make an inconspicuous mass of his large frame as he huddled over his teacup and poured from the milk jug. He had glanced furtively around the coffee house more than once since they had sat down; he supposed it was just out of habit now, for he was becoming increasingly sure that the Trustees always knew where he was.

"You're saying he wasn't ill?" she asked, unwilling to call him by his surname and suspicious of his credentials. When he had opened his wallet to pay for the tea she had seen something familiar in the licence holder: the diagram of a fish. Her father had a similar card on the shelf of his car, to designate his affiliation to the Baptist church, together with a laminated card that read: *I asked Jesus how much he loved me. In answer he stretched out his arms ... and died.*

"It depends how you define ill. He had nothing that could be cured with surgery or medication."

"It wasn't even agoraphobia?" she asked, uneasily. She wished she had had more time to think before accepting his invitation to talk.

"Not even that," he said, now risking a furtive sip of his tea. She glanced around, against her will drawn into his sense of discomfort. "*Trapped* would be a better word than 'ill'."

"What do you mean?"

"I've seen other sufferers ... of the same condition."

"Really...?" She was very suspicious now, wondering whether he had planted the fish in his wallet on purpose. He certainly hadn't made a point of returning his wallet to his jacket quickly, so allowing her to pick up that vital clue to his identity. She wasn't of the breed who allowed people to make fun of her family's faith and she certainly wasn't in the business of conversion, in spite of what her parents told her about being a good witness. Her look of sceptical mistrust must have been acute, for when she saw her brother coming back from the toilet his face was livid. Her expression immediately softened and she waved to him.

"Stefan looks after me," she said, as her brother sat down at the table. "I'm sorry, I was looking very serious just now and it might have upset him."

Stefan was twenty years old; he had a shaved head and was so thin Honeyman wondered whether he only ate when forced to do so at gunpoint. When he had approached the two of them outside, he had recognised a mildly bewildered look in the young man's eyes.

"I'd be protective too if I had such a nice sister," Honeyman said, offering his hand. Stefan saw it but didn't take it, his mind filled with the potential threat to his sister and so unable to cope with social pleasantries.

"What do you want with my sister?" Stefan grumbled, a sinewy hand going defensively to one of the braces of his dungarees.

"It's alright, Stef, he's a friend," Tarn said. "Mr Honeyman's a friend of Mr Sorensen's."

"Just Honeyman."

"Mr Sorensen?" Stefan murmured. "You mean Mr Sorensen in Heaven?"

"Yes, that's right." She touched his elbow and he shrugged with embarrassment at this show of affection, but didn't pull away.

"I think I've seen your handiwork," Honeyman remarked. "Didn't you build that charming cabinet of drawers in the late Mr Sorensen's kitchen?"

Tarn beamed with pride as her hand settled on her brother's captive elbow. "You're so good at DIY, aren't you Stef? You're so clever."

Stefan smiled and looked away, adopting a serious air as he nodded in agreement.

"Did you know Mr Sorensen, Stefan?" Honeyman asked gently.

Stefan nodded again.

"Did you like him?"

Tarn looked suspiciously at Honeyman.

"He was scary," Stefan answered.

"But always nice to us," she suggested, prompting another nod of agreement from her brother.

"How would you have described him?" Honeyman asked. Tarn's eyes flashed a warning in his direction, which he answered with a slow wink of his right eye.

"Mr Sorensen was..." Stefan began.

Tarn and Honeyman held their breath.

"He was like Sigmund," Stefan finished. He had found a teaspoon and was turning it around in his free hand. An inquiring look from Honeyman prompted Tarn to mutter:

"Sigmund's our budgie."

She thought about Stefan's answer, with dark looks for both the bearded stranger and her brother.

"He's a smart lad and don't let anybody ever tell you any different," Honeyman remarked to Tarn, as he pictured the caged bird. "He has intuition."

She had a blank expression, not daring to allow her feelings to show over such a precious thing as a good opinion of her brother, but in her mind she thanked the stranger. A warm glow was spreading through her body at the thought that her brother was not a joke, that he had ... he had...

Intuition.

Yes, that was a quality that even the wisest didn't always possess.

"You were saying that you've seen others like Mr Sorensen?" she asked.

"Yes, yes indeed," Honeyman replied, but sipping his tea without amplifying; she guessed that her brother's return from the toilet had made him think better of confiding in her. With a final wink that told her that there would be another time, he asked, "Are you looking after Mr Sorensen's daughter?"

"She's sacked me," Tarn murmured with a face of unhappy resignation.

"Sacked you? Why?"

She shook her head in reply.

"Ah, have you fallen out? I suspect it's all those secrets and promises: the things Mr Sorensen told you to hide." Stefan, to his right, gave a vacant blink of his eyes.

"I don't know what you mean," she answered warily.

Honeyman stirred his tea. "I think I see your heart, Tarn Hughes. When you make a promise you build a door with a bolt lock six inches thick. Am I right?"

She didn't answer, but a raise of her eyebrows reluctantly accepted there was some truth in the metaphor. "Ellen knows that I'm hiding something," she confessed.

"Hiding something?"

She shook her head, realising the words had left her mouth with her guard dropped.

"Don't punish yourself," Honeyman suggested. "You're the best person to know whether a promise needs to be kept or a thing needs to be hidden. Mr Sorensen was stronger than most, much stronger in fact, but at the end he wouldn't have been thinking clearly. He would've been acting purely on impulse."

"Impulse? What impulse?"

Honeyman shrugged, but was thinking:

Hide.

Protect.

"Just impulse. When someone is sinking in quicksand every action is prompted by desperation. So don't burden yourself with promises you might have made to him at the end, no matter what he made you swear. You know where the need is: you're here, Mr Sorensen isn't. Some vows made to the dead only punish the living. Some vows are unbearable loads. These are the vows that are better broken."

As she was considering this she caught Stefan's eye. She smiled at him but he didn't smile back; he seemed troubled and confused by Honeyman's words.

"I thought I said you were fired," Ellen said as she opened the front door.

Tarn was standing cautiously on the porch. She blinked slowly. "This is yours," she said, handing her a sealed envelope that was strapped down with many lines of Sellotape, most of which looked as if they had been ripped with teeth. The Sellotape lines were so numerous that the envelope was almost plastic in consistency.

"What is it?"

"Something that your father asked me to keep safe. Something he never wanted you to see."

Ellen accepted the offering suspiciously and Tarn stepped away from the door.

"He didn't want you to see it, because he wanted you to hate him. That's why I said you should leave, that he'd want you to leave. He made me promise to tell you that. He made me *vow*. But some vows are better broken."

"Why would he…?" Ellen began, but Tarn was already running down the steps to the road; with her prepared speech delivered she was eager to get away.

Ellen decided to open the envelope in her bedroom under Cody's gaze. She pulled and ripped at the Sellotape and the final rip was severe, causing the envelope to tear. A photograph escaped onto the bed.

She gasped, recognising it immediately, for it was the graduation photograph, showing her in her black cap and gown, that she had sent to her father with a note that said, simply: *Sorry you weren't there.*

The photograph was crinkled and weary, as if it had been rolled into a tight tube and then straightened and pressed out by hand. On the back of the photograph were five words that were barely legible, for they had been typed with obvious difficulty on her father's typewriter. The five words were:

`I am so very proud`

Something caught in her throat as she silently repeated these words. She touched Cody's hand and the doll's eyes closed and gently opened.

"He did keep it. He did…"

And the tears came as she hugged Cody pitifully to her shoulder, and her grief escaped at last.

XII

All about guilt

"It's not a stranger," Ellen explained to her uncle, when he telephoned the following morning. "Whoever's sending the letters must have known Dad." She was referring to the letter she had found in Cody's sleeve, having told him about the visit by the Trustees. "Only Dad called me Ellie Sweet."

"But *I* knew he called you that," Martin remarked cautiously; he was thinking that this was the first time in recent memory he had heard her call his brother *Dad,* as opposed to *Father.*

"Sure, but *you're* not sending the letters. So who else could it be?"

"Your housekeeper?"

"That's what I thought, at first," she admitted. "In fact I was sure of it."

"But not anymore?"

With her mobile at her ear she went to the window of the day room, watching the cars go by as if she expected to find the answer in the traffic. "Look, I think I might have been wrong about her."

There was no response.

"Uncle Martin?" she murmured, wondering if the mobile connection was breaking up: he had explained he was travelling around the country on a series of chiropractic seminars he was hosting.

"Is the housekeeper still working for you?"

"No, I've sacked her," she admitted unhappily. She had left a message on Tarn's mobile but it hadn't been returned.

"Good. Probably better if there are no strangers in the house at the moment, do you hear?"

"We don't have to worry about Tarn," she replied, sensing some hostility in his tone; she supposed he was just being suspicious of everyone now as a matter of course. "I'm more worried about the man who's posing as a probate valuer: man called Honeyman."

He was silent once more.

"I was given this telephone number," she continued, "and it was his old church, in Flint. They didn't give me any details, but they said that he wasn't allowed in any of their churches and that I shouldn't trust him."

Martin cleared his throat, sounding dissatisfied with this information.

"They told me that the police are after him," she added.

"Why?"

She frowned with exasperation, wondering why her uncle was having trouble believing her story. "Probably for doing what he did to me: turning up after a funeral and cheating his way into a house. Perhaps he's just looking for antiques on the cheap, but maybe he's at the bottom of these letters." She paused. "Has Uncle Mikey done any checks yet?"

"No, he's still waiting for lab time. Ellen…"

"Yeah?"

"I don't like the idea of you being in the house on your own. Can someone come and stay with you?"

"There's Hugh, I suppose."

"Is there something else?" he asked at length. "Something you haven't told me?"

She sighed and told him about the envelope and the graduation photograph. Martin was smiling as she finished, for he understood her happiness: the envelope contained the proof that her father loved her. Everything else was unimportant with such a truth revealed.

He nodded in empathy, thinking of the note he had found at his brother's grave.

Forgive me…

142

"But *Tarn* had this photograph?" he asked cautiously. "Why did he give it to Tarn?"

"Because he didn't want me to know about it … but I suppose he still couldn't bear to throw it out."

"But *why* didn't he want you to know?"

She sighed once more. "I don't know," she conceded. "I'm hoping Tarn will be able to tell me."

The leaves and branches of the sycamores were shaking as a southerly wind found its way into the clearing, making the shadows dance.

"I thought I might find you here," Tarn said, as she approached through the trees from the direction of Penally church. Honeyman was sitting on the bench, with a packed lunch at his side and a large well-thumbed hardback book, the cover concealed by his sandwiches.

"You did?" he asked, getting up and then sitting down with her. She smiled in appreciation of this show of courtesy.

"All the talk about Mr Sorensen: this is where he's buried. My brother and I visit the grave."

Honeyman didn't comment. His mobile had appeared in his hand and he fiddled with it for a moment; she wasn't sure but he seemed to be sending a short text message.

"Were you here hoping to meet Ellen?" she asked.

"No, I was just having my lunch. I find it's peaceful." He closed the paper around his sandwiches and popped two sticks of gum into his mouth. He chewed awhile, without speaking.

"Don't you want to talk to me?" she asked uncomfortably, realising that this clearing was quite isolated, possibly unsafe, and wondering whether she should have made some inquiries about this man before speaking to him. He had seemed friendly at the coffee shop but perhaps that was only because they were in public. "I had the feeling you were about to tell me something yesterday," she said, "but you stopped because my brother came back."

He looked at her cautiously.

"You can trust me," she ventured. "If this is about poor Mr

Sorensen, then you can trust me."

"There's no need for you to become involved," he replied. "It's young Ellen Sorensen I need to speak to. Though if you could help me speak to her I'd be very grateful," he added, as a thought occurred.

She looked bemused. "Why not just knock on the door?"

He shook his head.

They've visited her now, he thought. *She won't see me.*

"She knows that I'm an impostor," he said, raising his eyebrows as he let this admission sink in. "Does that scare you?"

Tarn considered him carefully. "No, you don't scare me," she said at length. "You seem like an honest man and … well, I recognised an air about you, in the coffee shop. So did Stefan. You're a minister, aren't you?"

A twitch of the moustache betrayed his smile. "He's perceptive, that brother of yours."

"So you *are* a minister?"

"A banished one. Perhaps even a guilty one…"

Just like Reverend Green, he thought, the musing making him see Neville Parry, sleeping fitfully in his uncle's spare bedroom. His memory now found an image of the Cluedo board and the little girl wailing pitifully to her parents. He wondered again at the contents of the murder envelope, surely the cause of her tears; the nephew, as custodian, would be wondering too…

"Do you want me to get a message to Ellen?" Tarn asked. "She's left a message on my mobile so I'm going round to see her."

"Miss Sorensen's the custodian," he murmured absently, "so I need to speak to *her*…" His voice trailed off as he realised he had stumbled into speaking his thoughts aloud.

She blinked slowly. "Custodian? What's a custodian?"

With a shake of his head, he put the remains of his packed lunch in one of his pockets. "When I was at the house Miss Sorensen was talking about a photograph of her father," he remarked casually. "She said it was lost. Did it turn up afterwards?"

"Yes, it's in the kitchen."

"Is it now?" he pondered. His book, which she saw was a hardback novel but was still unable to make out the title, went into another pocket. "Is it now?" he repeated, to himself.

"Won't you tell me what this is all about?"

He turned to her with an expression bordering on suspicion. "How much do you know already?" he asked.

She hesitated, taken aback by his demand. "Well, Mr Sorensen asked me to get rid of a lot of the things that he owned. He kept hold of a typewriter, but it's missing and I can't think who could have taken it. And Ellen's receiving letters, written on the same typewriter. I know that something's not right and I want to help."

He was thoughtful for a few moments before he nodded, sadly. "I know you do."

"This is something spiritual, isn't it? I can sense it. Can't you tell me?"

"I'm afraid to."

"I'm of the Faith. If you're a minister, I'll believe you."

He shook his head once more, reliving the agony of his walk down the aisle of his church when he was rejected by his faithful congregation. There had been many rejections since, though none so public and so painful.

The leaves shook with a heavy gust of wind, causing them to both look up with startled expressions. "When will you be at the house?" he murmured.

"If Ellen takes me back I'll be working mornings."

"Then I'll come tomorrow morning." With a grimace, he stood up. "I'll come when Miss Sorensen has gone out. If you'll let me wait then at least I'll have a few minutes with her, before she throws me out."

"Why would she throw you out?"

Without answering, he smiled in thanks and farewell. He strode quickly towards the trees that led to the Penally road and left the clearing.

As she sat there alone, pondering on his words, the sun dipped behind the sycamores and the bench cast a square silhouette on the gravel. She wondered where this meeting would lead, whether she had done the right thing in approaching him; she had a sense of wonderful unease that was reminiscent of when she was converted, one ecstatic Sunday evening two years ago.

The delight of knowing the revealed truth, yet trepidation at the trials that would surely follow.

The first trial was the difficult explanation that she had to offer to Ellen.

There were only vows, she explained, not reasons; Mr Sorensen had simply made her promise to do as he asked. She was sitting across the kitchen table from Ellen, their cups of coffee empty and long finished.

She couldn't account for his actions; it was as if there was a shut-down system in his head that would make his brain crash if he discussed or even signalled his intentions. He would point to the items that he wanted removed from the house; they were too precious to destroy, he had managed to explain, but beyond that there were no explanations, only vows. Vows he had made her swear.

"What vows?" Ellen asked.

"To keep that graduation photograph forever, but keep it secret. He said you were never to know how proud he was of you, how much he loved you. He was telling *me*, and that was enough. He made me swear to tell you that he wanted you out of the house, and..."

"And?"

"To never attempt to be your friend."

You will not be her friend! You will make her hate you!

"Why wouldn't he want us to be friends?"

Tarn glanced at her, then looked down and shook her head.

Ellen studied her with a sad smile. "You've broken all your vows, haven't you?"

Tarn nodded mournfully.

Swear on your god, he had insisted and his whispered order as he had gripped her hand had been merciless. *Swear on your god!*

"I'm sure that in his mind he was trying to protect you," Tarn said. "Perhaps he thought that if you hated him you wouldn't stay."

Ellen pondered on this with a stifled sob.

"I know," Tarn agreed sadly.

It was left unsaid, the conclusion that had to be drawn: Nigel Sorensen possessed a strength and emotional courage that was difficult to fathom; he was prepared to sacrifice all possibilities of his daughter remembering him fondly, just to keep her safe.

"Your uncle wants you to leave too, doesn't he?" Tarn remarked, considering her empty cup with a worried expression.

"He's just paranoid. He thinks there's some letch out there."

"Perhaps it would be safer. You being so pretty and everything."

"Oh … rot…"

Tarn smiled. "You don't like compliments, do you?"

Ellen pretended not to hear the question, instead producing the list she had found in the drawer of Stefan's cabinet, which began:

> This
>
> ~~Vien m b~~
>
> ~~Dckns~~
>
> Piano N
>
> Tel N

Tarn's face was alive with curiosity as she scanned the columns, occasionally pausing as she worked out the abbreviations. "What's 'N'?" she asked, after a time.

"I think it stands for Nia: my mum. He only needed to remove the things belonging to *him*, but I don't know why. I also don't understand why Cody isn't on the list."

Tarn sighed. "Dickens," she said, tapping the list with her finger. "He adored those books, he was always looking at them … touching them. I think that's why they were the last things to go." She shook her head. "No … no, I'm wrong … the last thing was the musical box."

"It was treasured, that thing." Ellen put her head back briefly to banish the tears. "They honeymooned in Vienna and my dad adored Mozart."

Tarn sighed again. "What does *'this'* mean?"

"It must mean the typewriter itself. Writing 'this' was easier than writing 'typewriter'. But I can't understand why it isn't crossed off." She paused, thoughtfully. "Tarn, are you sure the typewriter's gone? Are you absolutely sure?"

"It wasn't one of the things I gave away and your father certainly didn't get rid of it. He barely had the strength to tap the keys, let alone lift the thing, and there's no way he could have taken it out of the house." She shook her head slowly. "It took him all day to type that letter on your graduation; I said 'let me type it', but he refused, saying he had to do it himself. He was very stubborn like that."

"That's Dad, alright." Ellen turned her cup round on its saucer. "I'm sorry for calling you a thief, but I suppose I was a bit jealous of you. It was because you were close to my father at the end … because you looked after him so well. It made me feel guilty." She winced. "It made me feel like shit, to tell you the truth."

"Don't feel guilty, Ellen. I know all about guilt. It was in me for years. It almost destroyed me."

Ellen looked at her inquiringly, seeing that she was rubbing a tear from her eye. "What's the matter?" she asked.

Tarn shook her head.

"Tell me," Ellen persisted.

She took a breath. "Stef wasn't born the way he is. We were playing with an air rifle, I was eleven, he was twelve." She wiped more tears from her eyes. "I did it. I shot him and damaged his brain. We were both laughing and the gun just went off in my hands. It just went off…"

148

Ellen offered her a helpless expression of regret. She glanced at the drawers by the sink, the middle one now jammed irretrievably half way out after her incident with her father's collodian, and tried to think of something nice to say about them.

"My parents, they told me that it was all God's purpose," Tarn continued, speaking to her empty cup. "Told me that God must have wanted Stefan to be that way, for we come before God as children and Stef will always be a child now. They said it was meant to happen and that we should pray for understanding." She looked up. "Do you think God meant it to happen? Do you?"

Ellen shook her head slowly. "But you have your faith," she suggested.

"Yes, I have my faith. I discovered my faith two years ago, one wonderful evening when my world changed. I was in torment until then … *torment,* finding no comfort anywhere. The guilt would have destroyed me in the end, I think."

For the first time, Ellen gave some thought to Stefan Hughes beyond his being just an annoying irrelevance, seeing him in the context of a sister's love. Her impressions had been formed at the wake, when he had been glaring at her until Tarn nudged him in the ribs, and on his one visit to the house when he refused to look at her, still cowed by his sister's censure. He came to fix an electrical short; Tarn kept a big mug in the house with the words *Workman on Duty* and with a serious face he drunk his tea from this mug as he tested all the light switches in the house. With a pencil behind his ear, he considered the fuse box and declared that they probably needed an electrician.

"I wish I had a brother," Ellen remarked, supposing that Tarn had never expected him to fix the short, that she simply wanted him to feel useful. "In fact a sister would do. All this would be easier to bear." She paused. "I get so lonely."

"I'm sorry," Tarn said, still tearful.

Ellen shook her head quickly, not caring for sympathy. "Anyway, it's nice that you and your brother are so close."

"I do try to look after him. And he's a lot smarter than people realise." Tarn was wiping her eyes when the telephone rang.

Dring-a-dring.

Throughout the house, they heard the delayed echo of the speakers blasting out the bicycle ring of the antique telephone. In the kitchen it was a small, tinny shrill but alarming in the fact that it should choose to ring at all.

"It's been ages since anyone telephoned," Tarn whispered, getting up nervously. "Your father changed the number. Only Mr Hobbs knows it: he was given it when he changed the will."

"Only Mr...?" Ellen began, remembering how the Trustees had hauled her out bed a few mornings ago.

"Your father didn't like the telephone ringing because he considered it an intrusion, but he couldn't bear to have it dismantled. He loved it ... it was the only thing in the house he ever talked about." She was halfway across the kitchen and had stopped, uncertainly. The telephone hadn't rung again.

Ellen frowned. "Who do you think...?"

BWAM BWAM BWAM!

They both screamed as there was a pounding on the front door, the dull thud so loud it sounded as if the door was being forced off its hinges.

They held their breath.

BWAM BWAM BWAM!!

This time the pounding worked as an alarm and they raced up the stairs. As Ellen made the last stair, she saw the letter waiting on the mat.

"Forget the letter – see who it is!" she shouted with a swiftness of mind that surprised her. She pulled open the door and they ran out onto the landing of the steps, looking in opposite directions along the road. They stayed on the landing until they agreed there were no candidates for the mystery postman. They came back in and Ellen picked up the letter. It was addressed to *Eleanor Sorensen* and bore a thumbprint stamp that was larger than before. This time the stamp was:

1331p

"The post is getting more expensive," she joked uneasily, her heart skipping a beat as she saw the number. A sudden impulse told her to attempt to rip the letter, to see whether it *could* be ripped; she put the impulse aside with horror, thinking it would be like mutilating a child.

"How could they have got away so fast?" Tarn wondered, looking through the small window above the pedestal that held the phrenological skull. She glanced down at the skull and instinctively stepped away.

Ellen was frowning thoughtfully. "He seems too big to be able to run so fast, so maybe someone's helping him." She glanced at Tarn who had turned from the window to look at her, questioningly. "It's the valuer guy, Honeyman," she explained. "It *must* be him."

"Why do you think it's him?" Tarn asked warily.

"The last letter was *under* the mat, so someone planted it. He planted a letter in Cody's sleeve too." She shrugged. "No one else has been in the house, have they?"

Tarn seemed troubled by this news; she hadn't mentioned her two meetings with Honeyman but it was on her agenda. "No one that I can think of," she muttered. "My brother, perhaps, with that electrical short."

"Don't worry, I know it's not your brother." Ellen offered her a reassuring smile, thinking that Stefan hardly had the brains to carry out this sort of elaborate hoax on instructions, let alone think it up. It was a mystery why her father had entrusted him with that drawer disaster in the kitchen.

Christ … why am I thinking about Stefan's stupid drawers … now of all times…?

In fact, with the letter in her hand, she was unable to shake the image of Stefan's handiwork. It was disrupting her concentration as if it were a pneumatic drill in her head: the letter was pulling at her through the cuticles of her fingertips, forcing her mind to look below the sink.

"Ellen, what's the matter?"

With a shake of her head, she unfolded the letter, finding that the fold was stronger than with the others.

"Oh my God."

"What?" Tarn asked.

Ellen handed her the letter. It read:

Find me

Ellie Sweet

XIII

Worthless, useless

Neville had pulled the dining table into the conservatory to enjoy the romantic setting of the garden, even finding some Christmas lights to drape over the nearby bushes and to trail along the earth of the small rose garden. They were blinking on a random program, the glass panels catching their reflection in garish blues and greens against the October evening gloom.

He was sharing a Chinese take away with his voluptuous estate agent Jenny Bond. She was wearing a low-cut top and a very promising French perfume but his attempts to get her tipsy on wine had come to nothing. She drank only bottled water, saying that her ex-husband had put her off alcohol for life. He uttered a silent *fuck* as he regarded his glass of wine with a smile of agreement, then took a sip and put it aside, pretending not to like it either.

This was the third time he had been alone with her, the second time being when she agreed to show the Trustees around the house. A look had turned into a secret clinch in the far corner of the conservatory, out of sight of the Trustees as they had strolled upstairs. She had since refused to talk about it, acting as if it hadn't happened.

Table talk this evening had revealed that she had known his uncle Lawrence, in fact had popped in most evenings to see whether he needed anything. She had arranged for a cleaner and meals on wheels because it was evident – and there had been a small accusation in her eyes – that none of his family were remotely interested. Often she would cook herself and a fond smile recalled those evenings, when she would insist that he struggle out of his chair and help with the food preparation in some small way. Once he had spent an hour grimly chopping an onion, refusing her assistance, his hand gripping the handle of the knife with ferocious resolve. She would bring a film for later and would explain the story as they watched, though his vacant eyes were never quite on the television screen, but somewhere just beyond it.

"He was an old dear with no family," she said, when questioned on her motives. "I became quite attached to him ... and him to me, I think."

"Hah ha. You were just looking out for the sale. You knew he was going to pop his clogs and you were thinking about your three and a half per cent commission on this place, right? I've seen his note with the will that instructs you: you and no one else." He paused. "So did you sign him up while you were serving him up his swede and mash?"

"Perhaps," she conceded. "Your uncle trusted me and I looked after him. Why shouldn't I get the sale?"

He produced two hands and a grin. "Not questioning it at all. Nothing wrong with being on the hustle."

She wondered how many times he had now said the word *hustle* during the meal. For Neville Parry, she supposed, it was not only his favourite word but some sort of all-knowing, all-redeeming panacea, his spiritual aspirin. His latest hustle, he had explained, concerned a real estate development in Canary Wharf, an ambitious timeshare complex on the Thames.

You can't sell Canary Wharf with a suitcase and a sun tan, she thought, as she listened patiently to his description of the penthouse suites with the marble Jacuzzis, the private harbour berths and the concierge parking. She discovered why the sad demise of his uncle Lawrence was so very opportune: he had already invested most of his savings in the project, the only security the promises of his partners, all of whom were unable to front the operation. When asked why, he explained that they had criminal records, but with a wave of a hand dismissing that as being a long time ago and all a

154

big misunderstanding anyway. She smiled and nodded, picturing him as the sly fox sneaking his way into the chicken pen, only to be confronted with wolves slathering at the jaws.

"Are you still trying to hustle that charity out of their inheritance?" she inquired, wondering if he would detect the irony in her borrowing his word.

"They aren't getting the painting or the game set. No fu... no way," he stumbled, sending another reminder to his brain that he mustn't swear in front of her. When he had first met Jenny and described his uncle and aunt he could see that his colourful but highly appropriate adjectives hadn't gone down at all well. Her sensitivity towards swearing was something rare for a forty-something seasoned professional. "Uncle Lawrence couldn't possibly have meant for the charity to choose such expensive items, right? Between them they've got to be worth around ten grand, possibly more if the painting goes up for auction and I can find an artist to replace the French doodle on the petition." He muttered under his breath as the pork ball he was trying to eat once again fell from his chopsticks; he wanted to use a knife and fork but Jenny was managing hers expertly and he didn't want to look like some peasant from the sticks. "I've collected together some memorabilia tat and holiday snaps, if they're interested in keepsakes. Or, at a pinch, they can take the television and the VCR. They're old anyway."

"What did the barrister say?"

He made a face. "Barrister says the clause is legal; he even sent me a bill for telling me so. *Advice* he called it." He stabbed at his sweet and sour ball as he thought of lawyers and again resisted the urge to swear. Stabbing worked, he realised, and he cheerfully put the impaled pork ball in his mouth. "Anyway, the charity ain't getting my stuff, right? I'll just bluff them out."

"I'm not sure I believe you," she remarked, looking away as he showed the food in his mouth. "I can't believe there's anything in the house that's so valuable it's worth all this trouble. Not to a successful man like you."

He smiled at the compliment but shook his head as he swallowed.

"I think you've got a fantasy about that woman," she declared quietly.

"What?"

"The very petite one, who works for the charity. That's why you want to string this thing out. I saw you looking at her, when they were here that time. She *is* striking, isn't she?"

"Is that why you pulled me in here, when they were going upstairs?" he asked, happily jumping on the event that marked the only time their lips had met, then losing his flow as the telephone rang in the hall. He made a point of concentrating on his chopsticks, but when the ringing continued, he said, "Leave it."

"I think you'd better answer. It's probably your wife."

He glanced at her to check her reaction: she seemed to be taking the insistent intrusion of his wife without too much worry and he hurried out to the hall. The telephone conversation lasted a few minutes, as he explained he had been sleeping and ... and *no*, he couldn't come back just yet and ... yes, it *was* necessary for someone to be in the house...

He retook his seat at the table to see that she was looking out at the Christmas lights in the rose bushes, as if in a dream. He grinned as he glanced at the Cluedo board, set up at the door of the conservatory.

"Fiddling with the game again?" he asked.

Her daydream was broken as her eyes returned to the table. "Hmmm?"

"The Cluedo board."

She shook her head with a bemused smile.

The moving signature was once more in evidence: Miss Scarlett forward one space, Colonel Mustard three spaces, and so on around the board, the leather beaker toppled, the dice showing 1 and 3. The pieces had been reversed one hundred and eighty degrees.

"I know you've been doing it when my back's turned," he said. "You did it the other day when you were showing that couple round, though I only found out after you left. Hah ha. Are you trying to wind me up or something?"

156

"Nev, what are you talking about?"

"The Cluedo set. You're moving the pieces, right?" He was still grinning.

"I've never even touched the thing," she muttered, giving the game board no more than a glance.

"Have it your way," he chuckled, getting up and walking over to the game. He stood the beaker up and picked up Professor Plum, replacing it on its purple square. It was heavy in his hand, heavier than it had ever been. "Is it some sort of kinky sex game you learned from your ex-husband? Turning me on by freaking me out? Don't get me wrong … it's working…"

Perhaps it was the reflection of the lights in the garden but the purple base seemed to be pulsing with energy. He was struck with the image of a leech having gorged on too much blood.

"We didn't play those kind of games," she replied, her voice subdued at the mention of her ex-husband. "He liked other kinds of games, the ones where the bruises never show."

Neville made no comment as he filed this information away with an air of satisfaction. He had suspected from her demeanour that her ex might have been handy with his fists and had pictured her by day showing her professional savvy to her clients, while in the evening being dragged around the house by her hair, admitting through the tears that she was 'a lying bitch and whore'. With a smile, he picked up Miss Scarlett to return the piece to its red base.

She saw that he had frozen in the act of leaning over the board. "What's wrong?" she asked.

He didn't reply.

"Nev, what's wrong?"

"Nothing," he muttered, quickly returning the pieces to their starting squares. As an afterthought, he decided to reposition them so that they all faced away from the dining table.

"Nev, I'm not going to stay, not tonight … not yet."

"Okay," he said, as he turned the last of the pieces. They had no faces; their silver features had been carefully filed down until just the hair remained.

"It doesn't feel right, and I'm not talking about your wife, honestly I'm not. Look, I know you'll call me stupid, but I was thinking about it just now when you were on the phone. I still feel him here … your uncle, I mean. Does that sound daft?"

"No," he replied, stepping back. The mention of his uncle made him look at Professor Plum, pulsing with purple blood and the only character on the board to have escaped the face removal.

Plum has eaten their faces…

"Come on, Nev, let's eat."

Neville didn't respond; he was considering the black envelope in the middle of the board, with the three cards that held the solution to the murder mystery. He was yet to look inside the envelope, but he now felt an overwhelming compulsion to do so.

"Nev, you okay? You're very quiet."

"No, no I'm fine. And it's okay, about you not staying, I mean."

"You're sure you don't mind?"

"No, let's take it slowly."

In fact, the sooner she left the better, for he wanted privacy. It occurred to him that he could discover the murder solution if he went through the pack; by a process of elimination he would identify the three cards that must be in the envelope.

A hazy memory surfaced of a little girl doing the same thing by looking through the pack, pausing now and then to close her eyes and memorise the cards. He had been talking to that crazy antiques dealer at the time and she was a faint background distraction, but there was now something about that scenario that bothered him. Another memory, this one very indistinct, pictured the little girl crying her eyes out in the garden.

As he retook his seat at the table, he tried to rationalise why it was important that he shouldn't just look in the envelope. It was an even more difficult task than trying to explain why he hadn't taken the game board and the painting out of the house, away from the clutches of the Trustees.

Uncle Lawrence put those three cards in the envelope. If I am to respect his memory then I shouldn't disturb them.

He picked up his chopsticks and smiled, everything in order inside his head.

It had started when that old man with the croaking voice had said those words, Neville decided a few days later.

You are the custodian...

Until those words were spoken the house simply had a gnawing sense of unease, an impression of pain and anger with no voice, no direction. But with the words spoken, and repeated...

Yes, it was important that he repeat it...

...the malice found its target. A courtroom that had been mumbling discordantly with a hundred dissenting voices suddenly fell silent, everyone present turning to look at him, in the dock.

And there was something else. Not only was he guilty, the object of all the hatred, but he was *tasked*. A tug in his brain reminded him he had to tend and administer to his charges, the game board and the painting.

He was, after all, the custodian. The position came with a gift of insight, for he was thinking differently; as he patrolled the house as if in a dream he *understood,* as he had never understood before ... he understood his guilt, and their pain...

It was the middle of the night and he was on the landing, studying the glass photographs of his uncle and aunt for the first time. Someone had vandalised them, he realised, finding that they each had a small rough borehole in a bottom corner, made with something like a screwdriver. His finger went to the hole in his uncle's portrait.

What are you doing there?

He had heard his uncle say that so many times in this house and imagined him saying it in the photograph, irritable as he realised he was being photographed. His uncle bore a resemblance to the original Professor Plum, he reflected gloomily, for he knew the faces of the characters of Cluedo as a prisoner knows the faces of his fellow inmates, having been forced to endure many long sessions of the game after his uncle's daughter had become pregnant. His father, Lawrence's older brother, said that they must play with enthusiasm and smiles. All this would secure his inheritance, his mother agreed. She had been very attentive to Aunt Jessica, explaining how wicked and ungrateful her daughter was, how right she was to turn her out.

His mother had less success with the rules of Cluedo, often forgetting to declare a card or hesitating after the dice had been rolled; she was invariably crying on their drive home, for Uncle Lawrence took the gameplay very seriously.

What are you doing there?

Standing on the landing of the house that was now his, thinking how happy his ambitious but poverty-stricken parents would be to see him here as lord and master, he realised that the smell of antiseptic was again drifting up the stairs. The air of sickness made him consider his aunt's glass portrait; after a time, when he had had enough of trying to understand why the photograph was fascinating him, he took it from the wall.

He was downstairs. *The Death of Marat* dominated the living room, for he had banished all the furniture to store rooms, to the kitchen, even to the garden. The room was now a hospital ward, functional and made ready for its patient.

He stopped in front of the painting. As he noticed the squeeze of pain in the eyes of the dying revolutionary the reek of antiseptic became overwhelming, as if a bucket of the stuff had just been tipped over the floor. With a frown he considered the portrait of his aunt in his hand and he held it up, moving it close to the painting. The key to the painting's distress was in the portrait, yet he knew that the worthless piece of glass was useless.

"Worthless, useless," he murmured, his sweating hand having left damp smudges on the smoky glass. Bringing the portrait to the painting had been like bringing cough mixture to a cancer patient.

There were no answers and there was no comfort.

His eyes went to the petition. "Treize trent et un," he read without any attempt at pronunciation, the words emerging as *trays trent ate un*. He smiled, encouraged, having beaten something that he thought was unbeatable; marshalling his courage he said, in English this time, "Thirteen thir…" He stopped, a painful lock turning in his head like a thumbscrew, as was always the case when he tried to repeat the Trustee's telephone number.

With a shake of his head he decided to go back to bed, supposing that it was possible that with a night's rest the painting's health might improve. A large square mirror hung at the foot of the staircase and as he went back the painting came fully into view in the glass. He supposed that his aunt had positioned the picture and mirror in this way, to give her a glimpse of her treasure every night when she struggled up to bed, one hand on her chest, the other on her lower back, for she had spinal as well as viral weakness. At least that is what she believed.

Leave me … just leave me…

He heard her saying this in her glass portrait, her head disappearing into her neck as she tried to escape the camera. It was her standard repost to her husband when he described her as *a damn fool hypochondriac*. She would refuse to kiss anyone in greeting, reluctant even to shake hands, for everything was contagious. In her youth she had caught the rarest of diseases, one that was only transmitted by parrots, though she never owned one, and her encyclopaedia of illnesses and infections, from achondroplasia to yellow fever, was her second bible. Her notes were carefully indexed and cross-referenced, generally with exclamation marks colour coded with different pens, depending on the severity of the symptoms.

Rubbing his eyes in weariness Neville paused on the first stair, thinking that what he had just seen must be the product of lack of sleep. He slowly stepped backwards until Marat's reflection veered once more into view.

The Jacobin's life was still draining away in his iron tub, his eyes closed.

His eyes were closed.

Of *course* they were closed...

XIV

Plum, Conservatory, Dagger

The glass front of Welsh Homes Estate Agents, Saundersfoot branch, reflected the sunshine of a cold but low morning sun. The occupants of the office uttered a groan at this freak intrusion, repositioning their computer screens as they reached squinting for their cappuccinos.

"I'm sorry that's impossible at the moment," Jenny said, smiling and leaning back in her seat. "No, it hasn't sold. Yes, it is near the harbour."

Seymour, her young colleague who sat opposite, tended to glance up at her when she answered the phone, feigning polite curiosity, but really to get another glimpse of her cleavage. She always leaned back and smiled when she answered the telephone, her mind becoming happy and relaxed, a good sales tip that she had never forgotten. "Parry house again," she whispered to him, putting her hand over the receiver. He shrugged and pretended to return to his work. "Yes, it is still up for sale," she confirmed to the caller. "The owner just wants to make some refurbishments. Can I take your details and ring you as soon as it's ready for viewing? Yes, that's right … no, I can assure you that it hasn't been taken off the market…"

The call ended, Seymour studied his biro as he turned it around in his fingers. His sallow face settled naturally into its sullen frown.

"What's up with this Parry guy? Why can't we view?"

"Refurbishments," she answered, copying her scribbled notes into her diary. "He said he wanted to get some decorating done."

"That's bollocks. He's negotiating a deal with another agent, trying to get a better percentage."

"You've seen that awful Anaglypta. I think a lick of paint is a very good idea."

"He's playing us for idiots, Jen. He probably doesn't like it that you negotiated a full three and a half per cent with his uncle. Mark my words: he's going to sell it with someone else on a cash deal, telling us he found the purchaser himself."

"He wouldn't do that, Seymour."

"Maybe we should ring our solicitors. There's the will, remember. It gives you complete rights."

"Leave him alone. As you said, *I've* got the rights over the sale, not Welsh Homes, and I say it's okay to let him do a bit of decorating."

"Why are you so keen to protect him?"

His smile said that the question was rhetorical. She threw an exasperated glance in his direction as she got up and walked to the glass front of the office. "He just doesn't want any visitors at the moment, that's all," she murmured. She was thoughtful as she looked out of the office front. "Sometimes people need a little bit of peace and quiet. His uncle's just died, remember."

"Still sounds like bollocks to me."

She nodded slowly as she noticed the vehicle that resembled a white hearse gliding slowly down the road and coming to a stop on the opposite side of the street. From the driver's seat, an old man considered his gloved hands on the steering wheel and then turned to look at her with an inquiring expression.

The occasional car was speeding along the harbour road in the early hours, the faint distant roar receiving Neville's full attention as he sat on the small bed in his uncle and aunt's drab guest room. He was unable to sleep, for whenever he dozed he felt the tug of

Sorrel's tiny fist in his brain.

It was an appropriate reminder of his duties. *They* could break into the house to steal what they considered to be their property; break in at any time, so he had to stay alert.

He was the *custodian*.

He was out of bed, rubbing the sleep out of his eyes, so tired he felt he was moving in a dream. His bedroom, this landing, the living room and conservatory were the only places where he existed now. There was nothing else, no world outside; if he walked through the front door, he would drop into a bottomless fog.

Now he was on the landing, under the glass portraits of his uncle and aunt. This was the staging area, before he went downstairs. It was necessary to pause here, to let his charges know he was coming.

"Worthless, useless," he muttered, now out of habit as he glanced at the photographs. As he turned to observe the house, he felt his uncle's eyes on him.

What are you doing there?

He didn't even register the walk down the stairs. He was in the living room, the lights on, his breath coming in shallow heaves. The smell, which had began as bath salts, had mutated into lavender and was now the reek of antiseptic, showcasing *the Death of Marat* in the bare setting of the emptied room.

Neville had been told that, in life, Marat had a disfiguring skin condition, the reason why he received petitioners in the bath, and that the painting was an idealisation. He appeared now as the eighteenth-century painter David might really have seen him, his face covered in weeping sores, his mouth a weak snarl, no longer the martyred sigh of resignation. The eyes were closed, but in gruesome agony.

The sores had appeared two nights ago when his last visitor to the house, a concerned Jenny Bond, had been turned away at the door with excuses, even though she said she was missing him. None of that seemed important now; it was as if he had entered a new reality with different rules and objectives, where money and sex were unimportant, where all that mattered were his duties as custodian.

165

"I am the custodian and must look after you," he murmured as he approached the painting, wishing he had the power to heal the dying man in the bath. His stomach turned as he saw that the sores were redder than the night before, some open and bleeding, others filled with yellow pus.

Leave me … just leave me…

He heard his Aunt Jessica, just as he imagined her speaking in her glass portrait. He supposed that Marat's disfigurement and martyrdom fitted with her idea of her afflictions; that she would have approved of the fact that the room was transforming into a hospital for one patient. Closer to the picture again, the reek of antiseptic was almost unbearable but he was fascinated with the eyes of the dying man. Marat liked to play games in the mirror by the staircase: when he caught the reflection in that mirror the eyes would spring open. He had the notion that Marat was waiting for him to turn away, that he hadn't realised he could be observed.

"Open them now," he murmured fatalistically, so tired that he wanted it to be over. He knew it was a matter of time, just a matter of days, hours or minutes, before Marat didn't care anymore whether he was observed, when his eyes would suddenly open wide in frustration and pain.

Then Marat would step dripping out of the bath, out of the painting, onto the floor and would tramp with slow, sodden footsteps up the stairs to the guest room, where he was sleeping.

"Open them."

The eyes remained tightly shut, though an annoyed flutter of the eyeballs made the membrane of the eyelids tremble briefly as the picture replied with a gust of antiseptic. Choking, he staggered out of the living room, catching a glimpse of Marat's face in the mirror; the eyes were still closed, yet as he turned away he felt them on the back of his neck as a thin, icy trickle of air. The painting was aware of his tricks now, no longer fooled by the reflection.

"Uncle Lawrence?" he asked cautiously, as he stepped into the conservatory.

It had been a dawning realisation that if *the Death of Marat* represented something fundamental to his aunt's character, the Cluedo set represented something in his uncle. It wasn't just that they had loved these objects in life. It was more than that. In the same way his hypochondriac aunt now lived so comfortably in a death bath, his uncle, who had been calculating and strict, was in his own psyche in a game with set rules, where guilt was hidden. Neville saw that the pieces had moved again, the moving signature in a one and three combination, the dice rolled to show 1 and 3, the leather beaker toppled.

He picked up each piece slowly and carefully, returning them to their starting squares with a resigned but kindly sigh, as if he were rearranging the blankets of a patient. Plum was again the heaviest, its base pulsing with purple energy, but this morning the base was made of skin, tight with liquid. The tiniest of silver tongues was poking out of the corner of the faint line of Plum's mouth, as if he had eaten his bodyweight.

The rest of the pieces had no heads. He suspiciously eyed the black leather envelope that held the three murder cards; it seemed to be the knot of pain causing all the game's muscles to go into spasm.

"Plum, conservatory, dagger," he said, having deduced its contents from the pack. With his uncle's portrait looking on from the landing, with the game board housed in the conservatory, all that was needed was the weapon.

"The dagger."

The board had no smell, no air of illness: with the game, the process of deterioration did not translate into sickness, but into treachery. His eyes settled on the tiny silver dagger; the 1940s rulebook placed the weapon in the dining room and his uncle had always insisted such details be observed, but tonight it waited in the conservatory.

He picked up the dagger and was surprised to find that it had no weight, that it made no protest at being removed from the board. He turned the miniature piece between his fingers, trying to keep hold of it, for it was so light and small it was difficult to grip. Then he saw that his hand was red. Flexing his fingers, blood oozed from the sliver cuts of a score of tiny lacerations. The dagger was as sharp as a razor, he realised with a grunt of surprise, slicing and biting through his skin like a piranha. He tried to reposition it and managed to find some purchase as he nestled it in his palm, where it found a large healthy vein to slice open.

With a snarl of pain he dropped it and it landed back on the conservatory square, the leather soaking up the blood like a sponge. For the first time he heard the voice of the game board: a greedy moan as the blood was sucked down.

"Oh, fuck," he muttered.

The shedding of his blood finally brought home the horror of recent nights, as Neville began to perceive the nightmare he was living through, and felt powerless to escape. Everything was happening naturally, as it should happen.

Marat was meant to be suffering.

Plum was meant to be cunning and cruel.

They were his aunt and uncle, their failings reaching the worst possible extremes.

And he couldn't leave the house; he couldn't leave because he was the custodian.

With a frightened, tearful whimper, he wrapped a handkerchief around the fingers of his right hand, the cotton immediately staining red. It was as if the tiny weapon had known exactly where to cut; which veins and blood capillaries to sever for the maximum effect.

Every night it gets worse, he thought. Where would he be tomorrow, or the night after that?

Uncle Lawrence is going to kill me, he realised.

He is going to kill me in the conservatory, with the dagger.

He reached for the murder envelope and let the three cards slide out. His face was deadpan as he turned them over, only a weary note of resignation and fear flashing in his eyes as he viewed each one in turn.

The cards showed the murderer, the weapon and the room.

The murderer was Professor Plum, the name appearing in white letters on all four sides of the black card, in keeping with the 1940s design. But Plum was his uncle, as he appeared in his glass photograph.

What are you doing there?

"I'm just looking, that's all," he muttered, his voice that of the shy youth he used to be.

What are you doing there, boy? Someone needs a sharp lesson in concentration.

The next card was the dagger, but it had a wooden handle and a long serrated blade. The picture was in black and white apart from the red tint of the gore spreading from the razor-sharp edges.

He let the two cards fall from his hand and they fluttered down onto the board.

There was another moan from the board, this time of delight.

The third card contained a glimpse of one of the glass panels of his uncle's conservatory; the setting was hazy and obscured, for in the foreground Neville was gagged and naked, trussed up on the floor, with long ragged wounds down his side. The wooden handle of the knife was sticking out of his back.

The telephone number was just a dead tone. Neville dialled it a dozen times before he gave up.

"But they made me repeat it," he muttered as he wandered frantically around the house, trying to think of a way to contact the Trustees. "They made me repeat it!"

He paused and considered the front door, longing to have the strength to open it and leave. Time passed and he was still watching it when the doorbell rang. Finding life in his feet and with joy on his face he raced towards the door and pulled it open, then staggered back as he saw the Trustees, who were waiting motionlessly.

"Are we here at your invitation, Mr Parry?" Wells inquired, as he looked up. "Or do you wish us to leave?"

Neville shook his head quickly. "No … no, you can come in."

Wells pulled petulantly at the joint of his index finger. "Are you sure we're welcome?"

"Please, please come in," Neville repeated, "I'm begging you."

The Trustees stepped in and walked past him. As Neville watched them go with relief, he remembered the words of the antiques dealer.

At the end you'll be begging for them to be taken...

It took several minutes for Wells and Sorrel to examine the game board and then *the Death of Marat,* by which time he was wondering whether he had made a mistake. The painting had returned to normal, the smell had vanished; his feelings of protectiveness and covetousness returned as he wondered if he had just had a bad dream. Once again he was unwilling to let them go.

"Don't doubt your decision, Mr Parry," Wells said. "Don't be fooled because they're at peace when *we* are here. They know we bring them succour."

Sorrel turned to Neville, her eyes a fist in his brain. The fist, he now knew, was her answer to his sexual fantasy of her, the means with which he had let her in: more intimate, more penetrating than he could have ever imagined in his wildest, most lustful dream. He stepped back, letting them take the painting from the wall.

"I know you've planned it all," he said. The accusation was no more than a sulky protest.

"We are merely Trustees," Wells remarked, glancing at Sorrel to ensure that the picture was level and then following her feet as they both stepped back slowly towards the front door. Their vehicle had been reversed to the door with the hatchback open, revealing many layers of cushioning black felt. Propped up near the front were two collodian portraits in brilliant colour.

"You hypnotised me, right?" Neville asked. "Is that how you did it?"

"If that comforts you." Wells paused, and with an eye signal to his colleague the painting was lifted gently through the open door and into the long cabin of the vehicle. The short distance took only a fraction of a second to cross but there was the faintest of squeals as the chasm was jumped.

"What does that mean?" Neville asked as he gloomily observed them walk back through the house and into the conservatory. Wells was studying the game board, scratching his chin. Sorrel touched his arm and made several gestures with her fingers; Wells nodded thoughtfully.

"I said what does that mean?" Neville asked in a louder voice.

"Whatever you want it to mean," Wells answered wearily. "When you return to that dismal existence you call your home, family and career and need to find a way to rationalise what you have seen, then call it hypnotism. Though I suspect you will simply forget it all, in time. You have little substance, I think."

"Fuck you," Neville managed, but with no challenge in his eyes.

"You have the skull and the bust in fair trade. We've left them under your very nose, for you and you alone. There can be no complaint."

"I couldn't give a monkey's about the skull and the stupid fucking..."

"Good, dispose of them then," Wells said in a flat voice. "You are the custodian and can do with them as you wish."

Sorrel had the pieces and cards balanced in her hands and Wells lifted the top of the board and slid it half way off. The inside of the board had cut out shapes to store the game pieces, and Sorrel rapidly proceeded to fill them. The playing pieces had their faces back, the knife was a soft blunt accessory, the murder envelope empty.

"Quickly," Wells whispered and she increased her pace. Before long she nodded, then reached down to the board lid. With a glance towards each other they slid the heavy lid carefully back into place.

"There now, there now," she purred, "don't be afraid." Her face was a mask of concentration as she turned towards the front door and effortlessly lifted her end of the heavy base, stepping in time with Wells as they walked through the living room. Mustering her strength for the final heave she again whispered, "There now, don't be afraid."

The chasm was jumped once more and the hatchback door slammed shut. They turned to Neville in a grim farewell.

"Do I have to sign anything?" Neville asked, eyeing them with hatred.

Wells shook his head. "Enjoy your inheritance, Mr Parry."

"Yeah and fuck you." Neville caught Sorrel's eye and hesitated; she was wearing a slinky black dress that showed off her legs and the elegant curves of her body. "You did hypnotise me, didn't you?" he asked uncomfortably, realising that one day he might wish he had asked more questions, no matter how badly he wanted them to leave. "That's why I've seen all these things, isn't it? Why I couldn't sleep…"

"When it's your time," she said slowly, "remember your dear uncle and aunty. Remember their torment, how they despised you for holding them here for profit. They would have killed you before long, never doubt it." Her eyes widened as a sigh of pleasure escaped. "I've just glimpsed your end, Neville Parry, and I see that you're alone and in despair. Illness racks you and failure torments you. You'll remember your uncle and aunt then, I think. They'll find you and make sure that you remember them."

"Go, just go," he muttered. When the door was closed he felt that he was finally free of them, apart from a fleeting moment when he heard the vehicle pull off the drive and Sorrel's fist let go of his brain. Before it vanished from his mind, it managed one final jolt of warning.

The tug of the fist said:

When it's your time, you will remember…

The Trustees were silent as they travelled through the night with their prize – the Parry vessels – in the boot, the black road in front of them outlined by cats' eyes. As they neared the Tenby turn off, Sorrel gasped and a rush of blood went to her face.

"What?" Wells murmured.

"Sorensen," she whispered.

Wells nodded, silent as he slowly negotiated a difficult turn, stepping down a gear before accelerating off down the country lane that would take them to their destination.

"Has he been found?" he asked.

Several minutes passed before Sorrel shook her head, her tight smile returning.

"No," she said, "but it's close."

XV

Find me

As Ellen returned home and shut the door behind her, her mobile started to ring from inside her bag. The summons made her groan in exhaustion; she just needed to slump onto the sofa and massage her feet. She had spent the morning looking in every likely shop in Tenby in the hope of finding the typewriter, for she thought that possibly whoever had been sending the letters had now passed it in to a second-hand shop, the joke over.

"Perhaps that's what *find me* means," she had reasoned, yet there was no Sholes & Glidden typewriter in any shop she had visited, no prank waiting to be uncovered. Then again, perhaps *find me* was referring to the letters themselves which, except for the letter with the 1331p stamp and the words *Find me, Ellie Sweet*, had disappeared.

She had looked everywhere but the letters were gone. When she told her uncle he hadn't commented. He hadn't even sounded surprised.

She walked into the day room and came to a sudden stop. Honeyman, seated on the sofa with his back to her, had turned round and slowly risen to his feet. She considered him suspiciously as she reached into her bag for her mobile; the caller was her uncle Martin ringing for his daily chat and she switched it off, deciding that the call could wait.

"I have to speak to you," Honeyman said.

She looked inquiringly at Tarn, standing nervously behind the armchair.

"He just wants a minute," Tarn said. "I think you should listen to him."

"Tarn, he's a conman." She turned to Honeyman. "What is it today? Double-glazing or phoney probate inventories?"

"I had to get into the house somehow. Surely you can see that I couldn't just tell you who I was?"

"And who *are* you, exactly? Your church seems to have a good idea."

He nodded with a grunt of resignation.

"Yes, I've spoken to them," she said, her eyes ablaze.

"I can see you're not ready to listen to me. You have my number when you are…"

"Are you sending me these letters?" she snapped.

He shook his head. "You know who's sending you the letters," he answered quietly. "You *know*…"

She reached into her bag. "Okay, if you're not out of here in two seconds flat I'm ringing the police." For some reason she wasn't scared of him, even though it occurred to her that he was a large, strong man who could easily overpower both of them in this room, the outside world none the wiser. She was simply angry, because she had liked him and trusted him. She felt betrayed.

"I'm going to tell you two things before I go," he said. "You can call the SAS as well as the police if you want, but I'm going to tell you anyway."

She waited, her thumb poised over her mobile.

"First," he began, "I told you last time that the collodians would be switched when the Trustees visited. If they haven't been switched then it means your father has bought you time. That time is precious. *Precious*. Believe me, when the typewriter is found they will come again and then … and then your parents are lost." His large hands reached out imploringly. "You must protect the collodians."

"Next?" she said, her mind reeling. Tarn had stepped back to the window and was staring at him with fear and dismay. He had seemed so polite; she hadn't imagined what would come out of his mouth.

He grunted his dissatisfaction. "I was hoping that we'd have more time to speak ... that it wouldn't be like this..."

"Next?" Ellen repeated in a firm voice.

He nodded. "Look at the serial number of your Jumeau. You'll recognise the number." With his head bowed he walked quickly out of the house, closing the door quietly behind him.

"Why did you let him in?" Ellen muttered as she went to the window and watched him go down the steps. "Do you know him?"

"I saw him at ... I just met him by accident. He knows stuff about your dad, Ellen. He said he's seen his condition before."

She huffed as she turned away from the window. "Pretending to be a doctor now, is he? Perhaps he should have some more cards printed."

"You don't believe him?"

"Why should I? Because he used to be a minister?"

"I'm as shocked as you are," Tarn admitted, "but I saw a fish in his wallet. The sign that he's a fisher of men ... a witness to the Faith..."

Ellen sighed, finding her housekeeper's naivety endearing. "I bet he made sure that you had a good look at it too, didn't he?" She slumped on the sofa and threw off her shoes. "You know that his church in Flint chucked him out, don't you? That he was expelled?"

"Expelled? What do you mean?"

"The church warden wasn't prepared to elaborate, but it sounds like he's been excommunicated, or whatever it is Baptists do."

Tarn was considering this with a slow, disbelieving shake of her head. "What was that he said about your parents' portraits being switched?"

Ellen gripped the sole of her foot with a mixture of pain and ecstasy. "Oh, that's more of his nonsense. When he did his rounds of the house he said that when the Trustees came that they'd swap the collodians, that they'd take away the good portraits and just leave worthless pieces of glass." She shook her head. "Well, they barely even looked at them … so he doesn't know what he's talking about. Either that or he has his eye on the pictures himself."

Tarn nodded thoughtfully. "I don't understand this thing about swapping them with cheap glass. Aren't they glass already?"

"No. The Trustees made Dad a present of the photographs. They're special."

"Special? How?"

Ellen considered her for a few moments and came to a decision. "Come on, I'll show you." She got up, flexing her bare feet for a few moments with a grimace, then went down to the kitchen, Tarn following behind. Taking a bread knife from the counter she picked up her father's collodian. "Watch," she said, and carefully ran the point of the blade down the smoky surround of the glass. It didn't scratch. She repeated the action, harder, with the same result.

"That's incredible," Tarn muttered.

With a deep breath, Ellen raised the photograph level with her neck and let it drop onto the stone floor. It landed with a heavy clatter.

Both girls turned to Stefan's cabinet as the photograph landed, the lower drawers convulsing as if a mini earth tremor had shot through the wood when the collodian landed.

"What was that?" Ellen muttered, startled by the faint and distant *whump*. "I think one of your brother's rivets just popped."

Tarn glanced at the collodian then looked at the drawers, suspiciously. "What was the second thing he said?" she asked in a distracted voice. "Something about the serial number on your doll?"

"All Jumeaux have serial numbers."

Tarn nodded, carefully picking up the photograph from the floor and placing it back on the counter. With a cloth she gave it a quick wipe, although the fall hadn't affected it in the slightest. "It's like he's here," she murmured, as she considered Nigel Sorensen, a blaze of colour in the glass.

"I know." Ellen tapped her head as she remembered something. "Shit, Uncle Martin. I'd better ring him back." She looked at the ceiling, remembering that her mobile was upstairs.

In the day room, Ellen took her call. Downstairs in the kitchen, Tarn was resting on her broom, having just started sweeping the floor. She was looking at the drawers her brother had constructed in the last few days of Mr Sorensen's life, with a puzzled and thoughtful expression. She snapped out of her daze when she heard Ellen's footsteps coming down the stairs.

"Everything alright?" Tarn asked.

"Oh, my uncle's getting all paranoid again. He's saying that I should get Hugh down here as soon as possible. Really overreacting, in fact. He says it's not safe me being in the house by myself."

"Hugh?"

Ellen shrugged. "Boyfriend," she said, the word more of an admission than an answer. "I had to agree just to shut him up."

Tarn smiled. "Nice to have a boyfriend," she said.

Ellen shrugged once more.

Tarn smoothed back her hair then took a firm hold of her broom again. "Why does your uncle keep ringing you? Why doesn't he just come round?"

"Oh, he's travelling around the country on some courses. He's semi-retired but he's been doing this chiropractic teacher training for the last few years. It sends him all over the place."

Tarn paused, resting her weight on the broom. "He's here," she said.

"What do you mean?"

"Your uncle's here, Ellen, in Tenby. Stef said he saw him yesterday on The Esplanade."

"I think Stefan was mistaken," Ellen remarked with a smile.

Tarn gave her a quizzical look. "I don't think so," she murmured.

Mr Sorensen, he had said, *but with glasses…*

"No offence, Tarn, but he's mistaken. Your brother probably

just saw someone who looked like my uncle Martin."

It was a careless statement, planting a chill in the air as they considered who could be mistaken for Nigel Sorensen's identical twin.

"I'm sure you're right," Tarn said, pretending to make nothing of it. Picking up the broom again, she went back to sweeping the floor.

They had made a quick sweep of the Saundersfoot house, which seemed empty now even though the sales particulars said it was being sold fully furnished.

Honeyman had arranged to be shown around the Parry's house by posing as an interested purchaser and his tour had been brief, just long enough to note that *the Death of Marat* and the game board were gone. The phrenological skull and bust were also gone; he suspected they were in one of the black bin bags at the back of the house.

For some reason that he couldn't explain, for he was sure they were simply the Trustees' motifs, he always experienced a pang of regret when he heard that the heads had been disposed of.

"You'll forgive me but I was hoping to be shown round by Jenny Bond," he said to the estate agent as they walked out of the house onto the paved drive. "She was recommended to me," he clarified. "That's why I asked for her especially."

The estate agent was a sullen young man who had introduced himself as Seymour; he was in a rush to go on to another viewing. "Yeah, she doesn't deal with this property any more."

"Why not?"

Seymour glanced at his watch. "Company policy. The owner took a bit of a shine to her, so we decided to keep her away from the house in case he was hanging around."

"Where is the owner?"

"Gone back to Bristol, I think."

Back to his wife and failing retail estate deal, Seymour thought, recalling Jenny's words after Neville's last telephone call, when she had insisted that someone else look after the Parry house. He offered his hand. "The price of this place is rock bottom because the owner is looking for a really quick sale. If you're interested, you don't want to hang around."

"Thank you, I'll be in touch," Honeyman murmured. He didn't notice the stab of pain in the young man's eyes as he shook his hand, nor did he feel them on his back as he walked to his Land Rover, deep in thought.

It was pointless making contact with the nephew, he reflected, who by now would have constructed his mental barriers, explaining away everything that had happened, citing lack of sleep and maybe some subtle hypnosis. Perhaps he had even forgotten everything thanks to his brain's healing process: some of the custodians did, for the level of healing depended on the level of faith. The less faith, the easier the recovery.

As Honeyman pictured Neville Parry he shook his head, certain he would be of no help. He was running out of leads; Marion Coates would die soon and when the last of them was dead, it would end.

"It will end," he muttered, as he sat in his Land Rover. He watched the estate agent drive away then threw a farewell glance at the Parry house. At moments like this he wished more than ever that he could pray, that he could call upon the mercy of God and the protection of Jesus, but that was lost to him. Instead, he closed his eyes to picture Lawrence and Jessica Parry, then sighed and returned to his dashboard.

Once again, he heard the shrill laughter of Sorrel Page. He had never heard her laugh, having only watched her from a distance apart from one brief meeting, but he believed he knew how her laugh would sound; researching people created an imagined intimacy.

There had been many Trustees of The Divine Sentiment, his research had revealed. They always worked in pairs, a man and woman of different ages, although sometimes it was the woman who was older. It was a mystery how they were recruited, for there was no group interest, no organisation or society to which they all belonged, no common factor from their childhood that he had been able to identify. There was not a criminal conviction among them. Many of them had stable family ties: Sorrel Page was a mother of two, presiding over Eisteddfods and charity country fetes, proud of her elderberry jam and married to a respected ophthalmic surgeon. Wells was a retired professor of Law, a lifelong bachelor living on his pension but who had been ill in recent years, going through chemotherapy after a throat operation.

It had been an easy matter to collect the names of the previous Trustees, they were recorded in the charity's public records, but they had smoothly returned to their former vocations after their tenure was up. He followed the progress of a few but their activities led him nowhere. It was as if ordinary law-abiding people were simply plucked from their lives and transformed for the brief period of their service, which averaged at around a year. The Divine Sentiment called on its members as a form of national service and never drew attention to itself through a dominant personality. It operated within its constitution, a volunteer organisation with no centre of operations. Returns were filed and accounts drawn up to continue the charitable status. The lawyers were in Switzerland and through these lawyers, the charity jealously preserved the mark of royal patronage.

As a brief but timely historical boon, the charity had received funding from Edward VII when he had first come to the throne. The charity's contact with the playboy monarch had terminated abruptly shortly afterwards, the king requiring all records of the society in his diaries or letters to be destroyed, although he didn't withdraw the licence to use the royal crest on their stationery. The king was the most prominent of the many wealthy people who had been duped by The Divine Sentiment, no doubt under the promise of communing with departed loved ones. They all withdrew their support when Scotland Yard briefly took an interest, but none of them made their experiences public.

Honeyman believed there were many eminent Victorians held in the temple. In the twentieth century The Divine Sentiment became a more low-key operation, preferring to search out the weak and lonely, having gorged itself with the proud and arrogant.

As Pembroke came into view he was mentally turning the pages of his lever-arch files; passing the castle, he was still trying to find that innocuous piece of information in his notes that would give him that all important clue. It was frustrating. No matter how hard he worked, no matter how much he uncovered, none of it seemed to make any difference: he was still unable to confront the Trustees.

The laughter of Sorrel Page again echoed in his imagination as he stepped out of his Land Rover, wondering what possible help Marion Coates could be to him now. He was hoping for something unexpected, perhaps an accident, most probably a miracle, that would set a light at the end of the dark tunnel.

There was no answer from the terraced house. He crouched down and opened the post flap, then with his notebook pushed open the second post flap on the inside of the door. He had a letterbox line of sight into the hall.

"Marion, answer the door," he called.

"Go away," she murmured. She was sitting on a hard chair in the hallway, looking vacantly at the longcase grandfather clock. On the wall, a little way to the right, he could just make out the collodian of her husband, Henry.

"Let me in, Marion," he persisted, "it's not too late for me to help you."

She didn't turn round. "You're lying again," she muttered. "I know that your church has disowned you. At least … at least the others didn't lie to me."

"But they deceive you none the less. Think of everything that you've been told … everything that you've been promised. Is there one single word of comfort there?" He groaned, knowing it was useless. "Is there a single word of comfort, Marion?"

"At least I'm with Henry." She glanced at the letterbox accusingly. "You shouldn't have lied to me. How could I trust you after you lied to me?"

"I'm sorry, but I had to get into the house, somehow … and my church, well … I know there's nothing I can say that will

182

satisfy you…"

"Leave me alone, I'm tired." She got up from her chair and shuffled slowly into the front room. Before long, he heard the loud, upbeat chatter of a television game show.

"They'll come back next with a skull," he called. "It will be their last visit, your last chance to escape them. I'll be waiting outside when they call. Come to the window and I'll know you want me to help."

He straightened up, groaning at the stiffness in his back, not even sure she had heard him over the television. Glancing across the road, he sighed in resignation as he saw himself slumped in his vehicle for any number of days and nights, waiting for the Trustees to return.

It would be their final visit to a living subject, he realised.

This time I must confront them.

He swallowed, tasting his fear.

I have no choice but to confront them.

The blows of the sledgehammer were shattering the wood with clean swings and Ellen watched with muted surprise as Stefan methodically destroyed the kitchen drawers he had so lovingly constructed. He was a lot stronger than his thin, sinewy frame suggested.

"Tarn, I've got no problem with smashing up these drawers," she said in a voice loud enough to be heard over the thump of lead and crack of wood, "but what's this got to do with my father?"

Tarn jumped slightly as the bottom drawer cracked. "*Find* me," she said. "That's what the letter said."

A glimmer of understanding appeared on Ellen's face as she turned to watch Stefan finish his work. He had put aside the sledgehammer and was pulling out the wrecked structure of the cabinet. With the bottom panel of wood forced up from the securing nails, a makeshift hole in the ground was revealed. He reached into the hole and carefully picked up a small metal machine.

Her jaw dropped as Stefan, at last allowing himself a small sigh of exertion, placed the machine on the stone floor.

"Dad's Sholes & Glidden," she whispered. "In the ground? I don't understand."

"He buried it," Tarn explained. "Your father asked Stefan to bury it, then hide the hole with the drawers."

Ellen nodded, attempting to register this information. "Then there must be another typewriter…"

"I don't know. Is there?" Tarn asked.

The machine was more than just an antique; it was a dark grey contraption that always made Ellen think of the skeleton of a typewriter. The refurbished keys were all in place, on the ends of thin metal fingers with two angled joints, but there was very little else to it other than its small paper roller and the flimsiest of bases. In spite of its time in the ground, it seemed surprisingly clean. It was gleaming with oil.

"Probably not," Ellen conceded. She shrugged, refusing now to let her imagination wander. "The letters were obviously written before it was buried."

Stefan had collected several reams of the watermarked paper from the hole; there was no Cellophane wrapping but the paper also appeared to have survived its internment with extraordinary resilience. He shook the paper slightly and all the earth fell away.

"Mr Sorensen made me promise," he murmured, avoiding eye contact with Ellen.

"It's okay, Stefan, I understand."

"Made me swear," he added miserably. "But he didn't like it. Didn't like being underground. That's why he wrote to us."

Ellen picked up the typewriter and placed it on the kitchen table, stacking the paper neatly nearby. She cast a cautionary glance at Tarn then smiled at her brother. "Stefan, whoever's sending the letters typed them *before* my father asked you to bury the typewriter." She stepped away from the table and considered the machine. "Why did Dad ask you to bury it?" The question was asked in a casual manner, as if the answer was wholly unimportant; she was aware that Stefan was shaking, his hands clutching at the handle of the sledgehammer. She didn't want to say anything that might alarm him.

"So *they* wouldn't get it," he replied, his eyes to the floor.

"That's all your father said," Tarn explained. She pressed back her hair; it had been difficult wringing the truth out of her brother last night, for they had the same approach to vows. "Your father didn't say who *they* were."

"Dad must have meant the Trustees," Ellen frowned, trying to make the fact of the buried typewriter fit with some logical theory. "He knew the Trustees would want the typewriter, so he hid it."

Tarn was unconvinced. "Why not just change his will?"

"Perhaps he'd signed a contract or something." Ellen shook her head. "He wrote the letters as a clue before he buried it, then arranged for them to be posted ... planted..."

"By whom?"

"Oh I don't know," she replied, a little irritably. "Mr Hobbs?"

"I suppose," Tarn said, seeing that Ellen wasn't inclined to test her theory too closely.

"That's why the stamps give the Trustees' number ... their telephone number, I mean. It's a clue."

"Yes, I see that." Tarn was careful not to say the number *thirteen thirty-one*: Ellen had shared all her knowledge with her now and she knew that she didn't like even to hear the number, let alone say it.

"But maybe the Trustees knew he was hiding it," Ellen continued, her eyes narrowing. "They *knew*. Perhaps that's why they didn't take anything last time they were here." She paused. "Why they said they'd come back when it was found."

She probably only needed a few seconds of silence to reflect; to reach the conclusion that this was why the Trustees didn't want the collodians on their last visit. Given a few seconds more, she might have even reached the next logical plateau, that this meant Honeyman wasn't lying or mistaken about the intention to switch the collodians.

Those seconds weren't granted to her.

Just as she finished speaking, the doorbell rang.

XVI

Delightful

Tarn and Stefan were sitting at the table, considering the typewriter, when Ellen stepped down into the kitchen with a warning flash of her eyes. The Trustees were close behind.

"Um, this is Tarn and Stefan Hughes, my housekeeper and handyman," she said by way of introduction as she walked to the counter.

The Trustees moved a few paces into the kitchen. Wells was wearing a roomy beige raincoat with large pockets and carelessly stepping on the broken wood, his shoes noisily cracking the fragments of the drawers. Sorrel was in her tweed skirt suit with a utilitarian matching handbag; her eyes went to the broken wood then flicked suddenly to Stefan.

"Hello Stefan Hughes," she said.

"Hello," Stefan grunted, recoiling as her voice created his name.

"Are you *really* a handyman, Stefan Hughes?" she asked, her eyes widening.

Stefan stood up abruptly, his chair falling to the floor. He turned and stumbled past the antique telephone into the pantry; Tarn followed without hesitation.

Ellen watched them go with disbelief. "I'm sorry about that," she whispered, after a time. "I don't know what's wrong … he's a little, you know…"

"Retarded?" Wells asked, too loudly.

"No, I wouldn't say that…" she replied, as quietly as she was able.

"Just a bit slow?" he suggested in a loud croak.

She shook her head as she glanced at the pantry. "Excuse me a minute," she said and hurried across the kitchen. In the old pantry, now just a small room with empty shelves, she found Stefan sat on the floor, shivering.

"Stay in here until they've gone," Tarn said, her hand on his elbow.

Ellen nodded. "Yeah, there's nothing for them to see in here and they've already examined the telephone."

Stefan looked at his sister imploringly. She said, "We won't let them come in here, Stef. I promise. I *promise*."

Ellen was anxious to return to the kitchen. "Actually Stefan, I've been thinking we need another set of shelves in here. Now that we've had to break the drawers, I mean. While we're showing the people round the house, could you measure up in here? Give me sort of an estimate perhaps?"

Stefan looked at her blankly for a few moments. "Shelves?" he muttered.

"That's what I need," she repeated.

He nodded and found a smile. She smiled back and then looked at Tarn imploringly.

"When you've finished I'll make you some tea," Tarn said to her brother, as she got up.

"In my workman's mug?" he asked.

"Absolutely."

The Trustees were standing around at the table looking at the typewriter, seemingly impervious to the interruption.

"Tried to hide it, did he?" Wells asked, referring to the typewriter.

"Well it was hidden, yeah," Ellen answered cautiously. "Don't know why."

"How confused he must have been to think he could hide it," Wells remarked. "That he could *bury* it. Bury it! The man's wits must have been failing."

Ellen's eyes narrowed, disliking the criticism of her father. "Yeah, whatever. But you're still in his house, so show a bit of respect. Okay?"

Wells turned to her. "Respect?" he asked.

"In his house, yeah. If he tried to bury the typewriter, well that's his business."

"Our business too, according to a clause in the last will and testament, Miss Sorensen."

Ellen shrugged, inwardly on the verge of tears but outwardly defiant; she supposed she had something of her father in her after all.

It was Sorrel who spoke next, as her tiny hand passed over the pile of letters as if giving a blessing. "And you thought that he'd given everything away." She glanced briefly at Tarn, a twitch around her eyes. "Didn't you say it was your housekeeper who gave everything away?"

"On Dad's instructions," Ellen clarified.

"On your father's instructions?"

"That's right."

Sorrel nodded thoughtfully. "So you no longer believe she's a thief?"

"I never said she was," Ellen replied through gritted teeth, hating the woman.

"Oh my, then I'm mistaken."

There was an uncomfortable silence as the typewriter became a magnetic focus for all eyes.

"But I do remember," Wells said eventually, "that the three of us agreed that she had busy hands."

"Big misunderstanding," Ellen said, briefly taking Tarn's hand and finding that it was icy cold. For some reason she seemed terrified.

Wells now surveyed the wreckage on the floor, as if seeing it for the first time, then his eyes settled on the sledgehammer against the far wall. "Was it the housekeeper's busy hands that hid this wonderful machine, I wonder?"

There was a pause.

"Please don't talk about my friend that way," Ellen said quietly, hoping that Stefan wasn't hearing any of this, or if he was, that he wasn't understanding it. She was making a big effort to keep her voice calm on his account; she remembered the maniacal look on his face as he had been swinging the sledgehammer.

"I didn't realise you were friends," Wells remarked, glancing at Sorrel for comment; she wrinkled her nose.

"Well we are," Ellen murmured. "Look, would you like to see the rest of the house now?"

And get this over with, she thought.

Wells took a long breath through his nose, savouring the air of the kitchen as if it were a vintage wine.

"Perhaps you'd like a cup of tea?" Tarn inquired, then looked at the floor as the Trustees studiously and completely ignored her.

To Ellen, Sorrel said, "I'm so looking forward to seeing your Jumeau."

"The Jumeau, okay," Ellen replied, as if it were something of no importance.

"My, isn't she charming?" Sorrel declared as she knelt down in front of the wicker chair. Ellen was in the doorway of the bedroom with one eye on Sorrel, the other on Wells; he was on the landing, admiring the collodian portrait of her mother.

"A beautiful lady," he declared.

"Thank you," Ellen said, switching her attention to the landing.

"But Cody is beautiful too," Sorrel purred. "Aren't you Cody?" She took a bisque finger between her own finger and thumb and shook it a little too harshly. The blonde wig shuddered ever so slightly.

"Please be careful," Ellen said. "She's very…"

"Valuable?" Wells murmured from the landing. Her eyes switched to him, then back to Sorrel.

"Well not valuable, no," she lied. "I mean she's broken."

"Poor thing," Sorrel said.

"Oh it's okay, I don't mind. I'm just saying she probably wouldn't fetch much." There was a lingering silence as she looked at Sorrel, then Wells, then back to Sorrel.

"I think something's wrong," Sorrel murmured at length.

"Wrong? What's wrong?"

Sorrel pulled the doll's finger again and the hair shook.

"Don't do that!" Ellen said in a loud voice.

Sorrel looked concerned and confused, as a nurse who had just come across a new and terrifying disease. With surprising ease, given that she had no leverage on her knees, she swiftly whipped the wicker chair around one hundred and eighty degrees in one fluid motion. Cody's eyes were at their left extreme, the movement jerking them to their right, then back to their left.

Ellen nearly screamed with panic as she reached down and stroked the doll's hair, in the hope that whatever had upset the mechanism in her head would correct itself.

"Have I broken her?" Sorrel inquired.

"No … no, she'll be okay. She just needs to readjust, that's all. Let me turn the chair back round so she's facing the window."

"Shall I help?"

"No!"

Ellen shook her head. "No," she repeated quietly, managing a smile. "It's just that she's broken, as I said. You have to be careful with her, that's all. She's very delicate."

Sorrel glanced over Ellen's shoulder to the landing and found her tight smile. "Perhaps we can trouble you for that cup of tea now."

Ellen nodded distractedly, smoothing the golden wig, then smiled as the eyes at last returned to their central position. She had intended to give the impression that the doll meant nothing to her but this plan was abandoned as she gave the doll the most earnest of hugs, then a kiss on a porcelain cheek.

"You love this doll," Sorrel remarked.

"One porcelain doll circa eighteen eighties, thirty-two inches tall," Wells muttered, coming into the bedroom. "A French Jumeau *Bébé* – that's with a face of a little girl – *Cody* – that's long-faced, with original pink satin chemise."

Ellen glanced at him and stood up with a sulk, remembering the description in her inventory for Mr Hobbs. She carefully turned the wicker chair back round so that the doll faced the sea.

"Almond-shaped blue paperweight glass eyes," he continued, now considering Cody's hand on the armrest. "Honey blonde, mohair curls, blush cheeks. She has a soulful expression." He gave a fragile sigh of pleasure. "Delightful," he finished.

"So you've seen my list. So you know how important she is to me."

"Important?" he inquired.

"I ... look I can't explain it."

"Can't explain it?" he mused, with an air of dissatisfaction. "Oh do try."

She closed her eyes briefly as she took a breath. "Look, my psychiatrist ... my counsellor ... has explained this to me. She says I identify Cody with my mum, because ... well, Cody belonged to my mum and she comforted me after ... you know…"

"Psychiatrists are such clever people," Sorrel remarked.

"There must be a big book of knowledge somewhere, which these experts consult," Wells agreed.

"Anyway," Ellen said with a shrug, her eyes ushering them out of her bedroom, "now you understand. Now you know why I could never ... you know ... let her go or anything…"

She was watching the Trustees carefully as they descended the stairs in front of her and she was halfway down before she realised she had forgotten to kiss her mother's portrait. Quickly stepping back, she kissed her fingers and touched the glass, then bounded down to the hall to catch them up.

Her fingers left behind a smudge of her anxiety on the smoky glass.

The soft opening notes of the Moonlight Sonata were gracing the day room once more, rising in harmonic triplets as Sorrel took her place at the piano.

"You play beautifully," Tarn said cautiously, placing her tea nearby, the cup and saucer rattling. Sorrel acknowledged neither the compliment nor the tea, though her concentration seemed to increase. Wells was in the armchair and his eyebrows raised as the tea was placed before him, bemused as if it had floated down in mid air.

"Sit down, Tarn," Ellen suggested from the sofa, annoyed at the Trustees' treatment of her friend. She patted the spare cushion and Tarn nodded wearily, taking her seat with a miserable expression.

"So has your psychiatrist been a help to you?" Wells asked carefully. He held back a smile as he noticed the housekeeper cast a quick, surprised glance at her employer.

"I suppose," Ellen returned uncomfortably, her sessions with Wendy being the one topic she hadn't shared with Tarn. "Actually, counsellor is the correct term ... she just helped me get over Mum's death..."

And didn't expect payment for it either...

"And was your counsellor successful?" he inquired. Sorrel moved her left ear closer to the keys as she played.

Ellen glanced at the piano, finding the music irritating. "I suppose so. Look, have you decided what you want?"

Wells looked up and said, "As you'll have guessed ... the typewriter."

She agreed with a shrug, thinking that it could have been worse. She felt little attachment to her father's machine, though she had the surest feeling that an attachment would have grown, with time, until she loved it almost as much as her doll. It was a relief that the wrench was therefore quick and painless; like hearing of the death of a parent who had never been known.

"What else?" she asked. "The telephone?"

A wide smile gave her a glimpse of his gums, which looked swollen with disease. "You *are* keen to get rid of that, aren't you?

I suspect you love the Wall Street telephone every bit as much as your father did." He looked at Tarn, who blanched and considered her knees.

"It's an antique, and almost solid gold," Ellen said with a pout, though secretly admitting to herself that she hated it. "So, what's the second thing?"

Sorrel stopped playing in an abrupt fashion. The resonant memory of the final chords drifted aimlessly into oblivion.

"I fear it has to be the doll," Wells admitted sadly.

Ellen closed her eyes, attempting a calming breath but failing, for she was too angry. "What?" she said, as she opened them.

He didn't reply; both Trustees were glaring at her.

"I told you," she said, attempting to sound both weary and bored, "that's not an option. I thought I explained to you how important she is to me."

They didn't answer.

"You're not having my doll. That's final. Choose something else. Choose the piano even, but you're not having Cody."

Wells sighed and stood up. Sorrel also rose, slowly and serenely.

"Look, just take something else," Ellen repeated. Tarn was looking nervously on as the Trustees made their way to the door.

"Call us when you're ready to respect your father's wishes," Wells said.

"I *am* respecting…"

"His will and testament, that is. There'll be no need for us to challenge this in the courts, Miss Sorensen, for I've no doubt you'll see the error of your ways."

Ellen now got up and grabbed Tarn's hand, finding strength in her friend's skin. "Right, that's it," she whispered. "Tarn's brother's downstairs and he's got a sledgehammer, okay? If I just raise my voice…"

The Trustees looked at her with feigned surprise.

"I mean it. Now piss off, both of you. Piss off and don't come back. And if you try anything I'll have you on *Panorama* or something. Good story: con artists preying on the bereaved and helpless, ripping off the next of kin."

"We're a registered charity with a royal licence," Wells remarked, his fingers going to his throat as if the words struggled to find moisture. "But we'll leave if that's your wish. This is your house after all and we're merely your guests." He walked into the hall with Sorrel following and pausing by the front door he said, "Look after our possessions, Miss Sorensen..."

"Right, whatever."

"...for you are the custodian now."

"Yeah and take tootsie with you," Ellen called as they walked out of the house.

As the front door was closed and she heard their footsteps fade, she allowed herself a look of surprise. "I am the custodian," she said to herself, a trace of pain appearing around her eyes. She looked inquiringly at Tarn and noticed that she was smiling. "What?" she asked.

"Can't believe that I took you on," Tarn said admiringly. "Didn't they scare you?" She put a hand over her mouth. "Scared me," she admitted.

Ellen shook her head. "Don't know what came over me, but it was like … I don't know … it's how I would imagine it would be if someone came and wanted to take my children. You know?"

Tarn frowned.

"I can't explain it," Ellen said. "Anyway, you're ten times tougher than them. You actually made me cry … and the only time I ever cry is with my shrink. That's a Sorensen patented personality trait: we only cry to our shrinks."

Tarn had the beginnings of a smirk but lost it as something occurred to her. "They didn't seem to care, though. I think … I think they were almost *expecting* you to throw them out."

"Can't believe they wanted Cody, after what I told them," she murmured, not really listening.

"What did he call you, as he left?"

Ellen shrugged. "Custodian, I think," she replied, uneasily.

"That's the word Honeyman used." The mention of his name gave Tarn a tremor of foreboding in her stomach, as if something had gone horribly wrong.

"What's the matter?" Ellen asked.

"I think we should look at the back of Cody's neck. Didn't Honeyman say that you'd find something?"

"I'll find the serial number. All Jumeaux have a serial number."

"Then why did he say it?"

Ellen considered this.

She looked up at the ceiling.

Under the words TÊTE JUMEAU Cody's serial number was impressed into the porcelain bisque in the back of the neck, branded and stamped long ago with a hot tool after the head had been fired and baked. The doll had a jointed composition body and the back of the head came away to give access to the eye mechanism, but the neck and the face were one piece.

"It's one piece," Ellen muttered, shaking her head in confusion.

The serial number was 1331.

As the white hearse pulled away, the house was screaming in panic and alarm.

XVII

Where is thy sting?

The Trustees' vehicle was parked near Pembroke castle, the dark tinted glass in the sides and rear hiding the contents of the long, wide boot. The driver's cab was free of any clutter or homely connection to its owners and only a pair of neatly folded leather gloves, left behind by the driver on this occasion, would have offered any clue that the vehicle had a function over and above attracting the curious glances of pedestrians. Those passers by who knew a little about mechanics might comment that the vehicle was a hearse on the chassis of some long, very powerful off-roader, possibly an army vehicle. Others might simply have noticed its registration plates.

The plates were a shining, brilliant white, identical to the bodywork, and carried no registration. This was only at first glance, for a closer inspection did indeed reveal a series of numbers and letters, the code for many nightmares and fears, causing the overly curious to hurry along chasing forgetfulness.

This was the temple transport and it contained the consciousness of all departed Trustees; it was riveted and upholstered with souls in a parody of the vessels the temple collected as its own. It had evolved but carried its heritage with it; an engineer who delved underneath it would have found the remnants of a canopy of a carriage, the black leather painted white and stained with horse manure, amid the welded chassis of many different vehicles, the oldest of rusted iron.

It was a form of peerage for the Trustees, their occupancy of the transport after their days, so that they could still be of service. The vehicle acted not only as an alarm when vessels were ready to be collected, or collodians needed to be switched, but also as a watchdog. The registration plates were its eyes and which were now ready to jump to attention as the vehicle waited patiently outside the house of Marion Coates, guarding the serving Trustees from intrusion.

The Trustees had been in good spirits as they alighted, having come directly from their encounter in the house overlooking North Beach unperturbed by their failure to collect their two items from the Sorensen estate. They had taken their cargo from the boot, gently unwrapping it from the folds of black felt, playfully aware of the green Land Rover parked near the castle on the other side of the road.

"We've yet another present for you, Marion," Sorrel declared as she handed Marion something spherical and wrapped in porous white linen. As Marion took it, her bare arms revealed kitchen burns for her reactions were now a fraction behind her mental commands. She weighed the gift uncertainly in both hands; it was light. The linen fell away to reveal a skull, grey with age and chiselled exquisitely with lines and numbers.

"There's no need to be frightened, it's just a phrenological skull," Sorrel explained. They were sitting on the settee, facing each other.

"Phren...?"

"Phrenology: it's a science of the mind. Remember that, in case you're asked. What is it?"

"A science of the mind," Marion whispered.

"Oh, well done. We've got some books too, to place somewhere in the house so it looks as if you have a general interest in the subject."

Wells was at the folding dining table by the bay window, re-arranging the photographs to make a clear space and dusting the table with irritated movements. Then he collected the skull and placed it in the space he had made on the table. He moved his head from

197

side to side as he measured the impact of the light on the bone. "It doesn't matter where you put the skull," he said, "provided it's in the house and on show. It is important that it's on show. In a place where your nearest and dearest will see it…"

Marion heard the rest of his sentence, the part that was unsaid.

When they are picking over your estate…

"Why have you brought it?" she asked weakly.

Wells moved the skull further onto the table so it would cast fewer shadows. "As Mrs Page has explained, the skull is a phrenological artefact because The Divine Sentiment began as a phrenological society. There's a number ingrained into everything we do, for the society is now a temple, and every temple belonging to the Father has a number. But the skull records the crime; a terrible crime, which enabled the temple to be sanctified." He adjusted the skull slightly then stepped back, satisfied. "It isn't important that you understand the history: it's only important you understand there was a crime. And that you understand *your* crime, Marion."

"My crime…?"

"Against Henry," Sorrel clarified, taking her hand. "You chose to keep him here. You kept him here, *trapped* him here, against the will of his god. Yes, against all the laws of Heaven." She looked up in despair. "Oh death, where is thy sting? Oh grave, where is thy victory? Isn't that what your god tells you? What he promises you?"

Wells glanced up from the table with the briefest of smiles.

"You promised we'd be together," Marion protested, pulling her hand free.

"And so you will," Sorrel confirmed solemnly.

"And so you will," Wells agreed. "You'll wear something in this house and, with Henry, you'll sing for us."

Sorrel nodded. "For the Father. In penance for your crime."

No one in the room moved, the only sound the small hammers of the hall clock. Suddenly Marion tensed and looked around the room.

"If you're wondering, I suspect that it'll be your charming, charming dresser," Wells remarked, placing a hand near the skull as if he were testing the frequency of the air around it. "That's the only thing you love which I believe could effectively communicate. Consider the dinner service that belongs with this dresser, the Sandringham that you're so proud of, that you took such trouble to collect." He raised two fingers of two hands in the direction of the dresser, then one finger, making a square as if he were checking the dimensions of a piece of art. "Arranged in a certain way, using the different shelves as decimalisation, they'll be able to offer numbers. Like a bean counter or some ancient calculator."

"I'll destroy it," Marion whispered.

"No you won't. You don't *dare* destroy it."

"Really Marion, you don't," Sorrel agreed. "You won't need to be coaxed into something you love, as was the case with dear Henry. You're destined for the temple because of your crime and a vessel will take you regardless. Destroy everything that you love and you risk falling into something vile. The first thing your soul finds in this house, in fact, until a suitable vessel is found. Even stripping the house wouldn't help: we've known condemned souls become trapped in a bug's larva in a carpet, or in a fly's vomit on a window, in their attempt to escape their judgment."

Marion shuddered.

Sorrel went on: "Far better to make the best of yourself, to wear what you loved, what you were proud of, so when you keep Henry company he won't feel ashamed."

"Yes," Marion said, forlornly. "I must make the best of myself." She felt as if she were heavily sedated, understanding everything but capable of only a limited response.

Sorrel regarded the dresser with a wistful air of regret. "The wood will never scratch, the iron never tarnish, for this is the vessel that will hold you. The plates will be indestructible … as souls are indestructible. Oh death, where is thy sting? Oh grave, where is thy victory? You can trust our promise, for it comes from the Father and He does not lie."

Marion swallowed and looked at the skull, then at Wells. "How long will it be? Is it forever?"

"Not forever," he replied. "You'll sing until the last temple is built, though that may seem like forever."

A spring juddered in the hallway, as the clock stuttered. The mechanism was unstable but working without rest, although the hands always showed five minutes past three o'clock. Sorrel heard the spring with a momentary widening of her eyes. "Now there are some important details and you need to listen very carefully. Are you listening, Marion?" She paused. "First, have you made arrangements to be buried, like Henry?"

Marion nodded mutely.

"Good. Now, you need to change your will. You do have a will, don't you?" When Marion nodded once more, she took a package from her bag and placed it on the coffee table; it was addressed to a Pembroke solicitor, with her telephone number. "Ring this solicitor, make an appointment and give her the package. Everything she needs to know is in the envelope, including our strict requirements on confidentiality, and the steps we'll take if that confidentiality isn't observed. The solicitor isn't one of us, Marion, so she'll ask many awkward questions: be ready, say that you're not prepared to discuss anything. Just tell her you wish to leave a gift to a charity that's helped you but they have strict requirements that must be followed. Do you understand?"

"Yes, I understand … I'm not prepared to discuss anything…" She gestured with her hand to imitate her manner with the solicitor.

"Oh my, that's very good. Give the solicitor the envelope and say it contains all necessary instructions."

"What instructions?"

"We'll take two items from this house after your death. We need to be sure that the contents of the house will not be tampered with before we make our selection, and so the instructions contain not only the necessary clauses for the will but also explain the inventory that needs to prepared before our bequest is revealed to anyone. In short, we need protection from your children."

The mention of her children angered Marion, though it didn't show in her face, which remained in an exhausted stupor, rather in her restless hand, which gripped the arm of the settee. She got up with an effort and walked slowly over to the bay window, where she pulled aside the chintz and looked out, her eyes searching the road.

"He can't help you," Sorrel remarked. "You had your chance to listen to him."

Henry's clock again broke the silence, the ticking tripping forward this time. Eventually Marion turned from the window with an expression of tired resignation and returned slowly to the settee. "You've promised me nothing," she muttered, the settee rocking as she heavily took her seat. "You've given me no hope at all. Neither me, nor Henry, though Henry is innocent. You've shown us no mercy."

"There is no mercy," Sorrel sighed.

"So why should I cooperate? Why shouldn't I make things as difficult for you as possible?"

Sorrel took her hand and held it tight, ignoring her attempts to pull it away. "Because you know we'll look after both of you. Imagine Henry's clock being given to some uncaring relative, or a junk shop for scrap." She found her tight smile. "Imagine your dinner service wrapped up and stored away in boxes as an investment. The shelves of your dresser bare, stripped and naked, possibly in some storage garage somewhere."

Marion shook her head with a distressed face.

"Your children won't know, you see. They won't understand that you need to be looked after. That's why you need us to come to the house and take you away … to keep you safe."

"Yes I see that," Marion agreed, with a slow nod. She reached for the hem of her skirt to wipe her eyes but her energy failed.

"We've arranged for someone to visit you on a regular basis, to look after you as you approach your time," Wells muttered. "You won't see us again in this life."

Marion looked up at the old Trustee. "Was my crime so great? Was it so bad that I deserve this punishment?"

"Death, where is thy sting?" he said in answer. "You've conquered death, for Henry, solely for your own selfish whim. You've committed the gravest of sins and your god has abandoned you."

She opened her mouth to speak but nodded instead with a weary sigh.

"Only the Father loves you now," Sorrel said. "He will protect you, so long as you obey Him." She paused, now taking a deep breath. "Obey Him in everything: understand that He is merciful but will not countenance disobedience. In the certain knowledge of His power we are strong; in the sure promise of His mercy we are pious; in the dread certainty of His vengeance we are obedient."

"Amen," Wells said automatically, as if she had just recited the last stanza to a famous psalm.

"Amen," Sorrel concurred.

The seconds were counted by the ticking of the clock. Marion was coming to understand the language of the mechanism, the irregular tap and thump; it spoke now of helpless despair.

Say it Marry! For pity's sake!

"Amen," she said at length, to relieve the pain.

"Ring the solicitor," Wells said, his tone carrying a trace of satisfaction. "Only think about the details now and let nothing else distract you." He nodded and smiled broadly, producing his teeth and gums. "You will soon be at leisure and there'll be plenty of time to ponder on your crime."

On the path of Marion's small lawn Wells stopped abruptly and waited for Sorrel to come to his side. Honeyman was guarding the front gate a few yards away; he was crouched slightly, his hands defensively in the pockets of his overcoat.

"We sometimes wonder whether we should knock the window of your vehicle and say hello," Sorrel said by way of greeting. "We know you like to hide, and you believe yourself so good at it, so we pretend not to see you."

"I know you see me," Honeyman retorted. "I don't care any more. Release Mrs Coates' husband, let him go. Let them both go."

"Let my people go!" Wells laughed. "We have Moses before us, Mrs Page."

Sorrel's eyes were alive with the vision of the large man blocking their path. "Moses indeed," she purred, "attempting to part the Red Sea. Doesn't it trouble you, Baptist? Doesn't it trouble you how little help you receive in your endeavours? Even Moses got a pillar of fire…"

Honeyman didn't reply; he was struggling to move his legs. When he had seen Marion appear at the window he had bounded out of his Land Rover and raced across the road, but his attempt to enter the house had failed. As he had hurried past the removal wagon he had been unable to avoid catching a glimpse of its rear registration plate, which had brought him to a breathless stop and weighted down his feet, at the gate. The plates had been his downfall a year ago, when he had tried to jot them down in his notebook and they had drilled into his subconscious. That was when the attacks had started.

"Aren't you in awe at our latest prize?" she asked. "Letters have been sent. The machine was buried … *buried*, yet still the letters were sent. Don't you see how powerful the temple becomes? How it is sanctified?"

"I see that it is cursed," Honeyman muttered. "As you are cursed. I know that God has put me here to destroy you."

"All that you know," Wells croaked, "all that we've allowed you to know, all that you will ever know, is how you will die."

"With earth in your mouth," Sorrel added, "your limbs shattered."

"The pit is narrow and deep," Wells continued, "and it has been dug for you." He inhaled greedily. "We'll not countenance trespass. We're peaceful and holy, for we are priests, but the Father permits us to deal with such sacrilege. You are warned."

"You are warned," she repeated simply and a mere flicker of her eyes made Honeyman clutch at his chest. "Know that if we talk again, it'll be at your painful and lingering death."

Honeyman groaned and with a huge effort, his legs apparently weighed down with lead, he stood aside from the gate.

The Trustees strode past him but the sense of suffocation stayed with him until the removal wagon drove away, Sorrel casting a thoughtful glance back in his direction.

From the bay window, Marion watched the scene on her path with detached interest. After Honeyman departed, staggering across the road to his vehicle, his hand clutched to his chest, she returned to her narrow hallway and took her seat in front of the oak clock.

It was ticking at a slow, regular pace. Henry was sleeping.

"Forgive me, Henry," she murmured, after what seemed like a long time. It may have been hours; she had a vague sense that she was starving, but was unable to find the will to leave her chair.

The mechanism had slowed to a crawl. When the doorbell rang, perhaps the next day, her energy returned and she was able to rise and walk to the front door. She stood at the door but hesitated to open it.

"Mrs Coates, open the door," came the voice from the other side. "I'm here to look after you."

XVIII

The custodian

"This is Tarn, my new friend," Ellen announced, as Hugh put down his holdall in the hall. "She was kind to my dad. Oh and this is Stefan, Tarn's brother," she added.

"And friend," Tarn suggested.

"And friend, absolutely," she agreed, her eyes going up into her head at her foolishness. Stefan looked shyly at the floor, not caring about the mistake.

Hugh was in his early thirties, with light brown curly hair and chubby cheeks. He was smiling as he shook Tarn and Stefan's hand in turn.

"Ellen's told me all about you," Tarn lied, having pictured a tall, good-looking professional type, all vanity and airs.

"She has?" he asked, sounding a little surprised.

"When time's allowed," Ellen muttered.

He nodded, a little lost for words. "Ellen's told me a lot about you, too," he said to Tarn. "You're a … you're a … well you go to church…"

"Oh dear, is that me defined?" she answered, hiding her amusement as she saw Ellen put a hand to her forehead in embarrassment.

"You know what I mean," he said.

"I know."

"I mean … it's great."

"Yes it is," she agreed, good-naturedly.

With a sigh of relief, and with a huge effort of concentration as the thesaurus in his head filtered out any words or acronyms remotely connected with *slow, stupid* or *backward*, Ellen's favourite terms for the housekeeper's odd-job brother, he turned to Stefan. The young man was waiting expectantly, ready to like him.

Hugh punched his shoulder playfully, prompting another embarrassed shudder from Ellen. "You're a Wing. Am I right?"

"Wing," Stefan confirmed, his face lighting up.

Tarn took her brother's elbow, the action making him look away in embarrassment. "He's wonderful to watch on the pitch, he really is. Like a bullet from a gun, aren't you Stef?"

Stefan shrugged, then nodded.

"Rugby," Ellen groaned. "The further west you come, the worse it gets."

Hugh rubbed his hands together. "Anyway, I thought we could all go out for a meal tonight. My treat."

"There's really no need…" Tarn began.

"No way," he insisted. "You've both been such a help to Ellen."

"I'm sure we haven't," Tarn remarked, a hand going to her hair.

"Yes you have," Ellen said. "Hugh's right, but I'm paying. I suppose I'm wealthy now, what with Dad's money and everything." She paused. "Hugh's only on payroll where he works."

"But with partnership prospects," he clarified quietly.

"Oh I'm sure," Tarn agreed.

"Whatever," Ellen murmured, noting her reproving glance and sensing that she was being scolded. "See you in the Lifeboat around seven?"

It was a good few minutes after Tarn and Stefan had left before she spoke again.

"Didn't know you were such a charmer," she remarked. Hugh was trying to find a suitably inconspicuous place in the day room for his holdall, having declined the invitation to sleep in her late father's bed. She had half a dozen sensible reasons ready as to why he couldn't sleep with her, none of which had anything to do with sex. After putting so much time into their preparation she was a little miffed she hadn't had to use any of them.

"What do you mean?" He was regarding the sofa as he would a difficult snooker shot.

She made a face of exasperation. "Oh, let me take you out for dinner and everything."

"Just trying to be friendly," he said, his eyes still on the sofa.

"And I'm paying, too."

"Hey, that was your idea, not mine."

"Tarn's *my* friend, not yours."

The statement just fell out of her mouth, without the weight of her mind behind it. She put a hand to her mouth and looked down.

"I know she's your friend," he said carefully. "I don't want to take your friends away from you, Ellen."

"Don't know why I said that," she muttered from under her hand.

"It's okay. I understand."

"Understand what? *What* do you understand?"

In his head, he counted to three. "I don't know," he admitted quietly.

She glanced at him accusingly. She had discussed her friends with Wendy; why one day she was so clingy with them, the next day ready never to speak to them again for being two minutes late outside the students union. They generally had a short shelf life. Wendy had suggested that all her anger and mistrust was simply grief, in another form; water when boiled becomes steam, but it's still water…

She wondered about this, and she questioned her impatient treatment of Hugh, but logic told her that she was within her rights. If she were being unfair, he would have protested.

"Must have seen your uncle Martin today," he said, in an attempt to change the subject.

"What do you mean?"

"As I was driving through the town I saw him going into a hotel down on The Esplanade. God, he *is* the spit of your father." Hugh was aware of her father's appearance from the photographs in her digs, taken with her mother about three years ago. He remembered them because he had considered it unusual for an undergraduate to have photographs of parents so obviously on display.

"Couldn't have been Uncle Martin. He's travelling around the country at the moment."

"Well if it's not your uncle Martin," he joked, "it must have been your dad."

There was a pause, and with a sigh that acknowledged his error he reached down to his holdall; he was trying to diffuse the tension with a look of intense concentration, rummaging through his belongings as if he had to find something very important.

"You are such an arsehole," she whispered.

"Sorry, Ellen," he muttered.

"Such a complete fucking arsehole!" She stormed out of the room and bounded up the stairs.

He nodded to himself with a sigh of resignation. Eventually he spoke to the sofa.

"Hi there. Looks like we're going to be good friends."

In the Lifeboat Inn on the slope of Tudor Square, underneath hanging nets and in front of a large ornamental frigate wheel on the wall, Stefan eagerly showed Hugh his rugby photographs. Hugh made a point of finding something different to say with every photograph, even though the majority of them involved Stefan stopping to study the camera in bewilderment.

Tarn was beaming as she looked on, a coke with ice occasionally touching her lips, while Ellen considered her red wine with a sullen air. She had stayed in her room for two hours and her shrug when she eventually came down was the closest she came to an apology.

Hugh searched for a topic to turn the conversation away from the photographs. "So, these charity people have visited?"

"Bad people came to the house," Stefan said, putting the

photographs back in his large leather wallet, which was otherwise empty.

"They frightened Stefan," Tarn explained quietly.

"Bad lady, angry eyes."

"That's enough, Stef," she whispered, patting his elbow.

Hugh raised a lower lip in his much-used pose of thoughtful reflection. "I've been doing a bit of digging on these people, The Divine Sentiment. The word 'sentiment' has nothing to do with caring or counselling by the way: it's referring to a lobe in the brain. They used be a phrenological society."

Tarn nodded. "You've seen the skull in the hall, and the bust under the stairs. They were both gifts from the charity."

Hugh glanced at Ellen for clarification, but she didn't look up from her wine; he supposed she was still upset over their argument, for she had been quiet since they had left the house, barely even wanting to speak to her uncle when he rang on the walk down. "You won't find anything about The Divine Sentiment on the web," he said, "no matter how hard you look. Had to go back to grass roots to find out about those guys. I've got a mate who works in the Hall of Records and he cross-referenced some archived newspaper articles and other materials."

"And?" Tarn asked.

"There still isn't much. It was founded by a chap called Thomas Wilkinson in the eighteen sixties: he started out as a lay preacher but was thrown out of the church."

"Just like…" Tarn said to herself, then shook her head and urged him to continue.

"Well, Wilkinson claimed they'd discovered the existence of the soul." Hugh paused. "In the brain," he added.

Tarn was taken aback. "The soul … in the brain?"

"Soul's in *here*," Stefan remarked, with a hand going to his chest. Tarn nodded with a smile for her brother, though her full attention was on Hugh, who was continuing to surprise her.

"He marketed it as some kind of discovery, saying that phrenology could prove the place in the brain where the soul was stored. You know, if the brain is a house with a lot of rooms, the soul lives in the third spare bedroom. In bed probably, watching TV..."

"Don't joke, Hugh," Tarn whispered.

"Right, sorry," he agreed, his serious face falling back into place. "Anyway, that's what he believed and he seems to have had a lot of support in the early days."

"Only in the early days?" Tarn asked.

"Well, all these phrenologists were amateurs, trying to prove their theories without applying an ounce of scientific objectivity. I mean that George Combe, the guy who prepared the list on Ellen's chart, was one of the worst. He wrote a massive book setting out all his research. I've read some of it." He groaned. "There's all these chapters explaining each of the individual sentiments, describing all these people he'd examined and referring to plaster busts of criminals and the like. Thing is, whenever he found something which seemed to prove the location of a certain organ, or sentiment, he put it in. Whenever he found something that disproved it, he called it an exception..."

"What's your point, Hugh?" Tarn asked. She glanced at Ellen, noting that she had been quiet for a little while now; she had barely touched her wine.

Hugh nodded to acknowledge he was wandering off course. He had started his research in the hope that he would find a few snippets of information to impress Ellen, just enough to play along on what he had considered to be one of her paranoid journeys, yet he had quickly become quite fascinated with the subject.

"My point is that Combe was pretty typical of phrenological thinking. Phrenology was supposed to be the big break through in modern science, so the phrenologists needed to be vindicated. Think of it – Combe creates a chart that he says is effectively a map of the human condition, listing and numbering every talent and temperament. Now, Combe thinks: 'If I'm right, then I'm the new Aristotle. If I'm wrong, then I'll be the laughing stock of this and future generations.' It's little wonder phrenologists dedicated their lives to their subject and went to their graves defending it and so of course were on the look out for anything ... *anything* that might prove them right." He hesitated. "But they *still* wanted nothing to do with The Divine Sentiment." He hesitated once more, letting this information sink in. "Even to phrenologists, Wilkinson and his supporters were screwballs."

Ellen looked up from her wine, her eyes searching his face, but she had nothing to say.

"You okay, Ellen?" Tarn whispered to her, tapping her hand. She shrugged quickly in response.

"Anyway, Wilkinson took it badly," Hugh continued, throwing Ellen a concerned glance. "There's a statement filed with the Phrenological Society – did you know that that organisation wasn't disbanded until the nineteen sixties? – officially confirming that their theories had, and I quote, *no sound or rational substance in science or religion.* It refers to tests that were *ill conceived* and *inconclusive.* It contains a warning to avoid them."

"What tests?" Tarn asked.

Hugh's lower lip went up again. "I don't know, but my friend says the complete lack of material is suspicious and that the case was probably turned over to Scotland Yard." He shook his head. "He says that the only time he's seen a trail lost so completely is when there's the involvement of a royal. That's what he reckons happened here, that maybe one of the royals got mixed up with the charity." He grinned. "But that's just guesswork and my mate's a real conspiracy nut: he reckons that they never caught the Ripper because there was a royal..."

"What happened to Wilkinson, Hugh?" Tarn interjected, with a smiling apology for bringing him back on track.

"Yeah, right. Wilkinson disappeared. He left all his money to a charity and after enough time had passed to presume him dead, the charity appeared in the form of bereavement counselling. They inherited Wilkinson's estate and they kept the name of the society out of gratitude to their founding benefactor, even though all his previous supporters, you know the financiers and patrons, seemed

211

to melt away."

Ellen spoke at last. "Honeyman explained that … that 'thirteen' was a special number for phrenologists, that it represented the divide between animals and humans." She was speaking slowly, with effort, and winced when she said 'thirteen'.

"Thirteen is the sentiment of 'benevolence': if we accept Combe's list, that is. There were a few different ones, but Combe is the acknowledged authority, if that's the right phrase." Hugh smiled briefly, then was thoughtful again. "Honeyman – that's the ex-vicar guy?"

Tarn nodded, while Ellen stared back at her wine glass, touching it uncertainly with one finger.

He threw her another concerned look, this time more than just a glance. "Perhaps that's where they thought the soul was housed. In lobe thirteen, I mean. But you also mentioned number thirty-one, and that's 'time'. I'm not sure what…"

"It's just the reverse of… it's just the reverse," Ellen muttered, with a pained expression.

Stop saying the numbers!

"That's what Honeyman thinks, anyway," she clarified. She was finding it curious that she was accepting his information as being accurate, even though she had assessed him as a conman.

"Cody's got the number too," Tarn said. "It's carved in the back of her neck."

Hugh nodded. "Someone got to her when they planted the letter in her sleeve. Someone's obviously been in the house."

Ellen shook her head, but didn't speak.

"Ellen says that's impossible, because the neck is part of the face," Tarn said. "Though she never really looked at the serial number. It could just be a coincidence."

Hugh took a swig of his lager. "Well, I think it's time to change the locks, whatever the case. I also think we should get some legal advice on this clause in the will." He tried to catch Ellen's eye. "When you refused to let them take the doll and the typewriter did they threaten to sue you?"

212

Ellen didn't seem to hear him and Tarn spoke for her once more. "They seem to think she'll just come round. They said they'd come back when she was ready to respect her father's wishes."

He considered this with a chuckle. "I think they'll be waiting a fair while, then. I know how much the doll means to her…"

"And the typewriter," Ellen muttered. Her attachment to the machine had grown in the last twenty-four hours.

"Right," he agreed cautiously, taking another swig of his drink and noticing she still hadn't touched her wine. "Ellen, you okay?"

Ellen slowly shook her head, the small frown of her eyebrows signalling her confusion. "I don't want to go for a meal. I want to go home. I want to go home *now*."

Hugh put down his drink. "Why? What's wrong?"

Ellen got up. "It doesn't feel right being away from the house. I need to look after…" She hesitated then put on her coat.

"Look after what?" he asked, also getting up.

She buttoned her coat with decisive speed. She felt as if she was attached to a long elastic rope, which had now found its limit. "I have to look after my parents' things. They left everything to me so it's my job to look after them. I'm … I'm the custodian."

As she uttered the word, *custodian,* it clicked into place in her head, as if something had locked.

There had been a visitor while they were out. Not only was there another letter under the mat but the phrenological skull had been moved.

"Mr Sockets always faces away from the window," Tarn explained excitedly, having noticed the new angle almost immediately as they walked through the door. "Now he's looking at the day room. Someone's been examining it."

"Locks and alarms tomorrow," Hugh declared, a reassuring hand going to Ellen's shoulder. In spite of the evidence of an intruder she seemed herself again now they were back in the house; she was holding the letter thoughtfully, unopened.

"Locks and alarms," she agreed, reading her name, *Miss Eleanor Sorensen* and checking the 13p stamp. The malaise in the Lifeboat Inn seemed a distant memory.

He noticed other obvious signs of the intruder: the cupboard door under the stairs was open and the light was on. He checked the cardboard box and found that the bust in the straw was still there. "The burglar's been careless," he remarked, pushing the box back into the cupboard with his foot. "He must've left in a hurry. Perhaps we surprised him."

"Surprised him?" Tarn queried.

"Well, we were meant to be going out for a meal, weren't we? I'd booked the table."

The question lingered in the air, unsaid.

Who knew we were going out?

Hugh was about to remark that Ellen had told her uncle they were going out for a meal when he rang on the way to the Lifeboat, but thought better of it; he had already mentioned the uncle once today and it had got him into trouble.

They filed down to the kitchen, but nothing in this room appeared to have been disturbed. Ellen's hand hovered over the reams of watermarked paper; they were still neatly stacked. Checking the typewriter, she considered how small it was, and how basic; as an experimental prototype only the parts of the machine that were essential to its operation had been fitted.

She sighed, having fallen a little in love with the metal contraption and understanding why her father had so carefully refurbished the keys and kept it gleaming with oil. She frowned as her finger found a rough ridge of ochre rust along one of the jointed fingers of the letter keys; she didn't remember seeing it before.

"No sign of a forced entry," Hugh said, checking the windows. "Someone's been sneaking into the house to plant the letters and it's someone who's got a key."

"Someone with a key," Tarn agreed, "who also knows Ellen as *Ellie Sweet*."

"Anyone could steal a key ... but the name narrows it down,"

214

Ellen conceded. She had spent her teenage years guarding that name and had been mentally flicking through every friend she might have mentioned it to, at one time or another. No one came to mind. "Not even Hugh knew about 'Ellie Sweet'."

Hugh smiled, finding the *not even* part of the statement encouraging, thinking that he must occupy at least some vacant corner of her heart. The reflection sparked the image of Stefan putting his hand to his heart in the pub and he suddenly realised how patient the young man had been since he had put away his rugby photographs, how he hadn't uttered a single word. He felt a twinge of guilt at not having made the effort on any subject other than rugby; he turned and caught his attention. "What do you think about all this, Stefan? You've heard us ramble on enough."

Stefan's eyes were baleful. "I think Mr Sorensen is writing the letters," he said. He was embarrassed by the silence. "I think he's writing them from Heaven."

"Oh Stef..." Tarn muttered, with a look of apology for Ellen and Hugh.

There was a silence as they all wandered through their own thoughts.

Ellen was recalling her argument with Tarn, when she was mimicking the finger of her father coming down on the machine.

Tarn was remembering Honeyman's description of her brother, that he had ... intuition.

Hugh was thinking of a joke. "Shame he didn't send a postcard. Love to see what it looks like."

Tarn blinked slowly to dispel the misplaced humour. "What does the letter say?" she asked. "Is it the same message again: 'find me, Ellie Sweet'?"

Ellen unfolded the letter. She considered it blankly for a few moments, then shook her head and handed it to Tarn. It read:

The temple is reversed

XIX

This is our pain

It was the most comforting of nightmares for there was a detachment from the horror, as if she was watching a film she had seen countless times before, in the company of a dear friend.

I have to get you out of bed now ... I'm sorry Ellen, but I have to...

It was the voice of the little girl. Cody was standing up on her chair, one bisque hand settled on the chair's back and the other raised, a finger pointed towards the wardrobe door.

The inventory said the wardrobe was empty ... just some blankets and coat hangers...

She was out of bed, walking towards the wardrobe, her feet not making contact with the floor. On the landing, the image of her mother was gone from her portrait, only the black smoke of the glass remaining.

Don't be afraid, but we need to show you what we see...

Her hand was on the wardrobe handle door as she looked around. Cody was still pointing but her eyes were white, the eyeballs completely in the skull. It didn't matter, for a warm blanket of reassurance and safety wrapped around her as the door was opened. So she wasn't afraid as she saw herself propped up in the wardrobe, stiff and upright: a corpse.

This is what we see...

She regarded the rotting cadaver with detached sympathy, finding it no more alarming than some Egyptian mummy behind a glass cage in a museum. The little girl leading her through this dream had given her the freedom and ease of a spirit, but she sensed that the bubble of protection was fragile; she imagined it would take just a shake of the wardrobe, a coat hanger to fall or a shelf to fail, for the illusion of safety to pop.

When she would see herself as a corpse.

This is our pain, Ellen. We have to show you … we're sorry, but we have to show you our pain…

"Why must you?" she whispered. A trace of sadness was in her eyes as she considered the perished fate of her skin.

Because you are the custodian…

Ellen's eyes opened slowly.

It was early morning and Cody was a dim outline on the wicker chair at the foot of the bed. She took a breath and realised she was calm, wonderfully calm.

Almost too calm; as she moaned and closed her eyes, she felt as if a powerful sedative was running through her veins.

"I'm going to look after you," she murmured, picturing the doll and the typewriter.

She took a troubled breath, the sedative failing as tears of horror came.

"I am the custodian."

She pushed off the sheets and crawled to the bottom of the bed, stroking her Jumeau. The paperweight eyes responded. "I'm going to look after you," she repeated. "No one's going to take you away from me." She stroked the porcelain cheek protectively with her right palm and the blue glass eyes rocked once more.

Returning to her bed, she pulled the sheets tightly around her. As she tried to sleep, she was clenching and unclenching her right hand. Her palm was tingling. It was some time before the sensation disappeared, absorbed into the electrons of her nervous system.

Timothy Hobbs had stopped making notes and sat back with a grunt of dissatisfaction. He glanced at Hugh, who was sitting next to Ellen with an embarrassed smile.

"Have you got any of these letters?" Hobbs asked. Handed the letters he studied them briefly, passing them back across the desk with a raise of his eyebrows. "And you believe these were typed on your father's machine?"

"My uncle's carrying out some tests," Ellen said, "but the typeset looks identical and it's definitely his paper. The stamp design with all the bunched up numbers may have been created on a computer."

"Very well," he muttered, inviting her to go on.

She shrugged. "Well that's it, really."

Hobbs was still confused about the reason for this urgently convened meeting. "When you came in you said you were worried about the charity, the … the…"

"The Divine Sentiment."

Hobbs found the will. "The Divine Sentiment," he read slowly and deliberately, as a warning to her not to finish his sentences again. He looked up inquiringly.

"Well I think maybe it's the charity which is sending the letters," she explained.

"But they were typed on your father's typewriter?"

"Yes, but…"

"Which was buried?"

Hugh noticed Ellen catch her breath, saw her demeanour change as it had done on the way here, when they turned the corner and the house went out of view. "You okay?" he whispered and she nodded. "There's something not quite right about the Trustees of this charity," he said, turning to the solicitor. "I haven't met them but on the last occasion they frightened Stefan, the odd job man."

"That's young Stefan Hughes?" Hobbs asked, considering Ellen for a moment with a concerned frown.

"Yeah, he was very upset, apparently."

"What did they do?"

Hugh made to answer, but shook his head instead. Saying *the woman looked at him a bit funny* had sounded a lot more convincing back at the house.

"They want the typewriter," Ellen murmured, her breathing

returning to normal. "And they want my doll."

"Ah…" Hobbs declared, sitting back with a look of relieved satisfaction at having untangled a stubborn knot.

"My Jumeau doll. It was my mum's, Mr Hobbs."

"I see. I know you're fond of that doll, my dear. I know because your father told me so."

"He did?"

"He was very fond of the doll himself. Cody, isn't it?"

She nodded. "Yes, how do you know?"

"Because…" and the solicitor scratched his neck uncomfortably, "because your father introduced me to her."

"*Introduced* you?"

He gave a theatrical wave of his Mont Blanc pen. "Perhaps 'introduced' is the wrong word. He said *this is Cody,* or something of that sort."

She thought about this. "But Tarn said that you saw Dad in the kitchen … that you didn't go round the house."

"Indeed so. The doll was sitting at the kitchen table. Your father said that's where she always sat."

"Rubbish!" she snapped.

Hobbs considered her with a blank expression.

"Sorry, Mr Hobbs," Hugh said.

"Yeah, sorry," she agreed, remembering herself.

Hugh tapped her hand. "She's been under a lot of pressure. These letters and everything…"

"I understand of course."

"It's just that Tarn hasn't mentioned that he moved the doll around the house," she said.

"Have you asked her?"

"Well, no." She was thoughtful for a moment. "Was anything else moved, Mr Hobbs?"

"Such as?"

"Well there's a glass portrait of my mum on the landing. Did he move that too?"

"Portrait?"

Ellen shook her head. "It doesn't matter." Something told her that the portrait was there, in the kitchen looking on, and she didn't need the solicitor to confirm it. "Didn't you find his behaviour strange? Keeping a doll at the kitchen table, I mean?"

Hobbs sighed. "I've handled matters for a number of elderly widows and widowers, my dear. Your father was without doubt the most curious of them all, but elderly bereavement is, I have to admit, a phenomenon that defies understanding. People cope in different ways. Your father, I suspect, was playing a little game with himself…"

"What game?"

"Ah, to trick himself into believing that your mother was still there. I think Cody was a replacement for your mother. Someone he could talk to, as he used to talk to *her*." He paused. "Don't think badly of him, my dear: he wasn't mad."

"I don't … he wasn't…" she murmured. She was thinking of the many evenings that she had spent speaking to her Cody doll, the hugs she had given her, the mohair feeling so comforting on her skin.

The way she imagined Cody spoke to her, with her eyes…

In that moment she experienced the strongest of urges to go home, and not to walk, but to run, to run as fast as she possibly could. Once again, she felt that she was on the end of the long elastic rope, stretched to its limit. She felt Hugh's hand on her wrist and she shook it away irritably.

Hugh turned to the solicitor in exasperation. "But don't you think it's inconsistent that Mr Sorensen would allow the doll to be given away, given that he was so fond of it?"

Hobbs considered this. "Let's look at that proposition from a different angle. Given that he was so fond of the doll, we can assume there is no possibility … no possibility at all … that he could have overlooked her. Now, when he changed the will, leaving his bequest to the charity, he didn't tell me to exclude the doll. That means…"

"He didn't mind the charity having it," Hugh mused, taking

the point. Hobbs looked at him blankly, again not caring to have his sentence finished.

"But the Jumeau is valuable," Ellen muttered. "Can't we challenge it?"

"Challenge it how?" the solicitor asked.

"Say that they're con artists?"

"Then they'd have taken the piano. They're a registered charity, my dear, under royal charter."

"But I told them how important it was to me. And they didn't care. Honestly Mr Hobbs, they didn't care one jot. What sort of bereavement counsellor ignores the wishes of the next of kin?"

"But who knows *why* they've chosen the doll?" Hobbs answered. "Perhaps your father *wanted* them to have it, but on private instructions. What would be your answer to that?"

There was a pause.

"How *could* I answer?" she muttered.

"Indeed. That's why if this matter goes to court, which now seems highly likely after having ejected them from the house, then you'll lose."

"I don't think they'll sue," Hugh remarked. "They didn't mention legal proceedings. They just said they were sure that Ellen would come round by herself, or something like that: that she'd respect her father's wishes." He considered this statement. "Now to my ears, that sounds like a veiled threat."

Hobbs wasn't impressed. "Or perhaps they were simply expressing the hope that Ellen should respect her father's wishes." He looked down at the will and his eyes flashed at them in turn. "I would express that hope too, and not only because I predict a troubled and unsuccessful litigation."

"They're not getting them," she said to the desk. "They're not getting them, and that's that."

Hobbs studied the will for a few moments longer before gathering up his papers with a sigh of disappointment. "Well, you've heard my advice on that subject. Perhaps you'll be lucky and they won't take the matter any further. Now, returning to those letters, and this possible intruder. That isn't a matter for me: you need to contact the police."

She nodded, but with no intention of involving the police; the police might take the typewriter away, to have it analysed or something. She pictured them picking it up and hauling it up the stairs, then out through the open door, its keys chattering furiously.

"We're going to change the locks," Hugh said, unhappy over her refusal to contact the authorities, the cause of a heated discussion last night. "We're also going to see about getting an alarm installed."

Hobbs concurred by sitting back with a reflective twirl of his pen. "If the charity contacts you again then give them my details. You may wish to remind them that there's a protocol to be followed, given that I'm acting in the estate. They shouldn't have contacted you directly."

Ellen had stood up and was shouldering her bag. "But haven't they already been in contact with you?"

The solicitor answered with a blink of his eyes and a small shake of his head.

"But they must have ... to collect my inventory."

The solicitor put the cap on his pen. "The inventory is still on file, my dear. Your father specified that you should prepare one. The instructions were *very* specific on that point. But the charity hasn't called for it. They must have read the notice of the death and decided to go straight to your house."

"I don't understand," she murmured.

"What don't you understand?"

She tried to answer, but found nothing to say.

Ellen had only a vague recollection of stepping out of the front door of the solicitor's office and following the cobbles of Upper Frog Street, for it wasn't until she smelled the salt of the sea and saw the steps leading up to her front door that she came out of her daze. On the sofa, in the day room, she was herself again, the journey home an unpleasant dream.

"*What* didn't you understand?" Hugh asked, for the umpteenth time.

"Wells knew about Cody," she muttered.

"So? He'd probably seen the doll when he was helping your father."

"No, I don't mean that. He knew the description ... *my* description, on the inventory." She whispered it to herself.

Honey blonde mohair wig...

Almond-shaped blue paperweight eyes...

"That could fit any number of antique dolls," Hugh remarked with a smile. "He read it in a catalogue or something."

"Delightful," she murmured, finishing the description to herself.

Delightful...

She heard Wells whisper the word in synch with her, as if he had borrowed her thoughts for the occasion.

The old Trustee would play a part in her dream that night, as she walked to the wardrobe door; he would be on the landing, considering her mother's portrait and reciting Cody's description on the inventory with a dry voice. The doll was again standing on her chair, pointing at the wardrobe door, the beautiful Sorrel Page covering the doll's face with the bat wings of her indigo gown, whispering, "Hush now..."

Hush now...

The wardrobe door was open and the air was rancid with the smell of her corpse.

This is our pain...

Ellen's eyes opened onto the dark room. She replayed the dream in her mind, then with a groan climbed out of bed and made her way downstairs to the hall. In her eagerness to leave the bedroom she neglected to kiss her mother's portrait, remembering only as she calmed herself on the bottom stair but one, looking at the front door. She was surprised and confused by how easy it had been. Her lips going to those two fingers, going to the sheen glass, had always come so naturally, as naturally as breathing itself.

"Ellen, is that you?" Hugh called quietly, from the sofa in the day room.

"Go back to sleep."

"Are you okay?"

"I said go back to sleep!"

A mumble of discontent was heard in the day room as her eyes returned to the front door. Beyond the door, she saw only a bottomless fog.

XX

And not by works

"Oh, you're not going out again, Tarny?" Mrs Hughes grumbled, as she came through the door with her shopping to see her daughter making sandwiches. "I won't be late," Tarn answered.

"Aren't you going to eat with us? This is the third time this week: your da thinks you've left home." The walk across the common had made her hollow cheeks and stork neck red with exertion.

Stefan chuckled from the Formica kitchen table fixed to the wall, where he was making a kit aeroplane. Mrs Hughes turned to him and considered the gluey mess of newspapers; she smiled in spite of herself and with a sigh put the shopping down on the floor. The council house was small and busy and they were used to being in a clutter.

"I've left a hotpot in the oven," Tarn muttered. She glanced at the table. "We'd have to eat on our laps anyway."

"It's not that, Tarny. I worry about you, that's all. You work so hard. And if you're not working you're with those friends of yours…"

"Now don't start. They're good people."

"They're not church people."

"Marmy, the church hasn't got a monopoly on helping others. Some people do it just because it's the right thing to do." She was referring to the volunteer organisation based in Carmarthen, which operated outreach programs to the homeless and needy. It met only once a week but organised quite a few charitable events, which took her all around West Wales and used up the few weeks holiday she had.

"And not by works, lest any man should boast," her mother quoted.

"I know. I know you can't get to Heaven with good works. But what's *wrong* with good works?"

Mrs Hughes shuffled the shopping bags with her feet, unable to think of an answer. "It's all very well, this outreach program, but I wish you'd spend some time with girls your own age. Going out perhaps..."

"What, drinking and dancing? Meeting boys?"

Stefan sniggered.

"I didn't say that. Anyhow, I've been hoping you'd meet a nice boy in the church." Her hand cupped around her long chin as she considered her daughter, who so reminded her of herself at that age; a genetic bond refused to let her believe that her daughter was anything but beautiful, in her own unique fashion, a selective memory having blocked out her own pubescent difficulties in finding romance. "Are you seeing those people this evening?"

"No, not this evening." Tarn folded up the sandwiches and placed them in her rucksack.

"Where are you going?"

"Just out."

"With sandwiches?"

"I'm visiting someone and I don't want to be a burden. I'm taking them in case I get hungry."

"Is it that Sorensen girl again? Stefan says you've become quite friendly with her."

Tarn glanced at her brother. "What if I have? She's nice."

"She's a spoilt little madam."

"Marmy!"

Mrs Hughes' hands went sternly to her narrow hips. "She's another one who doesn't go to church. And she's rude and ungrateful: she barely spoke a word to me at her father's wake."

"You hardly spoke to *her*."

"You leaned over backwards for her father. You virtually lived in that house and I didn't hear her say one word of thanks at the wake. Not one word."

A flash memory had Mrs Hughes considering the proud, made-up Sorensen girl at her father's wake.

All is vanity, she thought, but her dislike of the girl went beyond an objective assessment of her sin. A twitch on an invisible umbilical cord told her that the pouting Sorensen girl meant danger; it warned her of her children's doom. *My Tarny*, was all she could manage to say, as she protectively took her daughter's shoulder, unable to articulate her fears.

"Ellen's really nice," Tarn insisted, "when you get to know her."

"Oh, it's *Ellen* now."

"She *is* nice," Stefan murmured, smiling shyly as he twirled the propeller of his model. "She wants me to build some shelves for the pantry. I've given her … I've given her an *estimate*."

Mrs Hughes looked suspiciously at her son, then at her daughter. "So it's Ellen now," she repeated. "Is she your friend or your employer?"

Tarn shook her head. "Mr Sorensen was my employer, and still is, given that I'm paid up by him until the end of the year. Ellen's made me her friend, that's all."

She lifted her rucksack over one shoulder.

And as her friend, I'm going to find out who broke into her house.

Tarn had been waiting on the bench in the Penally clearing for several hours and was eating her sandwiches when she took Ellen's call. The voice was a distant crackle, the sycamores interfering with the reception.

"You're breaking up," Ellen said. "Where are you?"

Tarn looked ahead of her, the grave of Nigel Sorensen just in view. "I'm outside," she said simply.

"Can you hear me?"

"Yes, I can hear you." Her eyes narrowed as a shadow darkened her line of vision; she leaned to her left and angled her head slightly.

"Look, I went to see the solicitor yesterday," Ellen said in a loud voice, "and he told me about the time he came to the house to change the will. He said that my dad had Cody in the kitchen. He reckons he carried Cody around the house with him … he even *introduced* her, as if she were a real person. Is that true?"

She didn't answer.

"Tarn?"

"Yes. Yes, he did." She didn't raise her voice, making no concession to the bad connection. "I moved Cody back to your room, and put the picture back, before you came home."

"The *picture* was in the kitchen too?"

"Yes. Your father carried it with the doll."

There was a silence on the other line. She leant further to her left, her eyes almost slits as she tried to find the creator of the shadow at the grave.

"Why didn't you tell me?" Ellen asked.

"You didn't ask." She straightened up with a look of satisfaction as the owner of the shadow came into view.

Yes, I can see you…

"I'm not going to let them take her," Ellen said, her tone cautious.

"I understand."

"I mean it."

She nodded. "I understand," she repeated quietly. "Really, I do."

"I can't hear you, Tarn."

"I know." She switched off her mobile, waited for it to say *Bye Bye Tarny,* and then returned to watching the grave.

The man was down on his knees now, dusting away the top layer of earth that filled the trench where the remains of Nigel Sorensen lay in their elm coffin. She remembered her sandwich and took another careful bite.

"I knew it was you," she whispered shortly. The man stood

up from the grave and shook his head. "I knew it was you," she repeated as Martin Sorensen's face came fully into view, as he leant back down to check the earth.

What were you looking for in the house?

What did you find?

"Should I tell Ellen?" she wondered aloud, eating the last corner of her tuna sandwich. She supposed there was little to be gained in Ellen knowing that her uncle was prowling around Tenby, intent on her being ignorant of the fact; that he had waited for them to go out before he had sneaked in, using the key he had kept after the funeral. That he had tampered with the phrenological skull.

She nodded slowly. No, there was little to be gained.

"I can see you," she murmured, as she watched him walk away.

When Ellen recounted the conversation to Hugh she didn't mention that Tarn had sounded a little distant, even unhelpful, having put her non-responsive tone down to the bad connection.

She had noticed that Hugh didn't have many nice things to say about her new friend and she felt protective of her, wanting to shield her from criticism. She had come to rely on her; with Tarn holding her hands she had unburdened her grief, guilt and regrets over her parents and the result had been a thousand times more therapeutic than the professional but detached sessions with Wendy. She had a real friend who had known her father and was genuinely interested in her.

"So it looks like Mr Hobbs was telling the truth," she concluded.

"But why didn't Tarn *tell* you that your dad took the doll everywhere?"

They were in the kitchen and Hugh was frying lamb mince for his famous homemade Moussaka, her contribution having been to chop the parsley. With a shake of the pan, he threw her a questioning glance.

"Why *should* she tell me? What difference does it make? Having the doll near him made Dad happy: that's all *I* care about." She was sipping wine and a mellow Coldplay track was drifting from her portable stereo; she had loosened up during the afternoon and was finding not just the wine but the smell of the seasoned lamb, onions and garlic intoxicating. She was starting to think that she could stay in this kitchen, in this house, forever.

There's no reason to leave …

I am the custodian …

She shuddered with the memory of a recent dream.

Hugh tossed the mince with a dissatisfied shake of the pan. "Just because Mr Hobbs was telling the truth about the doll doesn't mean he's telling the truth about the inventory. He *must* have told the Trustees about the inventory, if they repeated it, word for word. What other explanation is there?"

"Who knows?" she murmured, wincing. "As you said before, Cody's description is probably commonplace … I'd probably seen it in an advert or something and remembered it." She took a longer sip of her wine and found her smile. "I'm glad you're here," she said, refilling her glass and enjoying watching him cook. It was a relief to escape into the smell of the food, with the help of the wine.

He threw her a quick smile. "You're glad? Really? And it's not just my Moussaka?"

A salacious sip of her wine served as her answer. "Do you think we're crazy, my dad and me? Do you, Teddy?"

It was her affectionate name for him; she had only used it twice before and on both those occasions, he recalled, she had been tipsy.

"I think you've both got an unhealthy obsession with that doll," he remarked, turning off the heat and moving the pan to a rear hob to let the mince cool.

There was a silence.

"Her name's Cody," she said quietly. "She's not *that doll*."

He sighed, recognising in her tone the end of the intimacy. Glancing up, he noticed her reproachful look. She shrugged to acknowledge that she was over-reacting but was unable to rescue

230

her smile. "I can't keep walking on egg shells with you," he said quietly. "At some point you're going to have to let me in."

She made to answer, but changed her mind. "I know," she said to her wine.

"Are you going to tell me what's going on with this typewriter?"

She looked up. "What do you mean?"

He found his glass of wine and briefly examined its colour. "These letters … finding them on the mat, *under* the mat, in your doll's sleeve … was this a game you played when you were a kid?" He took a deep breath of courage. "Did you and your dad send each other notes, like treasure hunts or something? It's okay, Ellen, you can tell me, I'll understand. You want your dad to be here and the game makes it seem as if he is. I understand, really I do…"

She looked at him sullenly for a few moments. "Is that what you think of me?" she murmured, a tear lurking in one of her eyes. "You think I've made all of this up…?"

He hesitated. "I'm sorry," he said, realising from her reaction how far off beam he was. "I'd make a crap detective, wouldn't I?"

"Yes, you would."

"I mean, really crap."

"Oh yes."

Her glass was empty. She refilled it with a weary shake of her head.

"If all this isn't made up, then I need to tell you something," he announced quietly.

"What do you mean?"

"I believe you now," he said warily. "I didn't before, you see … not entirely, anyway. I knew that you were having genuine problems with this charity, but I thought that these letters were just some therapy game you were playing. That maybe you wanted to believe that your father was talking to you, just like I know how the doll helped you when your mother died…"

"Hugh, what are you talking about?"

He nodded, wondering what his fate would be. "Now don't get

cross, but I've found another letter. I found it last night, under the paper." From under the stack of watermarked paper, he produced the folded letter; she snatched it from him, saw that it was addressed to *Miss Eleanor Sorensen* with a 31p stamp, then pulled it open. "It must have been left last night, when whoever got in here left the other one under the mat. I'm sorry, Ellen, I didn't mean…"

"It doesn't matter." She gave a shrug that suggested she was too tired to be angry, although secretly she was quite impressed with the way he had spoken out and challenged her. It was a reasonable theory, that therapy idea, with a body of evidence in support; perhaps he wasn't the doormat or the fool that she had supposed.

"What does it say?"

She handed it to him.

```
Th  t mpl  is r v rs d

Look insid
```

"The 'e's are missing," he remarked. "The temple is reversed, look inside… inside *what*?"

She gently touched one of the double-jointed fingers of the typewriter. This finger was only half formed, the metal having dissolved half way between the first and second joint into an ochre stump. It was an isolated wound, with nothing else in the machine having been affected, as if the finger had been dipped in acid before being fitted.

"What's happened to that?" he asked, as his eyes followed her hand.

"It's as if it's dissolved."

"Acid?"

She shook her head slowly. "There was rust on this key, yesterday."

"Rust? Are you sure?"

"At least it looked like rust."

His finger also now traced the half-eaten metal, carefully keeping a half-inch space between the key and his skin. "Must be acid," he murmured, "although it has been underground, I suppose, and it's really old. Maybe it's reacted with something in the earth. Better if we don't touch it, just to be on the safe side."

She looked at the letter, frowned, then picked up a page of the watermarked paper and carefully fed it into the mechanism.

"What are you doing?" he asked.

"I'm just curious. Push some keys."

"Why?"

"The keys," she said impatiently. "Just push some."

He found a teacloth and wrapped it round his hand. He tapped the 'J' button. Nothing happened.

"You've got to push it quite hard," she explained.

He thumped the 'J' with his protected index finger and the jointed metal key made a slow arc towards the paper, speeding up quickly in the final few degrees and stamping a solitary

ȷ

He chuckled, finding the erratic movement of the key amusing.

"Do some more," she suggested.

He hit more keys, getting the hang of the tight mechanism.

yylp

Pressing the shift key, he typed

GPQX

"Not a bad little machine," he said, "considering that my printers usually have a life expectancy of about eighteen months. How old *is* this, by the way?"

She considered the letter again:

Th t mpl is r v rs d

Look insid

"Try the 'e' key," she said, ignoring the small talk.

He scanned the letter keys and smartly punched the round 'e' button. This time the paper didn't respond with an ink-impressed letter.

"Try again."

He hit the key again, but with greater force.

The half-dissolved finger reared up from the machine, paused, and returned uselessly to its nest: a snake that had lost its fangs.

XXI

Your own cadaver

The Land Rover had been left in the car park where the roads ended and the forced hike through the mountain lanes was in the direction of Manorbier, turning off at the cliffs near the beach haven of Barafundle. On a rise overlooking the sea, guarded at first by a clutch of bramble thickets, then revealed in bleak isolation, stood the house of Thomas Wilkinson, the founder of The Divine Sentiment.

Honeyman sat with his overcoat huddled tightly around him, clutching a flask of hot tea. The huge, decaying house would originally have been painted in a duck-egg blue with large, sea-facing windows, but time and complete neglect had turned the stone a bleary yellow; the windows, without exception, were boarded up. From his vantage point on the rise, he could see that most of the roof tiles were missing though no birds had set up residence amongst the moss, and he pictured the various leaks dripping into the bedrooms when it rained. If indeed any bedrooms remained, for he knew it was impossible to get upstairs, the huge double staircase having collapsed. The Trustees, as a matter of principle, did not carry out repairs; the house would be left to rot, as a wine is left to ferment.

He had found the house on foot, having followed the wide tracks of the white hearse he had seen outside the houses of Paula Fields and Teresa Danes, two members of his congregation who had died only weeks after losing their husbands. Paula Fields was a gentle, softly spoken woman whose favourite topic of conversation was the loose state of the country's morals, but in the last weeks of her life she had found other obsessions. She occupied her waking moments with a glass photograph of her husband, her music box and a night sky globe; she insisted that the globe always showed the thirteenth constellation, Virgo.

The globe was a myriad of pearl stars set in anthracite that swivelled when it was touched and it did indeed always return to a position where the light in the room illuminated the thirteenth constellation. He would see the globe again, from a distance when two people were removing it from the house. One of them was a diminutive woman who appeared to be whispering to it as if she were comforting it. At this time, he knew that the children of the late Teresa Danes were in dispute with a charity, refusing to give up an illustrated copy of Robinson Crusoe and he was pondering on that book as he watched the globe being lifted carefully into the boot of the vehicle. Chapter thirteen of the book and the thirteenth constellation: with the number, he found the first link.

His curiosity had led him to Tom Wilkinson's house, where a woman introducing herself as Sorrel Page beckoned him into a huge lobby dominated by an incomplete double staircase. In contrast to the stench of damp and decay, the woman had a fresh smell of apples and was wearing something that resembled a negligee, her bare flesh pressing provocatively against the cream lace. His eyes were on the small of her back as she walked though the double doors to the room beyond and as if her sexuality had cast a spell his eyes remained on those doors until she appeared again. Afterwards, the periphery of his memory would register there was a room to the left, which was creating moving shadows in the lobby where he waited and a corridor to his right, which ended in darkness.

He would explore neither the room nor the corridor, nor would he see what lay beyond the double doors; he was innocent then, expecting only explanations or lies and shortly he would be retreating from the house in confusion and alarm. For he was shown Paula Fields, now in her music box. As the ornate shell lid was lifted, the four opening lines of 'Silent Night' chimed. The final note of the tune was missing – later he would realise there were only thirteen notes left to it – and on the beat of this missing note Mrs Fields' voice briefly drifted through the lobby on a breeze of pornographic obscenities. He could hear her gentle and careful inflections, the character preserved yet mutated.

He had dropped the box and ran but would soon discover that it was not so easily left behind. For it carried a curse: the Trustees' punishment for trespass. The following Sunday a sense of unease was growing in his stomach as he heard the chiming of the music box while the congregation sang 'Thine is the Glory' and again while his deacon read out the notices. He found he was humming Mrs Fields' incomplete 'Silent Night',

Silent night, holy night…

disguising it with the occasional clearing of his throat, hiding his mouth behind a large fist. He was barely a few minutes into his sermon, one involving Peter and the other fishermen's first meeting with Christ, when the bells sounded again.

All is calm, all is –

"I will make thee fishers of men … I will make thee … I will make thee…"

On the rise Honeyman's hand covered his eyes, even now finding the memory so painful; he had repeated the sentence with the music box chiming in his head, the word *fishers* transforming on his tongue.

Fuckers … fuckermen … I will make thee fuckers of men…

He had escaped down the aisle after several equally disastrous attempts to recover himself, only the children looking at him with shocked delight. The Elders had visited him the next day and had listened patiently to his explanation that he was under some mesmeric spell. The spell, he said, must work in the same way that hypnotists can induce strange behaviour on hearing a certain word or trigger. They wanted to believe him; after all, he was the celebrated Flint Pastor, his church boasting an enormous congregation for the size of the community. He was also highly respected in secular circles, sometimes acting as an expert witness for insurance companies. It was well known that he had rejected highly lucrative offers for putting his expansive knowledge of art and antiques to good use.

His nomadic existence wasn't even a possibility in his mind at this point but he was aware that he was thinking differently. Sorrel Page's curse had come with the equally horrific gift of knowledge: an insight into the history of the coven, the structure of its temples and the powers of its servants. He was encouraged by the Elders' silence and described the incident with the music box. He went on to explain his then fledgling theories on The Divine Sentiment, which included a reference to Robinson Crusoe, a white off-roader that resembled a hearse and a rotting house in Manorbier, where Paula Fields was held captive with her husband. The Fields were not lucky in their children, he remarked as he finished, for they had given up their parents without a fight.

His experience with the music box had made him careless of the practical realities of imparting information. He learned the lesson quickly and painfully. Not only did any doubts that the Elders had about dismissing him promptly vanish, but the Synod also issued a nationwide circular that he was never to preach in their churches again.

The circular, as it turned out, was unnecessary; he could not sit in a church even as part of the congregation without hearing Mrs Fields' 'Silent Night'. He had tried, only to remain standing at the back of a church after the first hymn had finished, waiting until enough people had turned round to look at him

All is calm, all is –

then vomiting out every swear word he had ever heard, and even some he hadn't.

The entire world was his church now, he supposed. It was a strange inversion that Sorrel Page must have found ironically amusing, just as it had amused her to twist dear Mrs Fields' words in her music box. Whereas most people swore but would never dream of doing so in church, he was the reverse.

He realised his mobile was ringing. Forgetting which pocket he had left it in, it rang a little too long before he answered it.

"Honeyman," he said quickly, finding with relief that the line wasn't dead. He sensed that he had caught the caller on the very last ring.

"Mr Honeyman…"

"Just Honeyman," he replied, automatically.

"Okay," came the cautious voice. "My name's Hugh Sims, I'm a friend of Ellen Sorensen's."

Honeyman put down his flask and wrapped his overcoat more tightly around him, rapidly trying to organise his thoughts. From the echo in the voice he knew that Hugh's mobile was on speakerphone. "Hello Hugh. Does Miss Sorensen know you're speaking to me?"

"Yes, she's here with me." There was a pause. "But she doesn't want to speak to you."

"I understand. She's the custodian: things are difficult for her at the moment."

"Difficult how?"

"I know the typewriter has been found and that the collodians have been switched…"

"How do you know about the typewriter?"

"It doesn't matter. I know. The vessels will attempt to come to terms with the cheap glass imitations, but will fail." He shook his head. "They'll go into distress."

"Distress?"

Honeyman cast a glance at the house. "Their earthly image is now contained in worthless glass, yet it's the *same* image, so they'll try to hold on to it." His voice slowed. "Imagine sleeping with a corpse of yourself: waking up every morning next to your own cadaver."

There was no answer on the other line, but he thought he heard Ellen whisper something.

"Are you still there, Hugh?"

"Yeah," came the response, the scepticism and caution evident. "So … how will we recognise it … if they go into … what did you call it?"

"Distress. All vessels are unique, so I can't make any predictions. The best I can say is that you'll know … the vessels won't allow themselves to be separated from their images."

"Their what?"

"The collodians. The photographs in the glass."

"What have the photographs got to do with any of this?"

"The souls are trapped in the vessels, but they've been tricked into believing their bodies still live, that they have an existence here … on this plane. Body and soul, Hugh … they can't be separated."

There was a silence.

"I can imagine what you're thinking." Honeyman was thick-skinned after a year of such conversations and was waiting patiently for the laughter or the abuse that would end this call. Hugh's tone, however, remained neutral.

"Look, I'm ringing because I'm worried about Ellen, because she's getting the same symptoms of agoraphobia, or whatever it is that her father had. I'm trying to persuade her to see a doctor because maybe it's something genetic, but she's refusing to leave the house. You said that you knew what was wrong with her father."

"Who told you that?"

"Ellen's odd job man mentioned that he talked with you in a coffee house."

He nodded, but didn't comment.

"Well, *do* you know what's wrong with her?"

"She'll be well again, Hugh. When she lets go, she'll be herself once more."

"What do you mean 'lets go'? Lets go of what?"

"These are difficult times for her, as I said, and she must keep her faith. Miss Sorensen, if you're listening, you must keep your faith. The vessels won't lash out with hatred, they'll try to warn you, I think. Your mother and father were good people and they loved you, but in the end they'll do whatever is necessary … whatever it takes, to return to their images."

There was a long pause as he heard a muttered dialogue that he couldn't make out, though most of the words sounded as if they were whispered by Ellen. He suspected he had gone too far.

"We've had some more letters," Hugh said reluctantly, returning to the phone.

"What do they say?" Honeyman asked, suspecting Hugh was being prompted by Ellen.

"The temple is reversed. Look inside."

"The temple is reversed," Honeyman muttered to himself.

"What does that mean?"

"A temple is a holy place. For everything holy there's a reverse, a reflection of what that holy thing could be if it were perverted … corrupted."

His thoughts trespassed to Mrs Fields' music box, as he heard her utter those profanities in her sad, gentle voice.

All is calm, all is –

Your greasy cock, Honeyman…

"It's important that the holy know they can be unholy," he continued, shaking the memory away. "That is Satan's triumph over the Lord's creation."

"Who?"

"Satan, Hugh." Two bushy eyebrows raised in expectation.

"Okay, I'm ringing off now," came the quiet response.

"I understand. Call me when you're ready to talk."

"We're not going to be calling again. Don't come near the house again, is that clear?"

"As you wish."

"We *will* call the police," Hugh warned.

"As you wish."

The call ended, Honeyman looked at his mobile for a few moments before returning it to his pocket, his hand re-surfacing with his hardback book; the cover was Thomas Harris' *Archangel*, though he had pasted the dust cover to the leather some time ago to avoid unwelcome eyes when he was reading. The book underneath was the New Testament.

Sometimes he just needed to hold it, as was the case now. He looked at the crumbling house and shivered with the cold, but also gave a nod of satisfaction. That was the first call he had been hoping for; the second would be Martin Sorensen, ringing with the results of the laboratory tests.

Cody was no more than a dim shadow outline. She was propped against the wing of the wicker chair, pointing at Ellen's sleeping partner under the sheets.

The bed was cold.

This is our pain…

The toes and hands were freezing, Ellen realised, for their bodies were entangled, their arms wrapped around each other's shoulders, legs around each other's calves, heads nestled into each other's necks.

"Hugh, is that you?"

This is our pain…

"Hugh, why are you so cold?" she whispered.

She untangled herself and pulled the bed sheet away.

Her corpse stared back at her.

Ellen woke in the middle of the night, with a start. She switched on her side light and reached down the bed to run a hand through the doll's hair; she saw that her eyes were closed. With a frown, she put a palm to a porcelain cheek, then the forehead, as if Cody were a child she had decided to keep home from school. Shortly, the eyes gently rocked opened.

"What's wrong?" she whispered, trying to dispel the memory of the dream. Honeyman's words drifted back to her.

Like waking up with your own cadaver…

Once more, she was aware of a tingle in her fingers and palm, no longer just a suggestion, some neurological rumour, now she could actually feel it. The bisque porcelain had been vibrating furiously with some kind of energy or friction that had passed into her own skin. It was as if Cody was struggling against something, or struggling to contain something…

She shook her head, knowing that her imagination always went into overdrive when it came to her Jumeau: the tingle was in her fingers, not the doll, and just the residue of a frightening dream. She turned off the side light but got out of bed, feeling her way out of the bedroom. She descended the stairs, again forgetting, in the darkness and in her confusion, to kiss her mother's photograph.

The phrenological skull was a dim outline in the hall but she was determined not to turn on any lights, feeling more comfortable in the darkness. In the doorway of the day room, she whispered Hugh's name. Shortly his head poked up over the sofa.

"Are you okay?" he murmured.

Her hand was on the door. "I'm scared," she admitted.

"Scared. Why?"

"Can I come in with you?"

She didn't wait for his response and his eyes squinted as he attempted to adjust to the light. He could see that she was wearing pyjamas with the smiling face of a teddy bear as she slipped under the blanket, but he was naked and there was little remaining room on the three cushions.

"Let's go up to your bedroom," he suggested.

"No, stay here…" she whispered, as she let him kiss her neck and find that part of the elastic in her pyjama bottoms that would gently roll them down.

"There'll be more room," he said, his breath quickening.

"Shhhh…"

He obeyed her command, though he didn't understand it. His feet struggled with the tangle of her pyjamas, finally kicking them off; they were breathing and sighing in unison. When he was on the verge of crying out she would kiss him, whispering another *shhh* in his ear. His libido was convinced he was a teenager with his parents upstairs. With Ellen naked in his arms, the act silent and forbidden, he couldn't remember a time he had been so aroused.

"I don't know what love is," she murmured unexpectedly, her words in defiance of her body and the act it was performing with such ease.

"Yes you do," he whispered back. "You do…"

"Then I love you," she replied. "Look after me…"

At some point they had fallen asleep and no dreams troubled her.

When she woke, Hugh was already up and making breakfast. He had gone to a local baker to buy some croissants and the smell of warm bread and fresh coffee was wafting up from the kitchen.

This is *our* smell, she thought, as she stretched on the sofa; not some contrived aroma to give the house that 'lived in' feel.

The house *is* lived in, she decided, with a smile of satisfaction. *No corpses here…*

"Is there any reason why we had to be so quiet last night?" he asked, after they had kissed in the kitchen. "Who were you afraid would hear?"

"I don't know," she answered uneasily. "It's my parents' house. Habit, you know."

"You're in the habit of making out on the sofa, then?"

"Never like that," she admitted with a smirk, taking some plates to the table. "What about you? Didn't your parents have a sofa?"

He didn't answer.

"Hugh?"

As she turned, she saw that he was studying the typewriter. "What's the matter?" she asked.

His hand was hovering over the machine. Overnight, more of the metal fingers had dissolved and now boasted red rust. The paper was still in the machine and he pressed some of the keys. "Y, S and P are missing," he said at length. "Oh, and L … and R," he added, tapping a final key.

He noticed her unease. "Hey, it's some slow-acting acid or something," he said, in his most reassuring voice. "Whoever got in here that night must have coated some of the keys. Either that or it's just rusting away. Perhaps your father had a way of preserving it we don't know about and that's why it's going to pot."

She was unconvinced. "It's going into distress, just like Honeyman said," she whispered.

He paused, carefully thinking through his reply, looking at the typewriter. "Writing instruments do not go into distress," he remarked in a level voice. "This is a *thing*, not a *person*. It's made of metal, Ellen. *Metal.* Just like your doll is made of porcelain."

"And wood and glass and real hair," she muttered.

"Okay." He was still looking at the typewriter. "How is she? Is she melting?"

She gave him a tired look, not in the mood for an argument. "Cody's fine," she conceded, but she was aware of the tingle in her fingers as if it were a memory locked into her skin.

"That Honeyman's off his head: I don't know what possessed you to listen to him. Besides, didn't you say that he gave you some bullshit before, about swapping photographs or something?"

She nodded, reluctantly. "He said the Trustees would try to switch them, but when they first visited they didn't even seem interested in them."

He nodded. "Why they'd want to swap them *at all* is a mystery to me." He had wondered why she'd raved about those two glass photographs during their telephone conversations; he hadn't said anything but couldn't see what all the fuss was about.

"What do you mean?"

"They're just cheap glass, Ellen."

"Cheap glass?" she replied incredulously. "Watch." She took her father's collodian from the counter and held it with an outstretched arm.

"Careful…"

"It won't break. They're like, indestructible."

"Surely not…"

"No, really, it's a special process they use. Watch."

The collodian portrait dropped to the floor with the sullen acceptance of gravity and error. Hugh instinctively backed his chair away as the first corner collided with the tiled floor and then the whole thing landed square on the stone with a dull clatter. The portrait had shattered into three pieces and countless grains of traumatised glass.

He sighed sadly; she was staring at the pieces in disbelief.

"Maybe we can salvage it," he suggested.

She had a horrified expression as her eyes went slowly to the ceiling.

The collodian of Nia Sorensen was also nothing more than a piece of cheap glass, light in her hand and, on closer inspection, with the colour image faded and blurred. Ellen shook her head as she considered her mother's image, supposing that she was so used to seeing it in vivid colour that she just imagined it that way, and so hadn't noticed when it changed.

"They swapped them," she said. "The bastards swapped them."

"We don't know that." Hugh was still sceptical about the story of the indestructible glass that wouldn't even smudge.

"They must have done it when they were last here. Honeyman was right." She paused, thoughtfully. "Though he expected them to swap the photographs the *first* time they called." Her eyes narrowed. "But they didn't swap them because … because Dad's typewriter hadn't been found."

"What's the typewriter got to do with it?"

Her eyes darted to him. "Why start the clock ticking, when they're not ready? Honeyman said that they wouldn't allow themselves to be separated for long."

"*What* wouldn't?"

"The vessels…"

"Vessels? What vessels? Ellen, what are you talking about?"

She looked away and shook her head.

He groaned. "You're not saying you're taking that man seriously? Tell me you're kidding – please!"

She didn't seem to hear him. "It must have been Wells who swapped it," she murmured. "I was watching him but that bitch distracted me with Cody." She nodded, remembering how Stefan running into the pantry had meant that she and Tarn had to follow, leaving the Trustees alone in the kitchen; that was when her father's collodian would have been switched. She now visualised the Trustees' clothes: the man's roomy overcoat with the big pockets; the woman's large handbag.

Is that why I've been forgetting to kiss Mum's portrait? I always thought it was something natural ... but I was wrong ... I had to start remembering to do it...

"Mr Hobbs has got to act now," she decided. "This is theft." She blanched at the prospect of another walk through the town. In fact, she couldn't even picture the road outside the house; only the bottomless mist beyond the front door. "Will you go?" she asked.

"And say what?" he answered, uncomfortably.

With a shrug, she acknowledged the dilemma: how was any of this to be explained? And if explained, who would believe it? She took the photograph from its hook and a folded letter, which had been jammed between the picture, hook and wall, floated down to the floor. The letter was from her father's typewriter and addressed to *Miss Eleanor Sorensen* with a 13p stamp. She picked it up.

"It must've been planted at the same time as the others," she said as she unfolded it.

```
Th   t m    i    v    d

   ook in id

   M    ock t
```

She frowned. "More letters missing..."

Hugh was looking at the message. "We don't need your solicitor," he said.

"What do you mean?"

His finger traced the broken words on the watermarked paper. "This is a logic puzzle. We can work it out ourselves."

XXII

No loose tongues

"The first letter appeared stage by stage," Hugh explained as they sat at the kitchen table in front of the typewriter, "and this one's doing the same. Look…" and he held up the first instalment of this new letter:

```
The temple is reversed
```

Then the second:

```
Th  t mpl  is r v rs d
```

```
Look insid
```

"But the format is also mimicking the condition of the typewriter … the missing keys. When this letter arrived only the 'e' in the typewriter had gone. So the 'e's in the words disappear. That's why we haven't got all of *inside*."

"Because the typewriter can't punch the letter 'e'," Ellen agreed, with a frown.

"Well, that's what whoever's sending us the letters wants us to think. The missing keys are like a cipher. They must have treated the machine with some sort of dissolving acid … then timed the keys to dissolve … dissolve in a certain order…" He hesitated, aware that he was stretching the proposition to its limits.

"Why?" she asked. "Even if that were possible, why would anyone do it?"

"I don't know," he admitted.

"It doesn't make sense. If someone wants to communicate with me, why not just talk to me? Why put it in code?"

He acknowledged the problem with a quick tap of his fingers on the table. "Well, what's your theory?"

"You don't want to hear my theory."

"Try me."

She shrugged and said, "I think Stefan was on the right track, when he said these were letters written by my dad in Heaven."

"Ellen, now come on…"

"Give me a better theory and I'll believe it," she snapped. "My father's trying to write to me on the typewriter but he's stuck with the keys that have dissolved."

Hugh nodded briefly but didn't comment.

"If you want to go back to Cardiff, then I won't stop you," she said guardedly. "I wouldn't blame you. I know you think I'm crazy."

"You're not crazy, though maybe someone out there wants you to *think* that you are." He took her hand and pressed it. "And I'm not going anywhere. But your father's dead, Ellen."

"I know," she murmured.

"Dead," he repeated.

She snatched her hand back. "Honeyman said that the vessels would go into distress, okay?" She touched one of the dissolved metal fingers. "Maybe this is what he meant. He said that every vessel was unique, that he couldn't predict what would happen, but we'd know it when it happened. Maybe losing the keys is the typewriter's way of going into distress. Dad wants to tell us something but the typewriter's stopping him."

Hugh didn't comment.

"Anyway, let's carry on," she muttered, to put an end to the silence. "For the sake of argument, let's say this is someone who's just pulling my chain, okay?"

Looking relieved, and clearly needing this assurance, Hugh nodded and picked up the latest letter.

Th   t m   i   v   d

ook in id

M   ock t

"Right," he said, finding his pen. "First off, let's write down the keys that are missing." He checked the missing keys with experimental taps, writing the letters down as he found them. The crinkled rice paper greedily soaked up his ballpoint ink.

Leprsy

They both considered the cipher in silence for a few moments.

"Any reason why you wrote them out in that order?" she asked.

He shook his head. "Leprosy," he murmured. "Well, almost."

"Pretty appropriate, isn't it? I mean the typewriter's got leprosy, hasn't it? With everything dropping off, I mean."

"Coincidence," he said but thinking that he could have written the six letters in hundreds of different combinations, for there was no configuration on the keypad that lent itself to that order. "Are things dropping off your doll?"

"You've already asked me that. I've told you: Cody's fine."

At least she seems *fine…*

She slowly clenched and unclenched a fist, trying to erase the memory of the tingle in her fingers and palm.

"With the cipher we should be able to work out what this last line is meant to say," he said, taking his ballpoint to the letter. "Let's write in the letters we know are missing, okay?"

"Okay."

The temple is reversed

Look inside
M   ock t

Leprsy

They both studied the last line, cross-referencing with the cipher and silently mouthing the words and letters that were possible candidates.

"I think it's two words," he said at length.

"Yes, the 'm' is *my* something."

He nodded. "And it must be an 'e' between the 'ock' and the 't'. After all, it's the only vowel we've got, isn't it?" He paused and asked, "Shall I write it in?"

"Okay."

The temple is reversed

Look inside

My ocket

Leprsy

She frowned. "At first I thought it might be *locks*. I was thinking of Cody's hair."

He nodded, the word had also occurred to him. "Did your father have a locket: perhaps with a strand of your mum's hair or something?"

She shook her head.

"And I'm assuming he didn't own a rocket?"

"Oh Hugh … please, please don't," she implored, referring to the sense of humour that had a habit of gate-crashing the most unlikely parties.

"Right, sorry."

They looked at the paper a while longer.

"Pocket!" they said together.

"Look inside my pocket," she declared, uneasily. "What does that mean?"

He was thoughtful for a moment. "One thing I do know is that whoever's writing these letters wants you to *think* that it's your father writing. Hence, *Ellie Sweet*: his name for you. So…"

"So *my pocket* must mean Dad's pocket," she pondered.

He nodded slowly. "Where are your father's clothes?" he asked.

"With Oxfam. Tarn took them, but she said that she emptied out all the pockets. Anything she found she put aside for me."

"Such as?"

"Just some money, a set of cufflinks, some spare buttons: nothing important."

"Perhaps we should try the Oxfam shop?"

She shrugged her agreement but with the feeling that they weren't on the right track. Then her face dropped.

"What's the matter?" he asked.

"There was one set of clothes that Tarn didn't check," she answered quietly.

"Yeah?"

She spoke in a hushed whisper. "Uncle Martin took Dad's morning suit to the undertakers. He did it before I came back. Dad was buried in that suit. It was one he wore to Mum's funeral, it was a grey flannel, really expensive and Mum loved it. He said he'd never wear it again, except at his own funeral, so he'd be wearing it when he met up with her … you know…"

She glanced at Hugh, who was looking at the typewriter, unhappy with the implications of this discovery and the investigation it plotted.

"Look inside my pocket," she muttered, her mind's eye going to her father's grave.

Martin Sorensen was lying on the bed of the Tenby hotel room sipping brandy and watching the laptop and printer set up on the desk. They were waiting for an e-mail command, the lab boys having promised Mikey they would come back to him by noon. He wasn't wearing his spectacles and both machines were blurs.

With a rapid blink of his eyes it dawned on him that he was falling into a trance of brandy-induced boredom and to break the spell he sat up, glancing at his jacket on the chair, where three letters were lovingly folded within the wallet in his inside pocket. These were the letters he had found at the grave, typed with the Sholes & Glidden on the letterhead with the S watermark. They were his brother's letters.

"You're his twin brother," Honeyman had said without introduction or explanation as he approached the grave at their first meeting. "Who better to hear his thoughts?"

Forgive me…

They were such healing words. How could a stranger have known how badly he needed to hear them?

He had dismissed Honeyman as a crank but checked into a hotel on The Esplanade without informing his niece or Mikey. At that point, he was just being curious and didn't care for having to make difficult explanations to his nearest and dearest, but another letter was waiting for him in the peat earth the following evening. The stamp was numbered 1331p and the crease of the fold was much stronger than before, as if an iron spring had somehow been stitched into the paper. He prized it open and it sent him into shock.

Forgive me

Marty Smarty

Marty Smarty. It was Nigel's name for him when they were little, when they were inseparable, given to him when he boasted that he was the smartest even if Nigel *could* always wrestle him to the ground. As teenagers the name was an embarrassment, used by neither of them: later as adults it was all but forgotten. In fact, it took a while for the name to resurface in his memory, located and restored from the recycle bin of his mind with a gasp that emptied his lungs.

And that evening, even though they were locked away in a hotel drawer, the other letters disappeared. All that was left was the final letter with the 1331p stamp: *Forgive me, Marty Smarty*.

The following evening he received another letter

`p us`

which gave him a sleepless night until it disappeared, to be followed by another, again with the stamp 1331p. This one sent him into panic.

`Help us`

He had telephoned Honeyman then, for the ex-minister had left his card in the pigeonhole of his hotel. There would be only one further letter waiting at the grave and this time it was neither an appeal nor an apology, nor was it an echo from the past. At first it read:

`ear th  care`

and it stayed with him for several days. He had believed that the message *earth care* was asking him to tend the grave, to keep the peat smoothly raked, but the message eventually vanished and rematerialised with a second letter and a 1331p stamp as something very different.

It was a warning. Honeyman had nodded sadly on reading this final letter but the warning came as no surprise and was of little interest to him; he was more interested in testing a theory, one that would explain why there were no cremations.

Martin took a reflective sip of his brandy and considered the laptop and the printer. They came into focus as he put on his spectacles. Honeyman's theory had been outrageous, appalling, yet he remembered straightening Nigel's headstone and it made sense;

it was for this reason he had sneaked into the house while everyone was out, using the door key he still had, and photographed the phrenological skull with one of Mikey's x-ray cameras. Honeyman, who was watching the road from his Land Rover had telephoned to warn him that his niece was returning home earlier than expected; he was forced to leave the house in a hurry, but the films were safely stored in his camera.

"You should speak to your niece, tell her everything," Honeyman said as the Land Rover pulled away.

"I don't want her to know. If you're right, I *never* want her to know."

"But she can help…"

"Leave her out of this. My brother's writing to *me* … he wouldn't want her involved. Do you hear?" He had been furious when he heard from Ellen that Honeyman had been to the house a second time, smuggling himself in with the help of the housekeeper. They had only known each other a few days at that point and trust was still being built.

Honeyman was silent for a time. "Have the collodians been switched?" he asked at length.

"Well, they smudge." In the house, he had performed the tests as he had been instructed.

"Then we're too late anyway. Your niece can't help us now." He sighed.

"I'm sorry," he murmured, beginning to realise his mistake in refusing to let Honeyman get near his niece.

"It's not your fault, Martin. I'm *always* too late. It can't just be bad luck…"

His brandy was finished and he thought about Mikey, his partner of the last thirty years. Mikey knew he was staying in Tenby now and was covering for him with the story of the chiropractic courses, but that was because he had told him that he was trying to find Ellen's stalker without alarming her. He had posted Ellen's letter to be examined, only for Mikey to later sheepishly admit that it had disappeared. He couldn't explain it because the lab was completely secure; this was the same day Ellen received *Find Me, Ellie Sweet* and when she also mislaid her other letters.

As he waited now for the e-mail to arrive that would make the printer come to life he wondered whether he had done the right thing, keeping Mikey in the dark. Perhaps he should just tell him everything.

He wouldn't believe me, he reasoned once more.

No one will. Honeyman warned me about that.

He wasn't so sure that he believed it himself; not everything, anyway.

"Your brother must have been not only strong but incredibly resourceful to communicate in this way," Honeyman had explained. "Not only that, he fought off death for a whole year and that's unprecedented in my experience. It's extraordinary."

"Does that mean he can escape them?"

Honeyman shook his head, mournfully. "No, it simply makes their prize all the more worthy. They must've been greedily waiting for your brother to die, knowing that the result would be even better for the lengthy struggle … they're as patient as the hills."

He was downcast at these words; Honeyman gave him a slow half-wink of reassurance.

"But your brother's strength may also be their undoing. If he can ask his daughter to rescue him from where he had been hidden, and if he can write to you for help, then perhaps he can also write to us with a clue."

"A clue?"

"On how to enter the temple … and survive."

"Why not just tell us? Give us the answer?"

"It's not as simple as that, Martin. Just as he was trapped in life, trapped with prayers that worked like locked doors and that manifested themselves in that debilitating disease, he's also trapped in death. The Trustees are very careful, and there are no loose tongues in the temple. No loose tongues. In fact … in fact it's a miracle that he's writing to us at *all*. A miracle I don't quite understand yet."

With this agenda in his mind, Martin had made a careful note of every letter Ellen received, calling her every day, hungry for information. Honeyman had suspected early on that the typewriter was hidden underneath the badly fitting tower of drawers in the kitchen and had met with the housekeeper in order to get an introduction to her brother Stefan. During the conversation in the coffee shop he made a point of talking about secrets to Tarn, while reading Stefan's body language.

"He *has* hidden the typewriter," Honeyman declared after that meeting, "and he hasn't told his sister. Your brother tasked him in the last days of his life and made him swear not to tell anyone."

"Why? Why would Nigel hide the typewriter?"

"In giving away everything that was dear to him he was making certain that the typewriter would be his vessel. With that knowledge, and with Stefan's help, he smuggled himself out of the reaches of the Trustees." They had already discussed the list Ellen had found with all her father's possessions crossed off, apart from the typewriter. "It was doomed to failure, of course: it must have been torment being buried, out of view of his collodian image, and especially so given the phobia he suffered from. No wonder he wrote to her begging her to find him, even though his motive when alive had been to send her as far away as possible." A respectful pause acknowledged the hidden graduation photograph and a father's love that put aside any hope of being fondly remembered. "But he did buy us time. When the Trustees visited they were unable to switch the collodians. They were unable to switch them because they hadn't located the two vessels."

"Has buying time helped us?"

Honeyman had hesitated, unsure of the answer.

The printer was working. Martin jumped up from the bed and snatched up the first page that had fallen into the paper tray: it was a facsimile of the x-ray photograph of the phrenological skull in Nigel's hall, set against a computerised series of boxes. A light grey square showed up in the centre of the forehead; Mikey had highlighted this with a question mark.

It was a shadow from the camera or some other imaging error, Martin supposed, as he pressed his spectacles to the bridge of his nose. He picked up the second page now in the tray. This also had the background dressing of computerised boxes but was a photograph of Nia Sorensen and with a short sigh he gazed at his brother's wife, the wonderful woman he had loved as a sister. A third and final page from the printer was a short handwritten note from Mikey, with a lot of exclamation marks.

The explanations to Mikey could wait, he decided, as he studied the digital findings and his pulse quickened. He grabbed his mobile and pushed a speed dial; it was answered almost immediately.

"Honeyman? I've got it. Yes … yes, it's her. No doubt of it." He was shaking his head as he listened. "No, I'm not going to wait. Not any more, do you hear? I'm going to speak to Ellen and get her out of that house. Then I'm going to the police."

Because he switched off there, he didn't hear Honeyman's plea.

Remember your brother's final letter…
Remember the warning…

The Sholes & Glidden awoke in the middle of the night, having attempted to escape with sleep the ruinous disease that was stalking it. Six of its fingers had already been lost in its waking moments.

The smashed glass of the photograph was still in view, in pieces on the counter, in its broken state no more and no less able to provide relief. Upstairs could be heard the silent wail of the Jumeau doll as she fought her own, very different battle against the sense of separation; their bodies were far away now, with only cadavers left to comfort them. The agony was beyond torment.

More fingers were dissolving away into red rusted stumps, as easily as a crisp dissolves in the mouth. Every jointed finger that was once attached to a letter key was now gone and only the number keys remained. The numbers had been spared to let it chant the number of the temple, as a condemned man mutilated with torture is left his tongue with which to confess his guilt.

Two keys raised and fell, then raised and fell again, in reverse order.

In the hall a letter fell onto the mat. It was a watermarked letter, but not folded and with no smudge stamp. Another letter followed it, then another. The letters fell during that night as snow falls on a magical winter night, creating a paper heap in front of the door. They all read, simply:

1331

As the typewriter worked impotently through the night, the memory of Nigel Sorensen considered the brain tumour that had taken his wife. As she considered him from the hospital bed, the words in her mind that were *I love you* came out of her mouth as *comb your hair*. Her hands were erratic. The pages of her magazine were turned too quickly, with too much force, and as she finished with grim determination she would be at page one again. When the magazine was taken away, her index finger would draw squares on the food trolley, large and small squares, with only her eyes finding the strange impulse a curious development.

"Why are you doing that, Nia darling?" he had asked gently. She had merely shaken her head with a slight raise of her eyebrows, for the body no longer obeyed the mind.

The typewriter was seeing Nia's finger boxes as the 1 and 3 keys rose and fell, and hearing the words in her mouth that didn't correspond with the words in her brain. It was intending to type something quite different, hence the many repeated attempts, but the correct letters continued to elude it, as if it had a tumour of its own.

Only two numbered keys heard the trigger from its metal brain. Some of the fingers that had been beheaded stirred restlessly, as corpses receiving shocks of electricity, but otherwise didn't move.

The letters continued to drift silently down onto the mat through the night as typewriter continued to punch out:

1331

While downstairs, on the kitchen table, the mind of Nigel Sorensen was screaming:

Someone I love is going to die

XXIII

When the paramedics came

Ellen was aware of a cramp in her lower back as her eyes opened, after two nights the sofa was taking its toll. She didn't mind: the sun was shining and she had a delicious feeling of rested peace. Since she had slept in the day room, she hadn't had any dreams.

Maybe it's because I'm happy, she thought, with a stretch. As she took an energising breath, another thought occurred.

It's because I've been in a different room from Cody.

It was Cody directing all the dreams, standing on the wicker chair and speaking with the voice of a little girl. When she awoke, the porcelain skin of the doll was trembling.

Cody was sending me those dreams…

She noticed Tarn pass by the door in the hall and instinctively raised the blanket up to her neck. "Don't mind me," Tarn said.

"Stefan's not in the house, is he?" she muttered, reaching for her watch on the floor.

"Of course not. I wouldn't let him in while you're on the sofa, dressed as nature intended."

Ellen looked at her watch: it was just gone 10 am. "Drunk too much again," she murmured.

"What was that?"

"Nothing." She quickly pulled on her pyjamas and sat up,

glancing guiltily at the door. "Don't know how I ended up on the sofa ... must have been sleepwalking."

"I believe you..."

With a shrug, Ellen reminded herself that this was her home and Tarn wasn't her mother, but she was still unable to rid herself of the faint whiff of sin. "Where's Hugh?" she asked, attempting a carefree voice.

"He's with Mr Hobbs."

"Mr Hobbs? Why?"

There was a pause. "Ellen, there's something you need to see."

"What?"

"There's something you need to see Ellen, now don't get upset. Promise me you won't get up upset."

Ellen hesitated then got up from the sofa and walked to the door, to see a heap of letters so big it looked as if there had been an avalanche. She picked up the nearest letter, then another, then another. None of them were folded or stamped and they all read:

1331

"They're all the same," Tarn said. "Hugh and I checked every one this morning."

Ellen let go of the letter she was holding, letting it drift to the floor, and took a deep breath.

"Now don't panic. That's the official message from Hugh and he told me to pass it on."

"Okay," Ellen replied quietly.

"He thinks they've probably been run off on a printer then pushed through the letterbox in the night, just to freak you out."

"Right."

Tarn blinked slowly. "There are one thousand three hundred and thirty-one of them," she said. "We counted them. There's something else. The typewriter ... all the keys ... that is, all the letter keys ... they've dissolved."

"Only the letter keys?"

"The numbers are still there."

"Of course," Ellen murmured, realising she was in a mild state of shock. "They'd have to leave the numbers, wouldn't they? To type these, I mean." She kicked at the edge of the paper heap and bit on her lower lip, trying to find some courage.

"I'm worried, Ellen."

"Me too. What do you think we should do?"

Tarn made to speak but changed her mind.

"Go on, Tarn."

"I think you should let the charity have the typewriter and the doll."

Ellen answered with a confused shake of her head.

"I understand how important they are to you ... how they're the last link with your parents. I understand that, really I do, but ... but..."

"What?"

"You're never going to get over the loss of your parents if you don't let them go. For the sake of your sanity, let them go."

Ellen thought about this. "This isn't about grief and closure, Tarn. There's a nutcase out there, plain and simple. Or two nutcases," she clarified, as she pictured the Trustees.

"Give them up and leave the house. Just let them have them. I'm afraid of what's going to happen to you if you don't..."

DRING-A-DRING!

Both girls jumped as the hall speaker blasted out the ring tone of the kitchen telephone. The ring seemed to shake Tarn in particular; she looked terrified.

"I'll get it," Ellen said. It was her turn to stay cool and for her friend to panic. "It'll probably just be Mr Hobbs. Didn't you say he had our number? He's with Hugh and wants to speak to me."

"But what if it's ... *them*?"

Ellen frowned grimly. "Then it's them. Okay? Let them bring it on. They're just con artists."

"Ellen, please. They're..."

Ellen was already walking downstairs to the kitchen. Tarn went

263

to the stairs that led to the bedroom floor and sat on the second stair in dejection, her eyes on the letter heap that Hugh had been clearing away from the door when she had arrived this morning.

She wondered how long it had taken Mr Sorensen to tap out all those letters, all one thousand three hundred and thirty-one of them. He must have a bee in his bonnet about something, she supposed, if there were bees in Heaven or Hell; but there was no doubt in her mind that these letters belonged to Mr Sorensen, created in some way by the old typewriter on the kitchen table.

"It's a miracle," she whispered to herself, "Father be praised." As always when she was witness to a miracle, her body went a little cold, her hands slightly numb, in realisation of her frail mortality.

"Father be praised," she repeated quietly, with her tearful eyes closed.

They opened as the sound of the telephone ended abruptly half way through its ring, as it was answered.

"Miss Sorensen?" Wells inquired.

"Oh, it's you," Ellen murmured, her tone indicating that she was on the verge of hanging up.

"I've something very important to tell you. It concerns your dear, dear mother…"

She hesitated, poised to slam the receiver back on its hook.

"She loves you very much." He paused. "That's why she's struggled to spare you pain."

Ellen shook her head angrily. "What are you talking about?"

"She's struggled so … didn't you feel her struggle?"

A chilling sense of calm descended, as the turmoil in her mind vanished; she was aware only of the Trustee's voice.

"In your fingers, perhaps, as you felt her skin? It's now several days since we last visited; she must have loved you a great deal, Miss Sorensen, to have resisted so long."

"My mother's dead," she returned coldly.

"Ah, if that were only true … what a happy daughter you would be." A croak of derision crackled through the receiver. "The body dies, it's true, but the soul is immortal. It is imperishable and it has to go somewhere, for it was built to travel through eternity."

"I don't know what you're talking about."

"We're waiting outside, ready to take them. Your mother and father are very sick now and need the care that only we can provide."

"My mother and...?" she murmured, but inside she felt no surprise. She had known that her mother was in her Cody doll: she had always known.

"Don't resist," he said with a trace of satisfaction, sensing that realisation had come at last. "You'll find that you're ready now, that your time as custodian is over."

She shook her head then shook it again, her eyes coming back to life. "You're not taking them," she snapped.

"If you're in any doubt, try to say the number. Try to say it."

She swallowed, not daring even to think the number in her head and to hear those keys turn again, the walls of her prison moving closer.

"Have you hypnotised me?"

"Believe that if it helps you but have no doubt, Miss Sorensen, that you must let them go. At the moment the vessels are simply warning you, imploring you, to release them." He paused. "Eventually, they will kill you."

"My parents would never hurt me."

"They will kill you," he repeated. "They'll rip your arms and legs from your body if they have to. You cannot comprehend their pain."

This is our pain...

She regrouped, the frail breath of the Trustee in her ear. "My boyfriend's with the solicitor as we speak. We know you've stolen my parents' portraits and he's going to get the law on you."

"Your boyfriend is going to get the law on me," Wells pondered with slow, careful diction, as if the notion were an exotic *hors d'ouvre* he was savouring. There was just the beginning of a dry but delicious murmur in his throat as she slammed the phone back on its hook.

"Who was it?" Tarn asked, as Ellen came up to the hall.

"The Trustees. They're outside. They're actually making threats now." She considered her pyjamas then the sofa blanket that was on the floor of the day room, with embarrassment.

"You don't have to be embarrassed with me, you know," Tarn said.

Ellen had collected her cigarettes and cake foil from the kitchen. She lit one and her eyes narrowed as she exhaled. "But you don't approve, do you?"

"There are lots of things I don't approve of, but I also know that some things are meant to be." Tarn nodded thoughtfully. "I think it was right that you slept on the sofa last night."

"And the night before," Ellen confessed, with a flick of her cigarette into her burnt cake foil. Regaining her composure, she carefully put the foil with cigarette on the floor as she kicked away a few of the letters that were straying from the pile. With a rueful glance at the front door, she came to a decision. "I'm going to get dressed. Then I'm going to ring the police."

She ran purposefully upstairs, without a thought of kissing her mother's portrait as she passed, and hopped onto the bed, where her jeans had been left sprawled. The small of her back found the mattress as she pulled them on.

"I'm not going to let them take you," she said to Cody.

Cody's eyes made no response. The doll was casting a lopsided shadow on the drawn curtains, as if the wig didn't fit any more. "You were here to look after me, now I'm here to look after you," she said, with a quick grimace as she buttoned her jeans. "That's how it should be, isn't it? That's what family is." She paused. "Shit," she murmured, remembering the cigarette she had forgotten to stub out and seeing a flash image of the heap of letters ablaze. She ran out to the landing, the bed shaking with the sudden movement, but as she reached the top stair, Tarn shouted up:

"Don't worry – I put it out!"

Ellen gave a sigh of relief. As she walked back into the room, Cody's shadow was quivering a little, the tremor in the spring of

266

the bed having found its way to the wicker chair. The wig seemed even more lopsided. She pulled off her pyjama top as she returned to the bed and then twisted round in search of a bra.

It was in the process of this turn, with her thoughts elsewhere, that she had her first glimpse of Cody's face. It was a terror only snatched, as something vile is at first a matter of curiosity and then, as it is examined, becomes a thing of dread. Ellen's expression quickly became traumatised, so that it was almost wistful as she froze and then turned slowly to look at her beloved doll.

The mohair wig was disarranged, for Cody's head had shrunk. The eyes were in their peaceful position, the eyelids about one third over the glass, which were as blue as ever, and the small lips were opening in their half smile, but both features were troubled with deep lines stretching out at their corners which gave the doll a fatigued expression. Her skin was bleach white, having completely lost the blush in the cheeks, and was a maze of ravines, hills and valleys carved into the porcelain bisque skin.

She had the wizened face of an old woman.

Ellen was sobbing without tears on the stairs, just her shoulders shaking. Tarn was sitting a few steps behind, comforting her by touching her shoulder. The Trustees were carrying Cody out of the house, their vehicle parked as close as possible to the foot of the steps. The typewriter had already been loaded.

"There now, there now," Sorrel whispered to the doll, which had a blanket over her head. "It's just a little way, just down some steps and then you're safe." She nodded at Wells and they quickly sidestepped out of the house.

Ellen raised a helpless hand in farewell and a shiver went down her spine, the scene reminding her of the day when her mother had collapsed and the paramedics had to carry her out on a stretcher, her eyes open but her body limp and as heavy as a lead weight.

It could just be blood sugar, one of the paramedics had remarked, but she had known that her mother would never come back through that door alive. Still, she had resisted the urge to pull the stretcher back; her mother wanted to go, needed to go, to be cared for and to be safe. The feeling was the same now: Cody loved her but was desperate to leave.

"Sick ... she's so sick. It's just like when the paramedics came."

She walked out of the front door and stood at the top of the steps and saw that the vehicle boot was closed. With a sullen sense of finality, she watched the Trustees drive noiselessly away, without any glance back at the house. She looked down at her feet. It occurred to her that she was outside the house in the plain light of day, the bottomless mist having vanished.

I am no longer the custodian…

"Thirteen ... thirty-one," she muttered; they were simply numbers like any other. With a sigh, she walked back inside, pausing to pick up something that had been left on the mat. It was a letter on her father's watermarked paper but folded and stamped. She put it on the pedestal, where the phrenological skull still lurked.

"Are you alright?" Tarn asked, with a sad expression.

Ellen found an ironic laugh. "No," she admitted, "but I will be. I'm going to let Hugh take me out tonight and get me absolutely fucking plastered."

Tarn looked down; when she looked up, she was smiling. "That's two things I don't really approve of. Drinking and swearing, I mean. But again I think I have to admit that you're absolutely right."

Ellen shut the front door and looked suspiciously at the skull. "They hypnotised me, didn't they?"

"What do you mean?"

"To make me see Cody ... that way. They must've hypnotised me." She frowned as she selected from her memory the particulars of their various visits. "Perhaps they used the piano. I've heard you can be mesmerised with music. And there was something else. It was ... oh, I don't know ... words."

She patted her clothes for her cigarettes then located the packet and the cake foil on the floor. Sitting down on the floor, with

268

fumbling hands she lit a cigarette; it was shaking in her fingers as she smoked it. "*Key* words: words they made me repeat. They made me repeat their telephone number, thirteen thirty-one, even though it wasn't a real telephone number at all. I remember this ... oh God, this chill going down my spine when I said it and after that, I found myself saying things and not knowing why. *I am the custodian.* When I said that, when I repeated it, it felt as if a lock was turning in my head. That I was being locked into a prison." She took a long drag of her cigarette. "Does all this sound crazy?"

Tarn shook her head. "No, it's not crazy. Certain combinations of words are important, I think. Numbers too. They're like prayers." She was still sitting on the stairs. "Don't grieve, Ellen. You had to let them go."

"So, you agree I was hypnotised?"

Tarn blinked slowly. "I'm sure that must be it. Perhaps it's just the mind playing tricks." She was remembering how Ellen had come running down the stairs, hysterical, opening the front door and screaming at the Trustees to come in. Ellen had warned her not to go into the bedroom and so her last sight of Cody had been when the Trustees brought her down, with a blanket over her. She had glimpsed gnarled, withered hands and on the last stair the blanket slipped and she saw the doll's face.

It was the face of a woman over a hundred years old. Older in fact ... much older ... older than anyone could be...

Another miracle, she thought, believing that Ellen would need the theory of hypnosis because her faith, if she had any, was so weak. "Is that a new letter?" she asked, looking at the stamped and folded letter on the pedestal.

Ellen glanced up at the pedestal. "It fell out of Cody as the Trustees were taking her out. It must've been in her sleeve." She stubbed out her cigarette. "I wasn't hypnotised, Tarn. I was caught with the words and numbers, like an animal caught in a trap, but I wasn't hypnotised. I wasn't the only one to see the keys on the typewriter, all dissolved away. Hugh saw it too."

"But didn't Hugh say it was some slow dissolving acid?"

Ellen's expression lost some of its certainty. "Okay, but the blanket slipped when they went past you, didn't it, and I know that you saw Cody. You *saw* her." She took a breath. "What did you see?"

Tarn blinked slowly again, her mind turning quickly.

"Tarn, what did you see?"

Tarn found a reassuring smile. "Nothing that frightened me, Ellen." She pressed back her hair. "Why don't you open the letter?"

Ellen glanced at the letter and with a shrug lit another cigarette, not caring that she was chain-smoking. "Why bother? I know what it'll say. The typewriter didn't have any letter keys left, so what could it possibly say other than *thirteen thirty-one*?"

Tarn nodded slowly. "You think the letters were written on the typewriter?"

"By my father."

Tarn blinked once more.

She isn't in denial. She believes her parents are in the vessels.

"Why are you looking at me like that?" Ellen murmured, uncomfortably.

"I'm sorry. It's just that you surprise me sometimes, that's all."

Once more, she realised that she might have underestimated Ellen Sorensen.

XXIV

All else is shadow

Martin Sorensen was out of hiding and waiting patiently at Ellen's kitchen table, occupying himself with his brother's letters.

He had made his approach along the beach and waited until the road was clear before making his dash for the steps that led up to the front door. Ellen had changed the lock but had told him there was a key under the slab of the fifth step, and in the hall he disabled the alarm with the code she had shared with him. As the alarm beeps ended, he cast a glum look at the skull. A quick inspection revealed that the doll and the typewriter were gone.

It was as Honeyman had predicted. It didn't matter that Ellen was their daughter: once the collodians were switched, it would be like holding on to an object that was steadily getting hotter, until the skin burned, until the bones boiled.

Nevertheless, they had now made a key discovery: the Trustees were handling the skulls of the recently deceased, stolen from their graves and then artificially aged and worked with phrenological markings. Ellen, as the next of kin, could order an exhumation to prove that her mother's body had been decapitated; tying this in with his photographs and Mikey's lab analysis, the police could make an immediate raid of the house near Manorbier, where Honeyman said the vessels were stored. The Trustees would be arrested, the vessels returned to their rightful owners.

Honeyman had rung as Martin walked along the beach, insisting that it wasn't enough to know what the Trustees were doing with the skulls; they needed to work out what it *meant*. He had believed the phrenological skulls were no more than motifs, totems of The Divine Sentiment's origins, like the books, charts and plaster busts, but perhaps he was wrong. After all, the Trustees took a great risk in raiding the graves.

Why? Why would they go to so much trouble, only to give the disguised skulls back to the next of kin?

"Because they're maniacs!" he had growled as he negotiated the uneven sand. "For God's sake man, they've got the skull of my brother's wife…"

"Why not your brother too?" Honeyman remarked, it appearing impossible to make him angry. "They disturb both graves but only one skull is returned." There was a pause. "These people are very careful and very deliberate, Martin. The skulls must have a purpose, just as the collodians have a purpose."

"When we close that house down and lock those bastards up then we'll find out. Do you hear?"

The suggestion was ignored. "Perhaps … perhaps that's why they chose a phrenological society and keep its tradition. Yes, a phrenological society is the perfect cover, the perfect *front* for an organisation that needs to deal in skulls…"

"Honeyman, it's time for the police."

"The police can't help us."

"What do you mean they can't help us?"

"Don't you think I haven't considered calling the police already? More to the point, don't you think that the Trustees have considered it?" His tone contained an imperative as he realised that his words were falling on deaf ears. "Don't do anything, Martin. We need to visit Marion Coates before we speak to your niece…"

"You've been visiting people for over a year, Honeyman. It's time for action."

"Martin…"

"I'll be in touch," he said, ending the call. He switched the mobile off as he continued across the sand.

Waiting now at the kitchen table, he wondered whether he

was being too hasty. Honeyman had assured him that Ellen was in no danger; quite the contrary, the only way she could wander into danger was if she became too inquisitive.

This was a war with no innocent bystanders, Honeyman had explained. Only believers were chosen; atheists, agnostics and members of other religions were barely even seen or noticed by the Trustees. They were shadows. No, Ellen was in no danger.

Martin thoughtfully considered the letters. Still, she had the right to decide whether she wanted to exhume her mother from her grave. Her father too. She had told him about the latest letter, which she had translated as *look inside my pocket*, believing there might be a clue in her father's morning suit.

He slowly shook his head. He had carefully checked that suit and there was nothing in any of the pockets, though that didn't rule out the possibility that someone had slipped something inside a pocket after he had given the suit to the undertakers.

With his thumb, he rubbed the letter he was holding thoughtfully. Perhaps the clue about the suit was just his brother's ruse to make them look in his grave. Only one skull was returned to the families, but in his stomach Martin felt the agony of his twin: when he visualised the blue felt interior of the coffin he knew, with as much certainty as he knew anything, that his brother had no head.

He carefully laid out his three letters on the kitchen table, ready to show them to his niece when she got home, then looked up as he heard the front door open and footsteps on the wood floor of the hall. He had rung Ellen earlier on a pretext and knew that she was on her way home from the shops; he hadn't told her anything, not sure who might be listening.

"Ellen it's me," he called, not wanting to give her a shock by surprising her. "I'm down here in the kitchen and I need to speak with you, alone."

There was a pause as the footsteps halted.

"It's about the skull in the hall. I've had it analysed."

The footsteps came down the remaining steps. He stood up and managed a smile as he saw that they belonged to the housekeeper,

Tarn Hughes. "Oh I'm sorry," he said, quickly collecting up the letters and returning them to his inside pocket, though not efficiently enough to prevent one falling back onto the table.

"I think Ellen's still in town," she said. Her eyes were following his hand as he snatched up the errant letter.

"Oh yes, of course," he muttered, putting on his coat. "I'll catch her again." A finger went to the bridge of his spectacles. "I thought you only worked mornings?"

She slowly took off her coat. "I've offered to cook this evening. My brother's helping too. Stefan's coming behind with the groceries." She blinked slowly. "Can I get you a drink, Mr Sorensen?"

"I'm fine," he said, with a vigorous wave of his hands.

"Something to eat perhaps?"

"No, really." He paused. "And how are you?"

"Very well. Thank you."

"And your brother?"

"Very well."

"Good, good." He checked his watch and his eyes signalled that she was blocking the stairs.

"Oh I'm sorry," she said, standing aside. He passed her with a nod, carefully measuring his speed as he climbed the stairs. On the third stair he found himself falling backwards, a dull sensation in his right calf having made his leg go numb. As he fell back into the kitchen, landing heavily on his back, he saw the sledgehammer, which she was struggling to lift even with two hands, and which had caused his collapse. The blow had barely tripped him, such had been the weakness of her swing, but his spectacles had shot across the floor. She hurried across the kitchen and stamped on them.

"What are you doing?" he gasped, the image of the young woman with the sledgehammer just a blur. His eyes narrowed as he realised she was struggling to raise the sledgehammer waist high. With the assistance of gravity, she brought it down with a short crack on his left knee.

This time there was no numbness but pain, searing heart-stopping

274

pain, which threw his survival support system into overdrive. He reached into his jacket and pulled out his keys, finding the longest one and making a short stabbing tool between the fingers of his fist. With his free hand he pulled himself across the floor, aiming his key at her face.

"I'll put this through your eye," he whispered. In spite of his peril, he was thinking of Mikey and the things he wanted to say to him; it was a pre-death thought, he realised, and fear choked in his throat.

She was looking around the kitchen feverishly, registering where the knives were stored and wondering whether she should make a dash for one. She didn't like the look of the key and Martin Sorensen was a strong man in spite of his age; she decided to stick with the sledgehammer, with the relative safety of its long handle. She readied herself for the heave of effort that would raise the sledgehammer to her shoulders, when they heard the front door open.

"Down here!" Martin shouted. "Hurry!"

The footsteps coming down the stairs were frantic. It was Stefan. As he came to a halt he dropped his groceries in confusion.

"Stefan, your sister's gone crazy," Martin implored. "She's attacked me."

Stefan looked at Tarn.

"Don't believe him, Stef," she said quietly. "He tried to hurt me."

"Stefan, call the police," he groaned. He suddenly realised what he had said and reached desperately into his jacket for his mobile, dropping his keys as he opened it. As Tarn lunged for the phone, Martin's two large hands caught her by the shoulders. She screamed, trapped and helpless, until Stefan pulled her to safety.

"The mobile," she gasped.

Stefan smacked the mobile out of Martin's hand. "Don't touch my sister," he growled.

"Your sister's ill," Martin said, attempting to keep his voice calm. He suspected he had made a grave mistake in grabbing her. "She's very ill, Stefan, and she needs our help. Do you hear?"

Stefan turned to his sister in confusion.

"You have to hold him," she explained quietly.

"Stefan, don't listen to her!"

"You have to hold him," she repeated. "Hold his arms."

Stefan reached down and grabbed his wrists. Martin, feeling his years, struggled helplessly with clenched teeth and shaking head as his arms were forced to the floor.

"That's it, good, good boy," she said encouragingly. "He tried to hurt me, Stef. Hold him down now."

"Stefan, please ... don't listen to her..."

With a heave and a sigh of effort, she lifted the sledgehammer up as high as she could manage. With a readying glance at her brother she said, "Move away from his head."

As she waited the tiny muscles in her arms screamed with the exertion.

"Tarn ... please..." Martin whispered helplessly, "think about what you're doing ..."

She brought the sledgehammer sharply down.

Tarn had been to the Wilkinson house once before when her local network enrolled her for the care programme, but she didn't get any further than the lobby of the derelict building, prevented from entering the chamber beyond the double doors where the wondrous vessels were stored. She remembered that the lobby contained a huge portrait of the founding member, Thomas Wilkinson, which she was now admiring again.

"It's wonderful," she whispered, once more breathing in the rancid decay of the house.

The temple's transport had collected them an hour ago and Wells was dragging Martin Sorensen's body, the face unrecognisable, into the room beyond the double doors where there was a place to bury him. This place was a pit, deep but narrow; Tarn knew about this pit because every temple had one, just as every temple had a number. This was Temple 1331 and it was both famous and revered.

"I found these in his pocket," she said to Sorrel, handing her

Martin's letters. The letter she had seen him pick up from the table was on the top and read:

Fear the carer

"*He* was getting letters too," Tarn explained. "I think he found them in the grave: I've seen him there. When I surprised the Baptist that time, he sent a text message. I think the message was to Martin Sorensen, warning him to stay away."

Sorrel nodded thoughtfully as she sifted through the letters. "Nigel Sorensen was both strong and resourceful," she remarked, with a trace of admiration.

"What is this place?" Stefan muttered, standing mystified behind Tarn.

"These people are my friends, Stef," Tarn said, turning and taking his elbow. "Don't worry."

"Are we calling the police now?" he asked. "To tell on the man that attacked you?"

"No police," Tarn muttered.

Sorrel agreed with a twitch of her nose then turned as she heard a dull thump through the double doors. Soon Wells appeared through those doors, his face livid.

"I had to do it," Tarn muttered. "He knew about the skull. He was the one who broke in the other night and I heard him say he that he'd had it analysed. Then I saw the letters…"

Sorrel sighed as she handed the letters back to Tarn. "You know the law. Trespass to a temple is the only time when we can take life. You murdered this man … forced us to conceal your crime … in this holy place…"

"But he knew … he was going to…"

"What? He was going to do what?" Wells hissed, closing the double doors behind him.

"Call the police?" Tarn suggested weakly.

Sorrel had a bemused expression. "Don't you believe the Father would protect us, Tarn? The Baptist has been stalking us for twelve months and knows far, far more than Martin Sorensen."

Tarn swallowed, unable to counter the logic. "I panicked. I only wanted to help."

The hand that briefly stroked Tarn's hair had the scent of apples; she was reassured, imagining a country fete with ponies and homemade jam. "I understand … I do…" Sorrel said with a smile.

"Tarny, I want to go," Stefan murmured.

Wells' eyes settled on Stefan and Tarn tightened her grip on his elbow. "You don't have to worry about Stef. He's safe. He won't say anything, not if I make him promise. Not if I make him promise…"

Sorrel considered the face of the confused young man for several moments. "I suspect you're right," she said at length. "He's probably a good boy." She cast a glance back at Wells.

"He is," Tarn agreed, nodding vigorously.

"Come here, Stefan," Sorrel whispered, "I want to share a secret with you."

Stefan's hand tensed.

"It's okay, go on," Tarn said, with relief. "She's a friend." She let go of his elbow with a forward motion as if she were launching a ship.

Sorrel held out a welcoming hand to ease his approach. "Bring your ear close to my lips, so I can whisper a secret that only good boys can hear."

The diminutive woman barely came to Stefan's shoulder and he had to stoop. "We absolve your sister's sin," she whispered, lovingly touching his cheek with one hand while the other whipped past his neck. He frowned, tensed, then found an expression of mild surprise as the blood appeared at the thin slit in his throat. He was vaguely aware of his sister's screams as he sank to the floor, unsure why the strength was leaving his body. Sorrel wiped the fine blade with a lace handkerchief she had produced from her tweed jacket. "There now, don't be afraid…" she said, her voice heavy with regret, "don't be afraid…"

"A messy business," Wells muttered, walking over. He bared

his teeth and gums with disapproval as he considered the blood on the floor. "You see? An unnecessary, messy business."

Sorrel's hand was on Tarn's shoulder, holding her still. The aroma was now of rotting apples, as if a hormone in the skin had fermented the scent. "There now, don't touch him, watch him die," she said gently. "He dies because of your disobedience."

"I've been a good servant!" Tarn wailed, as Stefan's bleary eyes focussed on her in the last few seconds of his life. The stench of the rotten scent in her nostrils acted as a sedative.

"A messy business," Wells repeated. "You have put us to a great measure of trouble."

Tarn had sunk to her knees, attempting a smile to comfort her brother as the last of his energy drained out of him. She mouthed the words *Don't be afraid*, and he read her lips with a nod. He smiled as he died.

"All true servants will have such tests," Sorrel reflected sadly.

"My brother wasn't a servant," Tarn murmured, her body in shock as she watched the Trustees drag him away.

"Your brother's purpose in this world was to test you," Sorrel said, pausing as Wells pushed open the doors. From inside Tarn could hear that the vessels were chanting and had joined their very different voices to find an unintelligible hum, as many colours mixed together become a muddy brown. "He tested you when you were young, when you damaged his brain ... and he tests you now, as you watch him die."

"There must be more..." Tarn moaned, her face having gone numb with grief.

"There is nothing more!" Wells barked. "There is only the Father and His servants ... and the Enemy. All else is shadow."

"All else is shadow," Tarn repeated, finding solace in that part of the Black Eucharist that reminded the servants that they must abandon their family when duty to the Father called.

Some vows are unbearable loads, she thought, remembering the words of the man she now knew as the infamous Tristyn Honeyman of Flint, who *the Venerable* Sorrel Page, presently Trustee of Temple

1331, referred to simply as *the Baptist*. The members of the coven had said that she had often described his death, here in the temple, for she had seen it and had said that it would be most righteous. Sorrel Page was beloved of the Father and had been favoured with the gift of sight.

"I am His servant," Tarn murmured, again reciting from the Eucharist, "and He expects me to be faithful."

Tarn was talking to herself, for the Trustees were now on the other side of the double doors. She flinched as she heard the dull, distant thump, which was her brother's body finding the bottom of the pit.

"All else is shadow," she repeated, wondering if one day she would be as celebrated, as wise and as beautiful as Sorrel Page. In that moment of ambition the last remnants of the love she had for the world, which had been twisted with a garrotte years before, finally expired.

XXV

The prayers that are keys

On seeing the police car parked outside his digs in New Hedges, Honeyman drove straight past, neither slowing nor increasing his speed.

Something warned him not even to glance at his temporary home, for fear of being observed, a habit picked up from observing the Trustees. A primordial instinct told him that if he could not see the hunter then the hunter could not see him, though he sometimes wondered how many hapless animals had found an early death on account of following this theory. Daring a glance behind him, he saw that the front door was closed, the police car empty.

He had already seen the police today, for he had visited the hotel on The Esplanade when Martin Sorensen failed to return his calls. It was Martin's partner, Mikey, who had probably put the local force on a state of emergency, he reasoned, but it would have been Ellen Sorensen who would have given them the name of *Honeyman,* sending the police computer into overdrive. The police were probably watching her house and he dare not go there.

Finding only dead ends, in a moment of uncertainty he glimpsed his suffocating death; there would be soon be nowhere for him to go, other than to the temple.

"Give me strength," he muttered, unable to utter the name of Christ. "Just a little longer, to let me finish my work."

The heavens chose this moment to open and the rain came down relentlessly as he drove, leaning forward and peering between the wipers, until he came to a stop in a lay-by on the Pembroke road. Amid the banging and tapping on his roof, he searched on his mobile for Hugh's number, pausing thoughtfully when he found it; if the police were there they would listen in on his call but he shook his head, deciding he had no alternative. He selected the number and the call was answered quickly, though the person answering didn't speak.

"It's Honeyman," he said.

"Yes?" came the reply. It was Hugh's voice.

"Hugh, the police won't be able to help you."

There was no answer.

"You have to listen to me. You have to trust me."

"Tell us where…"

Ellen came on the line. "Tell us where he is, you bastard! What have you done to him?"

He spoke rapidly, yet calmly. "Your uncle and I were working together, Miss Sorensen. The hotel will confirm it, if you have any doubts, for I visited him often enough." He paused for breath. "Are you ready to speak to me yet?"

There was no response.

"The Trustees have taken the doll and the typewriter, haven't they?" he asked.

"I … I let them have them…"

"You know that's not true. Fight it! Use your faith," he urged.

"I'm telling you, I let them have them!"

"Let them have them…" he remarked sadly, "yes, as if it was your decision. Just like when you tried to take your doll out of the house, then decided it would be better if you stayed. I know you tried: I saw it in your face, the first time we met."

"I don't … I don't know what you're talking about…"

"You would've succeeded in taking Cody, if you'd thought to take your mother's collodian at the same time, for that's how the vessels are transported. They've no attachment to the house, just the photograph, but I'm sure you've realised that … now. I'm sure

282

there are lots of things that you're working out..." He wondered how much her mind had been willing to retain; it would come down to the strength of her faith, for only faith could rationalise her experience. The first twenty-four hours after the vessels were taken would be critical.

"I've been hypnotised or something," she murmured, without conviction. "The Trustees hypnotised me."

"But Hugh wasn't hypnotised, was he?"

"Okay, Hugh saw the typewriter and he wasn't hypnotised," she conceded, "but he thinks the keys were lost with dissolving acid."

"And what about the number in your doll's neck? Didn't Hugh see...?"

"That's just a coincidence. It's the *real* serial number."

He shook his head, tiring of the game. "Just as Satan has a number, every temple has a number. The number of this temple is thirteen thirty-one and it holds your parents. You can only help me if you trust to your faith ... not the police and certainly not logic or science. Will you help me?"

She hesitated. Secretly, she had been waiting, hoping for him to call; there was a place in her heart where she trusted the ex-minister and yearned for explanations to the things she couldn't explain. "No, it's okay," he heard her say away from the speaker; he guessed that Hugh was trying to persuade her to hang up.

"What was it that made you give up your doll?" Honeyman asked. "What did she do?"

"What...?"

"I suspect she struggled at first," he suggested. "Then, knowing that the fight was lost ... that the struggle was impossible ... she made it quick and brutal, for she wouldn't have wanted to prolong your agony. Did she ... did she frighten you?"

"Yes," she muttered.

"You mustn't blame her: it was a mercy to have the thing over and done with." He listened, trying to read her thoughts in her breathing. "What did you see?"

Her voice was muted. "She went old ... so very, very old. Look, I know that I was hypnotised because Tarn was there and Tarn saw her face."

"What did *she* see?"

"She said that Cody was normal."

He grunted, dissatisfied with her answer. "What were her words? What were her *exact* words?"

"She said that she saw nothing that frightened her."

"And I believe her. Remember, she can't lie to you. She regards herself as pious but more importantly as a carer she's taken an oath."

"You mean because she's a born-again..."

"Because she's a member of the coven that services Temple Thirteen Thirty-one," he said simply, cutting her short.

"Tarn ... I don't understand...?"

"They always install a carer: to monitor the subject and to ensure that no one intrudes."

"I don't believe you. Tarn's helped me ... she..."

"Did she tell you to give up the typewriter and the doll?"

"Yes, but..."

"Why do you think your father entrusted Stefan with hiding the typewriter, rather than his more capable sister, even though he'd tasked her with disposing of everything else? Why do you think he made such a fuss about the telephone, which really meant nothing to him? To fool his housekeeper, of course, who was guarding the vessels, as a crow guards eggs in a nest." He shook his head. "You've met the Trustees, Miss Sorensen. You know they're careful and skilled. Do you think they wouldn't protect their precious cargo?"

There was a silence as she tried to assimilate this information; she was sifting through everything that Tarn had said to her, but was unable to call on anything that disproved his allegations.

I had a different path...

What I am doesn't concern you...

"The police have warned me about you," she said slowly. "Just as your church warned me."

"I know, but you have to listen to your heart now. You trusted me when you first met me, just as you *mistrusted* the housekeeper. Your instincts are very sound. Miss Sorensen, trust them now…"

There was another pause.

"My name's Ellen," she said.

He heard Hugh utter a moan of exasperation in the background. "I'm on the Pembroke road out of Tenby," he said gently but with immense relief. "You know my vehicle: I'm parked in a lay-by. I'll wait for you."

The thin, sharp-featured housekeeper of the late Marion Coates, Tarn Hughes, furtively opened the door to the Trustees. They entered quickly and silently, without making eye contact. She had rung them as soon as she had arrived at midday to find Marion slumped in the hallway. From the grimace on the woman's face, it seemed as if she had died of a heart attack; she had been told it was always the heart that gave out.

"Five minutes, no more, before you ring the ambulance," Wells muttered to her, thinking that neighbours may have seen her arrive. He went to the grandfather clock and regarded the broken moon dial with an air of satisfaction.

Sorrel stepped between the head and arm of the body to move into the sitting room. This was the first time they had ever visited a house with no custodian present and it was risky, because they couldn't explain their presence if they were seen; nevertheless, with this last precious collection they would not be entrusting the planting of the second collodian to the carer. This time there would be no mistakes.

Tarn had been certain that Nigel Sorensen would enter the antique telephone and indeed the collodian seemed content enough when she placed it on the kitchen counter. When the collodian went missing, she wondered whether it had been smuggled out of the house by the interfering twin brother, with whatever vessel it had found. Only later would she realise that it had slipped behind the drawers, in an attempt to get closer to the buried typewriter.

It still rankled with her that she had been fooled by Sorensen's elaborate display of affection for his telephone, while he made his secret plans with her brother. She had been quite stern with Marion in the few days allowed to her as a housekeeper, pandering to none of her whims. The carer's oath was to obey the bereaved in everything, the price the temple paid for the intrusion, but Marion didn't know that. She had made the fat old lump very miserable.

"Do we know where she is?" Sorrel asked. Tarn indicated the dresser with the Sandringham dinner service edged in blue and gold. A plate stood alone, then three plates were arranged in tight unison, then three more and finally a gap and the last plate. The pattern repeated itself on the two display shelves below.

Sorrel flicked one of the plates with her finger.

"Careful!" Tarn whispered involuntarily then quickly made a face of passive submission. Marion Coates was her second task for the temple and she was starting to find her duties easier, but still had trouble containing her enthusiasm.

The plate was wobbling, a few degrees away from toppling, until it snapped back into its original position, rigidly and without motion. The movement of the plate had produced a low chime, which sounded like a note made in a throat of china and wood. More plates were disturbed, each wobbling at its own frequency before rigidly snapping to a halt. The movement of the plates produced a discordant ringing harmony:

Helllllllllp meeeeeeee...

"Praise Him," Sorrel and Wells whispered in unison.

"Praise Him," Tarn agreed. Miracles such as this had accompanied her conversion two years ago, when she witnessed the sure proof of the divine that would allow her to set down her guilt and feelings of worthlessness. She had found no such assurance when she had prayed in vain to the Enemy all those years: the prayers that begged forgiveness for damaging her brother; the prayers that were never answered.

Sorrel took Marion's collodian out of her bag and handed it to Tarn, saying, "I think we should put it on the table with the other photographs."

Tarn complied, placing it near the skull of Henry Coates, aged and etched to resemble a phrenological tool. She blinked slowly. "Why can't we just take them? Take them *now*."

"Just take them?" Wells queried.

"Her children didn't visit, they didn't even telephone," she explained eagerly. "They didn't care about her at all: they wouldn't know what was here and what wasn't."

"There's the list with the solicitor," Sorrel reminded her, not engaging with the conversation; she was making a last check of the room to ensure they had touched nothing with their bare hands other than the plates or the dresser, which would tolerate no fingerprints.

"We could say you came and took what you wanted," she argued, her face alive with excitement. "I know the porcelain is valuable but it would be too late if the family protested. The vessels would be in the temple..."

"Quiet now," Sorrel muttered, her patience straining. She was wishing that she could have allocated Jenny Bond to this task, the able protégé she had found cowering in a women's hostel, but regrettably the Coates' circumstances were better suited to a hardworking housekeeper than an estate agent with a heart of gold. "The vessels can't just be taken, they have to be given," she sighed, thinking that Jenny wouldn't have needed an explanation, that she would simply have obeyed. Jenny was not only obedient but skilled; she remembered how she had so effortlessly distracted the nephew in Saundersfoot, luring him into a corner of the conservatory while they switched the collodians.

"Given?"

"Just remember your oath. Don't think, just obey."

It was policy in the coven not to repeat let alone explain all the laws to the lower ranks, for it was considered bad for morale if it was perceived that the Father was bound by so many rules. Far better to grow into this understanding as wisdom and experience allowed a fuller understanding of the nature of temptation and the duality of holiness.

Tarn nodded as she considered Sorrel's command, thinking gloomily of Nigel Sorensen sitting in his armchair with that sly look in his eye, tasking her with errands and entrusting her with secrets, knowing she had to obey. She had rationalised her decision to return the graduation photograph as an attempt to generate a friendship bond with Ellen, to get closer to her; it had worked, but she knew deeper motives were at play. She wished to thwart the will of Nigel Sorensen, who had wanted Ellen to leave the house, blissfully unaware of his fate. Her revenge against him would be the suffering of his daughter.

She was regretting it all now, just as she regretted tracking Honeyman down by the graveyard. Her blood had chilled when she found out that the coven knew all about the Baptist, when she reported back with the boastful news that she had found a servant of the Enemy who was on their trail. She feared she was making too many mistakes; that the temple's apparatus, working so smoothly to collect the vessels, would jam on her misguided acts of initiative.

Sorrel Page was wise to sacrifice my brother. Surely, my sin is absolved.

"You understand your instructions with the relatives?" Wells asked.

"Yes, yes *Veneration*," she answered automatically.

"Never in public!" he barked. "That name is for the coven only."

She once more lowered her eyes in submission to *the Venerable* Jasper Wells who was gifted, as was every elder Trustee, with *the prayers that are keys*. When she looked up, *the Venerable* Sorrel Page was considering her with her hard smile and a sparkle in her eyes.

She swallowed and looked away, wondering if the Trustee gifted with sight was seeing her death.

The rain had stopped but the air was still heavy with moisture as Ellen, ashen-faced, heard Honeyman recount her uncle's part in his investigation and she learned of the letters found at the grave. She was mourning her uncle, sure he was dead.

She had known it yesterday, long before the first anxious call from Uncle Mikey; she was in the town when she felt the sense of loss, as if a light had been switched off. Perhaps it was because Uncle Martin was her father's identical twin that she found this empathetic reaction: her father was grieving through her, the only human now carrying his blood.

"All my family are gone," she muttered dismally. She was trudging with Honeyman through the sodden field next to the road.

"It seems as if we've something in common," he said. Like Ellen, he feared the worst, yet had difficulty in understanding what had happened. "They're unable to commit an act of violence unless there's a trespass and your uncle understood that. There are rules. I don't know what went wrong but I am so, so sorry. First your parents, and now your only uncle. You're far too young for such loss."

"Why are there rules?" Hugh asked, leaning against the Mini parked behind the Land Rover in the lay-by. Reluctantly, he left the place from where he was keeping a sceptical distance and caught them up.

"Temples are built on crimes committed in the name of God," Honeyman explained. He came to a stop, the road still in view through the hedgerow; he had looked at every vehicle that had driven by. "That's what a Satanic temple is," he continued, "a solid enduring reminder to God that his chosen beings are imperfect. But Satan attempts to take the higher ground, so forbids violence and demands piety. It's a propaganda war reaching out for hearts and minds ... on Satan's part, anyway."

"And on God's?" she asked.

Honeyman shook his head. "I'm no longer qualified to speak of God's motives. I'm cursed. I used to think that Sorrel Page had bewitched me but I've wondered recently whether she simply stirred something that was always inside me. A questioning as to why God would allow this to happen." He paused. "I could never lose my faith but I lost my *trust*, my confidence that everything He works is for the good of mankind. When I regain that, I believe I'll be able to step inside my church again." He turned to watch a loud truck go past but his thoughts were elsewhere.

"Is Mr Hobbs working for them too?" she asked.

"No," he muttered, still looking at the road. "He's just an ethical solicitor following your father's strict instructions. There are plenty of lawyers in their coven, of course, but the fewer servants involved, the smaller the probability of mistakes."

She nodded with relief. It still hadn't properly sunk in about Tarn and she didn't want any more surprises. "I want to know where this temple is. I'm going there."

He nodded, he'd expected this. "I know that they'll permit you one visit. You're a custodian and so have an entitlement."

"Custodian," she muttered. "*They* used that word."

"With a temple everything must be given freely. At least, there's an element of free will involved," he qualified dryly. "The bereaved subject *willingly* captures the soul of the deceased. The custodian *willingly* gives the vessels to the Trustees. In their turn, and in the manner of *fair trade,* the Trustees give the custodian the phrenological heads from the temple…" He hesitated. Mikey would tell her about the tests on her mother's skull and he saw no reason to raise this now.

"So let me get this straight," Hugh said, his mouth twitching towards a smile. "You're telling us that this charity traps souls in … how did you describe it?"

"Vessels. Usually furniture, books or timepieces but the possibilities are limitless. There are just certain characteristics a vessel must possess…"

"Right," Hugh said, not interested in the details, "and this is achieved … how?"

"Will you believe me if I explain it to you?" he asked, wearying of Hugh's tone. "Explanations are useless anyway, for the vessels have only a perverse and ironic logic. A letter can appear, though the machine that types it is buried in the ground. It appears in the manner of the man who used it, slowly, word by word. When the keys to the typewriter are lost, the letter is similarly disabled. Hell savours the irony and the logic but don't think of these things in terms of natural phenomena…"

Ellen was studying him intently. "You think it's my father who's been writing to me, don't you?"

His small, dark eyes turned on her sadly. "I've no doubt of it. Your mother, meanwhile, has been trying to protect you, but she could only provide you with comfort, I think."

"No, that's not true. She was able to warn me…"

"Yes. Yes indeed." He smiled and nodded, encouraged that she seemed to be keeping a grasp of the facts and even interpreting them; that was a good sign at this point.

"Yes, she tried to warn me," she said to herself, remembering the dreams with the little girl, the first one just before Wells had telephoned to introduce himself. Her thoughts turned to the letter that had dropped out of Cody's sleeve as she was carried out of the house, the final joint effort of her parents, yet the letter was meaningless. It must have been a failed attempt to say something; perhaps they had simply tried to say goodbye.

"Come on, let's go," Hugh said, with a shake of his head.

"Your mother's ability to communicate through a doll was limited, but your father found a writing machine," Honeyman said to her. "He was a very clever man, knowing that if he isolated the selection down to one item there'd be no mistake and in keeping with the ironic logic of the temple, something he understood early on, he knew he could write to you. He also hoped that the temple would make mistakes. The mistakes are the small hole in the wall that's allowed him to breach the temple's defences."

"What mistakes?" she asked.

"I suspect that young Tarn Hughes has broken her oaths: her oath as a member of the coven, and her oath as a carer." He looked up thoughtfully for a moment as the possibility occurred to him, that the carer had killed Martin Sorensen.

Fear the carer...

"I don't believe this," Hugh muttered. "Can you hear yourself?"

"And so we need to consider what your father is telling us," he persisted, ignoring Hugh. "When he first wrote to you it was to release him from the agony of his prison. But when you found him, he wrote another letter..."

"The temple is reversed. Look inside my pocket," she said, reciting the second message. "I've looked through all his clothes and I couldn't find anything. We've been thinking that maybe there was something in the morning suit he was buried in."

"Your uncle said he looked through that suit," he remarked, not caring for the idea of Ellen exhuming the body of her father to find that he was without a head. "We've still got Marion Coates alive and she and her husband will be the last vessels to enter the temple. Trustees have been collecting the vessels for over a hundred years and if I'm right the Coates will be numbers one thousand three hundred and thirty, and one thousand three hundred and thirty-one."

"That's an *odd* number," Hugh said, jumping on a contradiction. "Under your theory all the vessels are partnered."

"Thomas Wilkinson is the first vessel," he murmured.

No one spoke. They had been standing in the same spot in the field for a long time and they now realised they were cold. Ellen shivered.

"Okay, let's go," Hugh said.

Honeyman's attention turned to the road once more. "I'll wait here. When you come back perhaps we can go somewhere to eat and talk."

"We're not coming back," Hugh muttered.

"Will they try to hurt us?" she asked, resisting Hugh's hand on her arm.

Hugh chuckled. "Hurt us? They're a tiny woman and a frail

old man, aren't they?"

Honeyman noticed the smile. "Yes, just a tiny woman and a frail old man ... who perhaps dance naked around a fire at midnight and pull the heads off chickens?"

Hugh had lost his smile. "So, *can* these Trustees hurt us?"

Honeyman's eyes followed the passage of a speeding car. "During their tenure Satan empowers them. The man has *the prayers that are keys*, always possessed by the elder Trustee. Triggers and traps, in words. It's akin to hypnosis but largely an ironic device, a tongue poked at the power of prayer, the medium through which we talk to God."

Ellen nodded slowly, remembering the lock turning in her head.

"The woman is even more dangerous. She has the gift of sight, a rare talent not automatically handed out to the Trustees. She's destined to rise very high in the coven, I suspect." He nodded. "Understand that they both have enormous strength while they act as Trustees. Their strength is a temporary armour given by the temple."

They looked at him mutely, their resolve collapsing. He noticed their disquiet and gave them a reassuring smile.

"But they won't hurt you," he said. "You're allowed one visit, as I said, and you'll be quite safe, I promise you. I'll wait here until you come back."

Your faith will determine how you deal with what you see, he thought. He looked up at the grey storm sky. "And at some point I have to find a place to sleep," he muttered.

"Can't you go to a hotel?"

"Too dangerous, and my room in New Hedges is out of bounds. It's fortunate I carry all my materials with me." He groaned, touching his lower back in anticipation of a difficult night. "No, I'll sleep in my vehicle tonight."

I only have one night left, he realised, shuddering as he felt the clod of earth on his face, his death vision suddenly before him again.

His eyes closed.

"Are you okay?" she whispered.

He nodded, his eyes still closed. When he opened them, he looked suddenly older. "Can you excuse me now while I return to my vehicle? I'm going to pray and I have to pray alone, I'm afraid." He grimaced and said, "I swear a great deal when I pray."

She nodded in confusion. "That's what the church warden said … that you were a profane man. That you had actually sworn in church when giving a sermon. He said they were the worst words he'd ever heard."

"It's a little joke Sorrel Page has played on me," he explained wearily. "But I can still pray nonetheless and I believe that God still hears me, through the profanities."

He ambled off towards the solitude of his Land Rover, now the only place of worship left to him. She lit a cigarette. "Well, you've heard him out," Hugh said cautiously. "Do you believe *any* of it?"

She sucked her cigarette, her eyes wincing as she realised she had taken in too much smoke. She didn't mind, for it acted as an adrenalin jolt. "Uncle Martin believed him," she said, with a cough. "And I saw the doll and I've read the letters. I've seen too much. I can … *remember* too much." She frowned, finding the distinction important but not knowing why. "Hugh, you have to understand my parents believed in God … and so do I." She shook her head. "I'm not saying I'm religious like Tarn … like I *thought* Tarn was … and I don't believe in zombies or vampires, Santa Claus or the bogey man. But I do believe in the soul, that there is such a thing as a soul. And I also believe in good and evil." She took another drag of her cigarette, with a resigned expression. "I'd understand completely if you just wanted to go," she said, with a tremor in her voice. "Perhaps I'm the only one who can help my parents now. Perhaps I'm meant to be alone…"

He smiled and said, "I go where you go." He glanced at the Land Rover and at Honeyman hunched down in the driving seat. "Although your minister friend seems pretty sure we're going to come back with our tails between our legs," he added uneasily.

"I don't care what he thinks." She went to stub out her cigarette as it was dropped but it had sunk into the wet mud. "My parents are in that hellhole and I'm going to get them back."

XXVI

Many mansions

"This is the house of Thomas Wilkinson," Sorrel announced as she admitted them into the lobby, her aroma mixing a pungent perfume with the damp ill health in the air.

The double staircase appeared. It would have been impressive in its day but had collapsed on both sides about two thirds of the way up; a jump of some ten feet would be needed to reach the balustrade landing. Nevertheless, a large oil portrait of a handsome man with staring pale blue eyes had found a place on the wall. Even though it was in such an inaccessible position the oil colours were still vibrant and the polished frame gleaming, impervious to the house's decay.

"We just want to collect Ellen's things," Hugh said, taken aback by how beautiful the Trustee was, having pictured her with something like a long chin and whiskers. "There's been a mistake and you shouldn't have taken them. We're prepared to reimburse you."

He and Ellen had a mild sense of shock when the door had been answered so quickly, with the words, *you are welcome*. A sense of unreality marked their footsteps; the feeling was like a mist, suggesting that they could put this experience aside as a dream or hallucination, as some odd occurrence that never really happened.

"Oh my, that's difficult," Sorrel answered in a pleasant,

conversational tone. "Once the vessels are in place they don't care to be moved."

"The vessels?" he asked suspiciously. Part of him had believed Honeyman, at least to the extent that the Trustees were involved in some sort of black magic ritual. He was prepared to accept that the charity was built on the ruins of a phrenological society and that in their enthusiasm they were manufacturing little hypnotic tricks that could make it appear as if the objects were changing or communicating; he had, however, expected them either to refuse to discuss anything, or to deny everything.

"Hasn't the Baptist explained about the vessels?" Sorrel inquired.

"Do you mean Honeyman?" Ellen returned.

She nodded. "I'm assuming that you've spoken to him … dear man that he is."

Ellen glanced up at the portrait on the landing. "Is anything he said…?"

"True?" The question prompted Sorrel to turn a full three hundred and sixty degrees with one arm raised, as if to introduce the house; she was wearing a cream lace negligee that was very tight at the rise of her thighs and Hugh fought the urge to salivate at seeing the full measure of her tiny but perfect figure. "All true, I can assure you. This is a temple founded on a crime, committed in the name of your god. Come and meet the founder."

The dreamlike mist of unreality snaked around them once more, but now with danger and alarm, as tendrils of smoke in a burning building. They were led to their left, to the door of a study where a collodian of a handsome man with a moustache was set in the centre of a table. The image was an identical photographic copy of the painting on the landing and revealed even more clearly his pale, piercing eyes. Next to his portrait was a boxed set of surgical equipment including a saw, callipers and several long knives that looked very sharp. The initials TW were on the felt-lined box.

"Thomas Wilkinson Esquire," Sorrel announced. "He

immortalised himself in collodian, a fashionable practice of the age and the dark room he used is in the right wing of the house. It's still in use." The windows of the study were boarded up, the air carrying a film of dust just above the height of the furnishings, which were fusty and covered with cobwebs.

"We're not really interested," Ellen murmured, "we just want…"

"You'll see your dear ones shortly, but as you're visitors I must introduce you to Mr Wilkinson. It's good manners." Sorrel indicated a couch in a corner covered with white sheets; a candle revealed large bloodstains. "This is the room where he carried out his work."

"What work?" Hugh asked.

"The experiments in search of the divine. He was helped and encouraged by the people who were eventually to take over and run this society."

"Satanists?" Ellen whispered.

"An old coven of high standing," Sorrel confirmed, taking no offence at the description. "The coven was far-sighted, its elders quite brilliant. They knew full well that phrenology was a ridiculous enterprise, soon to be abandoned as quack science, but in Mr Wilkinson and The Divine Sentiment they saw an opportunity for progress."

Hugh swallowed as he scanned the room. "What opportunity?" he murmured.

"Hasn't the Baptist told you how we achieve our miracles?" Sorrel asked, quickly scanning both their faces. "Oh my, I see you're still suspicious of him. He hasn't explained it yet, has he?"

Hugh was now feeling distinctly uncomfortable and tugged on the jumper of Ellen's elbow. She pulled her arm back angrily.

"Quite right, Miss Sorensen," Sorrel said, with a twitch of her nose as she noticed the gesture of defiance. "I've always preferred to trust my own judgment too." She turned, walked towards the double doors and said, "Follow".

The upper floor of Wilkinson's house had once boasted a suite of bedrooms where illustrious patrons and devotees were entertained. A prince regent had once been a guest, his visit prompted by rumour and the entreaties of a bereaved mother stricken with grief, but the trace of cigar smoke and murmurs of disillusionment no longer haunted the corridors for the floor had been demolished years ago. The balustrade landing led into thin air.

The chamber was accordingly very high and not secure to the elements, drops of rain or thin rays of light finding their way through the missing roof tiles. Today a grey, indifferent sky cast a pall of gloom on the cupboards, stacked against the walls and reaching the ceiling. They were of different sizes, constructed with no apparent method, many awkwardly overlapping a neighbour, with gaps that might have been left by a workman careless with his measurements. Some of the cupboards lay at an angle, or had panels of uneven lengths, some were shallow, others deep, protruding from the wall. The result was a busy, alien structure, as if termites had been the carpenters.

The chamber was also very wide, clearly the product of many rooms having been knocked through. One of these rooms at one time would have been the kitchen, for a working stone hearth was still in place, offering a glow of warmth and emitting smoke that escaped through a wide copper flue. This flue was vibrating with a hollow, discordant murmur.

"That sound," Ellen whispered. "What is it?"

"The chorus," Sorrel replied. "It isn't time yet, but they're impatient." All of the cupboards were closed apart from the one that she now pointed to, which was empty. "That place is reserved for the Coates. When they arrive the temple will be complete." She took a satisfying breath. "In my Father's house there are many mansions. Isn't that what your bible tells you?"

"Why are you telling us this?" Ellen asked. She noticed a dark area near the wall by the stove, which looked like a narrow rectangular hole.

Sorrel was looking around her with admiration; if she was a

regular visitor to this chamber then she was yet to overcome her sense of awe. "Because you're a custodian and so you have rights under the laws of this temple. If you wish to exercise them … most do not."

"What if we come back here with the police?" Ellen asked, glancing fearfully at Hugh who met her eyes with equal concern. Still, something was preventing her from running.

"Then they'll see a warehouse where a registered charity stores various items that have been left to it by grateful patrons."

"But I saw blood on that sheet," Hugh said, attempting to keep his tone neutral. "Blood…"

"Mr Wilkinson showed you that. I assure you this house is empty apart from the vessels and their collodians." Sorrel turned to them. "Be warned, though. Today you've been invited, for you have a right to one visit, but we're empowered to deal with trespassers. Inviting the police here would be seen as trespass and you'd pay dearly for it."

"Is that a threat?" he muttered.

"Oh my, yes indeed," Sorrel clarified, her eyes widening. "It's the most earnest threat you'll ever hear. Speak to the Baptist before you act hastily. That's his purpose, after all, and why the temple tolerates him." Her eyes relaxed. "The Baptist is useful for he knows enough about us, *just* enough, to fear us."

"I want my doll and my typewriter," Ellen whispered. "And the collodians. I want to take them and go." She gripped Hugh's hand, finding that it was cold.

"You can see them. And if you can take them, then you can have them. Follow." Sorrel walked to the wall to the left of the double doors. She touched the doors of one of the sealed cupboards then moved to its neighbour, putting an ear to one of the panel doors. With a shake of her head she moved on again then stepped back muttering "Sorensen". She took a tiny, ornate handle between the thumb and index finger of each hand and, with a fluid motion, opened both doors.

All the cupboards were purpose-built to house their vessels; this particular cupboard was about five feet square by three feet deep and divided by a shelf. On the shelf, on its side, lay Cody, her long face once again the angelic little girl, her eyes closed. The collodian of Nia Sorensen in all its vibrant glory was positioned at the doll's feet. Nigel Sorensen's collodian was on the lower shelf, where the Sholes & Glidden typewriter sat replete with its watermarked paper neatly stacked. All the fingers of the keys had been restored, the machine gleaming and oiled.

"Cody shouldn't be on her side," Ellen muttered. "She'll hate being on her side." As she stepped forward, the doll's eyes opened but only enough to reveal half an eyeball, the rest disappearing into the skull in an imitation of deathbed agony. The eyes went further into the skull as she took another step nearer, becoming solid white as she took the step that brought her close enough to reach out and touch her doll.

"They worship in their own way," Sorrel explained. "Something important that moved them in life is amplified."

Ellen, poised to reach out, glanced at the Trustee, fighting the urge to punch her.

Sorrel's nose twitched once more, as if she understood the impulse. "Your mother was so ... so serene. She was a little martyr to love, so she must imitate her deathbed for you."

"Shut up," Ellen murmured. "I'm taking her home."

"Boring in life ... yet interesting in death..."

"Shut the fuck up!" she shouted, yet the chamber effortlessly absorbed her voice, leaving her words muted and without any reverb. Ellen reached out her hand then snatched it back with a squeal.

The typewriter had quickly tapped some of its keys, but with insect-like speed. It resembled some giant beetle giving a warning rattle with a click of its legs and mandibles. She reached out again and the machine rattled once more, a ream of paper darting out at her hand like the whip of a tongue. Clutching her hand, she saw she had a paper cut. With a curse she reached for her doll again but quicker this time and avoiding the frenzy of the machine.

The doll's hand was cold. In her head, she heard her mother's voice.

So … my vain, selfish whore of a daughter is here…

She jumped back, her hand over her mouth. The doll's lips had parted just enough to allow a porcelain tongue to poke through.

"Fuck," she heard Hugh whisper.

"Hush now, there now," Sorrel whispered to the doll as she closed the cupboard doors.

"Let's get out of here," Ellen muttered.

"Where's Martin Sorensen?" Hugh demanded. The petite woman glanced at the rectangular shadow by the stove. "Has he been here? Have you killed him?" He stepped back, pulled by Ellen.

"Do you see how you distress them?" Sorrel remarked. She paused in reflection and her aroma became the reek of rotting apples. "Your invitation has expired," she decided.

"Let's get out of here," Ellen repeated. As if a spell had been broken or a heavy floating bubble popped, their faces became animated as they took in what they had seen. They raced through the open double doors then through the lobby, which seemed bigger than they remembered. A plaintive voice could be heard from the experiment room as they approached the door.

And they say it wasn't true … wasn't true…

A ray of light hitting the collodian played a trick with the smoky glass, casting a large shadow across the room. They glimpsed it for a split second as they ran past the room heading for the front door. The shadow would make them both believe that they had seen a man in a white surgeon's coat sitting on the couch, half of a red cranium in one hand, a bible in another. The box of surgical tools on the table was empty.

They were in a Pembroke inn, in a back room with an open grate, seated around a little round table. Honeyman waved a hand, refusing to answer a single question until his steak sandwich was finished, which he ate with the deft use of a serviette to keep his whiskers clean. Ellen and Hugh hadn't wanted to eat.

"Tea," Honeyman said to himself, then looked up and caught the eye of the barman. He could see that Ellen was traumatised, but he hoped that the natural, relaxed atmosphere and friendly surroundings would help her; he had an inkling of what they might have seen from the woman in Usk, the only other custodian to brave the temple. The fact that they could both remember the episode was a good sign, a sign of their faith, although he suspected that Hugh was finding his strength through his love for Ellen, the need to share in her experience. Love was always a random card, he had come to realise, defying rules he thought had been set in stone.

"Tea," the barman grumbled as he put the mug down.

The presentation didn't seem to bother Honeyman, who sniffed the tea with appreciation and then took two long sips. He was debating how much more he should tell them, having now mentally joined the young man and woman together in his strategic thinking.

She shook her head. "The souls of my mum and dad are in the doll and the typewriter?" she asked dismally. "And they're connected to the collodians…"

Honeyman nodded. "As the vessel traps the soul the collodian acts as the body. It's an imitation, a sort of a cheat…" He thoughtfully sipped his tea, always finding this part of the explanation difficult.

She frowned. "I don't understand."

Honeyman savoured the warmth of the mug in his hands. "I'll try to explain. The soul is trapped in the body in life and is released when the body dies. Now, when the Trustees trap the soul, prevent it going on its long voyage to God, they have to fool it with a body. That's why the bereaved partner holds a photographic image which is as lifelike as possible, preferably a very natural photograph and not posed. The soul must find it and be fooled into believing this is its body … and that the body…"

"Isn't dead," she murmured.

He confirmed her assessment with a raise of his eyebrows and a final gulp of his tea.

Hugh was considering this, in spite of the protests from his rational mind. "So, Ellen's parents think they're alive?"

"The soul never dies, Hugh, but yes, they believe they're still on this earth, in this life. They're *trapped* in this life." He paused. "Consider ghosts. Ghosts are souls refusing to leave this life because they're trapped by their anger, or their grief, so that they haunt the objects of their misery. The temple, however, traps souls with *love*: the love of a husband or wife."

Hugh touched her hand. "Ellen told me what the photographs were like before they were swapped and I didn't believe her. But I saw them in that house. They were … incredible."

"And indestructible," Honeyman added. "Both the vessel and the collodian become indestructible, for a soul is binding them together, mind and body." He nodded with grim satisfaction. "Diamonds are like egg shells in comparison to the soul that is built to travel through eternity." He reached into one of his pockets and produced sticks of Wrigley's Spearmint and Juicy Fruit, unwrapped them and popped them into his mouth.

"Why are they building this temple?" she asked.

"Why was the Sistine Chapel built? To worship their god. The vessels, once the proud souls of God's Christian children, now tormented and forced to chant the number of the temple, are like the crucifixes and altars in the Basilica."

"But how…?" she murmured. "How are they able to trap souls? I mean why does God let them?"

He nodded mournfully, saying, "The Trustees make the bereaved challenge God's will by trapping the soul; by stopping it from following its proper path."

"But that's just human weakness," Hugh protested. "It's natural to wish your loved ones back."

She nodded in agreement, picturing her father listening to the Moonlight Sonata as Jasper Wells explained how his wife could be returned to him.

"The Devil harvests *all* his souls through human weakness," Honeyman remarked sadly.

They sat in silence for a time.

"So what do we do?" she asked.

Honeyman readjusted his gum. "I'm going to visit Marion Coates tomorrow," he said, trying to give his announcement an encouraging air. "I'll break down the door if I have to, but I'm going to speak to her."

"So what *was* his crime? Wilkinson, I mean," said Hugh.

"Did you see him, in the temple?" Honeyman asked cautiously.

Hugh nodded slowly. "I saw his photograph." Ellen gripped his hand.

Honeyman considered this. "He's still there. I sensed his presence myself." He looked up at the beamed ceiling and took a deep breath, as if the air was precious.

"It was to do with the thirteenth sentiment, wasn't it?" she asked. "The first human sentiment, the one that separates us from animals: benevolence."

"The proof of the divine," Honeyman agreed.

"Proof?" she asked, with a smile. "How *could* he prove it?"

Honeyman shook his head, disapproving of her smile, which she quickly set aside.

"Brain surgery?" Hugh murmured.

A downward shift of Honeyman's moustache marked his frown. "*Butchery* would be a more appropriate description. I don't know the details of the experiments because everything was covered up after Wilkinson killed himself. There were a lot of important people involved, I dare say, people who at first were duped by the idea of bringing their loved ones back. I do know that criminals were smuggled out of prisons, some escaping the gallows … it was important that the subject be alive, I suspect…" A short sigh registered his disgust. "With his respectable support gone he enlisted new backers, the coven. They helped him, trapping him in death and using his crime to form the plot of land for their temple: that's why thirteen is a holy number for this temple. But keeping the phrenological theme alive is also useful because it allows them to distribute skulls." He hesitated, avoiding Ellen's eyes.

"Why do they distribute skulls?" she asked.

"They give them to the beneficiaries, the custodians. In fair trade..." he added, frowning again as the significance of this trade continued to elude him.

"And what about thirty-one?" she queried. "Maybe the sentiment of 'time' is connected with the skulls in some way."

"What, in the way they're aged, you mean?" Hugh suggested.

"I think they're aged simply to disguise them," Honeyman replied. "In the early days I wondered whether 'time' was a reference to *eternity* ... thirteen thirty-one, the divine in eternity ... but there are specific sentiments dealing with spirituality and veneration." He shook his head slowly. "No, thirteen is the important sentiment and Satanists, as with most fanatics, are very precise and careful. Thirty-one is simply the reverse of thirteen."

"Okay, but why reverse it?" Hugh asked, mentally repeating the phrase but with Honeyman's pronunciation.

The *ruvuss* of *thurteen* ...

"Because it's holy to the unholy..."

"No ... no, I understand the theory," Hugh broke in. "What I mean is why broadcast it? Why not just call the temple *thirteen*? Why give us the clue about the reverse?"

Honeyman looked at him thoughtfully. "What makes you think it's a clue?" he asked.

"Because of my father's letter," Ellen muttered, now picking up on Hugh's train of thought. "He wrote *The temple is reversed*."

Honeyman sat back. "So he did," he muttered. "So he did."

"And you've said that there are laws ... rules, the temple has to follow," Hugh added.

Honeyman nodded slowly, his eyes inviting him to continue.

"Well, perhaps giving us a clue is one of their rules. Perhaps they have to cut us a break."

"Look inside my pocket," she whispered. "What was my father trying to tell us?"

Honeyman had a pained expression, knowing that the breakthrough still eluded him. "I don't think that letter was finished," he said. "Martin told me that the attempts at the letter would disappear when the final letter came, with the thirteen thirty-one pence stamp."

Ellen nodded. "Yes, I lost the letters that came before 'find me, Ellie Sweet'..."

"And Mikey will tell you that the other one disappeared from his lab," Honeyman remarked. "The fact that you've still got the attempts at the second message tells me that the letter wasn't finished. Perhaps your father was trying to finish it that night all the notes appeared through the letterbox, but he couldn't finish it, because there were no letter keys. The temple had beaten him at last." A dark suspicion that Martin Sorensen was dead again crossed his heart as he wondered at what Nigel Sorensen had been trying to say as the last line of the message.

Someone I love is going to die...

They sat in silence a while longer.

"Anyway," said Ellen at length, "what's the best way to approach this with the police?"

Hugh sighed with relief. "At last..." he muttered.

"The police won't be able to help," Honeyman said. "I had this same conversation with your uncle..."

"But my uncle's missing. What do I tell Uncle Mikey? That we're trying to solve riddles with photographs and skulls?"

Honeyman considered this. It was his experience that even with friendly, receptive ears the result was always a decision to ring the police, which would prove to be a disaster. He had learnt this to his cost when he made his first ally in Usk, the daughter and sole beneficiary of a man who now occupied a toy, a wooden acrobat on a swing. She had run to the police after her experience in the temple, but not only was she unsuccessful in getting their help, she soon found herself on some trumped up offences. When he had later tried to visit her, having arranged a meeting by telephone, he had seen the police waiting for him.

"Let me speak to Marion Coates first," he suggested.

They didn't answer.

"I'll visit first thing," he added. "Then we can all go to the police."

"Fine," Hugh said. "But Mikey's arriving midday tomorrow and then we're telling him everything. He has a right to know."

Honeyman nodded. "I understand. Yes, perhaps it's time we let the authorities take care of this."

So it's tomorrow, he thought, the premonition of sleeping in his Land Rover for only one more evening becoming true.

Tomorrow is the end of the temple, or the end of my life.

He had no intention of letting Ellen ring the police. After his visit to Marion, he would go straight to the house of Thomas Wilkinson.

A sigh of regret sounded in his throat. "I have to tell you something now ... something that's going to upset you even more, if that's possible."

She looked at him with a blank expression.

"I wouldn't have told you at all," he admitted, "but you'll be seeing Mikey tomorrow and when he mentions certain tests he's carried out you'll put two and two together."

"What are you talking about?" she asked.

"It's about that phrenological skull in your house..."

XXVII

Where all roads end

Honeyman was met by Marion Coates, thirty years younger, as the door was opened. He knew immediately she was Marion's daughter for the resemblance was uncanny: the woman had the same plaintive features and figure, which at this time in her life was curvaceous rather than heavy. Her eyes invited his name.

"Is Mrs Coates in?" he asked.

"Mum died yesterday," the woman replied in a faint Scottish accent. "Heart attack: it was all very sudden and unexpected." The words were delivered with a flat finality; she had said them many times in the last twenty-four hours.

"I am so sorry," he murmured, looking downcast. "My condolences … she was a … she was a special lady." He was thoughtful for a moment. "Clare, is it?" he asked.

"Clare, yes. Clare McIntosh."

"Ah yes, you married the Scot." He patted his coat as if he were looking for something, though he was merely taking an opportunity to think; his first impulse was to hand the daughter the card that presented him as a probate valuer, though it occurred to him that she may have seen the card he had given to her mother. "I spoke to your mother about double-glazing," he said, deciding that he was stuck with that persona. "For the bay window."

"Oh I see," she said, with an apathetic shake of the head. "Well, the house will be sold now." She offered him a vacant smile as she made to close the door.

"But it's already paid for," he insisted. "Your mother took advantage of a special offer and it's due to be installed next month. I'm sure that double-glazing will help the sale value."

She was only mildly interested.

"I merely need to come in and do some measurements."

"No, that's impossible right now, I'm afraid. I'm expecting some people and they'll be here any minute."

"The funeral directors?"

She shook her head. "No, a charity. Mum left them something in her will."

"Already?" he murmured, glancing back at the road. "Can't they wait until after the funeral?"

"The funeral's going to be in Scotland. I'm going back tomorrow so I wanted to tie up all the loose ends." She glanced at her watch with an expression of exhaustion. She turned round and said, "Tarn, did they tell you what time they'd be here?"

Tarn emerged from the kitchen, wiping a saucepan. "They'll be here soon," she said with a cold look at Honeyman. "I've packed the Sandringham dinner service inside the dresser, Mrs McIntosh. It didn't need cleaning."

"What about that?" Clare asked, with a glance at the oak grandfather clock standing between them in the hall.

"They'll take that as it is," Tarn replied. With a nod and a sigh Clare turned back to Honeyman. A triumphant smile flickered briefly across Tarn's face before she returned to the kitchen.

"She's been a wee treasure," Clare remarked confidentially. She checked her watch again. "As you can see, I'm short of time…"

"There was a skull," he said, in desperation. "I noticed it when I was last here. A phrenological skull."

"Is that what it is?"

"I mention it because your mother suggested that it might be for sale," he began.

"It's been thrown out." Her smile contained some irritation. "I'm sorry but I'm really going to have to ask you…"

"Yes, yes," he said, nodding and walking back to his Land Rover. In the driver's seat, he studied the controls on the dashboard and took several deep breaths. "This is where all roads end," he murmured, as he turned over the ignition.

He drove quickly past the castle, then out of Pembroke picking up the road to Manorbier.

"What do you want to do with it?" Hugh asked cautiously.

Ellen had spent the night on the second step of the stairs, looking at the skull of her mother. Yes, it had been etched, numbered and artificially aged, yet she was still reproaching herself for failing to recognise her mother's bone structure: that high forehead and long nose, the genes they shared.

"It's evidence, I suppose," she murmured.

"Mikey should be here soon. We can discuss it all then."

"They'll get away with it, I know they will," she said in an acid voice.

He didn't reply. The problem was that if the Trustees denied they delivered the skull and the bust, there was nothing to link the skull to the charity except for the science of phrenology. A defence lawyer would point to the chart in the kitchen to argue that her father had an interest in the subject.

"I'm not even sure that we *should* follow it up," she sighed.

"I know," he murmured, in reluctant agreement. They had discussed this through the night and had arrived at a possible scenario where Nigel Sorensen was portrayed in court as some lunatic who, in the grief of losing his wife, took his interest in phrenology to the logical extreme, raiding his wife's grave and taking her head.

"I think we should just move on," she muttered. "I think we should bury it."

He nodded, having tentatively formulated the theory that they had been hypnotised in the Wilkinson house. She was reluctantly coming round to his way of thinking; the episode had instilled in both of them an urgent need to blank out the memory.

"I want to get rid of that chart, too," she declared. "I hate it." She pointed to the cupboard under the stairs where the Fowler bust was lurking in its cardboard box. "And that thing in there, as well."

They decided that the chart would be the first thing to go. Hugh, downstairs in the kitchen, hesitated as he reached up to pull it off the wall. Something had caught his eye in the sectioned diagram of the skull.

"Ellen, come down," he called. "I want to show you something."

He was considering the chart when she appeared behind him. His finger went to the two sentiments in the schematic face that bore the numbers 31, represented as small ovals above each eye.

"The reverse of benevolence," she agreed with a frown. "So?"

"Where are they?"

"What do you mean?"

"Whereabouts in the head are they?"

She studied the chart with a shrug. "In the forehead, I suppose."

"In the...?"

"*Temple*," she clarified, her fingers going to her forehead. "They're in the temple," she murmured, to herself. She looked inquiringly at him; he had his mobile to his ear.

"Honeyman?" he asked, as his call was answered. He turned to her and said, "He's driving. He's just going to pull over."

They waited.

"The temple is reversed," she whispered, her eyes giving the statement meaning.

Hugh nodded as he returned the mobile to his ear. "Honeyman, I think we've found something out. Ellen's second letter, the one with 'the temple is reversed' ... yes ... it isn't referring to the temple as in 'where you pray'. It's the temple as in ... the *forehead*." He listened then shook his head. "I don't know what it means..."

"Dad must be trying to tell us something," she insisted. She tugged at his shirtsleeve, annoyed that she couldn't hear what

312

Honeyman was saying.

"I don't know, maybe something needs to be reversed," he suggested, putting the mobile on speakerphone.

"But reverse *what?*" came Honeyman's crackly voice through a bad reception.

"I don't know."

"We know that benevolence reverses to evil," Honeyman said.

Hugh briefly shook his head. "That's too obvious. There's more to it than that, I'm sure of it. There's a clue here, I know there is."

Honeyman didn't reply.

"It must be something to do with Dad's morning suit," she broke in. "The pocket of his suit."

"Your uncle said there was nothing in the suit, Ellen," Honeyman called. They heard the Land Rover's engine turning over. "I'm on my way to the house now," he announced. "Marion Coates is dead and the Trustees are about to collect the last two vessels. That should occupy them long enough to let me have a look around. Maybe I'll find something. Perhaps what I've been waiting to find has been there all along and I've just been too afraid to face it."

"Honeyman, wait for the police," Hugh said in a loud voice.

"There's no time," he replied. "The temple's almost complete."

They heard the grind of a hasty shift of gears before the call was ended.

The Trustees considered the logistics of removing two large items from the Coates' house and decided it shouldn't prove too difficult, even though the garden path was at least ten feet long. When the vessels and collodians were given freely – the daughter had considered the pictures with a shrug saying *I've got other snaps* – the departure from the house was relatively easy. There was after all nowhere else for the Coates to go, having been so readily

313

abandoned by their nearest and dearest. It was with solemn approval that the Trustees had learned that the skull was already rubbish; if only all the custodians could be as efficiently accommodating as Clare McIntosh.

"Are you sure you can manage?" Clare asked, looking incredulously at the dresser and then at the tiny frame of Sorrel Page.

"I'm stronger than I look," she remarked.

"Shall I help you? Perhaps Tarn and I can take one end?"

Tarn looked up cautiously from the floor that she was mopping in the kitchen.

"No, it has to be just the two of us," Wells replied. "We're the Trustees."

This answer provoked an odd look from Clare, which neither Trustee sought to address.

"There is a small, final detail," Sorrel said. "You're entitled to one more thing from us, in fair trade."

"Fair trade?"

"For the gifts your parents have bequeathed the society. We were founded on a phrenological society and our gift is suitably appropriate."

"You're not going to give me another one of those awful skulls, are you?" Clare groaned.

"A cast," she clarified. "A phrenological bust."

"Keep it," Clare said.

"It's been ordered now," Sorrel explained, with a glance at the table that used to hold Marion's photographs. It was bare and gleaming with furniture polish. "It'll have to be delivered *here*, where your mother lived."

"Och, just keep it. All I'll do is throw it away."

"Then throw it away. It's yours to throw away, or destroy as you wish." She considered the clock that she was preparing to lift. "We usually deliver our gifts before we claim our keepsakes ... we're not accustomed to being satisfied quite so quickly."

"Well I don't want to have to come back unless I have to,"

Clare said uncertainly. Something was troubling her about this exchange but she wasn't sure what it was. She sighed, already forgetting Sorrel Page's words, as if they could find no foothold in her memory and were dropping out of her head. "It's a long drive from Edinburgh. Tony's been working a lot of night shifts and he's exhausted. He said I should get everything wrapped up here once and for all." Her eyes dared the two visitors to say anything about an ungrateful son in law.

"Very sensible," Wells agreed, pulling on his black leather gloves in readiness for the lift. "If only all old people had such sensible relatives."

He noticed that Sorrel was suddenly looking startled. His eyes asked her what was wrong.

"We have to hurry," she whispered.

There was a double lock on the door of the Wilkinson house, but it was rotted and surrendered without a fight to the heavy push of Honeyman's shoulder.

The lobby was exactly the same as on his first visit, for that memory was the screensaver of his brain. He muttered a prayer, which emerged as a string of obscenities; the house seemed to laugh in response, the floorboards shaking with mirth under his feet.

"He still hears me," he declared, looking around the house defiantly. "No matter what you make me say ... He still hears me."

The atmosphere in the house withdrew but in a bitter, calculating way, like an animal waiting to strike. He turned to his right; he had debated his route many times in his head and it was always along the corridor shrouded in darkness, towards the door that Sorrel Page had not allowed him to see.

And they say it wasn't true...

The stains of the damp corridor murmured to him as he walked. The high-pitched voice was of an excited middle-aged man, the words rapidly spoken and insistent.

At the rise of the cranium! There ... cut there!

He shuddered as he heard the faintest of screams from the other side of the house, possibly from the room to the left of the lobby. The scream wasn't faint because of the distance, which couldn't have been more than forty feet, but because it sounded like a recording that was being played back on the quietest volume possible, with only the lonely echo of the house giving it wings.

The scream came again and the stains on the corridor wall glistened salaciously. The screaming conjured the image of a hole drilled through bone, a set of tweezers removing a lobe from the front of the brain.

Now your soul is removed…

He stopped at a door. Opening it, he found a small room deep in shadows. To his right, he saw a bowl of solution with blank glass plates stacked nearby; to his left, he saw a large box camera, a Victorian creation fitted on a tripod surrounded with black cloth.

The scream was louder now.

Take his picture … his picture … his image will prove it…

His eyes closed as he saw the flash of the camera and a man with a bandaged head, looking down at the floor with an absent expression. "They were photographed," he murmured, opening his eyes. In the gloom, the box camera and its tripod loomed like a man, given life by the cloth covering that was moving in a breeze coming through the boards of the windows.

They say it isn't true … but I will prove it to be so… my friends and I will prove it to be true…

"Leave this place, Thomas Wilkinson," Honeyman commanded weakly. He suddenly had the feeling that he had lost track of time, that he had been staring at the tripod for far too long.

The experiments will begin again … lobe thirteen … yes, it is in the thirteenth lobe…

"There is no lobe thirteen. It's the figment of a vain man's imagination."

… look at the photographs … see how these men have no souls…

"Leave this place," he repeated wearily, with a shake of his head.

... see how the light does not cast them in shadow ... how they refuse to look at the camera lens ... how they fail to start when the flash goes ... I have questioned them, and they have no substance...

"History's marked you down as fools," he said in a louder voice. "Phrenology's a joke science. The photographs proved nothing."

Now see if I put the lobes, these disembodied souls, in these things of inert matter belonging to the criminals ... a watch ... a toy ... see how they shine...

"You're mad!" In the rapid but slurred diction of the voice he detected a reliance on morphine and an indulgence of cocaine.

My friends say that I can capture the image ... to prove my work ... to prove it...

He shook his head, realising his entreaties were useless. He wondered why he was here; what purpose he could possibly serve.

I remove the soul from the body and take the image of what remains ... yes my friends speak the truth, for I am indeed like God ... I am God in reverse...

He stepped out of the room and slammed the door. With a deep breath he turned, to find himself looking down at Sorrel Page. Beyond her, in the lobby, Jasper Wells was pulling Henry Coates' grandfather clock effortlessly across the floor.

"I always knew you'd go to the dark room," she said. "Do you know what you've been looking for?"

He shook his head. He was right, he had been in the dark room a long while, the strained dialogue with Wilkinson having taken the better part of an hour. Wilkinson had kept him here while the Trustees, alert to the intrusion, had hurried back.

Sorrel seemed to hear his assessment, for she said, "The phrenologists would've said you have a small lobe thirty-one: your perception of time has failed you, I believe."

He nodded at the grim irony.

"Shall I show you what you're looking for?" she offered, still smiling.

317

He made to push past her but found both his wrists in her hands. They were so tiny they could only grip half the bone, yet still held him like a vice. The grip was so painful that he dropped to his knees, the smell of rotting apples in his nostrils. She took his right forearm in both her hands and, with two expert tugs, pulled the bone out of the socket of his elbow. She repeated the process with his left arm. As he dropped to the floor, groaning, his thighbones were pulled efficiently from their knee sockets.

"Is this how you pictured it?" she asked, now dragging his limp, quivering body back down the corridor.

He muttered an obscenity, tears coming to his eyes.

"It is, isn't it?" she declared. "I'm glad you met our Mr Wilkinson. After all, we made *his* dreams come true too."

As if Ellen heard Honeyman's cries of pain, as if she sensed his helpless desperation, she rang a number she had told herself she would never ring.

"Hello?" Tarn said quietly.

"It's Ellen," she said sternly.

Tarn hesitated. "Ellie Sweet," she remarked, unable to resist the jibe.

"Shut the fuck up!" she spluttered, pulling away from Hugh's hand as he sat behind her on the stairs. He shook his head, thinking this was a bad idea.

"If you swear I'll hang up," Tarn warned.

"Oh yeah, I forgot you're so devout and everything."

"More devout than you could possibly imagine."

Ellen was looking at her mother's skull. "I know about the skull. I know you dug up her grave."

"I don't know what you're talking about," Tarn replied, thinking that the conversation was possibly being taped. Once more, she struggled with impulses, with the urge to tell the vain and spoilt Sorensen bitch what she thought of both her and her stupid, meddling father.

"You knew. You let me keep a skull of my mother in the house, knowing those bastards had dug it up."

"I really don't know what you're talking about."

"You even called it *Mr Sockets*: just to make me think it was the skull of a man."

"You're fantasising," Tarn said, tiring of the conversation and hanging up. Ellen got up, glaring at her mobile with an evil temper.

"*What* did she call it?" Hugh asked at length.

"What?"

"The skull," he replied, thinking hard. "What did Tarn call it?"

She glanced at him, her expression softening. "Mr Sockets," she murmured.

He frowned, then jumped up and went into the day room. He found the letter with his doodling, which read:

The temple is reversed

Look inside

My ocket

Leprsy

"I'm glad you rang Tarn after all," he announced, as he returned to the hall with the letter in his hand.

"Hugh, what are you going on about?"

"R and S are part of *leprsy*," he explained. "They're two of the missing keys." He stared at her, waiting for her to react. "Don't you see? It fits."

"What fits?"

He pointed to the phrenological skull, waiting patiently on its oval table. "Mr Sockets," he said, his voice trembling with excitement. "It's not *my pocket*. It's look inside…"

She soundlessly said the name.

Mr Sockets...

She looked at him and said, "Mr Sockets... look inside Mr Sockets."

XXVIII

And they said
it wasn't true

J asper Wells possessed three poles of differing lengths. He was
now using the medium-length pole to find and hook the
intricate handles on the doors of the higher cupboards and prize
them open. The doors at ground level were already released and
the hum ringing in the copper flue was oppressive, a triumphant
keening becoming steadily louder as the occupants of the temple
joined the chorus.

Honeyman was silent as Sorrel released the ankle by which
she had dragged him through the house, then through the double
doors, now closed behind her. The agony was not as great as he
would have imagined, the dislocation of his limbs having been so
expertly performed; he suspected the Trustees wanted to avoid
any chance of his losing consciousness. His overcoat was torn and
dusty from the floor, where the flagstones had broken to reveal the
dirt underneath.

Wells carefully set down his pole and took up the largest one,
feeding its length through his hands. Honeyman looked up and
followed the flight of the hook, attempting to block out the pain, for
he knew he needed to concentrate as never before. He recognised
many of the vessels and their collodion portraits on the ground level
and reasoned that the temple must have been built from the roof
down. Among the cupboards that were open, he glimpsed objects

of all sizes and description, some of them very large; the cupboard above the double doors held a grand piano, carefully positioned on its side and bound down with ropes.

The hook was hovering at the top level, where he could make out that the collodians showed nineteenth-century-style clothes and coiffure, for the vibrant detail of the photographs in the temple seemed to defy distance. He winced uncertainly, realising that if he concentrated he could see every occupant of every cupboard clearly, as if it were directly in front of his face. The largest, blocking the entrance to the broken landing in the lobby, contained an entire wardrobe hanging from the ceiling on chains. The collodian, positioned on the wardrobe handles, showed a strikingly beautiful woman with a wide hat and veil. Her eyes, sultry and proud behind the veil, were barely inches away from his face, so close he could see the reflection of the camera in her irises.

"No one can hide in here," Sorrel explained, aware from his expression that he was struggling with the distance perception. "Isn't that how your god operates? Under his microscope every second of every day?" She turned three hundred and sixty degrees, her mouth open in wonder. "I've been to the Basilica in Rome, Baptist. They marvel at the forced perspective, those architectural tricks that bring the floors and ceilings closer. Imagine if the poor Renaissance artisans could witness *our* achievement … the forced perspective here … would they not throw down their tools in despair?"

Honeyman didn't answer; another flawed but primordial instinct was telling him to keep quiet, that if the hunter couldn't hear him then it wouldn't trouble him. The copper flue erupted with renewed energy as more vessels joined the temple; the beautiful woman with the veil, released at last from over a hundred years of confinement, had joined the chorus with delight.

"Do you not think to repent?" Wells remarked as he hunted out the few remaining doors that were waiting to be opened. "Your time is near."

Sorrel was at the hearth stove, next to the narrow rectangular hole at the foot of the wall. "He won't repent. He's in an ecstasy of sin and error. He welcomes this end, his supposed martyrdom." From inside the oven of the stove she produced two shovels, the spades glowing red with heat.

"*Do* you welcome it, Baptist?" Wells inquired.

"No, I wish to live," Honeyman admitted. "Or to die painlessly," he added.

Sorrel had returned and taken his ankle; as she readied herself to drag him she looked into his eyes.

"You say you're holy," Honeyman muttered. "If you are, then you'll have mercy."

She seemed to be seriously considering the request. "If we were to let you go, would you stop hunting us?"

His breath was coming in heaves as he heard Wells throw down his pole; the last doors were opened.

"Don't you desire our destruction?" she pressed.

He nodded mutely, refusing to let a lie escape his lips at this time.

"The questions are somewhat academic," she admitted, "for your death is very important to us. The just punishment for your trespass will sanctify the temple." She twitched her nose. "Know that the pit, when originally dug, was very deep, for it's accepted many such as you…"

He winced as he felt the tug on his leg and then felt himself moving. In desperation, he found the Sorensen doll and typewriter and with a grimace of concentration they shot towards him. "Nigel and Nia Sorensen, help me," he called.

This resulted in a pause in the journey, as Sorrel regarded the Sorensen cabinet. Shortly the typewriter reacted with a swift rattle of his keys, as some insect disturbed during feeding. The doll's eyelids opened to reveal white sockets, the eyes going up into the skull.

Suffer as I suffer… he heard the doll say.

There is no mercy here.

He groaned as his journey through the jagged stone and the dirt resumed. His eyes turned fearfully to the pit. "Is Martin Sorensen down there?" he muttered.

"And Stefan Hughes too … regrettably…" she confirmed.

"Stefan," he groaned, breathing the name in through his nose then burying it with his eyes. The thought of the hapless young man made him instinctively reach for his pocket to find his bible but his hands didn't respond, for his arms were dragging limply behind him. He swallowed, now hearing Wells behind him. The Trustee took his wrists while Sorrel took his other ankle. As he was lifted cleanly off the floor, he uttered a prayer of obscenities.

There was a gleam of amusement in her eyes. "Is that how you honour your god, when you stand on the brink of eternity?"

"They are your words, not mine," he whispered, struggling with the agony of his dislocated joints as he hung suspended in mid air.

"They are yours, Baptist. Never doubt that they are yours." She glanced at her colleague, readying herself for the slight heave that would send Honeyman down the eight feet of pit and have him landing on the soft earth.

He was thinking furiously, using the pain as a means of focus. "The temple is reversed … you give the custodians skulls…" he muttered. His eyes widened as he remembered Tarn Hughes' name for the Sorensen skull. "The *forehead* is reversed. Look inside Mr Sockets."

Sorrel hesitated, throwing a questioning glance at Wells. "Who told you such a thing?"

"Someone who occupies this temple," Honeyman said, as bravely as he was able. "Nigel Sorensen has breached your walls with the errors of your servant. *That's* why he had to use Tarn's name for the skull in his letter. Only *she* called the skull Mr Sockets."

He paused, but the Trustees didn't speak. "The reverse is in the forehead of the skull," he muttered, wishing his back would touch the floor again, if only for one blissful moment. "But what reverse?" he wondered, attempting to engage the Trustees in dialogue. "What is reversed?"

Still the Trustees didn't answer. He looked back at the Sorensen alcove and glimpsed the collodian of Nia Sorensen at the feet of the doll. Concentrating, the face in the portrait was before him, in her attitude of laughing surprise.

"The collodian ... of course ... it's the reverse of the collodian. Hugh was right: you had no choice but to leave us the means of your destruction, because you're bound by rules. Satan controls this temple with no more power than a wayward child plays a game under the watchful eyes of an indulgent parent. The child believes the game is his own, but..."

With that he was heaved into the pit.

Hugh was grappling with the phrenological skull. His fingers probed an eye socket and he discovered that the channels of the eye cavities had been bored through, allowing his fingers to reach fully inside the head. Ellen was finding the scene traumatic, two hands on her own forehead, in sympathy for her mother.

"Hugh, be careful," she moaned, "please be careful."

"I'm trying," he said. His two fingers emerged from one socket and now went into the other. He was shaking his head.

"Found anything?"

"Nothing," he said, returning the skull to the pedestal. "Looks like we were on the wrong track."

She considered the skull in disbelief.

"I know," he said.

"Let me try," she murmured and gradually her expression softened as she considered the middle and index finger of her right hand.

"Ellen, there's nothing in there."

"I'm the custodian. That's why Dad had to write to me ... not to the police or to Honeyman." She tapped her chest. "To me. That's why the letters were for *Ellie Sweet*."

He shook his head sadly; his fingers had touched nothing but bare bone.

"The skull's fair trade," she continued. "The Trustees don't mind if I throw the skull away, in fact they'd *prefer* it if I threw it away, but they have to give it me, nonetheless. There's something in there for me and no one else."

"Ellen, please…"

She gently picked up the skull in her left hand and managed a reassuring smile, as if she were urging the skull not to be afraid. With the two fingers that she always kissed, the fingers that had touched her mother's collodian portrait at least four times every day, she reached in through the left eye socket.

"Ellen, don't punish yourself like this." His eyes widened. Her fingers had emerged with a square of what looked like tightly folded paper of sheen grey. She opened it up to find that it was the same size and shape as her mother's collodian but it was film, not paper. It showed her mother holding back her laugh, though her skin was black and her hair was white.

"It's a negative," he said. "They must keep the negatives of the photographs when they prepare the collodians. They're not destroyed after all."

She was smiling. "The negative's a reverse image, where black is white and white is black. Didn't Honeyman say that everything they do has a perverse logic? The temple is reversed: the negative is in the forehead. That's what Dad was trying to tell me."

He nodded slowly, remembering Honeyman's caution that while everything concerning the temple had an ironic logic, nothing followed natural laws. Ellen was right: only she could find the negative, because she was the custodian. A smile escaped his lips as he thought of her kissing her mother's collodian with those two fingers; it was as if they were always restless to make this discovery.

"But what do we do with it?" he asked.

"I don't know."

She looked at him helplessly and shook her head.

In the temple, Cody's eyes opened, but showed only white malice.

The first few clods of earth had fallen on Honeyman's face while the Trustees shovelled from above. A tremor in the flue manifested as a creak in the copper, as if it had been overheated and was now cooling too quickly. The tremor was followed by the urgent mutterings of the Trustees.

Honeyman's arms were twisted at his side and to spit the earth out of his mouth required him to gather it with his tongue and then blow. "They've found them," he called up. "They've found the negatives. The Sorensens have escaped."

Sorrel's hand was waving in the air, although in fact she was stroking Cody's hair as she concentrated and brought her close. The doll's eyes were still white, the eyeballs in the skull. "There now," she said with relief, then glanced at Wells, her smile having returned. She took up her shovel.

"Only the female negative has been found," was the angry taunt Wells threw down, with another shovel of earth. "They are partners in life and death and stand or fall together."

"Where's the other negative?" he called back pointlessly, shaking the earth from his face.

"In the forehead of *Mr* Sorensen, of course. Where else would it be?"

"But you only gave one skull! Where is your fair trade?"

Wells lifted up a heavy shovel of earth and nodded to Sorrel, who also had lifted the heaviest of loads. "Save your breath, Baptist. Indeed, at this point I would advise you to *hold* your breath."

"Oh Lord Satan, accept this offering from your true and faithful servants abased at your feet," she murmured.

"Abased at your feet," he concurred.

The noise in the flue erupted as the vessels came to life in a chatter of expectation, as they attempted in their way, within the confines of their form, to chant the number of the temple to the death of the minister.

"Nothing's happened," Ellen said as she laid the negative next to the skull. "Nothing's happened, I can feel it. Mum and Dad are still trapped. I know they're still trapped."

Hugh was looking around helplessly. "Where's your father's negative? Perhaps we need them both…"

She shrugged miserably. "There's only the one skull." She had checked again but found nothing further.

"But didn't they say something about fair trade?" He stopped pacing; he almost tapped the skull in time with his thought processes, remembering himself just in time. She followed his hand in horror and confusion. "Look," he said, "what I think they do is give the beneficiaries, the next of kin, the chance to save the people they've taken. Who else would save them but their nearest and dearest? That's why they put the skulls right under their noses. I mean this thing wasn't hidden away in the attic, was it? It's right here, at the door, for everyone to see. And if the next of kin don't care, if they just throw out the skulls, then that's that."

"Like those poor people in Saundersfoot," she remarked, with a frown. In the Pembroke Inn Honeyman had told them a story about the couple who had left their estate to an avaricious nephew: the only person that would have cared about them, who would have taken an interest in their artefacts, would have been their daughter. The daughter was estranged and living in Australia.

"Right," he agreed, also remembering the story. It must have delighted the Trustees to have a greedy nephew as custodian, with the daughter on the other side of the world.

"I understand what you're saying. Only I can save my parents." She looked at the floor. "Or leave them in that place forever," she muttered, a hand going to her forehead.

He nodded. "But don't you see...?"

"See what?"

"It means they have to return your father's skull too. They *have* to!"

"But they haven't, have they?"

There was a pause and then as one, they turned to look at the door of the cupboard under the stairs. In an instant the cardboard box was dragged out into the hall and the Fowler bust pulled clean out of the straw, its smoothed out features holding an expression of patient resignation.

"What do you think?" he asked breathlessly. "Should we ask

Mikey to analyse it or something?"

She considered her two fingers that kissed her mother's portrait and she pictured, with a twinge of guilt, the imitation photograph of her father in pieces on the kitchen counter. She had never kissed it. Rather, she had smashed it.

Smashed it…

Her eyes widened. "Smash it," she said.

"Smash it? Are you sure?"

Without hesitation, she picked up the bust and threw it to the floor. It cracked neatly down its centre, along a weak seam in the plaster that had been filled to hide the join. A skull rolled out.

It was a plain, untreated skull. "Oh my God," she murmured, picking up the skull and through the bored socket retrieving the negative of her father's photograph. She unfolded it with a momentary look of grief, regarding the negative image of her father before it dissolved into nothing in her hand. In a crackle of energy the negative of her mother followed, vanishing from the pedestal without a trace that it had ever existed, save for a smoke trail of iridescence that glowed briefly then popped into nothing like a microscopic firework.

Hugh instinctively stepped back, his face a warning. Behind him, he saw the heap of letters also dissolving away into nothing. "Put the skull down," he whispered, unsure why he was afraid. She looked at him questioningly then nodded and placed the skull of Nigel Sorensen on the pedestal next to the skull of his wife. She stepped back too.

They held their breath as the house seemed to groan, as if it were a ship keeling against a wave attempting to snap its hull in two.

Cracks appeared in the skulls with dull crunches.

The skulls exploded.

Cody's eyes opened to find the image of the Trustees, their shovels raised. The Sholes & Glidden typewriter had come to life and was tapping out a message; the message travelled along the wood, trembling through every cupboard, as the hormones of a queen bee find every worker and drone in a hive.

The copper flue yawned into silence, prompting the Trustees to drop their shovels. Sorrel's eyes were searchlights as all the vessels tried to hide from her.

"Where are you?" Wells murmured in a parched voice. "Who breaks the chorus?"

"Sorensen," she declared, her eyes widening.

Wells made for the Sorensen cupboard where the typewriter was working feverishly, Cody's eyes wide with alarm. Something stirred in a neighbouring and larger cupboard, the home of the Parry Cluedo board and *the Death of Marat*. The painting trembled as if shaken and water appeared on the floor as the bath in the painting rocked, causing the approaching Trustee to slip. He broke his fall with his hands.

"Hush now," Sorrel murmured, her hands attempting to soothe the air, "all is well … all is well…"

Wells gripped the floor; the temple had cured his throat cancer by banishing the disease to his teeth and gums, leaving him with no saliva, making it difficult to catch his breath.

"Hurry!" she called.

He got to his feet and was half-walking, half-sliding towards the Sorensen cupboard. A hand went to his chest as he felt his strength deserting him, feeling the age once more in his body. The warning told him he needed to be brutal: he would rip the doll's head off and together with the typewriter throw it in the pit, on top of the Baptist. The completion of the temple would have to be delayed until two new vessels were collected; it was a major setback but the temple would be saved.

"The Sorensen skulls have cracked, I feel it!" she shouted. Her expression froze as she saw her colleague pause. "What is it? What's wrong?"

Wells staggered and turned, one of his eyes a mess of blood. His hand reached up to the back of his skull, to feel the razor sharp point of a tiny silver dagger sticking through the bone. He looked at his finger, which was bleeding also, then collapsed to the floor as his brain expired.

There was a crack, somewhere towards the ceiling of the temple. The sound was like a bolt shooting out of the rivet of a submarine being crushed under the pressure of the deepest ocean.

Sorrel, now alone, looked up, attempting to find the source of the noise. Her eyes alighted on the collodian of the woman with the veil; the glass had a crack from the left top corner to the bottom right corner. The wardrobe had lost all its shine and polish; it looked a hundred years old.

"No," she murmured.

The sound of collodians cracking snapped all around the chamber, making her turn in circles of frustration. The copper flue creaked and with a violent tremor splintered in two. The fire in the stove was out.

"No!"

The collodian of Lawrence Parry cracked cleanly from top left to bottom right; his wife's collodian followed and the floor was dry again. The Sorensen typewriter was still chattering furiously, sending out its signal of rebellion to the captive vessels. Hearing a creak from above Sorrel just avoided a piano falling from a height, but in the crash wood splinters ravaged her face. Her hand went to the splinters imbedded in her cheeks and she gasped with pain as a moment of silence descended on the chamber, as if the vessels were pausing to gather their strength.

"Father, help me," she whispered, unable to see any future, all paths in shadow. A sound made her open her eyes and turn; the china plates were shaking ominously on the dresser of Marion Coates. She considered her shovel, thinking there might still be enough time to bury the Baptist before the vessels took her, then considered the double doors. She chose the double doors. She jumped over Wells' body as she raced towards them, pulling them open just as the vessels began their final onslaught.

As the doors closed behind her, she felt the thud and crash of crockery, wood, metal and leather, objects large and robust, or small and delicate, landing impotently on the other side. Her eyes were alive with adrenalin as she breathed a great sigh of relief; her heart still pumped, her brain still functioned and she knew her god watched over her. If she had been aware that her face had changed, the perfect symmetry of her eyes and nose having reverted to the pleasant but unremarkable features she had before becoming a Trustee, then she would have been afraid. When Wells had felt the cancer in his mouth, moments before he was impaled, he knew his doom was upon him.

She sprinted through the lobby towards the front door. As she passed the study of Thomas Wilkinson a shadow crossed her path and she glimpsed the flash of a surgical saw. She continued running for a few seconds, then slumped to the floor, her throat severed.

At the entrance to the study a two handed surgical saw with a stained serrated blade was on the floor. On the table, next to the empty felt-lined box, the collodian of Thomas Wilkinson had cracked; the glass was cheap, the dull, broken image no more than a lost, unhappy memory.

The dust of the room was swirling with the final words of its occupant.

And they said it wasn't true…

Down in the pit Honeyman still lived but was unable to move except to twitch in fear when he heard the bullet crack of a collodian smashing as the last and more stubborn souls found their release from the temple.

Within an hour, only the Sorensen collodians remained intact.

The typewriter, exhausted, finally laid down its keys. The machine lost its gleam, the beautifully oiled fingers becoming grubby with dust, a moment before the collodian of Nigel Sorensen cracked. The double doors had blown open, the front door having fallen away from its rotting hinges, and a wind haunted the chamber, picking up reams of watermarked paper and casting them into the air. From the depths, Honeyman saw the paper fluttering above and he uttered a prayer of thanks. Tears welled in the corners of his eyes, for his words were his own.

He couldn't see it, but the portrait of Nia Sorensen remained in vibrant detail at the feet of the Jumeau, the doll's eyes still wide with alarm as the cleansing wind continued to whip around the chamber. This was how Ellen found her when she entered the chamber and raced to the cupboard, leaving Mikey and Hugh to go to the pit, to the sound of Honeyman's calls. The police were lingering in the lobby, having stopped at the body of Sorrel Page.

"You waited," Ellen cried, desperately hugging the doll to her shoulder. The paperweight eyes closed and then gently rocked open. "You waited for me. I knew this time you'd wait."

The expression in the doll's face was of elated exhaustion as the porcelain eyelids trembled and then slowly closed, never to open again. Ellen felt the mechanism in the doll's head finally fail, becoming just a broken metal circuit, a secret of a French inventor long since dead. The jointed composition body was limp in her arms.

She sobbed out her grief and muttered her goodbyes, as the last collodian cracked.

The date and time

The Divine Sentiment was abolished swiftly and discreetly on account of its royal pedigree, the Wilkinson house torn down on health and safety grounds, the transport vehicle scrapped. The discovery of the bodies in the pit led to inquiries into all the living Trustees of the charity but none came to be questioned, for they relinquished their lives with methodical efficiency as their names were turned up. They would all be listed as sacrificial martyrs in the halls of the coven, alongside *the Venerations* Jasper Wells and Sorrel Page.

"There will be no prosecutions," Honeyman remarked from his hospital bed, when he heard that the police file had been closed. "Strong forces have always protected the coven. We helped your father destroy the temple and that's victory enough."

Ellen shook her head, still finding her father's motives difficult to fathom. "But he wanted me to hate him," she said, thinking of the hidden graduation photograph and his instructions to Tarn. "How was I supposed to help him, if he sent me away?"

Honeyman found the question amusing. "You'll be a parent one day, Ellen, and you'll understand. He wanted his *brother* to achieve his rescue: that's why he was writing to him at the grave."

"Uncle Martin?" she whispered.

"Your father wrote the first letter to you because it must have been such a torment being buried, separated from his image. He wrote the second letter when he knew that you weren't going to leave and that his brother was going to die." He grimaced with pain as he tried to move one of his arms. "They're getting better," he remarked, referring to his fractures. "I believe I'll reach sixty after all."

Hugh was also at the hospital bed, again looking thoughtful. "But only Ellen, as the custodian, could find the negatives. So how could his brother help?"

Honeyman shook his head. "The duties of the custodian were imposed by the temple but I believe that anyone who *loved* the person in life could free the soul in death. In the end, it came down to love, not rules: that was God's intervention, I've no doubt of it."

Hugh was unconvinced. "I still don't see how you can be so sure that Martin Sorensen would have found the negatives..."

Honeyman painfully clenched and unclenched a fist. "Because of the x-ray photograph Martin took. There was a grey square in the centre of the forehead: Martin saw the negatives, even through his camera. How could he have photographed it, if it wasn't there?" His eyes flickered and he shook his head.

"What?" Hugh asked.

"I've just realised something. The temple transport, the removal wagon, was a hearse painted white, its windows tinted black." He smiled. "It was advertising the black and white negative: the clue being driven under our noses. Yes, that would have appealed to their sense of irony."

They sat in silence for a time.

"Why didn't Dad just *tell* me?" she murmured. "Why not just say 'find the negatives in the skull' or something? Why all the riddles?"

Honeyman's head returned to the centre of his pillow, his eyes on the stark white ceiling. "Your father was bound by frightful powers, Ellen. Surely you understand that now, having had no more than a taste of the temple's malice yourself. We've been so incredibly lucky, so incredibly blessed. You see, I don't believe your father could have written to you at *all* if young Tarn Hughes hadn't broken her oaths. That's why he called the skull Mr Sockets and was

forced to use the temple's own prayer ... 'the temple is reversed'."
He paused, reflectively. "The temple was destroyed by its own rules.
The errant housekeeper is in great danger, I suspect."

Tarn had vanished, even though she wasn't a suspect in the
murders. The police reasoned that Martin Sorensen had been killed
by the murderer of Stefan Hughes and so the murderer could hardly
be Tarn Hughes, even if she was involved in some sort of cult. Ellen
hadn't been invited to Stefan's funeral. With a mother's antennae,
Mrs Hughes suspected that the young woman lately returned from
Cardiff was somehow responsible for the loss of her children, even
if she couldn't be blamed for it.

"Will you go back to your parish?" Hugh asked at length.

A twitch of Honeyman's moustache answered in the negative.
"The Lord has shown me my path now. There are more temples and
I'll hunt them all out, if I can, or die in the attempt." He groaned,
clenching his fists once more. "I owe it to the bones of the dead,
to the bones buried in the pit: Stefan, Martin, and those ministers
who have gone before me."

The remains of the dead ministers found in the pit received a
proper burial, as did Ellen's Jumeau doll and the Sholes & Glidden
typewriter. She placed them side by side in the hole dug by
Stefan, covering it with a granite slab engraved with his name as
well as the names of her parents. Such was the healing benefit she
received from this ritual that it gave her a mission, which would
turn into an obsession: she persuaded the police to let her find
the owners of the objects in the Wilkinson house, rather than see
them destroyed. She set up a website and while progress was slow
at first, people eventually came forward to claim them; she didn't
tell them her story, she simply entreated them to look after the
precious artefacts.

One of the owners she managed to locate early on was Neville
Parry, but she spoke to his wife as Neville was trying to track down
some people who had stolen all his money. Ellen had made contact
only to obtain the address of the Parrys' daughter in Australia,
which Mrs Parry gave with a warning that she was as poor as a

church mouse and would insist that all the telephone charges were reversed; after all, she hadn't even been able to afford a flight to her own parents' funeral.

The daughter of Lawrence and Jessica Parry was persuaded to return to Wales to collect her parents' things, Ellen buying her ticket. She didn't care that her cousin had the house and the investments, grateful simply to receive the game board and the painting in memory of her parents, to have something they loved. She and Ellen would become lifetime correspondents.

Ellen would come to recognise a pattern in the way the vessels and collodians were claimed. Often the person coming forward had no legal entitlement, rather just a claim to friendship or simply an interest in the ancestry; sometimes they weren't even sure *why* they had come forward. The motive never mattered, for she handed the items over simply when it felt right to do so. One thing, however, was always the same: the recipient felt better for having the items returned, even if the cracked photograph and old battered relic only belonged to some distant ancestor. It was as if some unfathomable knot in the deep reaches of space had suddenly righted itself.

The unclaimed vessels remained in a warehouse written under a trust she had created with Mr Hobbs. The Sorensen Trust provided for the rented warehouse to stay operational until all items were collected, or the trust money failed.

Ellen firmly believed that the warehouse would one day be emptied, with every vessel and collodian finding a home.

It was fourteen months since the temple had fallen. At almost half past four on the morning of Christmas Day, Tarn Hughes crept up the front steps of the townhouse overlooking North Beach. She was delighted to find that her key still fitted and she eased the door open, holding the bolt in place as she gently closed the door behind her.

She glared purposefully at the ceiling, blinking slowly to accustom herself to the gloom, then took the knife from the inside pocket of her coat.

Even though misplaced initiative had been her downfall in the coven, her plan was to seek forgiveness with the blood of Ellen Sorensen, the true cause of the fall of Temple 1331. As with her actions when she was the carer it was a plan only half thought through for, as she hitchhiked back to Wales after months of sleeping rough in London, logic told her that if the coven wanted Ellen Sorensen dead they could have achieved this themselves.

Still, she was here. She supposed in the end that it was just revenge she sought; she wasn't even sure that she had much faith left, in spite of the miracles she had witnessed. In her dreams, she still watched Stefan die with more peace and certainty than she had ever known in the frenzied spectacle of the coven rituals; too late, she had come to the nagging possibility that faith built on human certainties was built on shale. But she didn't care about that anymore; she just wanted that Sorensen bitch dead.

She knew that Ellen was alone because she had made an anonymous telephone call to Hugh earlier at his Cardiff address. Having tracked their movements for the last two weeks, she knew that they alternated between addresses but this was the first day they were apart, most probably through his family commitments at Christmas.

As she prepared to climb the stairs to the bedroom, a sidelight went on in the day room.

"Hello Tarn."

Ellen was sitting in the armchair, turned towards her.

So she isn't sleeping, Tarn thought, holding the knife in front of her. She was unconcerned; she wasn't as tall as Ellen, wasn't even as strong as her, but she had killed before.

"Have you come here to murder me?" Ellen asked, without getting up.

Tarn didn't reply as she approached the day room, the knife held in front of her.

"It's against the rules, isn't it?" Ellen queried. "Just as it was against the rules to kill my uncle. Or was it your brother who did that? I suppose you wouldn't have been strong enough to lift the sledgehammer and my uncle was such a big man."

She stopped and raised her knife, infuriated. "The Father gave me strength. The strength of ten men."

There was a pause. "So *you* murdered him?"

"I smashed his head in. And Ellen, after I've killed you I'm going to have *your* head too." She blinked slowly. "You owe the temple two skulls."

As she walked through the doorway, the knife was knocked out of her hand. Without hesitation, she screamed her defiance and lunged at Honeyman, who had emerged from the shadows, but his huge fist effortlessly knocked her to the floor. She lay in the hall, dazed, before he pulled her up and bound her hands behind her back. Ellen stayed in the day room, telephoning the police.

"How did you know?" Tarn snarled.

"Let's just say we had advance warning," he explained gently, briefly producing a miniature tape recorder before it was consigned to his pocket. She shook her head in disbelief as she struggled helplessly with her bonds.

"I'm a true servant and The Father will deliver me."

He rubbed his shoulder, still the object of physiotherapy. "There's still time to repent. There's *always* time. Your brother will be watching over you."

"My brother was nothing, nothing but a test for my faith."

He buried her words with a closing of his eyes. "Your brother watches over you still … and there *is* forgiveness."

In the day room, Ellen sighed, choosing not to share her information with the ex-housekeeper though she held it in one hand as she finished her call to the police. An instinct that she realised was just a little callous made her decide that Tarn should never have the satisfaction of knowing how she was expected. She now rang Hugh, who answered immediately.

"It's over," she whispered. She nodded. "Yes … yes, it was here. No, I'm fine…"

A little later she closed her mobile and looked at the letter again, wondering when it would dissolve, for it was the final letter written on her father's typewriter. At the end, her parents had managed with a joint effort to save her life, for the letter came from Cody's sleeve as she had been bundled out of the house, typed with the number keys left on the machine. It read:

25 12 2009

4 25

"The date and time," she sighed, with a glance at her watch. She kissed her index and middle finger and with those kissed fingers touched the letter. She had a Christmas present for her father and she would keep the letter inside it, until it was ready to leave.

The present was taken from her collection of Dickens first editions. To add to *Little Dorrit*, she had managed to recover *Bleak House* and *The Pickwick Papers*. One day, her grown up children would inherit a complete set of first editions and they would know the story behind its collection, but for now, the collection seemed rather small for the large dedicated table.

But she had acquired something new; it was something that Tarn Hughes had never touched, that her father had never seen and which she knew was the Christmas present that would have delighted him above all things. It was a first edition of *Martin Chuzzlewit*.

As she slipped the last letter into its cover, she supposed that sometimes objects had a meaning far beyond the function for which they were created and were loved in a manner that was disproportionate to the pleasure or comfort they could possibly offer. Her father's search for this book had really been the search for his twin brother, the hope of their reunion.

"You have *the Martin* now," she whispered, wiping the cover of the book and putting it on the table.